# A Taste of Temptation

She tilted her head to one side and he leaned closer to her exposed neck. He kissed her skin and licked the puncture marks. He could feel her artery pulse, could almost smell her blood. Closing his eyes, he opened the wounds with his teeth and soon tasted the sweet richness of her blood.

As she moaned with pleasure, he slid his hand into her unbuttoned dress. . . .

## Confession

*Don't miss the other novels of dark seduction by Lori Herter . . . OBSESSION and POSSESSION*

"A WORLD OF DARK FANTASY . . . SEXY."
—Kathleen Creighton

*Berkley Books by Lori Herter*

**OBSESSION**
**POSSESSION**
**CONFESSION**

# CONFESSION

## LORI HERTER

BERKLEY BOOKS, NEW YORK

CONFESSION

A Berkley Book / published by arrangement with
Goddard and Kamin, Inc.

PRINTING HISTORY
Berkley edition / September 1992

ISBN: 0-425-13358-3

A BERKLEY BOOK® TM 757,375
Berkley Books are published by The Berkley Publishing Group,
200 Madison Avenue, New York, New York 10016.
The name "Berkley" and the "B" logo
are trademarks belonging to Berkley Publishing Corporation.

PRINTED IN THE UNITED STATES OF AMERICA

10  9  8  7  6  5  4  3  2  1

*To my husband, Jerry*

# 1

# Honor was the only thing a vampire could hold on to

STRONG, PALE moonlight streamed in through the huge ballroom windows on the third floor of the Oak Street mansion. In another part of the house, a clock struck four A.M. David de Morrissey barely heard the chimes over the music coming from his large-screen television. Concentrating on his tap dance steps, he didn't concern himself about the time, since dawn was still a few hours away.

The varying gray and white light from the TV screen flickered over David's white shirt as he copied Fred Astaire's moves in the fireworks dance from *Holiday Inn*. He threw imaginary fireworks onto the floor and deftly jumped away from imaginary explosions, copying what Astaire had done. David smiled as he danced. The tap lessons he'd been taking were definitely helping him polish his technique. David's superior strength and agility gave him more energy than his two idols, Fred Astaire and Gene Kelly, combined could ever have possessed. But their rhythm, finesse, attitude—these were the subtleties David longed to master. He was satisfied with himself tonight.

When the dance was over, David stopped the videotape and turned off the TV. The silence of the night filled the empty, vast room, lit now only by the still brightness of the full moon.

David told himself he should go back to work on the screenplay he was rewriting, from which he'd taken a break. But instead he felt drawn to his favorite spot, the cushioned window seat of the nearest bay window. This was the place where he and Veronica used to make love every night, sometimes all night, while they were together. His memories of her—her

dusky hair and sweet mortal's eyes so full of love for him—
were clear and vivid, though years had passed since their affair
ended.

No, that was incorrect. Their affair hadn't ended. It was in
suspension, David reminded himself. He must continue, always, to think positively, and not give in to his natural pessi-
mism.

Shifting as he sat on the velvet cushion, David looked out
at the dark skyscrapers of Chicago, discernible as they contrasted opaquely with the midnight blue of the clear, starry
sky. Veronica was probably out there in the city somewhere,
and much as he wanted to use their supernatural bond to
pinpoint her with his mind, he forced himself not to. Though
he longed to make love with her again and taste her blood, he
had a promise to keep, a pact with her to honor. And honor
was the only thing a vampire could hold on to, if he was still
to consider himself at all human.

So David pushed his beloved Veronica from his mind and
thought instead of Darienne. What on earth had happened to
the diamond-laden, voluptuous, blond vampiress, his inter-
mittent companion for the past four centuries? Almost three
years had passed since he'd seen or heard from her. She'd
never gone this long without returning to him from some
corner of the planet, to taunt him and tease him—and seduce
him.

David curved his lips with ironic amusement. He knew what
had happened. Darienne, the sublimely independent, egocen-
tric femme fatale, had fallen in love. He remembered how
devastated she'd looked when he'd explained to her why she
felt so lost and bewildered. David had understood her confused emotional state only too well, because just as he had
fallen for Veronica, so Darienne had also fallen hopelessly in
love with a mortal.

And for making that beguiling, irresponsible, irresistible
mistake, both Darienne and David had hell to pay.

"I'm glad you like it so much," Harriet Dvorak responded.
Her cousin Veronica had just given her an enthusiastic compliment on the dress of mauve rayon Harriet had sewn for
herself. "It doesn't look too *Vogue* for me?" Harriet asked,

still feeling uncertain about her appearance. "I usually use Simplicity patterns."

Veronica studied Harriet's dress again, with its cleverly detailed collar and padded shoulders, as they approached the entrance of the hotel conference room. "No, I don't think so," Veronica said. "It's fun to see you in something really stylish."

"Better than the sweat outfits I used to wear?" Harriet chuckled, but she actually felt annoyed with herself for having allowed her appearance to get so frumpy.

Veronica shrugged. "You looked fine in sweats, too. You had kids to run after, so what else should you have worn? Does Ralph like your new wardrobe?"

The question deflated Harriet a bit. "I don't know. He hasn't said anything. Probably hasn't noticed."

"Hasn't noticed?" Veronica pushed her beautiful, long, dark brown hair back over her shoulder with impatience. She was a small-boned, willowy young woman who looked ultra-slim today in her navy skirt and patterned blouse. Harriet had always admired her cousin for her ethereal beauty and wished she had inherited some of the same genes. Instead, Harriet had her father's sturdy bones and his tendency to put on pounds.

"I don't know how you live with Ralph," Veronica was saying, her tone a mixture of sympathy and irritation. "It's no wonder you've started going to psychic fairs."

Harriet raised her eyebrows. "Now, let's keep an open mind about psychics," she instructed her younger cousin.

Veronica had always used to respond to a directive tone. Harriet had discovered this while she was a young adolescent and Veronica was still a child, and this trait of Veronica's had continued into adulthood. But in the last few years things had changed somehow, and Harriet found she could no longer influence her cousin the way she used to. Harriet could tell by the set of Veronica's mouth just now that she'd merely done Harriet a favor when she'd complied with her arm-twisting and come with her to the fair.

"My mind is officially open," Veronica told her in an indulgent tone.

Harriet had to be satisfied with that.

They entered the large conference room, which was in a modern hotel in Oak Brook, a few suburbs west of Berwyn, where Harriet lived. Veronica, who lived on the north side of

Chicago, had driven out this Saturday morning to visit Harriet.

Harriet had heard about the three-day psychic fair being held this weekend and had awakened that morning with an odd feeling that she should go today, that she'd learn something significant about herself if she did. When Veronica had arrived at her house, she'd begged Veronica to go to the fair with her.

They signed in at the registration desk and were asked with whom they would like to make appointments for readings.

"You go ahead. I don't want to," Veronica said, her dark eyebrows furrowing as she backed away.

"Oh, come on. You're here. Why not?"

"I'll just watch while you talk to your palm reader."

Harriet shook her head. "I check in with her once a week. I want to hear what some of the others have to say." She was following her feeling that, much as she relied on Madame Layla, she would get a special insight from someone new.

"One psychic's not enough?"

"Well, they have different gifts. One might be good at advising about relationships. Another about money. Some read cards or tea leaves. Others use a crystal ball or psychometry. The more of them you go to, the more you find out."

Veronica rubbed her eyelid above her long lashes. "How do you know they aren't all quacks?"

"If what they tell you turns out to be true, it seems to me that's pretty good evidence."

"Okay, you pick one and I'll watch."

"No, I want you to have a reading, too. My treat," Harriet insisted, turning to the sign-up sheets before Veronica could object further. Scanning them, she found a name, other than her palm reader's, that she'd heard of. The name seemed to have a nice ring to it, too. "My neighbor said Dorothy Cummings is really good. She's a psychometrist. I haven't been to one of them before," she told Veronica as she wrote both their names down for appointments and paid the fees to the woman behind the desk.

A chance palm reading three months ago at a school fund-raising carnival had opened up a whole new world to Harriet. There she'd met Madame Layla, a middle-aged, black-haired palm reader, adorned with Egyptian jewelry, who was donating her time and fees for readings to the school that evening. Harriet was dubious about the colorful psychic, but decided to have a reading for fun and to support her daughter's high school, which needed new gym equipment.

Madame Layla had examined Harriet's hands with great interest and—like fate, it later seemed to Harriet—had correctly ascertained Harriet's marital problems, while also offering sympathy and suggestions. Madame Layla had seemed to provide the direction Harriet needed in her life. In that one evening she'd given Harriet the shove she'd needed to look more attractive for her husband, in the hope that this might inspire him to be more attentive and romantic. Layla had also advised her to stand up to him now and then, because Harriet had confided that she'd begun to feel like a doormat at home.

So Harriet quietly began seeing Madame Layla every few weeks, then every week, and soon came to look upon the psychic as a close confidante. Finally she told her husband, Ralph, how much she was paying the woman and how often her visits were. Ralph got angry, put his large foot down and ordered her to stop seeing the palm reader. "No way!" Harriet retorted. And since then Ralph hadn't said another word about it. Harriet was impressed. Madame Layla had told her it would happen that way.

While waiting for their appointments, Harriet and Veronica walked around the fair for a half hour or more, perusing the tables of goods for sale, which included books on psychic phenomena, witchcraft, the use of crystals, and so on. Also for sale were crystal balls, tarot cards, herbs and potions, astrological jewelry, and pendants made from crystals. In the other half of the large room, about twenty psychics sat at separate booths, taking their customers' appointments.

Harriet led Veronica to the table where she'd spotted Madame Layla sitting, giving a reading for a young woman. As usual, Layla was dressed in a colorful, flowing caftan that draped her large frame. Her hands were covered with silver rings in the shapes of Egyptian symbols. Harriet had once thought all those rings—two to a finger, and thumb rings also—looked tacky. But now she understood that they were meaningful to Layla, who felt her psychic power was connected with ancient Egypt.

When Layla finished with her customer, Harriet walked up

and said hello. She introduced Veronica, who approached with reluctance.

"Your cousin," Layla said, her dark brown eyes bright as she studied Veronica. "You should bring her in for a reading sometime."

"I've been telling her that for weeks," Harriet agreed. "She needs help with her love life. Hasn't gone on a date with a man in years." Harriet had been teasing Veronica about her nun-like lifestyle the last few years. But beneath the joking, Harriet was beginning to grow concerned about Veronica's increasingly solitary way of life.

"Some poor fellow is missing a wife," Layla said to Veronica, who was studying the carpeted floor with a grim half-smile. "Maybe I can help you find him. Let me see your hands."

"No, I . . . I didn't make an appointment," Veronica hedged.

"For free, dear. Just a quick look."

"Go on," Harriet urged.

With a sigh, Veronica approached and held out her hands. Madame Layla examined one and then the other.

"You have delicate, poetic hands," the palm reader said with admiration.

"She's a writer," Harriet told her, proud of her beautiful, accomplished cousin.

"I see that," Layla said, tracing the lines in Veronica's palm with her fingertip. "You will write a book someday," she told Veronica.

"About what?" Veronica asked.

"That would come clearer to me over time," Layla said. "I'm clairvoyant, too, and the longer I know you and the more you trust me, the more I can see."

"She gets images in her mind," Harriet explained.

"Oh," Veronica said. "So what's the verdict on my love life?"

"You are a late bloomer," Layla told her, squeezing her hand in a comforting manner. "But all good things come to those who wait, don't they? You will meet the man of your dreams soon. But he will be a challenge. You must prepare yourself or you may be disappointed in love. You could wind up a spinster."

"Prepare myself? How?"

"That would take more time for me to tell you than I have at the moment. My next customer is waiting. Have Harriet bring you to my home and I'll give you a much more thorough reading. Then I can tell you what to do to win this man when you meet him."

"What if I meet him and don't want him?" Veronica asked, her tone quite ingenuous.

Harriet suspected her cousin was baiting Madame Layla. But the palm reader simply repeated that Veronica should come in for a complete reading and thanked them with a motherly smile for stopping by her table.

"Why did you ask that?" Harriet said when they were out of earshot.

"Because she was full of beans!" Veronica replied.

"How can you say that? She knew right off that you were a writer."

"You told her."

"*I* told her?" Harriet remembered then and felt confounded. "I guess I did. But I was only confirming what she'd said, that you had a poetic hand. Are you planning to write a book?"

"No," Veronica replied with a dry laugh.

"Well, you have lots of years ahead of you. Maybe you will."

Veronica shook her head. "I don't know what you see in her, except that she has a reassuring way about her. You're paying a lot of money for someone to hold your hand."

Harriet kept her patience. "You have to go to her over a period of time. She really gets in-depth about things."

"She'll get you in debt, too."

After taking a long breath to keep her good humor, Harriet replied, "Look, I don't drink, I don't smoke, I don't gamble— not even bingo at church. I don't have any expensive hobbies, unless you count making seventeen loaves of bread in one night, which I wound up giving away because my freezer was already full of my baking." She'd found that baking lifted her spirits. "Can't I have one vice?"

"I just hate to see you put so much trust in someone who may be out to fleece you, Harriet. I think she's a con artist."

"Now you sound like Ralph."

Veronica looked chastened. "I'm sorry. I know you're unhappy. But you'd be better off seeing a marriage counselor."

"Ralph would never go to a marriage counselor. He says if I'm not happy it's *my* problem. But, you see, Layla understands all that. She says she has instincts and psychic knowledge about people that counselors with all their college degrees just don't have. She's great at predicting Ralph, for example, just from what I've told her, even though she never met him."

"Well, *Ralph*—I could predict him, too. Tell me, honestly, has your marriage improved any, with all this psychic assistance?"

Harriet lifted her shoulders. "We don't argue as much." The fact was they barely talked at all anymore, but she didn't feel like admitting that just now.

"Well, okay, I've met the Madame. Can we leave now?"

"No. We have our appointments with the psychometrist," Harriet said, checking her watch. "I think I saw her table down in the far corner of the room. Come on."

Soon they approached Dorothy Cummings's table. A sign with her name on it was posted on the wall behind her. She was dressed in a pink-and-gray business suit. Her hair was smooth gray, almost white, in a simple, short hairstyle. Her face had a youthful appearance, and her light green eyes carried an air of quiet intelligence.

"She's pretty," Harriet whispered to Veronica as they waited for the person ahead of them to finish.

"She looks halfway normal, I'll say that."

Harriet laughed. "What's with this attitude you have? You don't believe people can have supernatural abilities?"

Veronica was quiet for a moment and her expression became grave. "Oh, I *know* there are people with supernatural powers," she said, as if thinking of some personal experience. This surprised Harriet, because she didn't know what her cousin was referring to. Veronica usually confided in her. They had been close for as long as Harriet could remember. But before Harriet could ask, Veronica continued. "It's just an area where it's so easy to take advantage of people who are having problems."

"*Gullible* people like me, you mean?" Harriet said, raising an eyebrow humorously.

"Well, you have fallen for this stuff hook, line and sinker."

"All I know is I feel better after seeing Madame Layla, and her guidance has been valuable. Don't I look better lately?"

"Yes, you do," Veronica agreed.

"I'm still working on the weight issue, but I bet she can help me with that, too."

Veronica looked as though she thought otherwise. She glanced at Dorothy Cummings, whose customer had just left. "Look, she's motioning us to come over. Let's get this over with."

Harriet approached the table with Veronica, disappointed with her cousin's attitude. Veronica had changed from the sweet, shy, dreamy girl she used to be. She'd grown more mature, more forthright, but also inexplicably grim, impatient, and often melancholy. Harriet was still terribly fond of her younger cousin, but sometimes felt as if she didn't quite know her anymore.

"Hello," Dorothy said with a smile as they approached. She introduced herself and asked their names. "Who's first?"

Veronica pointed to Harriet. "She is."

Harriet put aside her ruminations about her cousin and focused on the present. "You need something of mine to hold, right?"

"Yes," Dorothy said. "A watch, a ring. Anything you've had for a while."

Harriet took off her wedding ring. "Try this," she said with a sense of gallows humor.

"All right." Dorothy took the ring and held it tightly in her hand. She closed her eyes in concentration. When she opened them and began to speak, her gaze seemed to be focused on some point in her mind's eye. "You're very impressionable, Harriet. It's something you always need to be careful of. Your marriage is not going well. You married very young. So young!" Dorothy shook her head in sympathetic dismay. "You're religious," she continued in a more positive tone. "You love your home and your neighborhood. You have children—three. No, two. Two. They don't need you much anymore. And your husband has become distant. You feel all alone."

Harriet listened, her spirits sinking as she heard her life capsulized. She wanted to say "Yes, that's right!" but Dorothy seemed in deep concentration, as if interrupting her would break the messages she was receiving.

"You're an exemplary homemaker. But your efforts aren't appreciated." Dorothy paused, as if waiting. "I'm getting something about the future now. I see some upheaval ahead. Your relationship with your husband will be tested even more. Whether the marriage lasts or not depends on you. I sense there will be another man who will have a profound effect on you, how you think, what you do. I see this man acting in the role of a counselor or priest for you."

The psychometrist relaxed her hand and looked at the wedding ring. She nodded her head. "Yes, all the ambivalence you've felt about your husband lately will disappear over the next few months. You'll make a decision about him, and the decision will be all yours, I feel. He won't have much choice in the matter."

"How come?" Harriet asked, doubtful but greatly intrigued. Her heart rate began to accelerate. Was this the important information she'd had a feeling she'd learn today?

"Because you will be the stronger one."

"Me? Stronger than Ralph?" No, Harriet couldn't see how that could ever come about. "What about this priest? Have I met him? Is he at my church?"

"I don't know," Dorothy said with some puzzlement in her voice. She gave Harriet her ring back. "He may not actually *be* a priest. I saw a flash—a quick brightness—of sensuality around you. Be careful. He may become your lover. Nothing more than that came to me. Sorry."

"Thank you," Harriet said, feeling a little shocked as she slipped her wedding ring back onto her left hand. She wasn't sure what to make of the reading. Everything Dorothy had said about her past and present was right on the mark. But her predictions about the future seemed a little far out. Madame Layla had never told her anything about a new man in her life. It sounded exciting, all right. But for a plump, thirty-six-year-old housewife, who rarely met anyone new except other women in crafts classes, this was highly unlikely. Besides, there hadn't been a new priest at her church in years, and none was expected. Good thing, too, if this man might become her lover!

Amused now, Harriet decided that she'd better put any

future prescient feelings of hers aside, forget other psychics and rely on what Madame Layla told her. At least Layla made predictions that were grounded in reality.

"Shall I do your reading now?" Dorothy said to Veronica.

Harriet noticed that Veronica's previous expression of passive disapproval had changed. Veronica looked a trifle dumbfounded, probably because she knew the facts Dorothy had stated about Harriet's past and present were true.

Veronica began to take off her watch, but then stopped and slipped it back on her wrist. Harriet wondered if Veronica had changed her mind. But her cousin opened her purse, then a zippered compartment inside it, and took out a knotted handkerchief. She untied the cloth and took out two keys, one larger one and one smaller one. Harriet wondered what these separate keys were for. She knew Veronica kept her everyday apartment and car keys on a metal chain.

Veronica studied the two keys as if questioning which one to give Dorothy. She picked up the smaller one. With some hesitance, apparently worried if she was doing the right thing, she handed it to the psychometrist.

Dorothy took the key and, as she had done with Harriet's ring, held it tightly in her hand and concentrated.

"I sense a large house, a mansion. The third floor is important. But most important is a small room below the house. It's hidden. Always dark. Secret." Dorothy seemed to shiver a bit. She swallowed and continued in a firmer voice. "You're very attached to the house, more than to your own home. But you haven't been there for a long, long while and you miss it terribly. I sense a man who is overwhelming in his importance to you. You love him deeply. I can feel the love between you and him. It's . . . it's quite beautiful and profound."

Tears gathered in Dorothy's eyes. She spoke with feeling, as if taking on Veronica's emotions herself. "And terribly, terribly sad. Such a burden of love you carry! But it's made you strong. Everything you do, your whole life is lived for this man you love so deeply."

She paused and then uttered a sound of pain. "Ohh . . . ." Dorothy's hand began to tremble. Her voice diminished to a whisper. "He's ill! He's . . . cursed. I see darkness, darkness, nothing but darkness around him."

Dorothy straightened and blinked the wetness from her

eyes. She seemed to try to pull herself together, concentrating on the key, as if to discern a new message that was coming to her. "There's a remedy—a cure. I see this clearly. He can be cured, Veronica. A woman . . . far from here, across an ocean. She knows the way. She lives near a forest. You know of her. You must find her soon because she's very old and frail."

Her hand still trembling, Dorothy held out the key to Veronica. "That's all I can tell you," she said in a strained voice. "I'm sorry, this has exhausted me." She looked earnestly at Veronica. "But you *must* use this information. You have a great love to save."

Harriet glanced at Veronica as she took back her key. Her cousin was biting her lower lip to keep back a sob. A tear slid down her cheek. "Thank you," Veronica said in a hushed voice. "But I don't know who this old woman is. I've never been out of the States. How do I find her?"

Dorothy shook her head, her expression troubled. "I sensed some connection between you. I don't know any more than that. I'm sorry. I wish you well, Veronica."

Harriet and Veronica walked out of the conference room in silence. Veronica seemed distracted, almost dazed, and Harriet was afraid to say anything at first. Finally, when they had left the hotel and were walking to the parking lot, Harriet said, "You never mentioned you had a man in your life. Who is he?"

Veronica, who had stopped crying, paused and stared at Harriet, eyes wide and unblinking, as if a thought had struck her. "Will you help me?"

"Me? How?"

"I need you to tell someone what the psychometrist told me—about the cure. You remember everything she said?"

"I think so. Who do I tell?"

"There's a house on Oak Street on the near north side. I'll write down the address. I need you to go there, but only after dark. Knock on the door and wait till he answers. Tell him—"

"Wait. Who's *he?*"

Veronica swallowed and a look shadowed her eyes that was at once tender and frightened. "His name is David."

"He's the man? The one the psychometrist mentioned, the one you love?"

Veronica nodded. "Tell him you're my cousin, that I sent

you to see him. Tell him what the psychic told us about the cure. Just say I wanted him to know. I . . ." She looked down. "I hope he won't be angry with me."

"Why? Does he have a bad temper?" Harriet asked, concerned for Veronica.

"Oh, he'd never hurt you," Veronica assured her. "Don't be afraid of him."

Somehow this unsettled Harriet even more. "Look, I want to help, but I don't understand. Why can't you visit him yourself? Or call him on the phone? I gathered that you and he broke up, but can't you write him a note at least?"

"No. We aren't to have any contact. I can't tell you why."

"Can't tell me because *you* don't know why, or because you aren't supposed to tell?"

"Whatever you may learn about David and me, *he* must tell you, Harriet. And he may choose not to tell you anything. I know this all must sound strange. But I need you to do this for me. Please? Will you?"

"Well, sure, I suppose," Harriet said with a shrug. It was a more interesting way to spend an evening than watching TV while Ralph sat behind his newspaper, she decided. Besides, she was curious about this David, this man Veronica had apparently been in love with for some time. She had to admit, Madame Layla's reading for Veronica had been all wrong. "But what about his illness?" Harriet asked. "Is it catching?"

Veronica looked at her as if she didn't know what Harriet was talking about.

"Whatever it is he's got that he needs the cure for," Harriet said.

"Oh, I see what you mean." Veronica almost smiled. "No, it's not catching. He won't give it to you." Her eyes grew sad. "He won't even give it to me."

Harriet was too confused even to ask what *that* might mean. Yes, she'd better check this man out to see what sort of relationship Veronica had gotten herself into. "When should I go?"

"Tonight? Can you?"

"Sure. I just ring the bell and ask for David? Does he have a last name?"

"Let him tell you his full name, if he wishes. And there's no bell. David's . . . old-fashioned. There's a brass door knocker.

Keep knocking until he answers. Sometimes he's in a far corner of the house and doesn't hear it right away."

"What if he's not home?"

"Then I'm afraid you'll have to go back again another night. You must keep trying until you see him," Veronica said earnestly.

"I will. You can count on me. I just wish I knew more about all this. Isn't there anything else you can tell me?"

Veronica hesitated and new tears shimmered in her eyes. Her voice grew husky with profound feeling. "Only that I love him more than life. I would die for him—if only he'd let me."

# 2

# Sometimes nothing sure sounded nice

ABOUT SEVEN-THIRTY in the evening, David was sitting on his living-room couch, feeling increasingly tense and frustrated. Pencil in hand, he was reworking a scene for the screen version of his theatrical production *The Scarlet Shadow,* and it wasn't going well. He couldn't concentrate. The unholy desires of his vampire protagonist only reminded him of his own.

David had been living like a recluse, with Veronica off-limits and Darienne off *some*where. He'd suffered the misfortune of becoming involved in a disastrous affair with another mortal woman a few years ago and knew better than to make that mistake again. But sometimes his mind wandered into a fantasy that saw him walking down Rush Street, going into a singles bar, finding some available young woman, and taking her home with him. And while he tasted her sexually in his fantasy, he'd open the artery in her neck with his sharp teeth and taste her blood as well.

It had been years since he'd drunk directly from a human artery, years since he'd enjoyed blood, rich, warm, and fresh on his tongue. Refrigerated blood from plastic blood bags always had a dull, flattened flavor. And, God, how he longed to feel a woman in his arms again!

Annoyed with his wayward thoughts, David shifted his position. What was wrong with him—an educated, civilized, mature playwright, and all he could think about were his hungers? He'd fought these lusts for centuries, but lately—

Suddenly he heard the unwelcome sound of a knock at his

front door. It was drizzling outside. Who would want to come calling in this weather?

"Go away," he muttered as he erased a scribble on his script. It might be a reporter, fans, or pranksters. He'd had them all at his door at one time or another. Ignoring them was the best thing.

But when the knocking persisted, David impatiently put down the manuscript and walked out to the spiral staircase that led to the first floor. It might be Darienne, he started thinking. She always dropped in on him unexpectedly, though usually she did it by climbing in through his window. But one could never say for sure what the blond vampiress might do.

When he reached his front door, he opened it and found, not Darienne, but a stranger standing there. And she didn't look like a reporter. Or a prankster, either. She was of average height and, at first glance, was rather average looking, too—a rounded figure wearing a raincoat over her calf-length brown dress. A flowered scarf tied under her chin protected her head from the light rain. He guessed she must be a fan of his plays and wanted to meet him. She had that hesitant, slightly scared look.

"Yes?" he said with as much politeness as he could muster.

"Are you David?"

He hesitated at her vagueness. "De Morrissey?"

"Huh?"

"What David are you looking for?"

"The one who lives at this address," she said, showing him the damp slip of paper in her hand.

He felt a sudden frisson as he read the address—the handwriting looked so similar to Veronica's. "I'm David de Morrissey," he said, his pulse starting to beat faster. "Are you looking for me?"

The woman's dark, hazel eyes widened and probed his. "David de Morrissey," she repeated with awe, as if only now comprehending. "You mean, like . . . the playwright?"

"Not only am I like the playwright," he said with some asperity, "I *am* the playwright."

"You wrote *Street Shadows?* And *The Scarlet Shadow?*"

"Yes."

She smiled as if starstruck. "No wonder Veronica was always so anxious for me to see your shows. I loved them, by the way."

"Veronica?"

"I'm her cousin, Harriet. Gosh, I didn't know she *knew* you! I'm astonished! I can't believe I'm standing here talking to you—I mean, you're a celebrity!"

David remembered Veronica once mentioning a cousin named Harriet, of whom she was fond. But why was Harriet here? "I'm happy to meet you, too," he said. "Would you care to come in?"

She brought her hand to her chest. "Really? Well, I won't say no. I do have a message for you. Don't let me forget."

"A message?" he repeated with increasing anxiety as she walked into his oval, ivory-colored entryway.

Harriet took the scarf off her light brown hair and slowly pivoted as she gazed about the ornate, three-story hall with its pilasters and carved moldings. "You live here? This is so beautiful. What a gorgeous rug," she said, looking down as she stepped onto the colorful Oriental carpet that covered the middle of the marble floor. She glanced up. "A domed ceiling! This is like some of those homes pictured in *Architectural Digest*. And a spiral staircase, like out of a movie." She looked at him and grinned. "I'd sure hate to be the one who polishes the railing."

"My living room is upstairs," he said, trying to urge her along. "I'm sorry there's no elevator in the house. You'll have to climb the steps."

"I'd love to!"

She started up the steps and he followed. But along the way, she paused now and then to look at the interior of his home from new perspectives. When they finally reached the third-floor landing, she looked over the railing once more, down into the oval hall, and said with excitement, "I feel like throwing rose petals from up here to watch them float down. Did you ever try that?"

"It never occurred to me. My living room's in here," he said, guiding her through the door.

Once in the room, he patiently listened to more compliments as she perused his oak furniture, the chandelier hanging from the ceiling, the insect-and-flower pattern of his drapes and upholstery, the Oriental rug in front of the love seat. He surmised she must be a woman who had traveled little and seen little, to be so taken with his home.

As she made a study of his living room, he took the opportunity to study her. Her face was round, cheery, almost devoid of makeup. Her skin was fine and unlined, her figure rounded and quite feminine. Her large, dark eyes slanted just a bit and carried a lively, artless aspect.

When David took her coat, he noticed what a smooth, plump, white throat she had. His mouth began to water. He chastised himself as he hung her coat in the closet. She was Veronica's cousin, for God's sake!

After settling her in an easy chair by the draped bay windows, he took another easy chair placed nearby, at the other side of the windows. A small, round oak table stood between the two chairs. She placed her leather handbag on it.

"You said you had a message," he told her anxiously. "I was to remind you."

"Right," she replied, running her fingers through the damp bangs of her short brown hair. "That's why Veronica sent me here."

"She asked you to speak to me?"

Harriet's eyebrows drew together in a tentative expression. "She was afraid you might be angry about it. I don't know why. She wouldn't tell me much, not even your last name."

David understood by this that Veronica knew she was breaking their pact of total separation by sending a message to him. She was also trying to protect him by revealing little information. "I won't be angry," David said. "Veronica must have a good reason to want to contact me through you."

Harriet nodded. "Yes, she does. She was very concerned. I've never seen her so upset."

This sounded serious indeed. "So," he said, taking a breath in apprehension. "What is the message?"

"Well, I guess I can summarize it in three words: There's a cure."

This told him nothing. "A cure?"

"For you," Harriet said, averting her eyes, as though respecting his privacy now. "Apparently you have some illness. Veronica wouldn't explain. But we were told that there's a cure for the disease you have."

"Told? By whom?"

"A psychic. A psychometrist to be specific. You want to hear the whole story?"

"Yes, please," David said, rather dazed by all this.

"It was my idea. I've been seeing a palm reader for the last few months. Madame Layla. She's very good, usually. In fact, I thought she was infallible until she gave Veronica such a poor reading." Harriet paused to chuckle. "She told Veronica she'd meet the man of her dreams soon. And then I learned she's been in love with you all this time. The psychometrist got it straight, though."

"She went with you to see these psychics?"

"I talked her into going to a psychic fair with me."

"A fair?"

"It's held at a hotel and there are maybe twenty or thirty psychics there giving readings and so on."

"Good grief," David muttered.

Harriet seemed to take his comment with aplomb. "You sound like another skeptic. So was Veronica. But not anymore," she said with satisfaction. "Not after the psychometrist told her so much about herself and you."

"Go on," he said, anxious to hear this tale, wherever it led.

"Well, this gets a little personal. I don't know you, so I feel funny telling you about it."

David tensed a bit, on guard now. What had Harriet learned about him and his secret relationship with her cousin? "I appreciate your sensitivity, but I need to know what upset Veronica."

Harriet was studying him with her deep, dark eyes, whose color he couldn't pinpoint. Until now, his impression had been that she didn't have one of the greater intellects he'd ever encountered. But she had a surprising, penetrating gaze for someone with such wandering attention.

"You really do care for her, don't you?" Harriet said. "I can tell from your voice and your eyes. That's nice. That's . . . I wish I had someone who cared for me like that."

She smiled and shifted in her chair. David noticed she wore a wedding ring.

"Sorry," Harriet said. "Where was I?"

"The psychometrist told Veronica—"

"Right. She said Veronica was deeply in love. She described it as a great, sad love, and even started to cry. I think she took on some of Veronica's feelings from holding the key. She—"

"Key?"

"Oh, I forgot. Veronica gave her a key. I'd never seen it before. Actually, she had two keys. They were wrapped in a handkerchief. She took the smaller of the two and gave it to the psychometrist to hold for the reading."

David felt intruded upon. Veronica must have handed the woman the key to his secret room in the basement, the room where he rested during the daylight hours. He'd given it to Veronica years ago, along with the key to his home. Why had she given it to a psychic? Was she growing so desperate to know the future?

If so, he couldn't blame her. He felt desperate sometimes, too, to know the final outcome of their disrupted love affair.

"The psychic was able to discern that Veronica loved someone," David conjectured, trying to cast doubt. "Anyone might have intuited that."

Harriet shook her head. "She told Veronica about this mansion, even mentioned the third floor," she said, gesturing toward the room they were sitting in. "And she said you were ill. She used the word 'cursed.' She said she saw nothing but darkness surrounding you."

Again David felt shaken at the truth in her words. Over the centuries there had always been people who believed in palm readers and clairvoyants. He'd become convinced long ago that most of these fortune tellers were charlatans. But now and then, there would be one who seemed too accurate to be dismissed. Perhaps this woman was truly clairvoyant. "And she mentioned there was a cure?"

"Yes. She said she felt it very strongly. An old woman across the ocean knows about it. There was also something about a forest. But the part that puzzled Veronica was that she was supposed to know who this old woman was. Veronica couldn't figure it out. She wanted you to know what the psychometrist said. Maybe she thought you would understand."

David shook his head. "No, it makes no sense to me. I've never heard of such a woman. Besides, I'm certain there *is* no cure for me. I know of a scientist in Switzerland who has been working on discovering a remedy for decades. He's found none. She's right, in a way I *am* cursed. And cursed, I'll stay. I brought it on myself. It's my punishment."

"Punishment." Harriet studied him. "You think being sick is a punishment? Why? You seem like a nice enough man to me. And so talented."

"I'm punished for wanting to be more than I was born to be, for wanting more talent than I was allotted." David looked into Harriet's eyes. They seemed simple and confused now. He smiled. "I don't expect you to understand. I'm just trying to explain that the psychic's prediction about a cure was completely inaccurate. Though, I admit, she came close in describing my circumstances and my place in Veronica's life. Love is a strong emotion, easy to pick up, perhaps, for those who are sensitive."

Harriet made a subtle grin. "But isn't there an old saying that there are more things in heaven and earth than we can understand?" she pointed out.

"You're quite right," David said, pleasantly taken aback by her appropriate comment. " 'There are more things in heaven and earth, Horatio, than are dreamt of in your philosophy.' It's from *Hamlet*. Thank you for reminding me."

Harriet's eyes sparkled now with a mixture of pride and surprise. Perhaps she was as taken off-guard as he was that their minds had made such an easy and quick connection, for two people who seemed to have little in common other than an affection for Veronica.

"I'm sorry you don't believe the part about the cure," Harriet said. "Veronica will be disappointed and sad."

"How is Veronica?" David asked, conscious that he was guilty of abusing their pact by asking about her. But he had to know.

"Oh, she's fine. She's still my beautiful little cousin. I call her 'little' from when we were kids—she's several years younger than me. She got a job promotion recently. Maybe you didn't know. She's a full-fledged staff writer now at *Windy City* magazine. Writes feature articles regularly."

David was so happy to hear this, tears stung the backs of his eyes. "That's wonderful! That's what I wanted for her, to excel in her career. And does she still have the same apartment?"

"Yes. Same place. She's been redecorating it."

"She . . . lives alone?" David tried to ask nonchalantly.

"Oh, yes. She's been alone since Rob Greenfield left Chicago a few years ago," Harriet said, apparently surmising what David wanted to know.

He was relieved to hear Rob had left the city. David had more or less pushed Veronica into Rob's eager arms by advising Veronica to see other men, have an affair if she wanted, explore the world while she and David were separated. But knowing now that Rob was permanently out of her life gave David great relief. While he wanted her to live a full life and see the world, he was always afraid that in the end she might choose the daylight world of mortals instead of him.

"I was beginning to think she hated men. But now I see what she's waiting for." Harriet smiled and gestured toward David. "If you and she are so in love, why are you separated? Because of your illness? You aren't going to . . . I mean, is your prognosis not very hopeful?"

"I'm not going to die," David hastened to tell her. He couldn't very well explain that he was one of the "undead." But how could he explain his situation plausibly without revealing much? Harriet had been kind enough to come here on Veronica's behalf, and she'd told him things about his beloved that he'd longed to hear. He felt he owed Harriet some explanation. "I have a chronic medical problem that Veronica needs time to fully comprehend. One aspect of the problem is that I can't have children."

He realized then what Harriet might read into that statement. "Not that I'm . . ." David shifted in his chair uncomfortably, finding that he'd happened onto a very personal subject.

"I didn't think so," Harriet said, tactfully glancing away. "You look too good to be . . . nonfunctioning. That's why I wondered how you could be ill. You seem so healthy."

David studied her with appraising eyes, finding he was vain enough to appreciate her assessment of him. He hadn't gotten a compliment from a woman since Darienne left town. Harriet was really more attractive than he'd at first thought, he decided.

"Well, I am quite healthy, actually. I never get colds or flu, for instance. But," he said, growing serious again, "when I met Veronica, I felt she was too young to make a decision about entering into a permanent relationship with a man who could never give her a family. And I'm not easy to live with. I keep odd hours. I write during the day and must be alone while I work." This, of course, was not true. It was the lie he used to explain to mortals why he couldn't be bothered during daylight hours. "I have . . . unusual habits," he continued carefully. "She was too young to understand the consequences of a permanent relationship with me. But our attraction to one another was overpowering. So I felt the best way she could make such a decision was if she spent some years on her own, to mature, to know the world better before she gave it up for me. I live the life of a recluse, and to be with me, she would have to live that way, too."

"I see. You want to be fair to her."

"Yes, precisely."

"That's nice. I think people should wait and think before making any big changes in their lives. I wish I had been able to think before . . ." Her expression grew somber.

David hesitated, but decided to draw her out. "Your marriage isn't working out?"

She looked at him. "No," she replied simply, apparently not one to hide anything. "And it was for the reason you mentioned—we were too young. Ralph was eighteen and I was seventeen. He was our high school's football hero and I was crazy about him, afraid I'd lose him if I didn't give him everything he wanted. So pretty soon I was in a family way and we *had* to get married. In those days, in my neighborhood, you did that if you found yourself in such a predicament. I was lucky I managed to graduate high school at least. Never got to college." Harriet's downcast expression changed all at once to a smile. "But Veronica did. I was so proud of her. She was the first college graduate in our family."

"Her mother is your aunt?"

"Yes, my father and her mother were brother and sister. My maiden name is Benda. But of course I took my husband's name, Dvorak. They're both good Bohemian names."

"Antonín Dvořák was a great Czech composer. Could he have been a distant relation?"

"To Ralph? I doubt it. Ralph doesn't have any musical inclination. He sells insurance."

She changed her position and glanced admiringly around

the room again, as if talking about her husband depressed her and she didn't want to be depressed. David felt sad for her.

"Speaking of music," she said, turning to him, eyes lively now. "What's going on with *The Scarlet Shadow?* I read that it may be made into a movie. Is that true?"

"I'm working on the screenplay now," he said, pointing to the manuscript he'd left on the love seat. "The studio sent it to me to rewrite after some of the brilliant minds in Hollywood got their fingers in it and made a mess of it." David's tone showed his exasperation. Dealing with Hollywood people was proving to be a learning experience for him. They'd wanted him to fly to California to work with them on the script. But David preferred the comforts of his Chicago home and thought it best to stay off the Hollywood roller coaster. He would find it difficult to "do lunch" anyway, since he was confined to his coffin all day. So other writers had been hired, who had mangled his work. And now they'd sent it back to him to repair.

"When will the movie be made?"

"I have no idea. It could be years."

"Will Matthew McDowall star?"

"Yes, he's signed a contract, so that's settled, at least."

"Great! He was *so* wonderful in that role onstage. Veronica was surprised I got such an instant, huge crush on him. I thought he was even better than Sam Taglia was in *Street Shadows,* and Sam was excellent. I graduated high school with Sam."

David nodded. "I remember Veronica told me that. I haven't seen him in a while."

"He moved to New York and got married. I dated him for a time in high school, before I dated Ralph." She grew quiet again.

David sensed she was thinking about what might have been. Again, he found himself feeling sympathy for her. "Would you like some tea?"

She seemed taken by surprise. "Thank you," she said with a smile, "but I should go. I'm imposing on you."

"Not at all. I'm enjoying our conversation. The tea will only take a minute."

She tilted her chin. "Well, all right. Thanks. It's kind of cold and damp out, so some tea would be nice. It's been such a wet spring this year," she chattered, as if a little nervous now.

"I should have thought to offer you some sooner," David said, rising from his chair to go to the built-in wet bar in the corner of the room. He took out a small hot plate and teakettle from one of the lower cabinets, filled the kettle with water, and set it to heat.

"How come your shows are about vampires?" she asked, sounding composed again as she rose from her chair and walked over to the bar, where David was. "It's an unusual sort of hero to base a musical on."

"Oh, just an interest of mine," David murmured, lowering his eyes.

"Do you do a lot of research on vampires before you write your plays?"

"No, not really."

"It's a fun subject," she said. "My grandmother used to tell me stories about them. I like fantasy and folklore."

David smiled as he tended the heating teakettle and changed the subject. "Delivering this message from Veronica must have seemed odd to you."

"It did," Harriet said, leaning against the wood bar. "It got me curious. I didn't know she was in love. I wanted to meet you. Now that I have, I can see why she's hooked."

David looked up with delight. "You can?"

"Well—you're a celebrated playwright, handsome, you have a gorgeous home, you seem cultured, and you know how to talk to a woman. I'm impressed with my little cousin's taste!"

David again found himself pleased. He'd grown so vain! Where had his sense of humility gone? he wondered. He'd missed having a female around to converse with almost as much as he'd missed sex. "I enjoy talking to women. Your husband doesn't communicate well with you?" he asked, trying to shift the focus back on her.

"Hardly at all anymore," she said, looking down to trace her finger along the grain of wood on the bar. "I don't know, maybe it's my fault. *He* says it's my fault. Maybe he's right."

"Do you work?"

She looked up. "You mean, like, in an office? No. I work plenty at home, though."

"I imagine you do. Do you enjoy being a housewife?"

Harriet shrugged. "I do love to cook. I stay up late cooking sometimes. It makes me feel secure somehow. Productive. I like to sew, too. But doing dishes and laundry and so on—well, it's a lot of work and my family seems to take it all for granted. I'm tired a lot. My doctor gave me a blood test and said my hemoglobin was low. So he's got me taking iron supplements. Twice a day. I have to admit my energy has picked up since I've been taking them."

Again, David felt his mouth begin to water. "You must have rich blood now." He said this as if making a joke, though the remembered taste and texture of warm blood on his tongue invaded and awakened his senses. His pulse quickened. He swallowed, trying to quell his desire, which always came on at the mention of blood, no matter how civilized he tried to be. And lately the desire was overwhelming. He pressed his fingers onto the edge of the bar, trying to keep inner control of his frightful lust. She was the first mortal he'd been near in a long while, and she was here in his home—alone.

"With all this iron, I may rust out by the end of the year," Harriet was saying with a chuckle. As she looked at him, her expression changed. Her eyes widened and darkened with fear. David glanced away, wondering if she'd seen a hint of cobalt in his blue eyes, the involuntary vampire glow that came with any strong desire or emotion.

"How many children do you have?" he asked, anxious to change the subject as he tested the temperature of the teakettle.

"Two," she replied, sounding disconcerted. "My son, the oldest, is away at college. He's a freshman." As she spoke, she kept on studying him and seemed to relax again. Perhaps she'd decided she'd imagined the unearthly light in his eyes. "My son was always closer to my husband. They have a good relationship. My daughter is in her last year of high school, and she and I have been close. Until lately. She's been kind of growing up without me this last year. I used to worry she'd make the same mistake I made, but fortunately, she's a lot more sensible than I was. She doesn't get too involved with her boyfriends and she studies hard. She's talking about becoming a psychologist. I think it's because of what she sees at home. I'm glad she's learning from it instead of letting it get her down. She's a smart girl."

David had regained his composure and willed himself to conduct an interested, uplifting conversation with her and forget about her blood. "Has she seen a lot of arguing between you and your husband?"

Harriet leaned her elbow on the bar and rested her chin in her hand. "Not really. There hasn't been much of anything. We both care about the kids, and I think they know that. But the kids can sense there's not much of a relationship between Ralph and me. I don't know how it's come to this. We were so nuts about each other back in high school. But somehow that disappeared when the children came."

"Perhaps because you stopped focusing on your relationship with each other," David suggested. "You became a mother and he became a breadwinner. You both lost track of your own needs and forgot how to play the role of lover for each other."

Harriet stared at him as she straightened up, her dark eyes looking as though they wanted to pull every ounce of wisdom from David's brain. "I like how you put that. We did have a lot of rapport when we were dating. I love to think back on my days in high school. I even have recurring dreams about being in school again, dating Ralph. They're always wonderful dreams. I'm so happy in them."

David poured steaming water into a cup and dropped in a tea bag. "When you were in school you were still your own person, not someone's mother or wife."

Harriet took the teacup from him. "That's true."

"Unconsciously you want to go back to that time when you were free from the duties of motherhood and keeping house, to a time when you could focus on developing yourself, which is what being a student is all about."

She nodded. "I stayed home with the kids, while Ralph got his college degree working nights. Since then I've always felt that he thinks I'm inferior because I'm less educated than he is. And I gained weight. Maybe I shouldn't be surprised he doesn't pay me much attention."

David emphatically shook his head. "The sense of inferiority may be more in *your* mind than in his," he told her. "And I wouldn't worry about weight." He glanced briefly at her well-endowed bosom and, in his sexually deprived state, found he rather envied her husband. "Look at Renaissance paintings—Rubens, for example. Women with full figures were adored. If your husband loves you, I wouldn't think that would be a problem. He may have gained weight too."

"Oh, he has! But it doesn't matter so much for men," she argued. "It's women who are always supposed to look so good."

David gently shook his forefinger at her. "Don't you believe it."

She grinned as she studied him a long moment. "You know, I like talking to you! You've made me feel better tonight than my priest or my hairdresser or even my palm reader."

David was happy to hear he'd lifted her spirits. "This palm reader," he said, "are you sure you're wise putting faith in her? Does she charge you for her readings?"

"Well, sure, but—"

"Why pay her? You can come to me for free."

"Come to you . . . ?"

"I don't pretend to be able to predict the future, but if you've found talking with me is helpful, then, by all means, visit me again," he told her, though his conscience questioned if inviting her back was wise. She'd be a temptation. But he was lonely. "I . . . don't get out much. I like to have someone agreeable to chat with now and then. I need a new friend and I think perhaps you could use one, too." He had another reason, too, which he didn't say.

Harriet smiled slyly, a rather charming expression on her, which caused dimples to appear in her cheeks. "I've enjoyed meeting you, too. But it just occurred to me that you might have some other objective for wanting me to come back—so I can keep you posted about Veronica."

David felt a bit mortified but not surprised that she'd seen through him. "Please believe it's not the only reason. I do like your company."

Harriet looked thoughtful and a trifle shy. "That's the nicest thing I've heard from a man in years. Thank you. I will come again. I'd love to!"

Good, David thought, easily suppressing the misgivings of his conscience, because he felt happier than he'd been in months. He had a source of regular news about Veronica now.

This wasn't in keeping with the spirit of the pact he'd made with her, but he didn't care anymore. The pact of separation was to last a decade, but a decade was too long to go without any news of the woman he loved. If he and Veronica didn't see or speak to each other or send any further messages, receiving news from Harriet now and then wouldn't compromise the pact so very much, he rationalized.

And, he reminded himself, it wasn't only Veronica he was thinking of. He liked Harriet, and she had problems he felt he might be able to help her with. It would make him feel useful to be of assistance to someone else, instead of dwelling on his own loneliness all the time. At least he could save her from going to a palm reader. And he was sure he could keep his unsettling desire for her blood in check if she became his friend. His sense of loyalty and protectiveness would keep him from harming Veronica's cousin. In fact a friendship could only benefit all of them, including Veronica. Harriet would also carry news of David to her cousin, and Veronica would be reassured, as he had been about her, that he was well, and alone, and missing her terribly.

"I've just met your David!" Harriet said when Veronica opened her door. Harriet had stopped to see her cousin before driving back to Berwyn.

"What did he say? How did he look?" Veronica asked excitedly as she let Harriet into her apartment. She appeared frail in her slacks and thin gray sweater.

"He looked great! I can see why you're willing to wait for him. He's wonderful to talk to. I loved his European accent! He makes you glad to be a female. He even gave me a cup of tea."

Tears formed in Veronica's brown eyes, making them look wet and glassy. "He made you tea?" she said with a tender smile. "He used to do that for me."

Harriet swallowed, moved by her cousin's emotion. She gave Veronica a warm hug. "He asked about you," Harriet went on as they walked to the new plaid couch in the living room, which Veronica had had redecorated in shades of green, burgundy, and tan. "I told him you were fine. He was thrilled to hear you'd gotten a promotion. And he seemed relieved to know you didn't have a man in your life."

"Was *he* alone?" Veronica asked anxiously, hands between her knees, as they sat together on the couch.

"He looked pretty lonely to me. He even invited me to visit him again. I think he wants to keep tabs on you," Harriet said, giving her a between-us-girls look. "He explained why you and he were separated."

Veronica's wet eyes widened with what seemed like alarm. "He did?"

Harriet was surprised at her reaction. "He said he couldn't have children because of his illness and thought you were too young to make a decision about a permanent relationship. I assume by that he meant marriage."

Veronica made a vague smile. "What about the cure? You told him?"

"I told him everything the psychometrist said. But he thought the part about a cure couldn't be true. He said he knew of a Swiss scientist who's been searching for a cure for years and has never found one."

"Herman," Veronica said, nodding. "Darienne used to mention him."

"Who's Darienne?"

"She's a . . . a friend of David's and mine. I haven't seen her for a few years, though." Veronica bowed her head and seemed distressed. "I wonder what happened to her. She used to keep me posted about David." She looked up again at Harriet. "So David doesn't think there could be a cure? He didn't know anything about the old woman?"

"No. But he said something odd—that he thought his illness was a punishment."

Veronica's expression grew veiled. "He feels guilty about things in his past," she explained with hesitance, as if searching for words. "He has a deep sense of moral responsibility. Both Darienne and I have tried to change his ideas, but he won't change. He's set in his ways."

"Already? He looked a little younger than I am, and I hope I'm not set yet!"

Veronica laughed softly. "Well, if he doesn't think there's anything to Dorothy's prediction, I guess I sent you on a wild-goose chase."

*"No!"* Harriet insisted. "I was thrilled to meet the man who wrote *The Scarlet Shadow*. He was a little offbeat, even a tad

eerie, but he sure fulfilled the image of a recluse playwright. And we had such a great conversation! I wound up telling him about some of my problems, and he said a few things that made me feel better. He's so understanding."

"And reassuring and caring. I know," Veronica said, her eyes forlorn. "That's why I fell in love with him. Are you going to visit him again? You should. He'd do you more good than Madame Layla."

"That's what he said," Harriet told her. "But, do *you* mind if I visit him again?"

"Me, mind?" Veronica's eyes sparkled with eagerness now. "You can tell me more about how he is. This long separation is his idea, and I have to abide by his wishes. But if you see him, I'll feel closer to him through you—like I did when Darienne was in town." Veronica paused and a new light came into her eyes. "I just remembered what the psychometrist told you—that you'd meet a man who would act as your counselor."

Harriet stopped breathing for a second. "You think she meant David? But she mentioned a priest."

"In his youth, David wanted to become a priest."

"You're kidding!" she exclaimed with complete astonishment. "Gosh, you're right, she must have meant David." Harriet suddenly felt cold and awkward. "But Veronica, she also said he might become my lover."

Her cousin sat still for a long moment. *"Might,"* she said. "It may not turn out like that."

Harriet pondered the situation. "Now that I think about it, I don't see how it could. He's so in love with *you!* I could see it in his eyes."

Veronica's mouth curved into a tender smile and she looked almost happy now. "Then you have nothing to worry about."

But Harriet was having second thoughts. "You're awfully trusting. I'm still afraid Dorothy was right about too much to dismiss the 'lover' thing, even if it seems unlikely. If he's lonely without you, would he be the type to make do with a substitute—even a married housewife with flour under her fingernails? Not that *I'd* want to have to confess to a priest that I'd cheated on Ralph. But with a man like David, I wouldn't be normal if I weren't tempted."

Harriet already felt guilty admitting her "impure"

thoughts, as she'd learned to say as a child from her catechism instruction at church. She hoped Veronica wouldn't think badly of her, but they might as well discuss a potential problem before it happened.

Veronica bowed her head, looking at her hands in her lap for a few moments. When she looked up, her eyes seemed wise and placid, almost resigned. "David is unique," she said quietly. "All sorts of relationships are possible with him. I think he would be good for you right now, Harriet. Go ahead and see him again. Your conscience, and David's, will guide you to do whatever is right for you."

An hour later, Harriet was still pondering Veronica's words. After putting her car in the backyard garage, she unlocked the back door to her home, a sixty-year-old brick bungalow. Veronica had seemed so understanding, almost too complacent about Harriet forming an extended friendship with the man Veronica loved. Especially when Veronica could not see him herself. Harriet would have been jealous in such a situation, and she wondered why her cousin wasn't.

As she walked into her large kitchen, bright with the yellow wallpaper she'd put up five years ago, featuring a homey pattern of wooden spoons, bread, vegetables, and mushrooms, another thing still bothered her. She couldn't get out of her mind the radiant, almost neon light she thought she'd seen in David's eyes when they were talking about her hemoglobin. It had frightened her. But she must have imagined it, because when he'd looked at her again it was gone. And he'd seemed so pleasant, almost courtly, when he was serving her tea.

She left her purse on the wood breakfast table, covered with a yellow plaid tablecloth, and took off her raincoat. She peeked into her daughter's bedroom. Janet was cramming for a history test at her small desk in one corner of the room. Her blond hair, inherited from her father, was tied back in a low ponytail, and she wore jeans and a black sweatshirt. She turned from her books and smiled.

"Hi, Mom. Thought you'd get home earlier from the crafts exhibition."

Harriet felt a twinge of guilt about telling her family she was going to an exhibition downtown, but Veronica had sworn her to secrecy about David. "I visited Veronica afterward."

"You drove all the way to her place?"

"She seemed upset when we went to the psychic fair this morning, so I thought I should spend some time with her."

"Somebody gazed into a crystal ball and gave her bad news?"

"Something like that."

"Mom, I wish you'd stop going to those things. How can you believe that garbage?"

Janet sometimes behaved as if she were her mother's intellectual superior. But at age eighteen, that was natural, Harriet supposed. "I may stop going."

"Really? What about Madame Layla?"

"I may give her up, too."

Janet made an exaggerated sigh of relief. "Thank God! So how's Veronica?"

"She's fine. We had a nice talk."

"About what?"

"Oh, a man in her life."

"She's got a boyfriend?" Janet asked with interest.

"Sort of."

"One of those on again, off again situations?"

"Something like that."

Janet laughed. "Are you trying to set a record for vagueness?"

Harriet grinned. "Better get back to studying for that test on Monday. By the way, I got the spot out of your red sweater."

"Great," Janet said, turning back to her books. "Are there any potato chips?"

"Let me hang up my coat and I'll bring you some."

"Thanks, Mom!"

She'll probably want a cola, too, Harriet thought as she walked down the short hall to the closet. Harriet had probably spoiled her kids, but—oh, well, too late to change anything now. At least Janet had started saying thanks, lately. She was probably beginning to realize she wouldn't get the service she got at home once she went off to college like her older brother.

Harriet hung her coat in the closet. She got the chips and cola, brought them to her daughter, then walked to the living room, with its flower-patterned drapes and comfortable overstuffed furniture. The color TV was on, and there sat Ralph in front of it, asleep in his recliner, newspaper on his lap. He looked peaceful, snoring lightly. Harriet turned off the TV. He woke up at the sudden silence, looking groggy.

Ralph's blond hair was still thick and fell down over his forehead as it had when she met him in high school. Back then his face had angular contours and his eyes carried a constant whimsical quality. But now his face was more full and lacked definition. His six-foot-three frame had grown out of shape from lack of exercise and a penchant for big meals and home cooking. His gold-brown eyes, once so full of humor, carried a weary, uptight aspect much of the time now.

"Better go to bed," she told him when he looked at her in surprise. "We have church tomorrow."

"Yeah," he said, rubbing his eyes. "When did you get home?"

She might have told him an hour ago and gotten away with it. But her conscience made her be truthful about this much. Unfortunately, she'd have other lies to tell him. "Just now. I went to visit Veronica."

"So late? You saw her this morning, didn't you?"

"Yes, but we needed to talk more."

Ralph looked at his watch, shook his head and tossed his newspaper aside. "Always yakity-yak with your relatives," he muttered. "You can talk to *them* all day and all night."

"Why shouldn't I talk to my relatives?"

"I'm your relative, too."

"You want to talk to me? Talk."

He began to get up. "I can't talk any sense into you. The only one you listen to is your Madame Layla."

Harriet exhaled. "I probably won't see her anymore."

Ralph turned to look at her, his blond eyebrows drawn together over the bridge of his nose, once broken during a football tackle. "No?"

"No."

He seemed surprised, as if he wondered why she'd suddenly given up her palm reader. But, as was like him, he didn't ask. He began walking toward the bedroom and said, "Glad to know I won't have that draining my bank account anymore."

Harriet didn't feel like reminding him that their bank account was half hers, too. It would only lead to another lecture about how he earned all their money and all she knew how to do was spend it.

"You want an early breakfast tomorrow before church?" she asked.

"Not unless you fry me an egg or two. I'm tired of cereal and watery milk. How about waffles? You used to make waffles."

"Back when we were both thin. I'm trying to lose weight and you should, too. Cereal with nonfat milk is healthier."

He put his hand up. "Okay, okay, I don't want to argue." He disappeared into the bedroom. As Harriet turned to pick up the newspaper he had dropped, he poked his head out the bedroom door. "Coming to bed?"

"In a while."

"Well, don't stay up half the night baking. I can't sleep when you're up."

"Why not? I'm careful about not making noise in the kitchen."

"I can't sleep, I'm telling you. Why can't you come to bed at a normal hour?"

Harriet said nothing and folded the newspaper. He disappeared into the bedroom, not waiting for an answer. When he was gone, she collapsed on the couch, thinking with annoyance, Isn't this my house, too? Couldn't she stay up late without having to hear complaints about it? Why did he need her in bed with him?

Well, she knew the answer to that, didn't she . . .

Yes, she avoided sex when she could. Ralph's lovemaking technique had never evolved beyond the backseat-of-the-car approach he'd used when they were teenagers. She'd gotten tired of feeling shortchanged years ago. She didn't even really know what good sex was, except what she'd read in self-help books, which seemed too matter-of-fact and technical, and romance novels, which seemed over-passionate and vague. When she'd told Ralph once that she wasn't satisfied with the way they made love, he'd told her it must be *her* problem. He'd kept up *his* "end of the bargain," as he'd put it. What more did she expect? He'd sounded so certain of the matter that she'd never attempted to bring up the subject with him again.

Harriet wasn't sure anymore what she should expect from

her marriage. Someday, when the kids were out of college and well on their own, maybe she'd get a divorce. She hadn't mentioned this to anyone yet, because she still wasn't positive that it was the right thing to do. She had never liked the idea of divorce. She believed in honoring marriage vows and she'd always tried to be a good Catholic. If she did end her marriage, she certainly wouldn't marry again. It was against her religion to do so. So it was Ralph or nothing.

But sometimes nothing sure sounded nice.

# 3

# To have his nightly relationship with an audience

AT A theater in Sydney, Australia, Darienne Victoire sat fifth row center watching a performance of *The Scarlet Shadow,* her vision blurred by tears that wouldn't stop coming. Onstage, her lover, the charismatic American actor Matthew McDowall, kept the capacity audience mesmerized as he played Sir Percy Blackeney, the vampire role for which he'd won worldwide acclaim.

Any other man of average height, as Matthew was, might have looked less than powerful in the blond wig and elaborate eighteenth-century costume he wore. But on Matthew's lean, yet barrel-chested physique, the high black boots and black breeches lent a strong, elegant line. The black satin cutaway coat and dark red waistcoat accentuated his angular shoulders and deep singer's chest. His costume together with the stage lighting made him look larger than life, a striking, thoroughly masculine figure.

But more stunning yet was the way he glided across the floorboards with a stealthy dancer's grace toward his leading lady, also dressed in frothy eighteenth-century finery. Matthew's poignant manner of moving, which he'd developed himself, had become his trademark, along with his beautiful, emotion-filled, slightly eerie tenor voice. His portrayal had added new dimension to an old myth, indeed had set a new standard: Matthew's Sir Percy had now become everyone's idea of what a romantic male vampire ought to be. At least those who had had the privilege of seeing him perform in Chicago, New York, London, or Sydney could never again be satisfied with a commonplace Dracula.

He approached his Marguerite, played by a petite Australian actress, with ominous, sensual fluidity, each slow step, toe-heel, toe-heel, bringing him closer to her as she stood facing him, helpless, as if hypnotized by his eyes. Fingers extended, he loomed over her and ran his fingertips with tender, painful desire along the side of her throat, stopping at her pulse point. His head tilted to one side, as if he were contemplating the unholy thought of tasting her blood.

Then, turning his head to his shoulder suddenly, he backed away, head bowed in a tortured pose, as if caving into himself from guilt and anguish at his own bloodlust. Marguerite ran off, frightened, into the wings.

Left alone on the stage, Matthew bent his knees slightly and swiveled toward the audience, then rose up on his toes as he began to sing the song that would always be associated with him, "She Can Never Be Mine." His voice caressed Darienne's ear as it floated over the audience, soft, clear, tender with love.

New tears stung her eyes as she recalled that, years ago, this was the first piece she'd ever heard him sing. And tonight, at this, his farewell performance, it was probably the last time on any stage she would ever see and hear him perform this song and this role, which he'd made so convincingly his own. A movie of the musical was planned, but a movie would never be the same. She'd heard his fans say this over and over, and she agreed. Matthew would be wonderful in a film, but it could never match the experience of breathing in that rarified atmosphere that he alone could create in person, in real time, on the floorboards of a stage.

Darienne had first met Matthew in Chicago, where he'd begun working on what was then considered to be David de Morrissey's preposterous idea of putting a vampire into the *Scarlet Pimpernel* story line, from the book originally written by Baroness Orczy, and making it a musical. But Matthew had understood David's inspiration and gave life to a character that would make theatrical history. This had been confirmed when Matthew took the musical on to Broadway, where he, David, and the show later won Tony awards. With little rest in between cities, Matthew charged on to London, where he won the Olivier award. From there, he'd gone to

Sydney, where he'd received further rave reviews and accolades.

He'd been playing the heroic vampire almost nonstop for about three years. And in each city he received not only acclaim as a singer and actor, but a loyal following of fans, mostly women, who wrote him letters, sent cards when he was ill and on his birthday, brought flowers and gifts for him to the stage door, and waited patiently, even in the rain, for him to appear and sign autographs. By the time he left each place, there were fans who claimed to have seen him in the show fifty times and more, fans who spent their vacation time and money following him to the next city to see him perform again.

Darienne could understand their fervor, their devotion to him. She'd seen him in the show herself perhaps two hundred times. Yes, she could recite every line and lyric, and her mind wandered during scenes in which Matthew did not appear. But whenever he was onstage, he kept her enthralled in some profound way she still couldn't explain. She believed she could have gone on watching him play the role forever.

But that, of course, was impossible. Unlike his supernatural stage character, Matthew was only a mortal. And his mortal's body was worn out. His shoulders ached with bursitis from swinging on a rope from the proscenium to the stage every performance. Rope burns scarred the palms of his hands. He'd bruised and injured himself more times than he could count from the twelve-foot drop through a stage trapdoor that allowed him to disappear before the audience's eyes. Once, because of exhaustion, he'd fallen from the forty-foot ladder he had to climb backstage to get to the top of the proscenium. This had resulted in torn ligaments in his legs, for which he took pain killers in order to go on performing rather than resting and letting them heal. This was not to mention chronic eye irritation due to the contact lenses he wore to make his gray-green eyes a vivid blue, and the general drain on his energy from carrying the show, and from singing full force while moving his body in the slow, taut, gliding way he'd developed to give his vampire a visually eerie effect.

One night in London, after performing there for six months, he'd had to be hospitalized for exhaustion when he simply collapsed after a performance. Doctors ordered him to stop and take a long rest. But Matthew took only two weeks off, finished his run, then insisted on fulfilling his commitment to carry the show to Australia. Here, after renewed medical problems, a new set of doctors had advised him to rest for six months at least or risk breaking his health beyond repair and permanently injuring his overused vocal chords. Darienne had pleaded with him to take their advice.

Thank God Matthew had finally listened. And so tonight, though it pained Darienne to realize it, she was nevertheless relieved that this show would be his last. She alone knew that Matthew needed to quit the role not only to preserve his physical health, but for his mental well-being, too. Something had happened to him in the last year that she wouldn't have expected from the experienced, level-headed actor she'd met in Chicago: He'd become obsessed with his vampire character. This was the reason he'd refused, until now, to quit. He'd confided to Darienne that he couldn't stand the thought of getting up in the morning and not going to the theater. He hated the idea of another actor taking over where he had left off, though he'd had to accommodate himself to this fact in each city he'd left. In fact there were now several actors starring in the popular musical in various productions throughout the world. But Matthew psychologically needed to be playing the character he'd created somewhere on the globe, to keep on giving the definitive performance to which all other competitor *Shadows* would be compared. Even more profound was his fascination with his vampire, Sir Percy, originally an extension of his own imagination, but which more and more had begun to overshadow his own personality in importance, it seemed.

And finally there was the issue of the audience. Matthew needed, craved, would nearly kill himself to have his nightly relationship with an audience. Darienne, who had been in love with him all this time, his mistress for three years, knew her strongest rival for his attention was not his ex-wife, or any adoring fan who tried to throw herself at him, or any actress—and his various leading ladies had all fallen in love with him to some degree. No, it was the audience he loved the best.

And the audience loved him back.

Applause and shouts of "Bravo" deafened Darienne's ears as Matthew finished the last, powerful note of his trademark song. From her seat in the fifth row, Darienne could see the moisture glistening in Matthew's eyes in response to their approval.

Later, in the final scene, his voice grew husky with emotion as he reprised the love song with his leading lady, who had real tears streaming down her rouged cheeks. The curtain came down to thunderous applause. When Matthew came out last to take his final bow, he received his usual standing ovation, but this time from an audience who couldn't stop applauding, screaming his name and shouting "Bravo" for over twenty minutes nonstop.

Eventually the Australian actress stepped forward, and when the audience finally quieted, she officially bid him good-bye in a short, heartfelt speech. Matthew came forward then, carrying large bouquets of flowers that had been handed to him, and accepted more cheers until at last the audience grew very quiet, so quiet one could hear only the sniffs of his emotional fans.

"Thank you," he said, his voice sincere and out of breath. "I can't tell you what your affection has meant to me. I've loved being here in Sydney, working with this marvelous cast and this wonderful crew of 'mates.' I've been so blessed to have had the opportunity to play this splendid role for so long." He went on to thank individuals connected with the production, including David de Morrissey. He stopped to kiss and give special tribute to his leading lady.

He paused then, head bowed for a moment, and seemed to sway slightly as he stood there holding the flowers. Darienne grew alarmed. She'd seen him collapse before and hoped he was not about to again. But at last he raised his head as the audience stood so silent there was not even the sound of breathing or a distant cough. "I have loved playing this man, this . . . vampire," he added with a little smile, "Sir Percy. I have found in him so much human dignity, so much love. And it's given me the most profound gratification to know that you all love him, too."

The audience interrupted with new cheers. This seemed to throw him a bit, disturb his train of thought. He nodded almost reticently in appreciation and then continued in a voice that was due any moment to break. "I shall miss Sir Percy. I don't want to give him up. But I can no longer play him with

the energy required to do him justice. So I must leave him—
for the time being. I hope somewhere, someday, on some
stage, I will play him again."

More enthusiastic shouts and cheers rose from the packed
house. This proved too much for him. He closed his eyes as if
in pain, then pulled himself together enough to smile, wave,
and say, "Good-bye. Thank you all so much!"

The audience continued to shout his name as the curtain
came down. Darienne felt drained, wiping tears with a handkerchief, as fans about her blew noses and hugged each other.
Two well-dressed women, who looked to be in their early
forties and had sat in front of her, turned and seemed to notice
her. Darienne vaguely recognized them, having seen them
often at the stage door in a previous city. They clearly recognized her, too—probably as the mysterious veiled blonde
often seen at Matthew's side, sometimes appearing at the
stage door while he signed autographs to urge him to come in
out of the drafty doorway.

One of the women smiled hesitantly, then spoke to Darienne. "Tell him we miss him. We're from New York. The
actor who took his place there isn't half as good as Matthew.
Maybe after he rests he can play Sir Percy in New York
again."

Darienne lowered her eyes as she pulled down over her face
the black net veil on her small, sequined evening hat. "I'll tell
him what you said." She began to file out of her row to go
backstage, thinking that she wished the opposite—she wanted
Matthew to go to a secluded place where no one knew him,
where he could recover and forget the notion of ever playing
the exhausting role again. A place like Grindelwald, Switzerland. She'd already bought him his plane ticket and made all
the arrangements for him. He'd reluctantly agreed to fly there
tomorrow.

She went backstage, which was a madhouse of excited actors looking forward to the gala farewell party after the show,
delivery people carrying in more flowers, balloons, and gifts,
and reporters and TV crews waiting to interview Matthew.
The security guards reported that over five hundred fans had
gathered by the stage door waiting for Matthew to appear.

Darienne managed to squeeze past the confusion in the
hallway and into his dressing room. She found him sitting in

front of the mirror, shoulders slack, his body like dead weight in his makeup chair. Wendy, the attractive redhead who had been his makeup artist ever since he began the role in Chicago, hovered over him, removing his heavy stage makeup. He'd already changed out of his costume and was temporarily wearing a white undershirt and jeans. A makeup cape was draped over the front of him. His blond wig and skullcap had been removed, and his curly, graying brown hair clung about his head in short tendrils, dripping with perspiration.

Darienne smiled at Wendy and walked around them to stand at her usual place, to one side of the large mirror his chair faced. The makeup mirror had light bulbs framing it that illuminated the room in a warm, subdued glow. The corners of the small room were filled with more balloons and flowers. Cards were taped to the door and the walls. Plants, stuffed animals, and photos, all gifts from fans, filled the wall shelves.

Matthew's own ruddy skin tones were beginning to appear as Wendy gently removed his pale makeup with a sponge dipped in oil. He glanced up at Darienne with eyes reddened not only from tears but also from the removal of his blue contact lenses. His misty gray-green eyes appeared clouded with fatigue and spent emotion. There was an air of hopelessness about him, as if he'd just been sentenced to life in solitary confinement.

"It's done," he said to Darienne.

Darienne grinned at him and said in a bright tone, "The *show* is done, *cheri*. But the party is about to begin! Now you're going to have months and months to rest and have fun—with me."

He tried to smile and reached toward her. She took his fingers in hers and squeezed them in silent affirmation that she would be there for him no matter what. He returned the gesture of affection and let go. Then he grew silent and his gray, troubled mood seemed to overtake him once more.

This wouldn't do, Darienne thought. She lifted the black net veil, which covered her face to her chin, and pulled it back over her pink sequined hat. The cloche hat had been specially made to match the bright pink-and-black, low-cut taffeta evening dress she wore. Her face now uncovered so he could see her better, she sat down on the floor in front of him, caring more about him than wrinkling her expensive Paris dress.

She often sat at his feet like this, even at parties with others around. He seemed to enjoy it, and she loved to look up at him. When their relationship began in Chicago, Matthew was the stronger one of the two. He was the most strong-willed man she'd ever met. But now, because of his illnesses and emotional turmoil, she had become the dominant personality—but she didn't want him to know it. So at his feet she sat, so he could feel in control. Also, here in his dressing room, there was the mirror to consider. She needed to be either beside it or below it, so no one would notice that her body had no reflection.

"I hear there are five hundred fans waiting," Wendy said.

"Oh, God . . . ," he murmured as she scrubbed a last bit of makeup from the corner of his mouth.

"Don't do autographs. Just go out and wave," Darienne suggested.

"I want to get out of here," he said. "Leave by the back entrance, get into the limo, put in two minutes at the party and get it all over with. I hate this business of leaving. It's too emotional. I'm too drained."

Darienne knew better than he what he needed. "But you know how they love you," she said with gentle insistence. "They'll be disappointed if you don't at least appear for a moment. Some have come a long way. I just met two in the audience from New York. They want you to go back there."

"I wish I could."

"No you don't!" she said sternly, annoyed with herself now for telling him about the women.

At this point Wendy finished and took off the makeup cape draped over Matthew. The sight of him in his white undershirt distressed Darienne. Despite his deep chest, he looked so thin. She could almost count his ribs.

Wendy quickly packed up her tools, tossing a sponge into her plastic bag of brushes, powders and so on, as if she felt obliged to leave Matthew and Darienne alone. Wendy had always been sensitive that way, and Darienne appreciated it.

"Will you be at the party, Wendy?" Darienne asked.

"Sure will. I want to change out of my jeans first, so I'll go now. See you both there?"

"Yes, and thank you, Wendy," Matthew said, turning to her. He took her arm to make her pause beside his chair. "You've been wonderful—the best makeup artist an actor could have. I've appreciated your quiet efficiency, your putting up with my idiosyncracies." He pulled her down to kiss her cheek. "I'll miss you."

"I'll miss you, too," Wendy said, tears in her eyes as she smiled. "I'll have to get used to a whole new face now." She was staying on in Australia to do the makeup for the actor who was going to replace Matthew. Wendy had fallen in love with one of the Australian crew and had no wish to return to the States. "I'm glad you're going to rest, though," she told Matthew. "I'm relieved Darienne finally convinced you."

"You women are ganging up on me!" he joked. "Thank you for being so sweet. Let me know when you marry your Australian!"

Wendy exchanged a kiss with both of them. When she left, Darienne and Matthew were alone. Out in the hall, however, the noise and commotion could still be heard through the closed door, pressing Darienne to increase her effort to coax Matthew into a better mood.

"You see," she told him, resting her arms on his knees as she looked up into his eyes, "it felt good to say an affectionate good-bye to her. You need to do that for your fans, too. You'll feel better, I promise. Remember when you left the other cities? They screamed as if you were a rock star those last nights."

"I don't feel like a star," he said, fatigue in his voice. "I feel like a has-been."

"*They* don't think you're a has-been. Let them show you."

He exhaled slowly and glanced at the gifts on the shelves. "I do owe it to them. They've been so loyal."

"Exactly. But you'd better look happier about it than you do now, or they'll worry what's wrong."

"I'm an actor. I'll fake elation," he mumbled, rubbing his tired eyes.

"No!" she said with a playful push on his knee. "This is a special night in your life. You must live through it in a good frame of mind, or you'll lose the meaning of it."

He reached down to touch her nose with his fingertip. "And what does it mean, Blondie-Blond?" He sometimes called her that when he teased her, or when they made love. She took it as a sign that his mood might be lifting.

"It means you've completed a great accomplishment in your career. I'm very proud of you. Try to be happy tonight. For me, if not for you." She rose up a bit on her knees and leaned over his legs in such a way that he could gaze at her ample cleavage. "You're my sexy, brooding matinee idol," she told him in a throaty whisper. "Put on your tux and go out and wave and blow kisses to all those adoring women out there. While they're all screaming and jumping to have a look at you, I'll watch with a smug smile on my face. Because I know I'm the one you'll take to bed tonight."

He ran his fingertips lightly over the plumped mounds of her breasts, above her low-cut neckline. "Is that a promise?" he murmured, a subtle glimmer in his eyes.

"What?" she whispered, closing her eyes at the enjoyment of his touch.

"About taking you to bed. I thought you were going to make me pack for Switzerland."

She took his warm hand and pressed it between her breasts. "It's a promise—after you pack."

"Oh, so there's a string attached." He leaned forward, eyes devouring her now.

"Only a little thread, *cheri.* I'll help."

"It's a deal," he said. "But only if I get a kiss now." He gripped her upper arms and pulled her up between his knees. Bending toward her, he kissed her on the mouth with energy and kindling passion, his fatigue suddenly fading. Darienne had often gotten this reaction from him. Exhausted as he could get, his strong libido, his natural virility always lay submerged within, ready to be tapped. It was the very source he drew from to create his sensual stage vampire. From the first time she saw him perform, she'd guessed he had this deep, hidden reservoir.

Oddly though, when they first met, he resisted her overt advances for months. But once he'd given in and their affair had begun, he never resisted again. Darienne knew that this was her hold on him. Not love, she was sad to admit to herself, though she certainly loved him. Not even compatibility, for they didn't live together or have much in common. Oh, she knew he had affection for her, and lately he'd become dependent on her to bolster his spirits. But Darienne understood—because he didn't try to hide the fact—that his need for her was mostly physical. She was a voluptuous blonde who eagerly gave him all he wanted and asked for nothing in return—no promises, no vows, no commitment. Darienne was certain it was her strong show of independence that had allowed her to stay close to him for as long as she had. In his checkered past, Matthew had had enough of women who wanted more of him than he could offer and commitments that couldn't last.

"You seem to have regained some energy," she whispered with admiration as his lips left hers.

"You give me energy," he said, eyes shining with pleasure and a hint of amazement. "You're never tired, are you?"

"Because I sleep till noon," she told him blithely. "Tomorrow you can sleep in, too. No show to worry about!"

His expression sobered and he bowed his head. "God, what'll I do?"

She grabbed his shoulders and shook him gently. "I'll keep you busy, *cheri*. Your life isn't over."

"His is."

"His?"

"Sir Percy. I hear the other actors make him bloodthirsty. They don't understand him the way I do. He's going to be lost."

"There will be the movie, Matthew. Your Sir Percy will be recorded for posterity."

"You don't know Hollywood. They could destroy him in the cutting room."

Matthew was slipping back into a depression, and Darienne was growing nervous about what to do. His mental state was getting beyond her ability to handle. "Darling, don't think about all this now," Darienne told him, massaging his shoulders as she kneeled in front of him. "No one will forget your *Shadow*. Yours is the only one your fans will accept. Now be proud of yourself and strong. There are reporters waiting. And then you must appear for your fans. You'll be glad you did."

He exhaled and looked at her, a resigned sort of humor in his eyes. "I will, huh?"

"I promise, *cheri.*" She stroked his face. He'd aged in the last year. The creases around his eyes had grown deep, almost craggy, perhaps damaged from constant application and removal of stage makeup. He'd looked younger than his years when she met him. But now, in his late forties, he looked his age and it saddened her. Especially since she knew a way—a dreadful, yet miraculous solution—to stop the destruction of his looks. She put the forbidden thought aside and kissed him. "My handsome hero," she whispered. "Go and show them all how magnificent you are."

He smiled at her then, as if amused at her words. She knew he'd never thought of himself as handsome. Indeed, he'd begun his career as a comic actor. He placed the palm of his large hand over her cheek. "I don't know what I'd do without you."

Darienne's mind swam a bit at his words. A woman who didn't have both feet on the ground might interpret that as a declaration of love. But Darienne knew he'd meant simply what he'd said, that he didn't know what he would do if she weren't there. It didn't mean he wouldn't think of something—or someone—to comfort him. Matthew was a resourceful person.

He got up to shower and change into a tuxedo for his farewell party. When he came out of his dressing room, she looked on as he spoke to reporters, flashing his stunning actor's smile for the news cameras.

Darienne stayed in the background, out of camera range, veil pulled over her face again. The veiled hats she'd taken to wearing when she was at the theater were meant to protect her in case any fans or reporters should catch her beside Matthew in a photo. A vampire's image came out bluish in photographs. She hoped they'd blame their poor snapshots on her veil. As a consequence, however, she'd become known as Matthew McDowall's mystery lady, who rarely uncovered her beautiful face in public. Her invented fashion signature, it turned out, had added to his sex symbol mystique among his fans.

Darienne hurried to his side when he moved resolutely down the hall toward the stage door, as the reporters trailed behind. The security guard opened the door, which was at the side of the large theater, at the top of a short set of concrete steps enclosed with a railing. Women were massed on the sidewalk and into the street below. They held up banners saying, "We'll miss you, Matthew." Police were diverting traffic. As soon as Matthew appeared, a wail of cheers and shouts of "Matthew, Matthew!" erupted. Well-dressed, middle-aged women jumped up and down along with the teenagers beside them, waving, snapping photos and screaming.

Darienne stood to one side, smiling at the ruckus, thrilled for Matthew. She was also amused to see a number of women wearing veiled hats. Yes, she'd started a fad. They wanted to dress like Matthew's woman, perhaps fantasizing themselves in her place. And, yes, as she'd told him earlier, she did feel smug.

She gazed at him as he accepted flowers handed up to him. When he got too many bouquets, he gave some to Darienne. He waved, smiled, and turned slowly, looking over the crowd, as if to briefly make eye contact with each of them. The light above the door shone down on him and years seemed to slip away from his face. His eyes were luminous, full of joy, darting from one face to another in the crowd. His brightest grin reappeared and his satisfaction seemed profound.

Darienne beamed as she watched him and his fans indulge their mutual affection. Matthew craved this. He *lived* for this. Three years ago it had surprised and even embarrassed him to find his stage role had turned him almost overnight into a sex symbol. Even now he didn't look like a sex symbol or behave like one in real life. He hated being asked by reporters what it felt like to be one. But in moments like this, it was clear to Darienne that he'd learned to enjoy being such a male icon, with floods of adoring women at his feet.

After several minutes, Matthew made his final wave to the crowd. Turning, he took Darienne by the hand and they walked back into the theater. She could feel the new energy in his grip, the buoyancy in his step. He was ready for his farewell party.

He kept his good mood through the short limousine ride to the event, which was held at a hotel. Champagne flowed and cast and crew came up to wish him well. The Australian orchestra members played "Dixie," in honor of his home state, Georgia. His leading lady begged him to return when he'd rested, and young female dancers from the show gathered around to tease him. By one A.M., however, Darienne could see he was beginning to wear thin. His smile was artificial now, and the bleak weariness had returned to linger about his eyes.

She took it upon herself to begin making apologies to everyone for leaving early, saying Matthew needed to pack for his flight to Switzerland the next day. At last they left, and the limousine sped them to the furnished downtown apartment Matthew had used during his stay in Sydney.

When they walked into the living room, done in blue and white, he sat on the sofa, leaning forward, and put his hands over his face. "God, I'm tired," he said. "I can't think. I feel . . . numb."

"I know," she said, pulling off her hat and sitting beside him. She tossed the hat aside and ran her hand comfortingly up and down his back. "But all there is left to do is pack the rest of your things, and I'll help you with that."

"No, I don't want to leave," he said, leaning back and taking her hand. "I don't think I can face a long plane flight."

"Matthew, you must leave here." She knew he would be frighteningly depressed if he were still in Sydney when his replacement, a popular Australian singer, took over his role tomorrow night. Knowing him, Darienne sensed why he wanted to stay. He probably felt somehow that if he remained here, he could protect his character, Sir Percy, from being adulterated by a foreign interpretation.

"Why do I have to leave?" he asked, turning to her, a stubbornness darkening his eyes. "I've never seen Australia, except for what little I've glimpsed of Sydney going to and from the theater."

"You've never seen Switzerland either, have you?"

"No. So what? Why go there?"

"Matthew, you need a complete change." She began undoing the studs of his dress shirt. "Your emotions are tied now to this city, just as they were to Chicago, and New York, and London when you left them. If you stay here, you'll miss performing here. Go to a place where no one knows you, where they've barely heard of *The Scarlet Shadow*. The Alps are gorgeous in the spring, *cheri*. I've been there often. Grindelwald is a charming resort and you'll be able to rest there and relax, just be yourself—not a sex symbol, not Sir Percy, not anything but you."

"And after that—what?"

"Think about that later."

"That's no way to plan a career. I've got a momentum going now. This is no time to stop."

"You need to regain your health before you can go on," she reminded him. "You need to find out who you are again. There will be other roles and you'll be just as wonderful in them, but you need to get some equilibrium back before you can go on to the next thing."

Jutting his hips forward, he slumped and leaned his head on the soft top edge of the couch. "I'm too tired tonight to decide."

"Then let me think for you," she said, undoing his black bow tie and unfastening his shirt collar. "I'm trying to do what's best for you. You trust me, don't you?"

He turned his head toward her, amusement in his eyes. "I think you do what's best for *you*. But I know you care about me. I trust you."

She smiled and ran her fingers through his tousled, curly hair. "What do you mean I do what's best for me?"

"You've been that way from the beginning. When we met, you pursued me constantly, even hid in my dressing room to accost me. I kept saying 'no,' but did you listen?"

"You were happy when we finally made love."

He lowered his eyes to her cleavage. "I was delirious! I knew I had to be with you again just to be sure I wasn't dreaming." He looked in her eyes again. "And ever since, you've led me to places I'd never thought of going to, just because I couldn't disappoint you. You wanted me to take the show to London instead of Los Angeles, which paid better. You suggested Australia, when I had a great offer from Toronto."

"I do like to travel," she admitted. "But I wanted you to conquer the world. Why be content with North America?"

He narrowed his round eyes at her. "Sometimes I wonder what a simple Southern boy like me is doing with a worldly French woman like you. How did I make that leap?"

"I made the leap for you," she said, fondling his ear with her fingertips. "And I'll bet you never were simple, not even when you were ten. Your drawl is long gone and now you're an international star. Why shouldn't you be with me? I insist on only the best."

With a sly expression, he studied her face and her other attributes. "Then," he said, falling into a comfortable Georgia drawl, "why don't you take off that little dress, darlin', and show this superstar what you're made of?"

She closed her eyes at the touch of his hand on the inner curve of her breast. "But you have to finish packing."

"There's time tomorrow before I leave. And I won't see you for a few days, so I want my reward now," he said, leaning to kiss her near the mouth. "I still don't see why you can't leave with me."

Darienne couldn't explain that she needed to have herself shipped in her coffin to Zurich. From there she would be transported personally by her vampire friend Herman to her chalet in Grindelwald, all of which would take several days due to problematic time changes and inconvenient daylight hours. She hated being parted from Matthew those nights. It wasn't the best time for him to be alone, but there was nothing else she could do. If she'd left ahead of him to meet him there, she would have missed being with him tonight at his last performance.

"I need to shop for a few more things before I leave, *cheri.*" She said this in the manner of feminine French prattle. "I may not be in Australia again for a long while. You wouldn't want me to miss anything."

"I'll miss you."

The sincerity in his eyes made her pause. She leaned toward him. "Then you'll have your reward," she whispered, slipping her hands behind her back to unzip her strapless dress. It fell away, revealing a provocative lavender lace bustier, which pushed up her large breasts.

The lace edge played peekaboo with her pink nipples. She stood and bent to step out of the dress. She was gratified to see Matthew take a heavy breath as he gazed at her plump cleavage, which swelled as she bent forward.

The removal of the dress showed off her small waist, cinched tighter by the bottom of the bustier. Over her rounded hips there hung a narrow satin garter belt with garters extending down her slim thighs to hold up her silk hose. A wispy lavender lace panty over the garters barely covered her.

She sat on his lap, long legs astride him, and placed her hands on his shoulders, curving her own shoulders forward to increase her cleavage. She loved to feel her breasts ready to burst from the lace confines that barely contained their weight. She began breathing faster in anticipation, turned on by her own sexuality and by the sure knowledge that her body tantalized Matthew just as much as his sensuality onstage never failed to dazzle her.

"God, you're sexy!" he murmured, cradling her breasts and fondling them. He pushed down on the lace edges, revealing her pert nipples tilting up, peaked and hardening. Hands spanning her rib cage, he lifted her up and toward him to take one nipple in his mouth. She gave a little cry of delight as she felt his teeth nip her.

He'd learned he could play rough with her and she didn't mind. In fact she craved it. He began licking, then sucking on her nipple, hard, yet with a certain caring intimacy, as if worshiping her with his mouth, while his hands pressed her closer. The sensation aroused her, made her shut her eyes and moan. She yearned for him to bite and draw blood, as a male vampire would do. But she made herself be content with his mortal's lovemaking.

Matthew was the most wonderful mortal lover she'd ever had. And in her four hundred years, Darienne had had many. It wasn't because he was so innovative or expert in his approach. He was rather conventional, really. She was the one who introduced him to new ways of finding sexual delight. But he was the best because of his tender intimacy, and his actor's freedom of expressing emotion. It was the way he treated her as a unique and special person, and not as just a voluptuous female he desired. His sweet passion for her, if not his love, had become the whole focus of her existence. She would do anything to keep him.

Breathing hard, his eyes shining with sensuality, he gazed at her face while he slid his hands up her body. He ran his fingertips around the contours of her breasts and up her arched throat. The sensitivity and adoration she felt in his hands brought tears to her eyes. "I love the way you touch me," she whispered.

He smiled a bit, his hands cupping her face now, as he studied her features. "You're an exquisite woman. I can never quite believe you're real." He reached around to undo the chignon at the back of her head. When her thick, long hair fell free, he picked up gobs of it in his hands and brought it forward beneath her chin to frame her face. He studied her with bright, focused admiration, his eyes shimmering with desire and a sublime cherishing she'd never seen in any other man's eyes.

Oh, God, if she could just once tell him how much she loved him. But she didn't dare. Their relationship, their mutual passion for each other, rested on the freedom Matthew wanted. It was a freedom Darienne used to live by, too, though no longer. If she had her way, she would devote all of herself to Matthew and Matthew alone. He was the only man who had ever seemed to need her for who she was. And to be needed was enough. In fact, she wasn't sure how she would cope if Matthew ever began to love her.

He kissed her mouth warmly, and she returned the kiss in kind. As he smoothed her long tresses, his face revealed his enjoyment of the feel of her silky hair over her full breasts. The reddened tips of her nipples peeked through the strands of blond, and he fondled them with his thumbs. Breathing roughly, he pulled her to him once more, his large hands beneath her rib cage, and kissed and suckled her breasts again.

"Oh, Matthew, Matthew," she whispered as her body began to writhe with desire. She drew in her breath as she felt his hand move down the curve of her hip, over the top of her thigh, and into her wisp-of-lace panties. His fingertip slid into her pulsing moistness, and she gave a cry of pleasure mixed with the pain of need. "Yes! Oh, please, yes!"

"Is this what you want?" he murmured with a smile, nuzzling her cheek with his while he continued to tease her with his fingertip.

"Don't make me wait—"

"I never knew a woman could be in such a hurry until I met you."

"I just love the way you make love, Matthew."

"Mmm," he said, kissing her mouth. "I can't wait either. Do you want to take this off?" he asked, tugging on her bustier.

"No."

"Good! You look so damned sexy this way."

He took her by the upper arms to guide her off his lap and down onto the sofa. Eager to be compliant, she lay down on the couch and smiled when he pulled off her panties. He unfastened his pants. His arousal was obvious, and she gasped with anticipation, longing to feel him within her.

"Hurry, Matthew." She held out her arms, parting her thighs.

Not taking time to remove his clothes, he eased down on top of her, his chest making contact with her breasts. She closed her eyes as she felt the thick, engorged length of him slide into her.

"Ohhh, Matt . . . oh, be rough with me, my darling. Show me how much you need me. Oh, yes!" she cried as he thrust hard against her. "Oh, more! Harder!" She wished he had a vampire's strength and stamina, as David did. But Matthew was quite strong and virile for a mortal. And he was capable of channeling his passion in a way that made her rapturous, because he made her feel as if she were the only woman in the world. His sensual adoration was in his touch, in his expressive voice as he spoke in her ear while they coupled, even in the way he breathed—all acknowledging that she alone could take him to the heights they reached.

"Darienne," he murmured in a husky whisper as he looked down at her, resting his weight on his elbows. Her breasts rubbed against his chest with the back-and-forth motion of their bodies. "With you I always feel like I'm in some rare atmosphere beyond the earth."

Darienne had closed her eyes so he would not see their vampire glow. But he was sensitive enough to feel that sex with her was beyond the realm of normal. Many mortal men were too wrapped up in their own bodies' functions to notice subtleties. But Matthew truly appreciated all she could provide a man, even if he didn't understand it.

"I'm a magic woman," she said, smiling with her eyes closed. "And you're a magical man. Oh, Matthew," she said pulling him closer, "I could make love with you like this for a hundred years."

He chuckled, then moaned as he thrust into her again. "Oh, God! Darienne, I—"

"Yes!" she said with a gasp, running her hands over his back. "I'm ready." She writhed beneath him as his thrusting took her to the brink. "Ohhh—"

He drew out, then thrust savagely into her as she arched her neck and back. She'd reached the point where she knew it was about to happen—that point of brief suspension—the top of the roller coaster. Matthew plunged into her in one final, overwhelming thrust, crying out with his own fulfillment. All at once the tumbling, rapturous sensation overtook her. Her body rocked with pleasure as she gasped and screamed with joy.

In a few moments her body settled into satisfied relaxation, and she stroked the back of his head lovingly while he relaxed on top of her.

"You're wonderful, Matthew," she whispered, feeling his tousled hair between her trembling fingers. "You're magnificent."

He lifted himself up a bit and looked down at her. "I think I'm addicted to you," he said with a pleased, exhausted smile in his eyes. "You satisfy me so completely, I don't seem to need anything more." He stroked her hair back from her face. "Except my work. To sing on a stage and then to lie with you. That's all I could ever ask of life."

"Never mind the stage," she said, her hands running along the sides of his rib cage. "You'll have to make do with only me for a while."

His eyes glistened. "That may be more than I can handle!"

"Oh, no," she said knowingly, moving her hands to the small of his back, which she knew was an erogenous spot for him. "You can prove that to me now." She slid her hands further down to his buttocks, round and firm from the dance exercises he did every day to keep in shape for his role. As she caressed him, she kissed him on the mouth, her body keeping a slow, tantalizing, rhythmic undulation beneath him. In a few minutes she felt him swell inside her again. "Told you," she murmured, gently biting his ear.

"I'm starting to look forward to this vacation." His voice sounded rich with pleasure.

"Oh, *cheri*," she told him in a throaty whisper as she drew her legs up over him, "you'll love it! I promise."

# 4

# This is such bad timing

FIVE NIGHTS later Darienne was riding to Grindelwald, driven by Herman in his Mercedes-Benz. Herman was a wiry, bald, rather intense vampire, dressed in a tweed jacket and gray trousers. He was older than Darienne, perhaps by a hundred fifty years or more. Herman spent his nights in his medical laboratory searching out cures for viruses for normal humans as well as trying to perfect a sunblock lotion that would allow vampires to go about in the daytime. For the past century he'd also sought a remedy to make a vampire revert to normal, but he had made little progress in this area.

Darienne had known him for about a century and a half now. They'd met by chance at a Swiss hotel. A cerebral, inquisitive, incisive man, he'd quickly discerned she was a fellow creature of the night. He'd asked her questions about her experience as a vampiress, and over several evenings of conversation she'd willingly told him a great deal, including details of her active sex life. He'd always treated her as something of a case study, someone he might write about in a scientific paper on female vampires, though of course he could never publish such an article. It sometimes bothered her that he never got curious about experimenting with her himself.

But she'd gotten used to his unemotional, academic manner and admired him for his brilliant mind. They enjoyed an amiable conversation as they drove to Grindelwald from Lucerne. Her plane had landed in Zurich, where, after dark, he'd claimed the large metal coffin in which she traveled and brought it to his home in Lucerne. She rested during the day there, then at dusk stored her coffin at Herman's home and left with him for the resort town of Grindelwald, where Darienne owned a small chalet.

"You're in love with this actor?" Herman asked as he drove his Mercedes along a climbing alpine valley road. On either side of the road, moonlight illuminated the outline of snow-capped, sharp-edged peaks against a clear, star-glittered sky.

"Yes," she replied, unable to deny the obvious insight Herman had come to from listening to Darienne talk about Matthew.

"Not very wise," he muttered in his Germanic accent.

"I know."

"Is he interested in becoming a vampire? You say he played one onstage."

"He doesn't know it's possible. He doesn't believe vampires exist," she explained, pushing up the sleeve of her yellow sweater.

"You never told him?"

"No. I didn't want him to know I was so different from him. He might not have even believed me. I wanted him so, I didn't want to risk losing him."

"In three years he's never figured it out?"

"I told him from the start that I was very independent, that I liked to have my own place and not share his. I said I loved to sleep till noon, shop or read the rest of the day, then change into one of my extravagant dresses and go see him perform in the evening."

Herman glanced at her, doubt in his narrow gray eyes. "He believed a normal woman could live that way?"

Darienne chuckled. "I never told him I was normal. I told him I had inherited my family's wealth, which is true, and that I loved leisure, luxury, and the nightlife. Looking at me, anyone could believe this, *n'est-ce pas?*"

Herman nodded with dry amusement. "It's true."

"After the show there was often a party to attend or sometimes I'd just accompany him to a restaurant for a late dinner. I always claimed to have eaten already or to be dieting. And then we always went to his place to make love." Darienne felt a warm, sensual need overtake her just thinking about being with Matthew again.

"He never noticed your superhuman strength?"

She smiled softly. "I'm always gentle with him. No, he's

never suspected anything. Matthew is . . . well, I have to admit, he's rather focused on himself. When he was doing the show, he had to be, because he carried the show. He would be preoccupied before each performance, and afterward he'd be rethinking what had gone well and what hadn't that night. He was growing exhausted and worried about his health. Perhaps because I always seemed happy and carefree, he never thought much about what I was doing. Just so I was there, that was all he wanted."

She paused, ruminating, thinking it was nice to be needed by someone. Then she remembered Herman was waiting for her to finish explaining how she'd kept her secret from Matthew. "So if it seemed eccentric to live the way I told him I lived—well, he had too many eccentricities of his own to question mine. Before each show, for example, he'd meditate in front of a large green candle. He ordered them from a candle shop in Atlanta. He followed odd diets, trying to keep up his energy. For a while he lived on millet, tofu, and greens. Then he heard some other theory and ate nothing but seafood. He had a certain regimen of exercises he followed in exactly the same order every day. And—this was funny—at least once a week he'd watch a tape of one of the old Marx Brothers movies." Darienne lifted her shoulders, still puzzled by Matthew's habit. "He said the movies restored his sense of creative rhythm. And every evening, no matter how exhausted, he was always ready to make love."

Herman switched gears as the road grew more steep. "Why are you so attached to him? He seems to look on you as a convenient part of his routine."

"Yes, I'm his male sex fantasy come true. But I don't mind. When I first saw him onstage, I looked upon him as real-life fantasy, too. I pursued him solely to experience that rarified sensuality I saw him project on the stage. He stunned me like no other man ever had." She paused, watching the road but seeing Matthew in her mind. "When we finally coupled, I never expected to fall in love. It's my fault. I should have been more aware of what was happening to me emotionally. I can't blame him if he didn't fall in love with me. We'd agreed beforehand it was just to be a sexual fling, no strings, no emotional ties. I'm the one who hasn't quite kept the bargain, not he."

"Does he know you love him?"

"No."

Herman shook his head. "I'm glad I gave up on relationships centuries ago. Not worth the trauma. Better ways to spend one's time."

Darienne grew curious. "Were you in love once?"

"Long ago when I was a mortal. She was a vampiress and I didn't know it. She seduced me, bit me without explaining what she was doing and transformed me into a vampire before I knew what was happening. Though I've actually gotten to like being an immortal and watching the scientific world evolve over the centuries, I've never trusted women again. Swore off them."

"You tolerate *me,*" she pointed out.

Herman shrugged. "You're fascinating to observe. You're bright enough to sense without my telling you that I'm not fair game. Or maybe you just weren't interested. Anyway, I still *like* women—from a distance. And you're all woman."

Darienne gave him an impish grin. "Well, anytime you want to close the distance, just call."

"I'll leave you to your actor," he replied with a dry chuckle.

Darienne accepted his rebuff with good humor, but her smile faded as she thought of Matthew. "I hope he's all right. I hope he's here. He was thinking about staying in Australia, but I believe I talked him out of it."

They'd arrived on the outskirts of the town of Grindelwald now, and Herman pulled up in front of a charming old chalet. "Here you are. Place looks the same," he said, eyeing her quaint wood-frame home.

"Can you get back to Lucerne by dawn?"

"Easily. Need help with your luggage?"

"Yes. And thank you for the blood bags," she said. Herman always supplied her from his laboratory stock when she was in Europe.

"Happy to be of service." He got out of the car and went around to open the trunk. He took out her suitcases and brought them into the house. That done, he shook her hand. "Nice to see you again, Darienne. Stop for a while when you're in Lucerne again. It gets lonely sometimes. I'm still the only one of our kind living in Switzerland, that I know of."

"*Merci,* Herman. You're always so helpful. Don't spend so

many nights alone in that lab. Go out and mingle with mortals. Have some fun!"

"I'll think about it," he said with a smile, saluted her, and got back into his car.

As he drove off, Darienne entered her chalet and checked the small, tidy rooms, decorated with furniture that had been new when she bought it, but was now antique. She'd owned the home for over a century, one of several places she maintained throughout the world. A hired caretaker took care of the place in her absence.

It was too late, two A.M., to see Matthew, so she put the blood bags in her refrigerator, unpacked, attended to some bills left for her by the caretaker, then rested from dawn to dusk in her simple, varnished pine coffin, kept in a locked, hidden closet.

The next night, she rose at twilight and changed into a short skirt and provocative, low-cut, cream-colored angora sweater. She put on a leather jacket, for the spring night was chilly, and walked the quarter mile to the edge of town where Matthew was staying in a cottage she'd arranged for him. She'd told him her home was too small for two to live in the spacious manner they both were accustomed to, and that she still wanted to live independently from him, even on a vacation.

As she stepped up to the door, she saw lights on inside. She hoped this meant Matthew was there. But when she knocked, there was no answer. And then she heard someone singing in the distance, around the back of the house. She had no trouble identifying the silvery tenor voice. Walking through the small garden and around to the back, she discovered him singing in the Jacuzzi, steamy water churning around his chest. The tendrils of his graying hair were damp and hung about his broad face. His eyes were closed in a tender expression as he sang the final love song from *The Scarlet Shadow*.

Darienne couldn't help but think how manly and yet cherubic he looked. The sight of him after five days brought tears to her eyes. And yet she was annoyed with him. She said in a stern tone, "You're supposed to be resting your voice!"

His eyes opened abruptly and he stopped singing mid-note. He grinned broadly. Rising, he held out his hand to beckon her closer. "I thought you'd never get here," he said, taking her hands when she knelt beside the bubbling pool. "I was getting worried. How was your flight? How did you get here from Lucerne?"

"An old friend drove me. The flight was . . . peaceful," she said, thinking of her padded, velvet-lined travel coffin.

After leaning down to give him a long kiss, she asked, "How have you been?"

He shrugged. "I'm here, Blondie-Blond."

She surveyed his bared, broad chest and noticed beneath the water that he wore no swim trunks. The back of the house had a high wood fence and bushes to make the spa area secluded. "You've put on a bit of weight," she said with approval.

"I've discovered a pastry shop in town."

"Your face doesn't look quite so gaunt," she told him. "And the rest of you looks . . . well endowed."

He laughed and pretended to pull her into the water with him.

"Wait." She took off the jacket, the low-cut sweater she'd worn for his benefit and all the rest of her clothing, then stepped down into the heated water with him. The temperature was not too hot, but comfortable and warming. She sat next to him on the built-in ledge within the round pool. Her breasts floated on the frothy water as she nestled against his shoulder.

She smiled when she saw him admiring her. "And what else have you discovered besides the pastry shop?"

He took a deep breath as if to keep his advancing thoughts in check for the moment. "The mountains are beautiful. I have a spectacular view from my bedroom window when I get up in the morning. This is a restful place. You were right about that."

"But instead of resting, you're restless?" she said, picking up what he wasn't saying from his ambivalent tone of voice.

"Well, the first day I was so beat from doing the show and that endless plane flight that I slept for about twenty hours straight."

"Good," she said.

"The next day I went into town and explored. Very nice, really. Charming shops, friendly people. Goats with bells come through town every once in a while. And there's always the surrounding mountains to look at."

He paused to take another breath, then continued. "The next day, I decided to take the Firstbahn, since it's Europe's longest lift. The ride was beautiful—the clean air, the trees, spring flowers in the meadows. I reached the top, the lookout point. The view of the mountains and glaciers was absolutely magnificent. There was a place to sit down. It was chilly, but I had a jacket. And that's where I sat for maybe three hours, just . . . thinking."

"About what?"

"Myself and my life. And I found my thoughts kept going back to Sir Percy. I began to feel that I'd left the most important part of myself on that stage in Sydney."

Darienne touched her forehead, upset at what she was hearing. "Matthew, you can't play Sir Percy for the rest of your life."

"No, but I'd like to *be* him."

"He's an imaginary character. How can you be him?"

"I don't know. I mean, I . . . it's . . . the audiences loved him because he was courageous and caring. He took risks to save others. His tragedy was that he was a vampire, but still, he loved deeply. When I was up there on that peak looking at those glaciers that will keep on sliding down the mountains long after I'm gone, it somehow hit me that all I ever think about is me. But when I was playing Sir Percy, I was so much more than myself."

"But you must have all those good qualities within you. David always said you had such understanding of the character he'd written, that you'd made Sir Percy even more than David had imagined him to be."

"I have the feeling David is much closer to Sir Percy than I could ever be."

This statement made Darienne pause because of the hidden truth in it. "Why?"

"Just a feeling I have. I never got to know David well. But I sensed he has an altruistic nature, maybe even a need to sacrifice himself or make up for something. In his play, the reason for Sir Percy's courage was that Percy was a vampire and felt a huge guilt about his need for blood. So he went around rescuing people from the guillotine to feel he was worthy of even being on earth. I don't know what David's hang-up is, but he's always working, doing all he can—creating an exemplary stage character, for example—to contribute something good to the world."

"And so have you, *cheri.*"

Matthew chuckled ironically. "By playing a noble character? I ought to *be* a noble character. Look at my life—only a few close friends, one botched marriage, some broken relationships and a son I haven't seen in twenty years who probably hates my guts. A few movies, two TV series, and a hit musical don't make a life."

"But you've given your public so much."

"That's over for now. And where am I? I'm here in Switzerland, in the majestic Alps, coming to realize I have no life. And some warbling Australian is probably destroying what ephemeral good thing I managed to create. I need to play Sir Percy again, Darienne. I haven't learned all I should have learned from him yet. *He* was the one who had the love for humanity, the gift for life, not me."

Darienne tensed, even in the relaxing warm water. "He was supposed to be a vampire, darling. Would you really want to be him—I mean, not on a stage but in reality?"

Matthew shifted in the water and looked at her with puzzled amusement. "You almost say that as if it were possible. But since you raise the question . . ." He paused and his expression grew more serious. "There was another aspect to the role I've never talked about much, because it scared the hell out of me."

She drew her brows together. "What do you mean?"

"When I was truly in character, my own identity totally submerged in Sir Percy's, I could almost feel that power—the vampire's superhuman power. It got surreal sometimes. I could glide across that stage and sing as if I had all the strength in the world. And when I'd swing down from the proscenium on the rope to rescue Marguerite, I never felt the pain in my shoulders or the rope burning my hands. I could sing as if inspired. I felt I had such control. I felt like a god up there! And in the scene where I would bite Marguerite and put her under my spell—" Matthew's voice grew strained, but his eyes were shining. "I felt that power, that authority, and, yes, the lust to take from her and dominate her."

He shook his head. "Sometimes I wondered if I was going crazy. I felt possessed, and I loved it! But then I'd get the audience's reaction, all that shouting and applause, and I'd come out of it a bit and become aware of my surroundings again. And I'd gladly tell myself, No, I'm not losing touch with reality, I'm just one terrific actor, aren't I? To this day, deep in my soul, sometimes I don't know if I was acting or not up there on that stage. But I can tell you one thing—I need to feel that kind of high again or I'll go nuts for sure. Chalets and mountains, pastries and goats are fine for a few weeks maybe, but I'm going to need to get back on a stage, back in front of an audience soon. I need to play *him* again."

Darienne felt tears starting in her eyes. All she'd hoped for him—that he would recover his strength and regain his mental equilibrium—was dashed by what he was telling her, and the passion in his voice as he told it. If anything he'd grown more obsessed. She wondered if she should offer to make him a vampire. If it was power he craved, she could give him that. But would he hate himself then for what he'd become, as David and his stage invention, Sir Percy, did? Or would he come to enjoy immortality, as she and Herman did?

Should she tell him now that vampires existed, that she was one and could make him one, too? But she couldn't know for certain what Matthew truly needed to bring him out of his searching, deprived state of mind. All Darienne knew was that she loved him, and she was feeling more and more helpless trying to keep him on an even keel.

Matthew reached out to draw her into his arms. "Don't cry," he said. "This isn't like you. You're always the one cheering me up."

"You've changed, Matthew," she said, dabbing at her eyes with her fingertips. "I worry about you."

"Changed? Since we first met?"

She nodded. "You were so steady. You used to keep *me* in line. You seemed to know exactly who you were and what you were about. And now you seem so lost."

He held her for a while, nestling her head under his chin as the warm water churned quietly around them. "You're right, I am lost," he said. "If I seemed together before, it was probably because I hadn't become aware yet of what I lacked. It took at least a year of doing *Shadow* to show me I wasn't made of the stuff I could be made of—whatever Sir Percy is made of."

She pressed her hand against his shoulder and looked at him earnestly. "Ink and paper is what he's made of."

"No, he's far more than that," Matthew said in a low voice, almost a whisper. "A spirit hovering over me, waiting to revive me again and show me the way. That's how I feel him. He's a friend and he's still with me."

"Oh, God, Matthew," she breathed, stifling a sob. "Don't say that." She decided it wasn't the time to tell him her secret. He was too confused within himself to burden him with such a stunning revelation.

He tilted her chin up, making her look at him. "I'm sorry I'm putting you through this," he said with sincerity. "I know you'd like everything to be normal. But it's not. And I can't pretend otherwise for you. This is something I have to work through."

"All right, work through it. But don't assume the only answer is to go back onstage, at least not for six months. The doctors told you you mustn't."

He lowered his hand to the surface of the water, watching it churn between his spread fingers. "Doctors understand the body, perhaps, but not what the soul needs. My life is the stage. I'm not alive if I'm not on one."

"You may not live if you go back to the stage," she said, giving his shoulder a shake. "Where is your soul if you kill yourself working too hard?"

He slumped against the curved back of the Jacuzzi and gave a long exhale. "I don't know, Darienne," he said, seeming to study the steam rising along the edge of the water. "That old expression, the soul is willing but the flesh is weak, seems to have some kind of perverse truth here, doesn't it?"

"Recover first, then think through all this. Give your mind and body a rest."

His eyes shifted to hers. "But will I survive the rest period? That's the question. I don't know how to rest."

Darienne pulled herself together a bit. "Rest usually goes along with recreation, *cheri,*" she said with a smile, slipping her hand up his thigh under the water. "I'm good at recreation, if you'd like someone to play with."

He slid his hand beneath her breasts and his voice grew more sensual. "You made me spend five nights alone. No wonder I'm so restless."

She began fondling him while his hand moved upward to cradle her breast. "I can give you comfort, *cheri*. Some peace of mind—and body."

He pressed his hand wantonly into her soft mound of flesh and hotly kissed her throat. Darienne breathed in, closing her eyes at the delight of his touch.

His mouth moved down her body in slow kisses along her wet skin. She rose up slightly, bringing her breasts above water. His lips fastened onto her nipple. She gasped as he teased it with his tongue, then sucked hard, sending hot shivers of desire down her body and along her limbs. She buried her fingers in his hair and pressed him closer, groaning with pleasure and burning need. He cupped both naked breasts in his hands, feeling their weight, pressing them upward to watch them plump sumptuously.

"You have the most exquisite body," he whispered, gazing with eyes full of wonder and desire at her smooth, rounded flesh. "I could never imagine a woman more beautiful than you. God, I've missed you! Touching you, feeling you—"

"I've missed you, too, Matthew." She ran her fingers, trembling now, along his firm, masculine member. She gave a little gasp of joy as she felt his hardness. Suddenly she was beside herself with the need to feel him within her.

She rose to sit on top of him, her back to his chest, astride his lap. Pressing downward with her pelvis, she captured him within her pulsing femininity.

"Darienne—" he murmured as they began moving together in an age-old rhythm. "This is so good, so good," he said against her shoulder as he kissed her. His hand moved over her hips and thighs to the quick of her. As she gasped with heightened pleasure at his sensitive touch, he murmured, "This is better than anything . . ."

"Better than the stage?" she teased, breathing hard with each new wave of electric sensation.

"Better than anything, Darienne. You're so sexy! I could do this forever."

She twisted to look at him over her shoulder. "And be happy?"

His eyes were dark and glazed with the heat of desire, yet melancholy. "If there is such a thing as happiness."

"There is, *cheri!* Let me give it to you," she said with passion. "I'll make you happy, my darling. Oh, Matthew . . ." She faced forward and caught her breath as sensation overtook her, the feel of warm water swirling over her skin and Matthew thrusting within her. "We're so good together. I feel complete with you. Ohhh . . ." She made a choked sob as her craving need edged toward fulfillment and the sweet sensations inside her made any more words impossible.

He squeezed her thighs as he made a final, urgent thrust. A waterfall of sensations flooded through her body. She arched her neck as her body convulsed with pleasure, making her cry out until her fingertips tingled and she was out of breath. Matthew was breathing hard with his own release. She could feel his warm breath on her shoulder as he pressed her body close, holding onto her tightly and rocking.

In a few moments they began to relax. They sat for a long while in contented silence, except for the rippling noise of the steamy water. At last, Darienne turned to look at him and he met her gaze. His eyes were warm, pleased. His soft-spoken voice had a cozy intimacy. "You're good therapy."

"I want to be," she said with feeling, taking his hands in both of hers and pressing them over her breasts, still throbbing slightly with sweet, ebbing passion. "I want to give you everything you need, so nothing, not even the stage, holds any attraction for you. *This* is happiness, *cheri*—our bodies one, our passions aflame, enjoying each other just for the lovely thrill we can give each other. I love giving you my body. Take all you want from me. I'll always be here for you, my darling."

"That's quite a declaration," he murmured and kissed her neck.

He slid his hands affectionately over her back. Cupping warm water in each hand, he poured it over her breasts, then caressed her slick skin, enjoying her smooth, round contours. A soft sigh of pleasure escaped her as she felt his fingertips seeking out and teasing her nipples. Soon his breathing grew labored, his deep chest expanding, pressing harder against her back. She smiled as she felt him grow big inside her again, and her own ache increased.

She arched her neck back until her head was next to his. "Oh, Matthew, yes!" she whispered. "Yes!"

Soon they were in the throes of passion once more, gasping with the need for renewed gratification of their unquenchable desire for each other. If Darienne ever heard a footstep, her mind must have unconsciously dismissed it. Matthew seemed not to hear anything either. All Darienne knew was that when her tide of pleasure culminated in its last, overwhelming wave of bliss, she opened her eyes to find a woman standing by the narrow entrance between the house and the high fence. The woman stared at them in surprise, but not shock. It took a moment for Darienne to recognize the slim female, in her early forties, with well-formed cheekbones, a young face, and long, silvery-smooth gray hair, which looked almost like a halo in the moonlight. Darienne hadn't seen her for almost a year—not since London, when Matthew was in the hospital.

She was Natalie, Matthew's long-ago wife.

"I'm so sorry," Natalie said, her hand at her face as she stepped backward. "I knocked at the door, but no one answered. Then I heard voices . . . I should have phoned first."

As Darienne moved off his lap and ducked under the water further to cover herself, Matthew gazed at his ex-wife in astonishment.

"Natalie!" he said. "I . . . when . . . I didn't know . . ."

"This is such bad timing," she apologized again. "I should have told you—you sounded so depressed, I decided to fly out and see you. There's something I need to talk to you about. But I should have guessed Darienne would be here. I'm really sorry to have caused this embarrassment."

"It's all right," Darienne interjected, trying to smile.

Matthew glanced at Darienne, then looked back at his ex-wife in confusion. "What did you want to talk about?"

"It can wait," Natalie told him. "Look, I'll just go back to my hotel now. I need to unpack. I'll call you tomorrow morning, okay?"

"What hotel?" Matthew asked.

"The Grand Hotel Regina." She turned to leave. "I'm really sorry this happened."

"It's all right," Matthew and Darienne said, almost in unison.

When Natalie had gone, Matthew looked at Darienne. "I had no idea she would fly all the way here. I called her when I arrived to tell her I'd left Australia and was here on a long vacation."

"She must be concerned about you," Darienne said. Natalie knew about their relationship. Darienne had met her several times when Matthew was performing in New York, where Natalie lived. They'd met again in London, when Natalie had flown out to see him when he was hospitalized. In fact, she and Natalie got along rather well. Why hadn't he mentioned Darienne was following him to Switzerland? Why hadn't Natalie asked?

"I suppose I did sound depressed on the phone," Matthew said, brows drawn together.

"Well, maybe it's good she caught us in such a telling situation. She knows now that you're not *that* depressed, hmm, *cheri?*" She ran her fingers over his arm.

"She sure does," he said with a flush of embarrassment. "I'm sorry. I just didn't know she was coming here."

"Don't apologize. We're all adults. She seemed to take it in stride fairly well and so should we."

"I wonder what she needs to talk to me about." Matthew rubbed his chin. "She didn't mention anything on the phone when I called."

"What *did* you talk about?"

"The last performance. How tired I was."

Darienne nodded, understanding now. Natalie had probably asked how he was and he'd told her. And since Matthew had a one-track mind lately, the subject of Darienne, or anything else, probably never came up.

In a few hours, Darienne left Matthew, saying she had to attend to some business matters concerning her property here, since she hadn't been in town for so long. But when she left, she didn't go to her home. She went to the Grand Hotel Regina.

Natalie answered her door and seemed surprised to see Darienne standing in the hallway. "Would you like to come in?" she asked.

"May I? I thought we should talk a bit."

Natalie stepped aside, and Darienne walked into the tidy, attractive room. Natalie offered to call room service for tea, and Darienne declined. Darienne hadn't noticed before, but Natalie was wearing a chic green dress of raw silk with a slim skirt and long sleeves that showed off her fragile, well-proportioned figure. Her shoulder-length hair was held back with a matching rolled scarf near her hairline and was tied stylishly behind one ear. The premature gray color of her tresses was so sleek and uniformly bright that she always made Darienne a bit envious. Her fine eyes were brown, warm, and intelligent.

"Gosh, I'm still embarrassed at walking in on you two like that."

"As I told Matthew, we're all adults. So now you know he and I are still together," Darienne said with a light shrug of her shoulders, her airy manner covering her deeper intention of letting Natalie know Matthew was hers. Not that Natalie had ever shown any particular sign that she wanted her former husband back. In fact, it was only in the last few years that he and she had been on friendly terms again. But Darienne didn't want their renewed friendship to rekindle any bygone love.

"I'm unpacking. I had a glass of wine and a late dinner. I just got back to my room," Natalie said, picking up some sweaters that had been set on an easy chair. Her open matching red suitcases lay on the bed. "Here, sit down," she invited, indicating the chair. "I'm glad you came over, actually. I'd like to know what you think about Matthew. I got worried when I heard him on the phone. He sounded so devastated at not being able to continue in *Shadow*."

Instead of sitting, Darienne stepped up and took the small pile of sweaters from her. "Let me help," she said. "I know what you mean about Matthew. I'm concerned, too." As she assisted Natalie in putting her clothes away in the dresser drawers and wardrobe, she described Matthew's restlessness and confided many of the things he'd said that indicated his inability to let go of his stage character. "I manage to snap him out of it for a while, but his depression always returns." She paused, after putting a pair of designer jeans in a dresser drawer, and looked at Natalie. "Will you be here for a few days?"

"Maybe a few weeks," Natalie replied. "I need to go to London for a while, though. Why?"

"Matthew and I only see each other in the evenings . . . ," Darienne said, thinking aloud.

Natalie smiled. "I remember that from New York and London. You sleep late."

"I'm a hopeless night owl. And I need afternoons to attend to my business affairs," Darienne said, improvising. "That worked fine when Matthew was busy at the theater. But now, he's alone all day, and . . ."

"And it gives him too much time to think about himself."

"Yes. Perhaps you could help me get him through this roadblock. I think once he's gotten his strength back, he'll enjoy himself more and begin to think of other things. Right now all he thinks about is playing Sir Percy again."

"That would kill him," Natalie said grimly. "I remember how he looked when I first saw him in that London hospital."

"Oh, I remember that, too," Darienne said with a sigh. "You know, it's a relief to talk to someone who understands. I feel I've been trying to singlehandedly pull him through all this. If you could spend some time with him during the day—have lunch, go sightseeing, whatever—that might help," Darienne suggested, wondering all the while if she was wise to ask for Natalie's help. But Darienne felt Matthew needed company during the long days because he didn't know anyone in Switzerland other than Darienne. "You could see to it he eats properly. And you can keep his mind occupied with other things besides the theater."

"Sure," Natalie said, "I'll be glad to. You know, after our marriage ended, I hated him for years. But, in his way, he's always been caring toward me. I'd like to do what I can to help."

Darienne hesitated a moment, fingering a blue silk scarf Natalie had unpacked. Then she asked, "Why did the marriage end? Matthew's told me a little—said he was too preoccupied with his work and didn't devote enough attention to you."

"That was basically it," Natalie said, arranging her dresses in the wardrobe. "I was only nineteen when I married him, and then I had a baby. I'd expected a normal marriage. I didn't realize I'd married a genius." Natalie smiled as she closed the wardrobe. "Great artists aren't like the rest of us. Matthew can't relate to everyday life somehow. His career came between us, and it's only lately I realize that it wasn't that he wanted it to, it's just that he didn't know how to live a normal life. Still doesn't. His mind is too creative, too brilliant. It needs a constant outlet, an appreciative audience. A wife and child weren't enough for him." Natalie lowered her eyes. "That's what I need to talk to him about. You might as well know, too. Our son, Larry—" She looked up to see if Darienne remembered.

"Yes," Darienne said. "In London you were trying to locate him, but couldn't."

"Right. Maybe Matthew has told you about what happened when we divorced?"

"He did, once. I'd like to hear your side of the story, if you wish to tell it," Darienne said, sitting on the chair, since most of the clothes had been put away.

"Larry was five at the time. He was an adorable child," Natalie said, walking to the bed. "He loved Matthew—better than he loved me, I think. Anyway, I decided I wanted a divorce. The marriage just wasn't working. Matthew was always off doing a picture, or if he was in a play, then he was always at the theater, morning till late at night. During the divorce, there was a custody battle over Larry. Matthew wanted to keep him. I argued I could give him more attention. But Matthew said he could provide better for him because he made very good money and I had only a high school education and had never worked outside the home. The court battle got very bitter, and in the end, the judge awarded Matthew custody."

Natalie shut the open suitcase and snapped closed the locks. "Afterward Matthew admitted that he fought so hard for custody because he thought if he had our son he might be able to win me back. That made me even more angry, using Larry as a pawn the way he seemed to do." She picked up the empty suitcase and slid it under the bed. Then she sat on the bed, covered with a thick comforter, and continued. "So one day, after some secret planning between me and my parents, I kidnapped Larry from his school and took him to the airport. We flew to Scotland, where I had an aunt and uncle. I left Matthew a note saying I'd taken our son where he would never find us."

Natalie paused and lifted her shoulders in a sort of shiver. "It all seems so needlessly dramatic now, twenty years later. You'd think two adults could have worked things out better for their son. But I was too young to know how to handle emotional trauma. And Matthew, caught up in his career though he was, was still devastated that I'd divorced him. He never could understand what he'd done to deserve my leaving him. I couldn't get through to him that I wanted a husband—him—not his latest publicity photo."

Natalie looked up at Darienne self-consciously. "Sorry, I'm digressing. I took Larry to Scotland. Matthew eventually found out where we were, but he left us alone. I heard he'd realized that all our hatred and arguing was bad for our son. So Larry went to school in Edinburgh." She smiled. "He acquired a Scottish accent. He was so cute when he was young, talking with a brogue. He did well in school—to please me, I think. And he got interested in doing school plays. That I wasn't so pleased with."

She reached across the bed for the empty tote bag and pulled it toward her. "As you might guess, he had a natural talent for acting. He inherited a lot from his father. All he inherited from me, I'm afraid, was my anger toward Matthew. And—this is the part I regret the most—he took on that anger himself, the older he grew. He came to believe that Matthew deserted us, though I tried to explain that I instigated the divorce. Larry would say I did it because his dad was never home, never cared for him or me. And that wasn't true. I realized that when I heard Larry say it, how wrong my own assessment of Matthew was. Matthew wasn't around much, but it wasn't because he didn't care. He just had such a strong need to develop his unique gifts as a performer that there wasn't enough time in his life for us, too."

Natalie stared at the red tote bag beside her as if lost in thought. "When I first saw Matthew play Sir Percy in New York, I felt I understood him, finally. What an incredible performance. It was only then that I realized I'd been married to a genius, and that if I'd managed somehow to keep him home more, I might have deprived the world of a great talent."

Darienne grew a bit uneasy listening to her extol Matthew. "What happened to your son?"

Natalie glanced up suddenly. "Oh, yes." As if regearing her thoughts, she carefully zipped the empty tote bag shut. "Larry grew to despise Matthew, mostly because, as I said, I taught him to. I began changing my tune about his father when I realized how deeply Larry hated him. I tried to tell him, no, Matthew was never as bad as that, and yes, Matthew did love him. Matthew became a big star in the U.S. and 'Rick and

Rosie' was even shown in Great Britain." Darienne knew she was referring to Matthew's popular TV comedy series, still in reruns in the U.S.

"I made Larry watch it," Natalie continued, "so that he would know who his father was, could see his remarkable talent. My son would watch the show, belligerent and at the same time fascinated. And he would say, 'He's making lots of money in the U.S. and we're here just getting by on what you make as a secretary.' I was taking evening classes at the university, but I earned a living working in an office. I tried to tell him I'd refused to take the money Matthew had wanted to send us, but Larry would only say that if he'd been a decent father to begin with, I wouldn't have been forced to kidnap him and go off on my own."

Natalie sighed quietly and lifted the tote bag off the bed. She set it on the floor, looking distracted. After a few moments she continued. "Pretty soon, I couldn't even argue with Larry anymore. He just wouldn't listen. He began to get angry at me when I tried to be fair and take Matthew's point of view. One day when he was in college, we had a big fight. He took off. Sent me a note postmarked from London that he was fine and wanted to be on his own from then on. The letter had no return address. That's the last I heard from him."

Natalie lifted her shoulders, her expression full of regret, but not tearful. "I made an effort to find him, but couldn't. I got kind of lonely there, an American in Scotland, all by myself. My aunt and uncle had died, so I moved back to New York, where my parents lived. Matthew heard I'd returned and he came to see me. We talked about Larry. He felt terrible, responsible for it all. But we decided Larry was young and maybe needed some time on his own. I'd left word with neighbors in Edinburgh where I could be reached in New York, but as far as I know, Larry has never tried to contact me. A few years later, when Matthew came to New York again, doing *Shadow,* we met several more times—well, you know that. That's when I met you."

Darienne nodded, thinking she was still missing part of the story. "So have you heard something about—"

"Oh, yes!" Natalie said in a brighter tone, straightening her posture. "That's why I want to go to London. Matthew gave me money to hire a private detective in England to track down our son. Well, Larry's been found! He's still in London. He's changed his name and he does some acting and has a regular job as an announcer on the BBC. I have his address and phone. I need to tell Matthew this. I thought I'd go to London and try to see Larry. I'm not sure what to say or how to handle it, but I need to see him, to try to reestablish some kind of a relationship with him. We were so close when he was a boy. And I hope he can somehow be reconciled with Matthew someday. Gosh," she said, shaking her head, "I haven't seen Larry for five years. I may not even recognize him."

"How exciting!" Darienne said, happy for her. "I'm sure when he sees you, he'll be glad you've found him. He's what, about twenty-five now?"

"Yes. I hope he's gotten through his rebellious youth by now. Maybe he'll be ready to listen."

"This is good," Darienne said, thinking ahead. "Matthew needs a distraction and this is a wonderful one."

"I hope it'll be good for all of us," Natalie said.

"And what about you? What have you been doing?"

"I graduated college," Natalie said with a grin.

"Congratulations! Do you work now?"

"I run a business. I just became manager of a shop that specializes in women's clothing accessories. Belts, scarves, hats, and so on. It's called That Certain Thing."

"That's lovely," Darienne said. "I'll have to stop in next time I'm in New York. And what about your personal life? Are you still alone? Never remarried?"

"Oh, Lord." Natalie held up her hands and began counting on her fingers. "Well, I had an affair with a Scotsman in Edinburgh. But that didn't work out." She raised a second finger. "When I returned to New York, I got married again to someone my parents introduced me to. He was a solid man, a banker. It should have been a good match. But it only lasted about a year and then I wanted to be on my own again. I feel bad saying this—he was a wonderful man—but I was bored with him. After that," she counted a third finger, "I met someone else, and then someone else," she said, lifting a fourth finger, "but neither of those relationships worked out either."

She threw up her hands. "It seems I'm most attracted to men who can't make good husbands! I like men with creative minds, men who seem to live on a more rarified level than the rest of us. Try being married to someone like that!"

"Well, I'll tell you," Darienne said with some pride, "I've *never* married, and I'm perfectly happy."

Natalie leaned on one arm and studied Darienne, her rich brown eyes inquisitive. "But you're someone who lives on a different level, too, I think. That's probably why I liked you right away when we first met. I can see why you and Matthew are attracted to one another. You've been good for him. And you've managed to take care of him, probably better than anyone else could. When he didn't mention you on the phone, I was afraid to ask, thinking maybe you'd left him and that was part of the reason he was so depressed. But now I see—very demonstrably, too," she said with a laugh, "that you're still a pair."

"Did it upset you to see us . . . that way?"

"Why, because I was once married to him?" Natalie's eyes grew nostalgic. "He was my first love, the first man I ever made love with. And that was quite an experience"—she gazed at Darienne with an *entre nous* look—"as you can imagine. It was one of those love-at-first-sight, whirlwind romances. But that was so long ago, like another lifetime. And I've had other relationships. How can I object to his being with another woman? We're different people now than when we met. But I care what happens to him, and I'm glad that he's not alone. Sometimes he's gone along for years at a time with no one. I don't know why, but he has."

"Women are so easily attracted to him, they sometimes make demands and become a burden," Darienne said in a confidential tone as she leaned back in her chair. "I've seen them hang on him—some of his leading ladies, in fact—and he doesn't like that."

"He once told me he shies away from making commitments, because he couldn't live up to the one he made to me. You're smart. You don't make demands."

"We suit each other's lifestyle," Darienne said, sounding more smug about it than she felt. She didn't want Natalie to guess how much in love she was with Matthew.

"I'm glad," Natalie said, looking content. "I'll try to help out with him. Maybe you're right, that hearing about Larry will take him out of himself. If he stops talking about Sir Percy long enough to listen."

Darienne chuckled and nodded. "I know what you mean."

Over the next week, their plan to rehabilitate Matthew seemed to go well. Darienne noticed his spirits apparently lifting. She arrived one evening at Matthew's just as Natalie was getting ready to leave, after spending the afternoon and having dinner with him. The three of them talked for a few minutes. Matthew looked stronger and healthier. His mood seemed good and Natalie's manner was just the same as before. The former husband and wife seemed like friends, like family maybe, but in a cousinly sort of way. Darienne felt she'd taken a good step by inviting Natalie to spend time with Matthew.

That day Natalie grew animated as she told Darienne some news: She had just received a publicity photo of her son. She'd learned the name of his agent and had phoned the London agency to ask for his photo. "It arrived by mail at my hotel this morning," she said. Natalie picked up the photo from Matthew's coffee table and showed it to Darienne.

"Who does he look like?" Natalie asked with a big smile.

Darienne stared at the photo with a combined feeling of amazement and déjà vu. She turned to Matthew, who was standing nearby. "He looks exactly like you in your old films!"

"You would have to use the word *old,*" Matthew joked. He grew quiet and walked to Darienne's side to look at the photo again. "I think he's more handsome than I ever was," he said, studying the black-and-white image of his son. "His eyes aren't so round as mine. They're more like Natalie's. He's got her cheekbones, too." He glanced at his former wife. "The best of him is from you," he said with a soft voice that would have thrilled Darienne had he been addressing her. Darienne was immediately on guard. What was happening?

Natalie shook her head. "Overall he looks like you. And his speaking voice is exactly like yours, too. I noticed that the first time I talked to you after I moved back to New York. I was staying with my parents and you called me on the phone, remember? When I heard your voice, I thought it was Larry calling me from England. Then I realized the Scottish accent was missing."

"I remember," Matthew said in a rueful tone. "You were so disappointed it was me."

"Well, I'd hoped maybe he was finally trying to contact me. But I was glad to hear from you."

As they talked about old times, Darienne stared at the handsome, curly-haired young man in the photo who bonded Matthew and Natalie forever, by virtue of being their son. And suddenly Darienne felt like an outsider to this little family, broken though it was.

Natalie left the photo with Matthew, said good-bye and left, gracefully not intruding on Darienne's time with her ex-husband. Graceful was a good word to describe Natalie, Darienne thought. More and more, she had to admire the woman whom Matthew had once deeply loved, admire her for her quiet strength, her uncomplicated and unassuming manner, and her sensitivity—traits no doubt acquired through the difficult experiences of her past. Darienne also had to admire Natalie for being so gracious toward her, Matthew's mistress. Unfortunately, she had to hope that Matthew hadn't begun to rediscover the treasure he'd lost.

Darienne didn't see Natalie for several evenings. But about a week later, she once again arrived at Matthew's chalet to find Natalie still there. But this time the atmosphere was different somehow. Both Matthew and Natalie were wearing jeans and pullovers, and the color in their faces was high, as though they'd just come back from a hike in the mountains. They were sitting together on the couch, about a foot apart, and as soon as Darienne had been in the living room for a few minutes with them, she could feel that something had shifted in their relationship. Maybe it was the way they avoided looking at each other, though they smiled and made small talk with Darienne as though nothing had changed. But she could sense there was something they weren't saying, something they felt it best she didn't know. And there was more—she detected a subtle new awkwardness between them, as if something had occurred that they weren't sure how to deal with.

It didn't take Darienne long to imagine what had happened: They must have made love. After four hundred years of observing and participating in sexual relationships, Darienne could discern vibrations and tensions between others better than the people involved.

"What did you two do today?" she asked in a tone of casual interest as she sat on an easy chair facing them.

"Had lunch in town," Matthew said. "Then we went for a hike along a trail in the mountains."

Natalie smiled, but it didn't reach her eyes. "We were out for a few hours and then we came back."

Had it happened on the trail? Darienne wondered. Perhaps they'd happened on a spot in some secluded meadow, stopped to rest and found themselves giving in to a rekindled passion without pausing to think. And now that it had happened, their relationship was changed from what it had been, and neither was quite sure what it meant for them or what should happen next.

"Did you have dinner somewhere?" Darienne asked.

Both sat in silence for a moment, as if the idea seemed strange.

"We forgot to eat," Natalie said, as if surprised.

"It's still early." Matthew glanced at his watch. "Why don't the three of us go into town for dinner now?"

"I've already eaten," Darienne said. "But I could accompany you."

"Could we eat at my hotel?" Natalie suggested, sounding edgy. "That would be convenient for me, since I have to pack tonight."

"Pack?" Darienne said.

"I've decided to leave for London tomorrow. Matthew and I have talked about it, and it's time I go and see Larry." She looked at Matthew. "I wanted Matthew to come with me, but he thinks it's best if I go alone. I'm a little anxious about it."

Perhaps that's how it was, Darienne thought, envisioning a new scenario. Natalie was feeling nervous, perhaps guilty that her relationship with her son had gone wrong, and she wanted so much to make things right. Perhaps she began to cry. It was like Matthew to comfort a weeping woman. And that led to . . .

Darienne put aside her thoughts. "I'm sorry you're leaving," she told Natalie, though now she was secretly relieved. "How long will you be gone?"

"I don't know. If Larry accepts me, I might stay for a couple of weeks. I'd like to get to know him again. I hope I can convince him to meet Matthew."

"Don't hope for too much," Matthew told her, reaching to take her hand. "I don't blame him for hating me. I'll be happy enough if you and he can patch things up."

"But he should know you, Matthew," she said with feeling, making a fist with her other hand and gently bringing it down on his knee for emphasis. "If only he could know you, the way I've gotten to know you again . . ."

"Shhh," Matthew said, edging closer to slip his arm around her. "Remember what I said before. If it happens, that's wonderful. But don't count on it. I don't want you to be disappointed. Now take a deep breath. It's not good to get all upset again . . ."

Their eyes shifted away from each other and they avoided glancing at Darienne. Natalie pulled out of Matthew's comforting embrace and stood up. "Look, I think I better spend some time by myself tonight. I need to get my thoughts together before I fly to London tomorrow. And I have to get up early."

"I have my rental car. Should I drive you to Zurich?" Matthew asked, rising to his feet.

"The hotel has transportation."

"No, I'll drive you."

"All right." Natalie was silent for a moment, looking a little lost. She picked up her handbag from the coffee table and walked over to Darienne, who also stood up. "It was nice to see you again," Natalie said, putting out her hand with hesitance. She smiled. "It's up to you to keep Matthew away from the greasepaint for a while longer. I've done . . . all I can." Her smile faded as she said the words.

You've done too much, Darienne thought. Natalie was no longer quite the steady, together woman she had been when she arrived. Spending time alone with Matthew, probably making love with him, had clearly jostled her equanimity. No doubt Natalie was nervous about meeting her son again, but Darienne sensed it was her deepening relationship with Matthew that had thrown her off-kilter so suddenly.

Darienne could sympathize with Natalie's vulnerable, emotional state. And she genuinely liked her. But Natalie was becoming a rival. And at that point, Darienne had to draw a line, because Darienne fully intended to keep Matthew for herself.

"I'll take care of him. Don't worry," Darienne said with confidence as she warmly shook Natalie's hand. "I hope things go well between you and your son."

"Thanks. Good-bye until I see you again." She turned to Matthew. "Can you pick me up at six in the morning?"

"I'll be there."

Natalie nodded, her gaze lingering on him for a moment. Then she smiled once more at them both and left.

When the door had closed, Darienne gazed at Matthew. "Are you hungry? I'll sit in a restaurant with you while you have dinner."

He shook his head, his eyes focused inward, as if he was preoccupied and worried.

She walked up to him and ran her hands over his sweater, appreciating the expanse of his chest. "What happened, Matthew?"

"Hmm?"

"With Natalie. I can tell something's changed. I'm not angry, darling. These things happen. But I think we should be honest with one another and not keep secrets."

His eyes settled on hers, deep and still. "How do you know so much?"

"I know the way of the world, *cheri.* I'm wise about relationships." Except perhaps her own, she thought.

"We didn't plan it or want it," Matthew said. "It just happened."

"You and she made love."

He nodded. "She was getting apprehensive about seeing Larry. I tried to reassure her and . . ."

Darienne could at least be pleased she'd figured it out so well. "Your old attraction for her ignited?"

"Something like that."

"That's what happens when you comfort women, Matthew. You do it too well. They want more."

"It was just as much my fault as hers."

Yes, yes, be the gentleman and defend her, Darienne thought with irritation. "How do you feel about what happened? About her?"

Matthew turned away. "I don't know. Maybe it's because I'm still so at sea after quitting *Shadow.* Maybe I'm hoping to reclaim relationships in my life, get my bearings straightened out."

"There's nothing wrong with that," Darienne told him, stepping around to face him again. "But you'd better decide what kind of relationship you want. Most women want something permanent. That's what Natalie once wanted from you, and you couldn't give it to her. Be careful how you comfort such a woman. She may come to want more than you can give her, *cheri*. You don't want to hurt her again."

Matthew lowered his eyes, his face drawn and brooding. "No," he agreed.

She took his hands, placed them at her small waist and stepped closer. "You're so much safer with the easy relationship we have, *cheri*. You know I don't expect anything from you. When we make love, there are no consequences. We have pleasure with no worries afterward about why or what will happen now. Natalie is lovely," she said, kissing him softly on the mouth. "But she's vulnerable to you. We both like her and respect her too much to see her hurt, *n'est-ce pas?*"

He nodded, tension showing in his face. Though he agreed, there was still an element of confusion in his gray-green eyes. It was that remnant of doubt that troubled Darienne. Had Natalie rekindled something in his heart? Darienne had better put out that little flame before it grew.

"She'll be all right, Matthew. Don't worry. You have so much to think about lately. First your health and your career. And now Natalie and your son. Your poor brain is overloaded." She smoothed his furrowed forehead with gentle fingers. "Your emotions are stretched too thin. You must forget for a while. Relax. Relax, *cheri*. Let me help you forget. Let me help you . . ."

She kissed him again. Using all her skills, honed over the centuries in her explorations with men, together with her surplus of physical attributes, she soon had all his attention. After three years together she understood exactly how to tap his deep well of desire. Once she'd opened that channel, she beckoned him upward to that tantalizing plane of supernatural ecstasy to which only she could lead him.

When she left him asleep in bed at three A.M., his senses exhausted, she was quite sure she'd made him forget his afternoon interlude with Natalie. In fact, she wondered if he'd forget *Natalie*. She paused to set his alarm and write a note to remind him to drive his ex-wife to Zurich. After all, she thought as she left the note on his pillow, she wouldn't want Natalie to miss her plane.

# 5

# Cream cheese, apricot, and prune

HARRIET WALKED up the sidewalk to David's mansion, admiring its massive sandstone walls, its picturesque dormers and gables. She knocked at his front door, located beneath a high, sheltering arch, and waited for the buzzer to sound, which allowed her to enter. Once inside, she ran up the spiral staircase to the third floor, where David was waiting for her. In her hands she carried a plate of home-made *kolacky* filled with three assorted fillings—cream cheese, apricot, and prune.

"I was baking last night," she told him, smoothing under the edges of cellophane wrap before handing it to him.

"Looks absolutely wonderful," David said, appearing to admire the loaded plate of round, flat, yeast dough confections sprinkled white with powdered sugar.

They walked into his living room, and he set the plate on the bar, then came back to help Harriet off with her navy blue spring coat.

"You shouldn't go to so much trouble," he said, hanging up the coat. "I have the empty plate from last week for you to take home. Remind me to give it to you."

Harriet was glad to hear it was empty. She'd brought him coffee cake, houska—a Bohemian braided egg-bread—or kolacky each time she'd visited, which was about a half dozen times now over the past weeks. But she'd never seen him eat anything she'd made, and it disappointed her. She wondered if his illness was diabetes. Usually he wound up opening the goodies for *her* to eat while she drank the tea he invariably made for her. Come to think of it, she'd never seen him make himself a cup of tea, either. Sometimes he struck her as being awfully unusual—like the way he'd often look at her with eyes so still and unblinking that he'd seem to have become a statue. And there were the times she'd find him staring at her throat while that strange glow crept into his eyes, the one she'd noticed the night she met him. And then he'd seem to catch himself and the look would instantly vanish. It always gave her a touch of the willies. Yet he was so constantly gentle and reassuring, she'd put her wholehearted trust in him. Perhaps because he wrote about vampires, he'd become preoccupied with throats, she told herself.

"I found an old poem I thought you'd enjoy," he said to her with some eagerness. "Make yourself comfortable. I'll get it."

"Okay." Harriet sat down on the loveseat and adjusted the full skirt of the pink crepe dress she'd just finished sewing. One of the reasons she liked to visit David was that it gave her a chance to wear items from the new wardrobe she'd been making for herself.

David went into his small office adjacent to the living room and came back carrying what looked like a very old newspaper clipping. It was quite yellowed, almost brown. The edges were worn and its creases cracking.

He sat down beside her, leaving a comfortable distance between them. "It's an epitaph that was once seen in an old English churchyard. Listen." He began to read in his lilting, French-accented voice, which was so gentle she could easily have listened to him all night.

"Here lies a poor woman who always was tired,
For she lived in a place where help wasn't hired.
Her last words on earth were, Dear friends I am going
Where washing ain't done nor sweeping nor sewing,
And everything there is exact to my wishes,
For there they don't eat and there's no washing of
    dishes . . .
Don't mourn for me now, don't mourn for me never,
For I'm going to do nothing for ever and ever."

Harriet laughed as David looked up, eyes lively with amusement. "I like that!" she said. "Can I copy it?"

"Of course." He handed her the article. "I'll get you a pen and paper."

As he got up to go back into his office, Harriet looked at the clipping, astonished to see and feel how old it was. Studying it, she saw it was an epitaph quoted in a letter printed in a publication called the *Spectator*. The date was September 2, 1922.

When David came back into the living room with a fountain pen and a sheet of white paper, she asked, "Where did you get this?"

"I cut it out years ago. I ran across it last night when I was looking through a box of clippings."

"But it's dated 1922. That's way before you were born."

His movements slowed and he sat down hesitantly, as if thinking. "Someone gave me a pile of old publications once from a library that was getting rid of outdated material. I looked through them and found this."

"Was it when you lived in England?" she asked. He'd told her he was born in Paris, but later had lived for a while in Britain.

"Yes, while I lived in England."

Harriet took the pen and paper and began to copy the epitaph. David was always a little vague about his past, and Harriet sometimes wondered why. She, by contrast, told him *everything*. It sometimes embarrassed her to remember later some of the details she'd told him—how much she weighed, for example. He was so receptive, nonjudgmental and affirming—traits she didn't find in anyone else in her life—that Harriet found herself unburdening all her problems to him. And invariably he found things to say that made her feel better.

As she wrote, David said, "That's another lovely dress. Did you sew this one, too?"

She smiled and looked up. "Thanks. Yes. Some nights I've been staying up late sewing instead of baking. It saves us all a few calories, I figure. Except now I'm getting a closet full of dresses I don't have much of any place to wear."

"Have you thought of working outside the home?"

"Occasionally. I hate to imagine what Ralph would think of it, though. He'd take it as a criticism that he's not making enough money, instead of seeing it as something I might want to do just for myself. I don't know if it's worth the argument."

"You'd feel more independent if you worked. You'd feel as though you were a part of the outside world. Your life is rather insular." He smiled as if at himself. "Like mine is. But then, I'm a writer. People like me never quite fit in anywhere."

Harriet studied his face, seeing the strange sadness in his eyes. She almost wanted to mother him, but some instinct told her that wouldn't be wise. Besides, it wasn't what she really wanted. But she'd better not think too much about just what sort of relationship she might want with him if she had the choice. He was the most sensitive, most brilliant man she'd ever met. And one of the handsomest. Veronica knew what she was doing when she chose David!

"So," she said, changing the subject. "Which do you like best? My coffee cake, my houska, or the kolacky?" She waited, wondering how he would answer.

"You're asking me to make a choice?" he replied, a dumbfounded expression on his face as if he couldn't possibly pick one over the other.

"Well, if there's one you like less than the others, I'll stop bringing it."

"You don't have to bring me anything, you know. I'm very pleased just to have your company."

"Would you prefer it if I didn't bring anything?"

"Did I say that?"

"No, but—"

"I want you to do whatever makes you happy," he told her. "I can see it gives you pleasure to bring me your baked goods. And I very much enjoy the old-world custom of it—it's part of what makes you such a warm person."

Harriet was dying to ask him if he really ate what she brought him, but managed to keep herself from doing so. He was giving her roundabout answers and she could guess he must be hiding something. But his manner was so charming, she decided she didn't really care one way or another.

"Why do you stay up late cooking and sewing?" he asked. "It can't be good for you to lose sleep."

"I take a nap in the afternoon, sometimes. I have the best dreams in the afternoon—the dreams where I'm back in high school."

"Does your husband care if you stay up late?"

She lifted her eyebrows. "He doesn't like it."

David nodded in apparent understanding. "You do it to avoid him."

"Guess so," she admitted. She took a deep breath and exhaled.

"Is he that insensitive a lover?"

"He never got beyond his adolescent, get-her-while-you-can approach. When we *were* teenagers, I found it exciting just because it was all a new and forbidden experience. And I didn't know any better. I didn't know how sex was supposed to be or feel. I just assumed that since he was a guy, he knew what he was doing. My mother brought me up with the notion that men are supposed to have all the answers and know everything. I suppose she learned that from her mother. It's only the last ten years I've found out from watching Phil Donahue and Oprah, and reading magazine articles, that men aren't any smarter than we are." She glanced up at David. "Present company excepted," she said with a grin.

"Thank you," David said, chuckling. "But you're right. Men, too, are brought up to think we're supposed to be masters of the world. Our self-esteem is based on our competence. But we're not brought up to examine feelings very much. And that's a mistake."

"But you're different. How come?"

"I've had more years to—" He stopped and seemed to regroup his thoughts. "Because I'm a writer, I've spent more years thinking about people's motivations than most men do. I've made an effort to understand women. I don't claim to be an expert, but—"

"For a man, you're close enough!" Harriet said.

David laughed. "You're fun. You know, your husband is missing a lot. I wish he'd take the time to understand you better."

Harriet shook her head. "It's too late to hope for that. I don't think he even cares anymore. He refuses to see a marriage counselor."

"That would seem to him like admitting there was something wrong with him. It threatens his self-esteem."

"So what have I got? A two-hundred-pound workaholic with a Neanderthal sex drive and a fragile ego? That's what I've got to deal with?"

"I imagine he has a lot of emotions and unmet needs deep down that even he may not be aware of. If you can get to those, you might be able to make some progress."

Harriet was fascinated. "How?"

David thought a moment. "Well, it may not appeal to you at this point, but I would guess sex might be a good way to begin. That's probably one need he won't deny having."

She looked askance. "You men are all alike. And you stick together, too!"

"Now, Harriet," David said, laughing as he took her hand, "I'm on your side. But you're asking a man for his opinion, and that's what I have to tell you."

Harriet liked the feel of his long fingers covering hers. It had been years since any man had held her hand. She felt comforted and feminine. Trying to keep her mind on the conversation, she said, "But sex with Ralph is mostly a one-sided event. It's almost like he takes out his frustrations from work with me. I don't mean he's rough or angry. But I feel like I'm just there to make him feel less tense, because he's uptight from things that happened at the office. He doesn't seem to think about me, just about getting his physical release to feel better." She lowered her eyes as she breathed out a heavy sigh. "Maybe it means I'm a lousy wife, but I've gotten tired of accommodating him."

"Don't feel guilty. You have your own needs that should be met," David told her, shifting on the couch to face her more fully. He raised his forefinger for emphasis as he spoke. "But I think I understand where he's coming from. Men sometimes use sex as a way of communicating emotion without having to say anything—lots of different emotions, including frustration and the need for reassurance. For some men who aren't in touch with their feelings, sex is the only acceptable way for them to feel anything at all," he said, staring at her in that still way of his. "It is, as you say, a . . . release."

Harriet was looking into David's eyes as he explained this. And all at once, as he said the last word, a subtle light of admiration seemed to glimmer there. He looked away, and so did Harriet. And now her heart was beating fast. Her head was suddenly swimming with tantalizing, impure thoughts that she knew she would have to confess to her priest. But right now she didn't care. God, what a heady, wonderful, spinning feeling to have a man look at her, even for a sixteenth of a second, as though he might be longing to know what making love with her would be like. If Ralph would look at her with such appreciative eyes even once, she might give up baking.

"So," she said, trying to keep the conversation going smoothly without revealing her inner spontaneous combustion, "if he's using my body as a way to release emotion, where does that leave me?"

David's eyes settled on hers again, apparently at ease. Now she wondered if she'd imagined the admiring gaze. "You need to talk to him," David told her. "Get him to separate out his emotions. Ask him, is he really feeling romantic, or is he just upset about something that happened at work? And then you can try to explain how you feel."

Harriet nodded, thinking this over. "It seems like a reasonable approach. But Ralph isn't exactly one you can reason with. Talking isn't his strong point."

"You might have to ask him, are you feeling angry? Or sad? Give him examples so he knows what kind of answers you're looking for."

"Like a multiple choice quiz?"

David broke into a laugh, throwing his head back a bit. She noticed his teeth, for some reason. His eyeteeth were unusually sharp. But she let the thought go as she followed up with more humor, since her joking seemed to amuse David.

"I could say, 'Ralph, how do you feel: a. angry, b. depressed, c. frustrated, or d. just plain horny? Or e. none of the above."

David continued laughing, his shoulders shaking, and finally said, "I think you've been dreaming about your school days too long."

"That must be it," she said, chuckling. "It's not that I don't think your suggestion is good. I just can't quite see it working with Ralph."

"What is his general approach to sex, then? What does he say?"

"Nothing. If I get in bed while he's still awake, he starts, you know, groping me. And if I don't object to his advance, about five minutes later we're finished."

"Does he do anything to get you in the mood?"

She looked at him a little unsteadily. "Like what?"

"Touching you. Caressing you."

Harriet felt a slight thrill at those words pronounced in David's comforting European voice. She lowered her eyes. "Well, he does that, but . . ."

"Not so that you enjoy it. He doesn't seem to have your pleasure in mind?"

"If you mean, is it like in the romance novels?—No."

"I've never read one."

She glanced at him with a little smile. "No, I suppose you wouldn't have. Well, in them the hero always . . . well, does certain things . . ." Harriet was beginning to feel her face grow warm with this topic of conversation. Still she was eager to know what David would say. In fact, she'd love to know what *his* approach to a woman would be.

"And Ralph doesn't do them?"

"It's like—like he handles my breasts the way I might test cantaloupes at the grocery store. It doesn't exactly turn me on. Is it really supposed to?"

David stared at her thoughtfully, his blue eyes luminous and still. His voice grew soft. "If it's done right, it should."

She gazed back at him and thought, Could you demonstrate that theory? In reply, his eyes seemed to sharpen and grow inquisitive. Something electric happened then, a sudden charge in the atmosphere between them. Harriet glanced away in embarrassment, her breathing unsteady.

After a moment he said, "Perhaps we should put aside this subject for the time being."

*Oh, no!* she thought, but agreed, "Maybe we should."

The silence between them was telling for a moment, but soon David began a new conversation, as if the old topic had been forgotten. "Last time, you mentioned Ralph was talking about moving out of Berwyn. Has he said any more?"

"Oh, he's talked about that on and off for years," she said, trying to follow David's lead and continue as if nothing had happened. She began to chatter. "But just last night he was saying again that we ought to move to a more upscale suburb. Like Oak Brook. He says once Janet is away at college, we should move to a smaller home, but in a classier area. It upsets me. I like my neighborhood. I grew up there. So did he."

"He sees your present location as a negative factor for his career?"

She nodded, her misgivings about the possibility of moving bringing her spirits down. "The other men at his office all live further west, in new homes. And he thinks the Bohemian ethnic orientation in Berwyn is a joke that other people look down on. For example, every year he hates it when I go watch the Houby Parade down Cermak Road."

"The what?"

Harriet had to chuckle. "Well, it is sort of funny. *Houby* is the Bohemian word for mushroom, and every October we have a festival that celebrates mushrooms. There's a parade down Cermak, the main street that runs through Cicero and Berwyn, which together are the Czech stronghold in the Chicago area. But George Bush appeared in the parade when he was running for President. That's what I told Ralph—how stupid can it be if the President of the United States was in it?"

David's expression had a faraway aspect, as if he was reminiscing. "I remember traveling through Bohemia once, long ago. I was on my way to Prague. There were people with baskets in the Bohemian Forest having the most wonderful time searching for mushrooms. They made soups from them or dried them."

"Yes! I have soup recipes from my grandmother. She came from the old country when she was twenty. I'll make up a batch and bring you some."

David's eyes wandered, as if he didn't know what to say. Finally he said, "I'll look forward to it."

"Of course, we don't have the right kind of mushrooms here in the U.S. My grandmother always tells me that."

"I'm sure your soup is wonderful."

Harriet glanced at her watch. "Well, I'd better leave. I promised Veronica I'd visit her tonight before I go home. My family thinks I'm at a quilting class that ends at nine o'clock."

David's eyes seemed to grow pale. "How is Veronica?"

"I haven't visited her for a couple of weeks, but she was fine the last I saw her. She asked about you. I think I told you."

"Yes, I remember," he murmured. His face settled into a melancholy expression.

"Would you like me to tell her anything for you?"

David raised his eyes to hers. "No," he said softly. "No messages. She understands."

Harriet nodded and said nothing more. She wondered if it was because he missed Veronica so much that talking about sexual matters had made him briefly envision her as a surrogate for Veronica. She wished there was something she could do to bring him and Veronica back together, but David seemed to stick steadfastly to his reasons for not communicating with the woman he loved. And Veronica seemed to accept it. So what could Harriet do? It was none of her business, really, what they decided to do about their relationship.

Nevertheless, Harriet pondered the problem as she drove to her cousin's apartment. Veronica opened the door dressed in jeans, a T-shirt and a spotted apron. She hugged Harriet.

"Gosh, it's nice to see you," Veronica said, taking her coat. She laid it over the end of the couch. "I'm making a birthday cake for someone at work. I was just getting ready to frost it. Want to help?"

"Sure," Harriet said, and followed Veronica into her small, white-tiled kitchen. There was a round table in the center beneath the fluorescent ceiling lights. On the table were two chocolate cake layers, cooling on wire racks.

"You're better at this than me," Veronica said, handing her a table knife.

Harriet winced to see she'd already opened up a can of ready-made chocolate frosting. "Store-bought stuff?"

" 'Fraid so. The cake is from a mix, too," Veronica admitted. "You should have come sooner."

"Well, it looks pretty good anyway," Harriet said, holding up one of the cake layers. "They came out nice and even. Got a long, sharp knife?"

Veronica found one in a drawer and carefully handed it to her. As Veronica watched in horror, Harriet cut each layer horizontally, making four thin layers.

"We'll fancy it up a little," she said. "Got another flavor of frosting?"

Veronica looked worried. "No."

"Jam?"

"Raspberry."

"Good enough."

Veronica got the jar of jam from a cupboard and handed it

to Harriet. She dipped the table knife into the raspberry preserve and began spreading it on one thin layer.

"I've just seen David," Harriet told her as she worked.

"How is he?" Veronica's brown eyes looked eager for news.

"Fine. He always asks about you. He never gives me any messages for you, but I can tell he's sad not to be with you." She paused in her spreading to look at her cousin. "Is there something I can do or say to change things and bring you two together?"

"No. David will call me when the time comes."

"When is that?"

"A few more years."

"I don't know how you can wait. He's so attractive. And so understanding. I'd trade Ralph for him any day!"

Veronica smiled and took a dab of frosting out of the can with her finger. "I can understand why you would say that, but I know you wouldn't."

"How do you know?"

"You're too religious to do anything the church wouldn't allow," Veronica said, licking her finger.

"It's true. I don't like the idea of being an unfaithful wife. Especially since Ralph has never been unfaithful to me—as far as I know."

"Well, it's nice to know he has a good point."

"He's been a reliable husband and a good provider," Harriet felt obligated to point out. "And he's home every night. It's just that I can't communicate with him without it winding up in an argument. And the sex leaves a lot to be desired," she said, as she finished spreading the jam. "I was talking about that with David tonight, in fact."

"Really?" Veronica asked with interest. "What did David say?"

"He said I should try to get Ralph to talk about his feelings and then express mine to him." Harriet began to set the jam-spread layers on top of one another to build the cake. "And we talked a little about foreplay. But then we decided to drop that subject."

"Why?"

"It got too embarrassing." Keeping her eyes averted from Veronica, Harriet grabbed a clean knife to spread the frosting. "I don't know him well enough yet to talk with him in detail about that kind of thing. But I had the impression he's an expert on that facet of life. I . . . I found myself wishing he'd give me a how-to lesson." She glanced up at her cousin.

Veronica had grown wistful, her eyes luminous with a soft, sensual glow. "I know what you mean. I was a virgin when I met him. I barely knew what sex was all about, yet I wanted to throw myself at him. But I was scared, too. He helped me through it all, made me feel secure. He was patient, and so gentle. And when we made love," her voice grew husky, "it was such a profound experience. Beyond anything I could have dreamed." She paused and blinked. "Sorry. I didn't mean to go on like that."

Harriet stood there, chocolate-coated knife in her hand, and felt spellbound. "A woman can really feel that way with a man?"

"Sure," Veronica said, looking at her with surprise. "You must have felt that way about Ralph, at least in the beginning. Otherwise why would you have married him?"

"I had to, remember?"

"But still, you were attracted enough to Ralph to . . . to get pregnant by him."

"That was all adolescent hormones. I've never had the profound sort of experience you just talked about. But then, you were with David. And somehow I can imagine with him it would be . . . Well, no, I'd better not imagine." She went back to spreading the cake. "Too dangerous!"

Veronica studied her. "It's just like the psychometrist said."

"Don't remind me."

"Don't repress the feeling," Veronica told her. "You should understand what you've been missing with Ralph. David can show you. He can teach you . . . so many things . . ." Her voice trailed off poignantly.

Harriet looked at her in astonishment. "You sound like you want me to sleep with David!"

Veronica's eyes widened. She stared at Harriet for a long, unsettling moment. Harriet wasn't sure what her cousin was thinking. Then Veronica's eyes misted with tears, and she said with emotion, and frightening conviction, "If I can't make love with him, then you might as well. I'd be jealous—I'd be insane with envy. But I'd live on every word you told me about what he did and what he said, how he touched you. I miss him so much, I'd settle for being with him vicariously, through you."

Harriet's mouth dropped open; she couldn't believe what she was hearing. "Veronica, you must be crazy!"

Veronica sniffed and dug her fingers into her thick, dark hair to push it away from her face. "I just miss him so terribly!" she said in an anguished whisper. "My memories of him aren't enough anymore. It's frustrating to know you're seeing him. I feel like I want you to be with him for me. I know it's crazy. But I need him so desperately sometimes. I love him so much."

Harriet put down the knife, feeling deeply unsettled. And guilty. "I think I ought to stop seeing him."

"No!"

"This is too painful for you, Veronica."

"No! It's a comfort to know you're with him. Otherwise I have no connection with him at all." Veronica blinked and straightened her apron, as if trying to appear more composed. "And he's good for you," she argued in a more rational tone of voice. "I'm glad you're going to him for advice. I'd been getting really concerned about your frantic search for something better in your life. You were seeing that palm reader, who I'm sure was taking advantage of you. David won't take advantage. He's doing you good. I can tell."

"I know he's helpful, Veronica. But the truth is, I'm getting a little too attracted to David for my own comfort. And now you're making me even more uncomfortable, suggesting I get closer to him. I really don't want to be an unfaithful wife. I don't know what I owe Ralph anymore in this marriage, but I believe in God, and punishment, and that I have an immortal soul. And I don't want to face God someday and have to answer why I committed adultery. I'd be too ashamed to even confess it to a priest."

Veronica's mouth curved into a thoughtful smile. "You almost sound like David, saying that. He worries about punishment and the immortal soul. I should, too, I guess." She absently touched the side of her throat in a caressing way. "But all I can think of is David and how I long to be with him, no matter what."

As Veronica slowly let her hand drop back to her waist, she tilted her head in a dreamy way. Her hair fell away from her throat. Beneath the strong, fluorescent light, Harriet noticed two small, round, white scars on her neck, where Veronica had touched herself. Harriet could faintly see Veronica's pulse there, from the artery running beneath her skin. And for some reason, she thought of David's unusually sharp eyeteeth. Cold, prickly goose bumps made a chilling trail along her spine.

"What are those from?" she asked, stepping up to Veronica for a closer look.

"What?"

Harriet reached out to touch. "There are two small scars on your neck."

Veronica's hand swiftly came up to cover her throat again, and her eyes became guarded. "Nothing."

"You touched them a moment ago. What are they from?"

"I fell once. On some broken glass."

"It must have been deep to make those scars. I don't remember you ever mentioning it. Did you bleed a lot? It's right by your artery."

"I think you were away on vacation when it happened," Veronica said, backing away a step. "It was no big deal. I guess my skin just scars easily."

"Oh." Harriet pretended to chuckle lightly. "Sorry. I just remembered that David wrote those plays about vampires, and those marks look sort of like . . ."

"That's ridiculous."

"I know. Me and my ditsy mind. Well," she said, picking up the knife from the table with a shaky hand to make a last swirl on the cake, "how's it look?"

"Beautiful!" Veronica said, though Harriet could see she was still discomposed.

They talked a while longer about other things, and Harriet left to go home. But as she drove, Harriet kept pondering several things: She'd never seen David eat. She'd noticed there were no mirrors in what she'd seen of his home, not even in the bathroom. He had unusual teeth, and sometimes his eyes took on a strange glow as they made a study of her throat. He made odd slips in conversation. He wrote plays about vampires. And when Veronica had first asked Harriet to give David the psychic's message, Veronica had said Harriet could only visit him after dark. Veronica seemed so obsessed with him, beyond love, beyond anything Harriet had ever observed in anyone before. And now she'd discovered two marks on Veronica's neck . . .

Harriet had grown up listening to folk stories her grandmother, Anna, told her about vampires. Anna's parents in Bohemia had had a relative by marriage who was Hungarian. In fact, Uncle Miklos was married to Anna's aunt, who wasn't much older than Anna. Uncle Miklos had believed in vampires, folklore which had been rampant in his country as well as in Romania.

Now Harriet's grandmother seemed to half-believe the stories; though, since age twelve, Harriet had decided they were nothing more than dark fairy tales. Until now, perhaps. Now she was beginning to wonder. If David were a vampire, it could explain a lot of things—the odd change in Veronica she'd noticed over the past few years, for example. It would explain Veronica's almost hysterical devotion to David. It would explain the scars. And the psychometrist's description that he was cursed and was surrounded by darkness, nothing but darkness. It would also explain David's apparent fixation with Harriet's throat.

Harriet began to wonder: Should she be afraid of David? But he was so gentle. How could he be a vampire?

When she got home, she found Ralph in front of the TV, watching the evening news in his recliner. He'd changed into his favorite old sport shirt and a pair of tan jeans. As Harriet came into the living room, he turned off the TV with his remote control and looked up at her.

"I thought the class ended at nine," he said, his brown eyes pinning hers. "It's past ten."

"I drove to Veronica's afterward. You didn't have to turn off the TV."

He picked up the remote to turn it on again, but then seemed to think better of it and didn't press the "on" button. "Janet asked if she could spend the night at Sally's. They wanted to study together for a math exam. I didn't think you'd mind."

"No, I don't mind," she said, bending to pick up the newspapers beside his chair. "She'll stay there the night?"

"Yeah."

"Oh." So that meant she and Ralph were alone in the

house. Somehow that made her uneasy. "Why don't you turn on the TV?"

He made a study of the remote control. "Thought maybe we'd do something else."

"I have a headache, Ralph."

"I have an ache, too. Are you my wife or what? It's been months."

Harriet was about to argue, but then she remembered her talk with David. She sat down on the couch, feeling tense. As she set aside the newspapers she'd picked up, she said, "How are things going at work?"

He looked at her, puzzled. "Fine." He smiled a bit. "Even looks like I'll get my raise. I talked to the boss today."

"Really? That's great. So—you feel like celebrating. Is that why . . . ?"

His expression changed. "I need a reason to want sex? It's been months, Harriet. How long do you expect a man to go without? All this baking and sewing is driving me nuts. Don't *you* miss it?"

"Sex? I miss lovemaking, not sex," Harriet said, her tone a little bitter.

"What's that supposed to mean?"

"I mean there's a difference between going through the sex act and making love to someone. I'm just a handy tool for you. I could be anybody. Any female body would do. You don't care if *I* enjoy it." There, she'd said it, finally.

He looked at her, mystified, then pushed down on the recliner until he was in a sitting position. "What's this you're giving me? Anybody would do? I don't want anybody! I've never been with anybody else since we've been married. Are you accusing me of being unfaithful?"

"No. I know you're true to me. But . . ." She searched for words. "You're just so oblivious! You're not responsive to me."

"Responsive?" he said, imitating her. "You read too many books. Sex is sex. It's simple. Why make a big deal out of it?"

"If you made a bigger deal out of it, I might enjoy it more!"

He looked as if he were about to retort, but then seemed to stop himself. "Okay, okay." He shifted in his seat. "What do you want? I'm not virile enough to suit you?" In his eyes she could see a hint of fear.

"You're plenty virile, Ralph. That's not the problem. It's just . . . if you could spend a little more time at it, be more romantic about it."

He appeared a little stumped. Actually, she might have thought he looked kind of sweet, with his puzzled eyes and the blond hair falling over his forehead, if the problem hadn't meant so much to her. "All right," he said. "I'll . . . give it a try." He grew quiet, waiting for her reaction.

"Really?" She was genuinely surprised. Knowing he was getting a raise must have put him in a risk-taking mood.

"Something's got to give," he said. "You've been getting more and more distant. If I didn't know you better, I'd think you were interested in another man or something." He swallowed. "But I know you wouldn't do that."

Harriet froze. "Of course not," she muttered. She looked into his eyes. "Do you like being married to me?"

"Why shouldn't I like being married? We have a nice family—"

"But do you like being married to *me?*"

"Sure," he said with a shrug.

"Why?"

"Why?" He seemed at a loss for words. "Because we've been married all these years. I'm used to you."

Robert Browning he wasn't, Harriet thought. Still, he was actually trying to talk to her for a change. She gave him a smile. "Well . . . shall we go to bed?" She stood and held out her hand for him to take.

Ralph grinned, looking happier than she'd seen him in a long while. He took her hand, though he seemed to feel clumsy doing so. Still, it was sort of nice, Harriet thought. And it set a different mood from usual.

"I don't think we've held hands since we were in high school," he said, a little amused.

"No, we haven't," she said as they reached the bedroom.

When they walked in, she had an idea. "Want to undress me?" she said, looking up at him. He was almost a foot taller than she.

"Sounds good to me!" he said. He unzipped the back of her dress and even held it while she stepped out of it. "You've lost a little weight," he said, looking at her in her bra and half slip.

"Only five pounds," she said, wishing it were more.

"Looks great."

"Thanks," she said, truly pleased. She couldn't remember the last time she'd gotten a compliment from him.

"You've been looking really nice lately. Your clothes and all."

She began unbuttoning his shirt. "Thanks. It's nice you noticed."

While she undid his shirt, he reached around to unfasten her bra. Ralph was expert at this even when he was seventeen, and the undergarment was loosened in an instant. She let go of his shirt to pull the bra off entirely. As she set it on the dresser, he reached for her, his hands covering her breasts.

"God, you look good!" he said. "C'mon, take the rest off."

"Let's take our time—"

"I've gone too long without to wait." He pulled down her half slip.

She decided to cooperate and removed the rest of her clothing while Ralph undressed himself. When they were finished, he pulled her down with him onto the bed. He kissed her hard, his hand squeezing her breasts. It had been so long for her, too, that the feel of his masculine body next to hers was arousing. Suddenly, he pushed her legs apart with his thigh.

"Ralph, can't we go slower?"

"No, honey, this is too good."

In the next moment, she felt him enter her. Because she wasn't ready, it was uncomfortable at first. But then she closed her eyes at the pleasure the back-and-forth motion of his body brought her. By his labored breathing, however, she knew it wouldn't last long.

"Make it last," she whispered.

He didn't seem to be listening. "Damn, this is great!"

He made one final thrust, and then he was done. As he lay on top of her, recovering for a moment, Harriet shut her eyes tightly to keep back the tears.

He rolled off of her, and then he did something unusual. He leaned over her, held his hand to the side of her face and kissed her forehead. "That was nice, honey. You're beautiful." He turned over then, pulled the covers over him and went to sleep.

Harriet made a long, silent sigh as she pulled the blanket over herself. Well, he'd told her she was beautiful. That was progress, she supposed. But, oh, how different the whole experience would have been if it had been David with her. She had no doubt about that. He would have known everything to do to please her, to make their encounter lasting and satisfying. Oh, God! Would she have to go through her whole life never knowing the *pleasure* of life just because she'd married the man she'd married?

A tear slid from her eye, back into her hair. How she envied her cousin. Veronica had experienced David. Maybe Veronica was without him now and alone, but—she'd lived! She knew more of life than Harriet ever would. It wasn't fair. She wanted some part of David, too. Even . . . God, this was crazy, she thought, wiping away the tear . . . even if David was a vampire.

# 6

# Tell me about vampires again, *Babi*

HARRIET WALKED across the lawn, to the man-made pond, with Anna, her eighty-six-year-old grandmother. Anna was dressed in blue polyester pants, sneakers, and a sweater, and a babushka—a scarf folded into a triangle and tied beneath her chin—covered her head. The pond and park were located next to a facility for the elderly, where each person had his own small apartment and went to a central dining room for meals, and where activities were planned. Anna had been living there, happily enough it seemed, for a dozen years.

Anna carried a plastic bag that contained several dinner rolls. "I saved these from last night," she said in her Bohemian accented voice, her tone sly. "I always ask for extra and then hide them in my purse. This way the ducks eat, too."

Harriet smiled to herself, sure the ducks that inhabited the park's pond were well fed by the nearby elderly residents. She pointed to an elm by the lake that was getting its spring foliage. "What about the sign on that tree that says 'Do not feed the ducks'?"

"Oh, who would stop an old lady?" Anna said with a dismissive wave of her hand. "And the poor ducks need to eat!"

They approached a bench on the grass at the edge of the pond and sat down. Immediately, three white ducks began making Vs on the surface of the water, swimming toward them. Anna opened up her bag, took out a roll and handed it to Harriet, then took out another for herself. "Don't make the pieces too small," Anna admonished her, "or they get lost in the water. How's Ralph?"

"Fine," Harriet said as she tore a piece off her roll.

"Eating good? He always works so hard." Anna tossed a piece of bread into the water and the ducks dove for it.

"Oh, yes. His appetite's healthy." Harriet glumly watched the ducks flapping their wings. Since that night, Ralph had been giving strong hints that he'd like a repeat performance, but it only made Harriet more resistant. She thought of her grandmother's concern for Ralph and couldn't help but remember that Anna hadn't thought Ralph was such a fine fellow when Harriet was seventeen, unmarried and pregnant. Anna hadn't even wanted to go to the wedding. But once Harriet and Ralph's beautiful baby boy was born, all was forgotten. And Ralph, who indeed had become a hardworking, responsible man and devoted to his children, had been completely accepted by her family years ago. The circumstances under which they were married were rarely mentioned anymore, except perhaps in amusement.

Anna went on to ask about Harriet's son and daughter, and Harriet talked about them a bit. She also told her about all the baking she'd been doing, knowing her grandmother would approve. Harriet questioned her about the ingredients for a mushroom and sour cream casserole she remembered Anna used to make when Harriet was a child. Anna told her how to make it, but lamented that only the mushrooms she used to find in Bohemia had the flavor to do the recipe justice.

"How could you tell one mushroom from another when you went hunting for them in the old country?" Harriet asked, curious. "Some mushrooms are poisonous."

"Of course some are poisonous. The term toadstool, I think, must come from the German words *tod* for death and *stuhl* for stool. But in Bohemia we knew our mushrooms! We used to sense the time was right to hunt for them deep in the forest by the scent of the air. After a gentle rain in the night, in the morning the sun would shine on the wet leaves and soil and we'd feel in the atmosphere that the time was right. And we'd go off to the forest with baskets and hunt out our secret places where we knew mushrooms might be hiding. It was like a sport to us. We even told stories, like fish stories here, about how we had found the biggest or best mushroom. Oh, it was a wonderful time we'd have." She shook her head. "But those days are gone. My relatives write that the beautiful forests of

Bohemia are dying now from the industrial pollution of the cities. Such a shame."

Harriet pondered a moment on that sad note, throwing morsels to the ducks, who had doubled in number now and were becoming increasingly noisy with their quacking. She reminded herself why she had come for a visit today.

"Tell me about vampires again, *Babi*," Harriet said, breaking the last half of her roll into pieces. *Babi*, pronounced "bubby," was an affectionate Bohemian name, a shortened version of *babička*, which meant grandmother. "Do you remember what your Uncle Miklos told you?"

Anna adjusted her gray sweater, unbuttoning the top button. She was a plump woman, about five feet tall. Her white hair was pulled back with combs beneath the babushka. Her eyes were alert, but she put words together more slowly lately.

"The stories Uncle Miklos told me? You want to hear that again?"

"If you don't mind."

"Oh, I don't mind," she said, taking another roll out of her plastic bag. "I haven't thought of them in a long while. He was Hungarian, you know. He used to scare me with those tales."

"There were different kinds of vampires . . ." Harriet prompted her.

"Oh, yes, several kinds." Anna was quiet for a moment. "One was a spirit that could take the form of animals, like wolves and dogs and blackbirds. It could turn itself into a demon bird that flew at night. Such a spirit would sleep during the day, but at night it would meet with other evil spirits. And the female of this type were very wicked. They would suck the blood of children, spoil marriages, prevent cows from giving milk and cause diseases." She looked at Harriet in a searching way. "Why do you want to hear all this again?"

"Just curious. I was thinking the other day about all those stories you used to tell me when I was a kid. Wasn't there one that was like a werewolf?"

"Uncle Miklos used to say this was an unbaptized child. It would come out when the moon was full. And there were also the *iele*, he used to call them, a group of female vampires who traveled in groups of threes or sevens. They would attack a man while he slept and could paralyze him or drive him insane. The *iele* would leave yellow patches on the grass, where they played during idle moments in the night."

Harriet nodded. "I remember that now. How about . . . wasn't there a vampire like we see in movies? You know, like Dracula?"

"None of the old Hungarian and Romanian tales Uncle Miklos knew were exactly like what they show now in the movies. But he used to talk about the 'living dead,' a vampire who rises from his grave at night. It could appear in the form of a man, or a wolf, or a dog, so the howling of dogs sometimes meant that such a creature was near."

Harriet still wasn't getting from her grandmother the one type of vampire she most wanted to hear about again. "But wasn't there one who was handsome? Who visited women during the night and left them agitated the following day?"

Her grandmother smiled and folded up the empty plastic bag after removing the last roll. "You always wanted to hear about the most romantic one when you were little, too. You haven't changed!"

Harriet chuckled. "I guess not."

"That particular creature Uncle Miklos called the *sburator*. He was my favorite one, too. He took the form of a handsome man who entered a home through the window at night. He would kiss women in their sleep. And the women often would not even know he'd been there, except that the next day they felt tired and very unhappy."

Unhappy being stuck with their husbands, after knowing the vampire's attentions, no doubt, Harriet thought with quiet irony. "So with all these kinds of evil creatures supposedly roaming the countryside, what did people do?"

Anna offered Harriet the last roll, but Harriet declined it with a shake of her head. "Well, Uncle Miklos used to say the peasants would put up crosses in the middle of a field or on a mountaintop to protect travelers from evil," Anna told her. "They would hang crosses in their homes and icons, also. Sometimes they would make the crosses of garlic. They'd put garlic on the window frames and doorknobs to protect the house against vampires. Such creatures couldn't endure the smell of it. There were certain sayings to recite and charms they would wear. And when it came to finally destroying the vampire, they took a stake, made of wood or iron, and drove

it through the vampire's heart. That would keep the creature
in his grave for good. And then whatever bad was happening—droughts, or crop failures, or mysterious illnesses—
would stop. Uncle Miklos said he'd actually seen this done a
number of times. He'd lived for a while near Translyvania,
which once was a part of Hungary."

Harriet leaned forward and asked, "But how would they
know who the vampire was? Which grave to dig up?"

"They'd dig up graves of those who had recently died, just
before the bad things began to happen. If one of the bodies
was still healthy-looking and undecayed, and maybe turned
instead of lying on its back, they would assume that was the
person who had become a vampire."

Harriet was beginning to feel slightly ill. "Did you believe
these things Uncle Miklos told you?"

"When I was a girl? Oh, yes! I used to have a wreath of
garlic around a cross on the wall above my bed. And on the
third day of every February, Saint Blaise's Day, I used to go
to church and ask the priest to give me the Blessing of
Throats."

"The blessing with the candles?" Harriet asked, recalling
having seen someone have this done at her church.

"Yes. The priest would hold crossed candles against my
throat and say, 'Through the intercession of Saint Blaise,
bishop and martyr, may the Lord free you from evils of the
throat and from any other evil.' This was said mainly to
protect against sore throats, but I used to think it might
protect me from vampires, too. My mother used to laugh and
say I was listening too much to Uncle Miklos and his scary
stories." Anna made a little shrug. "She was probably right."

"Do you believe in vampires now?"

Anna's small, faded blue eyes widened with surprise.
"Now? Oh—I don't know. When I was a child, Uncle Miklos
had made it all sound so real to me. He was a wonderful
storyteller and I had a good imagination. Although—sometimes he would name names of actual persons who had been
thought to be vampires and were destroyed by fire or with a
stake. One of the most famous I remember was named Peter
Poglojowitz. I don't think he would have made that up. Some
of his stories seemed to be real and factual, not like the folktales. But whether such people truly were vampires, I don't

know. Maybe it was all due to the lack of education and the superstition of the times. Like the cure for vampires Uncle Miklos said he'd learned from a Hungarian gypsy. That must have been superstition."

Harriet's head shot up. "Cure?"

Anna nodded. "Uncle Miklos said he knew the ingredients to make a potion to cure a vampire and make him normal, and alive."

Harriet sat in shock, recalling the psychometrist's words. And then she vaguely recalled hearing *Babi* tell her this long ago when Harriet was a child. Veronica very likely would have heard it, too. "Do you know the cure?"

Anna laughed. "Oh, no."

"You can't remember any of the ingredients in it?"

"Uncle Miklos never told me. It was a secret, he said. But I think my Aunt Maria knew. She was his wife, so she probably knew."

"Your Aunt Maria? Is she still alive?"

Anna slowly shook her head with concern. "I don't know. She used to write me at Christmas. But I didn't get anything from her the last two years. My cousins in Prague still write me, and they haven't said that she died. So she may be alive."

"Where does she live?"

"In a small town by the Bohemian Forest."

Harriet could barely catch her breath for a moment. It was just as the psychometrist had said! And the "old woman" the psychic described did indeed have a connection with Veronica—she was a distant relative. Of course! Why hadn't they thought of this before? The only thing Harriet didn't know for certain was what David needed to be cured of—and that she would have to find out for sure, before she said anything to anyone or pursued this cure any further.

That night she told her family she was going shopping at the mall, but she drove to David's house. She'd been visiting him once a week, on the night she'd told her husband she had a quilting class. Since this was not the usual night for her visit, she'd secretly phoned David first, early in the evening. She'd told him she needed to talk to him about something, something that couldn't wait. If her great-great-aunt in Czechoslovakia was still alive, she must be very aged, and even the psychometrist had indicated there was no time to waste.

But how was she to ask David if he was a vampire? Would it make him angry? If he *was* a vampire, what would he do to her? Harriet didn't know under what circumstances he'd bitten Veronica. That is if such a farfetched thing could be true—if there was such a thing as a vampire, and David had indeed bitten her cousin.

Harriet began to grow nervous, even scared, as she drove on the Eisenhower Expressway into Chicago. Nervous that she might be getting ready to insult a brilliant playwright whose only malady was, perhaps, diabetes. And scared that if he *was* a vampire, he would find it necessary to silence her in some way because she'd discovered his secret.

Harriet reassured herself that David seemed far too civilized and scholarly to do violence to her, vampire or not. Even Veronica had promised that he would never hurt her. Harriet couldn't help but recall the other night in Veronica's kitchen, the way her cousin had serenely tilted her head, as if in a dream state, and lovingly touched the marks on her throat. Had Veronica willingly exposed her throat in just that way to invite David to . . . ?

Don't think about it now, Harriet told herself. First and foremost, she had to find out the truth, before she let her imagination get too carried away.

When she reached his home, David buzzed her in and she hurried up the spiral steps to his living quarters. He met her at the door wearing a beige sweater and brown pants. He smiled at her, yet his eyes were a trifle puzzled; he was probably wondering what Harriet had to talk to him about that could be so urgent.

Harriet walked into his living room, which looked so familiar to her now that it felt like a second home. And yet, tonight, she experienced a skittish nervousness being alone with David in his lonely mansion. She turned to him. "It's a nice night out. Could we go for a walk?"

He made an easy shrug. "A good idea. Let me get my jacket." He went to the closet, put on a camel-colored cashmere blazer, and walked down the spiral stairs behind her. But instead of going out the front door, he took her through a hidden hallway off the oval entryway, which led to a side door to the house. Here he took her by the hand down a very dark sidewalk alongside the mansion to the backyard. As she found her way through the darkness, she began to wonder if she were really any safer with him outside than she would have been inside.

The backyard was lit by the moon, however, and she could see better. He unlocked the back iron gate, and they went through it and into the narrow alley.

As they passed his neighbor's trash cans, she asked, "You don't like to use your front door to come and go?"

"Since I'm well-known for my plays in this city, I prefer that my comings and goings are not in full view for my neighbors or any nosy reporters to observe. When one writes vampire plays, it tends to invite curiosity."

"I can believe that," Harriet said. His penchant for secrecy only made Harriet wonder more about who or what he really was. The alley led to Rush Street, where there were lots of people and activity. This was Chicago's hot spot for singles, with its popular Irish pubs. The activity made Harriet feel more comfortable, but with so many people around, it was difficult to bring up a provocative subject like vampirism. When they had walked the half block along Rush to Oak Street, she asked if they could head toward the lake. David agreed, and they turned down his street, lined with brown-stones that housed boutiques, expensive shops and hair sa-lons.

They walked in silence for a while, as Harriet contemplated what she should say. About the time they reached the front of his mansion, David asked, "What did you need to see me about? Is something wrong?"

"Not exactly." Harriet made a hesitant sigh. How does one ask a man if he's a vampire? Just blurt it out? "David, can I ask you . . . well, kind of a personal question? A question that's probably going to be a little shocking?"

He turned his head, slowing his pace as he studied her. She noticed how his eyes seemed translucent in the light of the streetlamp they were passing—as if they carried the wisdom of the ages. "I doubt that any question could shock me," he said with a smile. "Go ahead, ask."

"Okay." Swallowing, she felt herself breaking into a cold sweat. She looked around briefly to make sure no one was about to pass by and overhear. "Are you . . . are you a vampire?" Her heart rate escalated to a rapid beat as she said the words.

His expression sobered as he looked deeply into her eyes, and then, without missing a step, he continued his previous pace, facing ahead. His manner was very smooth—a little too smooth, Harriet thought, her heart almost stopping in anticipation of hearing his reply.

"Now why would you ask me that?" he said.

"First of all, you write plays and musicals about vampires."

"Would you assume Bram Stoker was a vampire because he wrote *Dracula?*"

"No. But there are other things. I've never seen you eat. There are no mirrors in the rooms where you live. You're unavailable during the day. Your teeth are . . . sharp-looking . . ."

"There are explanations for all those things, Harriet," he said quietly.

"The psychometrist said you were cursed and surrounded by darkness."

"I can't help what a self-proclaimed psychic may have told you."

"But she's been right about everything else. And there's one more thing—about Veronica."

David turned and looked at her with a penetrating gaze. "What about Veronica?"

"The last time I saw her, I noticed that . . ." Harriet lost some courage under his close scrutiny.

"What?"

"She has two small scars on her neck, right above her pulse point. I noticed because she touched them without thinking while she was talking about you. And when I asked her about them, she became very guarded and said she'd gotten them from falling on glass—which I find hard to believe."

David continued to stare at her, his eyes growing more and more pale. He faced forward and continued to walk, his head bowed slightly.

"Veronica never told me about you," Harriet continued, words tumbling out of her mouth now. "She kept her love for you a secret for years, apparently. But now that I know and she's more free to talk about it, I find that her feelings for you don't seem exactly normal. She seems obsessed. She said once that she would die for you, if only you'd let her. I didn't know what that meant then. But I think I do now. And I think I know what your true relationship with her is. You . . . you took blood from her. And now she's under your spell. And that's why she's so agitated sometimes, why she lives only to be with you again, why other men don't interest her." As she said all these things and looked at David's handsome profile, Harriet realized how much she envied Veronica.

David stopped walking suddenly. His eyes were a vivid blue now, made jewel-like because of a sheen of tears. "She felt that way about me before I took her blood, Harriet. Initiating her only made our feelings for each other more profound."

Harriet took in her breath. "Then you *are* a . . . ?"

"Yes. You're right about everything. You're far brighter and more perceptive than you let yourself show."

She felt highly vulnerable now and possibly more exposed than he. "Now that I know, what will you do?"

"To you? Nothing, Harriet," he said in a reassuring tone. "I trust you to keep my secret."

"Really?" she asked with doubt. He'd let her go with this knowledge so easily?

"I know you would want to protect Veronica. And I think you've come to like me enough to keep this to yourself. Besides, who would you tell?"

She thought about this. "No one would believe me if I did."

"Exactly. Which leads me to ask, why did *you* believe it so readily? Most people would explain my odd lifestyle as the artistic eccentricity of a playwright."

"The vampire stories my grandmother told. Her uncle believed in them and so did she when she was young."

"Are you going to be afraid of me now?"

Harriet chewed the inside of her lip as she studied his grave expression. "Veronica once told me you would never harm me. At the time, I had no idea why she would say something like that. But now I understand, and I believe her. You've been nothing but kind to me. If you were going to, you know, attack me or something, I imagine you would have done it by now."

"I try to be a civilized vampire," David said with dry amusement. Harriet could see the melancholy in his eyes, beneath his humor.

"How do you . . . ? I mean, do you really have to have blood?"

"Yes. I rob blood banks several times a year. I mail in an anonymous monetary donation to ease my conscience. I never take from a person without much thought beforehand or without their permission. Veronica was right. I won't harm you."

Relaxing now, she fell in step again alongside of him as they continued east down Oak Street. "Can you tell me what happened between you and Veronica? This separation between you—it has to do with . . . with what you are, doesn't it?"

David nodded. "She was only twenty-three when I met her. Against my own better judgment I fell headlong in love with her. She fell in love with me. We began an affair. I pretended to be a mortal and didn't tell her my secret. But she eventually discovered it. At that point, we had to decide what to do, how to continue. A mortal woman in love with a vampire faces many problems. I gave her four choices: Ending our relationship. Going on as we were in a mortal-style love affair. Initiating her. Or making her an immortal, like me."

Barely breathing, Harriet watched his profile as he calmly told her his story.

"She chose initiation," David said, regret in his voice. "She wanted to be under my power. And I wanted it, too. Because I knew it would give us a physical and spiritual unity such as mortals can never know. I was lonely and I loved her dearly. I wanted and needed to be that close to her. And Veronica—I think at the time she not only loved me, but she wanted an escape from the world, a world she found too harsh and complicated for her delicate personality. She knew I would love her and protect her and she wanted that. So—one night I took her blood."

Harriet was beginning to feel slightly dizzy from not breathing properly. David had stopped speaking and was blinking his eyes, as if overcome for a moment by emotion.

"What happened?" she asked in a quiet, empathetic voice, wanting to hear the whole story, even if it made her faint.

"She was under my power then. And it was an exhilarating experience for both of us. It deepened our love. We were inseparable. And that became the problem. Veronica found it more and more difficult to cope with her job in the real world and carry on her nightly relationship with me. She wasn't getting enough sleep, and as you say, she became completely and utterly obsessed with me, with being with me, and eventually, with becoming *like* me. She thought it would solve all her problems. She would become a vampiress, quit her job and her life in the real world and come and live with me, as I lived."

David took a long breath and shook his head. "She was only twenty-three—well, twenty-four by that time. She was far too young to make such a decision. How could she decide to give up the world for me, when she knew nothing of the world, had no concept of what she would be giving up? I told her we must spend ten years apart, until she was thirty-four. This was the age I was when I became a vampire. During this decade apart, I wanted her to have no contact with me, to let the bond between us go dormant. I wanted her to live a full life, succeed in her career, travel, even have relationships with other men. I wanted her to *know* life before she gave it up. Because what I live is not a life. As you perhaps already understand, Harriet, I'm not really alive."

Harriet nodded as tears came into her own eyes. She hated to think of David as . . . as undead, as in her grandmother's stories. "Do you have a coffin?"

"In a secret room in my basement."

Harriet paused, remembering that the psychometrist had mentioned this, too. "How old are you?"

"I died in 1616."

"Gosh."

"Yes. When I stop to think of it sometimes, that's my reaction, too. I was born in France, but I went to England and studied with William Shakespeare."

"You knew Shakespeare?" she said with astonishment, almost tripping over her own feet as they walked down the sidewalk.

"Shhh," he said, indicating with his eyes that people were about to pass them on the sidewalk from the other direction. When the couple had passed, he continued. "He was my beloved teacher. I wanted to become a playwright of his ilk. When he died, I feared he and his works would be forgotten by future generations. That was why I traveled to Transylvania to seek out a vampire, so that I could be transformed into one myself. If I was immortal, I thought, I could make sure his works did not perish. And I could have forever to hone my own inferior skills as a writer.

"It wasn't long after my transformation that I realized what a mistake I had made. An irreversible mistake. The bloodlust, the alienation from other humans and from God, the thought of never seeing the sun again, never having a normal relationship with another person—I realized all these consequences too late. And the irony was that it was all for nothing. Shakespeare's works have survived very well without ever needing my help to preserve them. And if I live for two thousand years, I'll never be able to write a single sentence with the philosophic insight and poetic cleverness Will had. I wasted my life for immortality. And now my punishment is just that: immortality."

"But you'd still consider making Veronica immortal? Is that what will happen when your ten years are up? She can choose then to be with you forever?"

"Yes. I've told her she would do best to turn her back on me and forget she ever met me. For her sake, I hope she chooses to live out her mortal life without me. And for my sake, I hope she chooses me. I'm in a dilemma, and I put her in one, too. Love shouldn't be so perverse." He stopped speaking, eyes and head downcast.

"W-what if there were a cure?"

He looked up at her abruptly, yet with some confusion in his eyes. "A cure? What that psychic told you?"

"Yes. What if there was one?"

"It's nonsense, Harriet," he said firmly. "There is no cure."

"But, just pretending, what if there was? What would it mean for you and Veronica?"

His eyes looked both bleak and yet filled with fantasy. "That would be the perfect solution, if it were only possible. I could live with her as a mortal, and she would never have to become such a vile thing as I am. We could be together, grow old together, live like normal human beings. We could be a part of the world. And then we'd die and have eternal peace. At least, Veronica would. I hate to think what God would do to me. But she would have peace. And that's what matters most to me."

"You think God would punish you for having been a vampire, even if you were cured?"

"I *chose* to be one. It's the sin of pride, of wanting to be like God, to have power over life and death. Why would God forgive me for that?"

"But you could go to confession."

"The priest would think I was a lunatic."

"Maybe not. The church does exorcisms and so on. They believe in the supernatural."

"I don't know what would happen, Harriet. I might go to confession, take communion, and find the wafer scorching my tongue. My sins are too great, and have gone on too long to go unpunished."

"I don't believe that. God forgives."

He smiled at her in a fatherly way. "Then go on believing, Harriet. You have nothing to worry about."

They turned and began walking back to David's home. She asked him many more questions about himself, about a vampire's existence. He told her of the many places he'd lived over the centuries, for he had to move every few decades in order to keep his secret. People would eventually notice that he never aged, but continued decade after decade, to look thirty-four. She was intrigued to learn he'd visited America in the 1800s and didn't like it. He told her it was only later, when he came to New York City in the late 1930s and lived there throughout the war years, that he came to love America almost as much as France and England.

When they reached his home, she told him she wished to leave then and visit Veronica. "Can I tell her I know everything now?" she asked.

"You might as well. It's easier on us all not to keep secrets. I'm glad you figured it out, actually. You're one of the few people who didn't run in panic from me when they discovered my true nature. I'm grateful for that, that you treat me almost as if I were normal."

Harriet leaned up and kissed him on the cheek. "I wish I knew more people who were as normal as you," she said. "Good night. I'll come to see you again."

"I cherish your visits, you know," he told her, deep sincerity in his gentle voice. "I really do."

She hugged him before getting into her car. He waved as she

drove off. When she arrived at Veronica's unannounced, her cousin let her in with a smile of surprise.

"I didn't expect to see you again so soon," Veronica said. She'd answered the door in her bathrobe. "Excuse how I look," she said, patting her wet hair with a towel. "I just took a shower and washed my hair."

"Sorry to come so unexpectedly, but I have something important to tell you."

"Okay. Come into the bedroom with me, so I can comb my hair."

"Sure," Harriet said. She took off her coat and laid it on Veronica's bed. As Veronica combed tangles out of her long, wavy hair, Harriet took a deep breath. "I know about David."

Veronica turned from the mirror, her comb caught at a knot in her hair. "Know what?"

"That he's a vampire. I guessed and he acknowledged that he was."

"You—you what?" Veronica looked shocked and frightened.

"It's okay. I won't tell anyone. He trusts me and so should you."

"How did you guess?"

"Well, the little things I'd noticed that I mentioned last time I was here. But most of all it was those marks on your neck."

Veronica pulled the comb out of her hair and briefly touched her throat. "Oh. I should have been more careful," she said, sounding remorseful. "I shouldn't have given him away."

"It's not your fault. He wasn't angry. He still loves you."

Veronica looked up at Harriet, a tear running down her cheek. "Does he? What did he say when you told him you knew?"

Harriet related the whole story. Veronica sat on the bed and listened. When Harriet had finished, Veronica said, "I'm glad you know. It makes everything so much easier. You weren't afraid?"

"Not much. You told me David would never harm me. I remembered that."

"I was petrified when I found out," Veronica admitted. "I opened his refrigerator and found the blood bags he stores there. Like you, I'd had some suspicions, and when I saw the blood bags, I knew. He tried to calm me, but I ran out of his house fearing for my life."

"What happened then?"

"He came here to my room. He opened the window even though it was locked and climbed in while I slept. I wore a cross around my neck, thinking it would protect me. It only amused him. Soon I realized he wouldn't hurt me and I wasn't afraid of him anymore. He gave me the four choices he told you about."

"The cross didn't work?" Harriet asked, puzzled.

"No. That's only an old superstition, like those stories *Babi* used to tell."

"Oh," Harriet said with concern.

"You sound disappointed."

"But what about mirrors?" Harriet asked, pointing to Veronica's dresser mirror, where they could see themselves. "That part's not superstition, is it?"

"That's true, David can't be seen in a mirror. He says it's because he really shouldn't still be here on earth. But the stuff about garlic and crosses and so on is nonsense."

"What about a stake through the heart?"

Veronica pulled her robe closer around her. "David told me that would destroy him. And the sun would also kill him. I used to stay by his coffin and hold his hand at dawn. I could feel through his hand, through our bond, the intensity of the sun's rays as they hit the stones of his mansion. Only his coffin and the soil from his homeland beneath the satin lining protected him. And then as the deep lethargy of his daytime sleep came over him, I would have to let go of his hand, or else I felt that I would fall into a deep sleep, too," she said, her voice near a whisper. "That's how close we were. As if we were one, as if our hearts beat in unison."

"That's what the bond with him is like?" Harriet asked with awe.

"Yes."

"What's it like to be . . ."—Harriet wanted to say *bitten,* but instead used David's term—"initiated?"

Veronica smiled, took a long breath, and closed her eyes. "It's unreal and wonderful. I felt like he took me up with him into some rare atmosphere. There were shimmering lights and colors and I felt so languid and filled with bliss. There was no beginning to me and no end, and I lay there with him as if I were floating, as if he and I were one forever and forever." She opened her eyes, but they were still shining and transfixed. "And after that, I could feel what he felt and he could feel what I felt. We were so close, so . . . close. It was beautiful, Harriet. And it didn't fade. If I was away from him, he could call me and I would hear his voice as if on the wind. I could hear him in my mind. And he would call to me and tell me he loved me. And I could tell him things and he would hear me. We had that mental bond that kept us so close."

"Is it still there?"

"Yes." She lowered her chin. "But David blocks my thoughts from his mind when I call to him now. I know. I've tried. And he never calls to me. He's determined that we should have no contact for ten years. Sometimes I don't know how I'll survive the time remaining without him."

Harriet listened to her cousin with unabashed envy. She wished to God she could feel that kind of closeness with a man, particularly David. Never in her life had she experienced anything like the relationship Veronica described. Harriet wondered if she should ask David to initiate her, too. But she said nothing for the moment to Veronica, because she wasn't sure how Veronica would react. Her cousin might be jealous, or on the contrary, she might encourage Harriet to follow through, or both. Harriet decided she'd rather make up her own mind without input from her obsessed cousin. And then, for the first time, it occurred to Harriet that if she did ask David to initiate her, *she* might become obsessed, too. Harriet had only to look at the sensual, mesmerized glow in Veronica's limpid eyes to decide that being obsessed might not be all that bad.

"Maybe you won't have to be without him for too much longer," Harriet said, pushing aside her own thoughts for the moment. "Remember the cure? Guess what—the old woman across the ocean, near a forest, is *Babi's* Aunt Maria, our great-great-aunt in Czechoslovakia."

Veronica seemed very quickly to come back to the here and now. "The one who was married to the Hungarian?"

"I'd forgotten, and you must have, too, that he knew of some gypsy cure for vampirism. *Babi* told us about that when we were kids, and she brought it up again this morning when I asked her about those old stories she used to tell. She thinks her aunt might know the cure. If she's still alive, that is."

Veronica raised fingers to her lips. "I remember *Babi* used to tell those scary stories, but I don't remember anything about a cure. One night after she told us some of those tales, I had nightmares. It was at Thanksgiving and I was only about four, I think. After that my mother would never let me listen to those stories again. So maybe I never heard the part about the cure."

Harriet nodded. "I remember now your mother always pulling you out of the room when *Babi* started telling stories. But I used to sit there and hang on every word." Harriet reached to touch Veronica's arm. "What do you think? Should I get Aunt Maria's address from *Babi* and write to her? *Babi* could translate it into Bohemian for us. We could ask if she knows the ingredients for the cure."

"Did you mention this to David?"

"Not really. I just asked him, if it were possible, would he like to become mortal again. He said he would, because then he could live a normal life with you."

Veronica grew quiet, and an unexpected, troubled aspect came into her eyes. "I'm not sure I'd like that," she said.

"Why? You prefer him as a vampire?"

Veronica hesitated. "I don't know. I've never known him as a mortal. Our bond would disappear, I imagine. We'd be like any other man and woman. I think I would miss that wondrous closeness. But then, too, I'd want David to be happy. And he's never been happy as a vampire." She paused and then said with some reluctance, "Yes, this is something we should do, Harriet. I'll go with you to talk to *Babi* about writing to her aunt. We need to do it for David."

"Should I tell him?"

"No. What if Aunt Maria is dead? Or she's lost the recipe for the cure? I wouldn't want to build up his hopes."

"That's what I thought," Harriet agreed.

Veronica smiled with irony. "Although David might not even believe a gypsy cure would work. For a vampire, he's pretty skeptical."

# 7

# I don't think many
# women get the chance

DAVID CHATTED with Merle Larson, the producer of *The Scarlet Shadow,* as they sat in the audience waiting for the show to begin.

Merle was a short, stocky man, nervous and ulcer-prone. They had known each other for years. Merle had produced some of David's previous shows, too. Though they got along well, Merle did not know David's secret. He apparently chalked up David's reclusive lifestyle to the eccentricities of a creative mind. Merle lived in New York now, but was in town to check on the Chicago production of *Shadow.*

"Where is Matthew now?" David asked Merle as he unbuttoned his suit jacket.

"I think Matthew's recuperating in Switzerland. At least that's where Darienne told me he was headed when I was in Australia the week before his final performance." Merle ran his hand over his gray crew cut, a mannerism of his. "I went there to see how his Australian replacement was coming along in rehearsals."

"Darienne was still with him?" David asked.

"Oh, yeah, she's been with him ever since he left Chicago," Merle said, keeping his voice at a level just loud enough for David to hear over surrounding conversations in the audience. "You didn't know?"

"Not for sure. I haven't heard from her in a long time."

"Matthew's fans all know her. She started a fad with the veiled hats she wears."

"Veiled hats," David repeated with puzzlement. And then

he thought for a moment and realized why she would wear them.

"You don't keep up with things, do you?" Merle teased him. "Still holed up in that mansion of yours, eh? This is the first time I've seen you in what—two years?"

"The Tony Awards was the last time," David said. "When you talked me into going to New York."

"Because I was sure you'd win. And then you refused to be photographed with your award! Our reluctant genius," Merle said in a chiding tone. Then he added with sincerity, "I'm really glad you decided to come to the show tonight. When I called and left the message this morning that I'd be here, I doubted I'd actually see you. I figured you'd phone me back as you usually do and leave it at that."

"I thought I owed you a personal visit. Besides, I decided it might be a good idea for me to see the show again. I'm having trouble putting the *Shadow* screenplay back together after it was mangled by those Hollywood writers. They shifted the emphasis to horror and horse chases! I thought if I saw the stage production again it might put me back in touch with my original concept."

"Relax. Take your time with the screenplay," Merle advised. "We might as well make all the money we can off all the stage productions before the *Shadow* movie comes out to compete with them. Not that this Chicago production is making us rich anymore."

"Ticket sales are dwindling here?" David said. "I suppose after three years, it's inevitable."

"Yeah." Merle adjusted his silk tie. "Ned's beginning to wear thin, I think." Merle was referring to Ned Holt, the actor who had replaced Matthew McDowall in Chicago as Sir Percy. "I saw him backstage before he got into makeup and he looked beat. The theater manager agrees he's running down. His contract's almost up. We need to replace him or close the show."

"Isn't Ned only about thirty? Matthew's well past forty, so I can see why he got worn out. But Ned's a young man."

"Ned's been doing the show for two-and-a-half years, with only a few weeks off for vacation," Merle reminded David. "Even a young guy has limits."

"Perhaps I forget how strenuous the role is." David knew

the physical demands of the show would be nothing for him, but then he wasn't like the mortal actors who were being asked to perform some of the feats a vampire could do.

The houselights dimmed and the show began. David settled back and cleared his mind, trying to absorb the show as if he were someone who had never seen it before. Somehow he had to get a fresh inspiration, so he could weed out the nonsense added to his screenplay.

He found, after a while, that he was truly enjoying the show. Ned Holt had a fine voice, and if he lacked Matthew McDowall's maturity and anguished sensuality, he nevertheless portrayed the role with energy and youthful bravado. The actor didn't seem tired on stage. But then he remembered that Matthew could give a stunning performance while ill with the flu. Covering fatigue was part of an actor's job.

Toward the end of the first half, they reached one of the musical's most memorable scenes, used in ads for the show, where Sir Percy appears at the top of the stage's proscenium. The proscenium framed the stage and was made to look like the intertwined trunks of two trees growing up from either side. On stage, Marguerite is about to be abducted by two evil-minded Frenchmen. Sir Percy swings down from the tree trunk on a rope to rescue her. When David had written this into his play, he wasn't even sure such a thing could be done. But experts in stagecraft had managed to rig a heavy rope in such a way that it pulled Sir Percy inward and onto the stage, sweeping him in a bit like Tarzan to snatch Marguerite out of her captor's grasp. Audiences always gasped at the stunt.

David watched now in anticipation, looking up at the top of the proscenium. Ned, in costume, took hold of the rope and wound some of the lower portion around one booted leg. He pushed himself off the tree trunk, forty feet above the stage floor, and began to lower himself.

But instantly David sensed something was wrong. Ned hung a few feet below the proscenium for a moment, looking as if he were trying to maintain his grasp. The rope unwound itself from his leg. He began to slide down the rope anyway, which is what was supposed to happen, but he seemed unsteady. The audience began to gasp, but in the wrong way.

All at once, the actor lost his grip. He fell sideways about thirty-five feet onto the edge of the stage. There he landed with a sickening thud and then slipped off into the orchestra pit as musicians stopped playing and scrambled to get out of the way.

"Oh, my God!" Merle exclaimed as the audience reacted in horror. Marguerite rushed to look over the edge of the stage in shock. Stagehands hurried to the orchestra pit.

Merle got up from his seat to run down the aisle to the railing surrounding the pit. David followed as people began to shout and scream. When David reached the railing, he looked down to see Ned crumpled in a heap between musician's chairs, apparently unconscious, a viola smashed beneath him. His wig was askew and he was bleeding from the head.

The sight of the blood made David back away instantly, for no matter how tragic the young actor looked, David's lust was immediately aroused by the red liquid running down his face. Hating himself for his lack of humanity, David turned and left the scene. He went backstage, deciding he could be of more help seeing to it that an ambulance was called than being at the actor's side.

The show was canceled, and the audience was asked to leave. An ambulance arrived. Later David saw the paramedics pass by in the backstage hallway, carrying Ned on a stretcher. He'd been wrapped in splints and bandaged. He seemed to be conscious now. Merle followed the stretcher out to the ambulance and then came back to talk to David.

"How is he?" David asked as they stood in the hallway.

"Bad," Merle said, his hand shaking as he rubbed one eye. "The paramedics said it looked like five broken bones, a smashed jaw, and a concussion. Maybe internal injuries, too. No way he can do the show again."

"How did it happen? What went wrong?"

"I don't know. Ned couldn't talk. It looked to me like he didn't grab the rope right. Might have been due to his fatigue. I hear he's been going blank on his lines. It happens when you do a show too long. He might have just gone blank on how to do the stunt properly—you know, just did it mechanically, too tired to think about what he was doing, and didn't remember to be careful."

David shook his head in dismay, feeling responsible because he'd written the stunt into the show. "Poor fellow."

"Yeah," Merle said. "Feel like getting out of here? Taking a walk?"

"Sure." David followed Merle past actors and crew who were still lingering, stunned and upset, and left by the stage door. They walked up the side street to Michigan Avenue. The night was brisk, the air clean and fresh as it blew off the lake. It had rained, and the wide street and sidewalks were wet, reflecting the car lights and streetlights. The tall buildings looked formidable and majestic against the black sky. Fast-moving low clouds added a silent, ominous backdrop to the city atmosphere.

"Looks like Ned's understudy will have his hands full for a while," David said.

"He'll do a good job. But we can't go with him as a permanent replacement. We need to find a name—fast. Or close the show."

By "a name" David knew Merle meant an actor who was well known and would be a draw. But this wasn't David's area of expertise. "Who would be available on such short notice?"

"Well, if we could get someone who's already played or is playing the role, that would cut down on some rehearsal time."

"Steal the lead actor from New York?" David suggested.

"He just renewed his contract there. Besides, why would he leave Broadway for Chicago?"

"If you get the British actor who's doing it in London, you may have problems with Actor's Equity."

"Mmmm," Merle said. He gave David a sly glance. "What about Matthew?"

David shook his head. "He finally quit because of exhaustion, didn't he? I read in the paper that his health's not good."

"Maybe it's not. But that wouldn't stop him from giving great performances," Merle said. "I saw him in Australia. He was better than ever. And he loves the role. I bet he'd do it, if we asked him. And, boy, would that make Chicago ticket sales skyrocket! His fans here are constantly writing letters asking to bring him back."

David shrugged. "It will depend on Matthew. If he feels he's recovered, then it's a perfect solution."

Merle put his finger to his upper lip, as if considering a

strategy. He looked at David. "Do you have his number in Switzerland?"

"No. I didn't know he was there until you told me."

"That's right, you didn't," Merle said, disappointed. "I thought you kept up with Darienne."

David chuckled. "No one keeps up with Darienne. She always contacts me, when she feels like it. Now that she has Matthew, I guess I'm negligible."

Merle sniffed. "I wouldn't say she 'has' him."

David raised an eyebrow. "How do you mean?"

"I don't know," Merle said. "Just a little undercurrent I picked up in Australia. She fawns over him and he lets her. I have the feeling he stays with her for the sex—which, by the look of her, I imagine ain't bad!" Merle's laugh was a bit lusty. "But from what I observed, she seemed much more focused on him than he was on her."

David studied the wet sidewalk as he listened. He wondered how Darienne was coping with this new situation in her life. In the four hundred years he'd known her, he'd never seen her truly in love. And then she met Matthew. David had watched her fall hopelessly for the charismatic actor, all the while marveling that Darienne had no idea what was happening to her. More than that, she'd fallen in love with a mortal. David knew the snares that awaited her. Perhaps it was just as well Matthew didn't entirely return her feelings. Their relationship could end simply.

Merle exhaled in a heavy way. "Well, I'd better go to the hospital and see what they have to say about Ned. Want to come?"

"No. But let me know, will you? And give him my best wishes. Are you really going to contact Matthew?"

"Yup. His agent must know where he is. I'll call tonight. No time to waste."


The next evening, David had just picked up his ringing phone when he heard Harriet's knock at the door. He was expecting her, since it was their usual night to meet. "Hello, can you hold on a moment?" he asked whoever was on the phone.

"I'm calling from Switzerland—"

"Darienne?" he said, astonished to hear her unmistakable throaty voice.

"Yes!"

"Well, hold on, will you?" David said. "Someone's at the door." He set the receiver on his desk before she could protest and rushed to the living room to press the buzzer, which allowed Harriet to enter. He went out to lean over the railing and called down as she walked in. "I'm on the phone, Harriet. Come up and make yourself at home."

She smiled up at him. "Take your time."

David hurried back to his office and grabbed the phone. "Darienne? I'm shocked to hear from you. It's been years!"

"I know, David. I'm sorry I haven't had a chance to see you in so long. How are you?"

"Fine. Where are you?"

"Grindelwald. It's three A.M. here. Matthew's asleep in the bedroom."

"You're still with him?" David said, pretending ignorance. "I never imagined you'd stay with one man for so long."

"Neither did I." There was poignance in her voice.

"Does he know about you?"

"He's never guessed. Listen, David, I need your help. Matthew heard about the accident. His agent called, and Matthew told him he'd play Sir Percy again in Chicago."

David sat down on the chair in front of his rolltop desk. "Merle will be happy to hear that."

"No!" Darienne said, her voice so strong David had to pull the phone away from his ear a bit. "You can't let it happen! You must stop this. Matthew hasn't recovered."

"He must feel fit enough to do it, if he's agreed."

"You don't understand. He can't let go of the role. If he does *Shadow* again, he won't want to stop. I'm afraid he'd go on playing the role until it killed him."

David couldn't believe what she was saying. Matthew was one of the most sensible, solid men David had ever met. "You must be exaggerating, Darienne. Or you have some ulterior motive for keeping Matthew off the stage. You want him all to yourself, without his fans tugging him away from you, is that it?"

He heard her sigh into the phone with frustration. "David, I know what you think of me, but you must believe me now.

Matthew hasn't recovered. He hasn't even had the six weeks his voice coach said he needed to rest his voice. He hasn't gained back all the weight he lost, and he still looks tired. His injuries haven't healed. If he goes back, he might fall off the rope, too. I worried every night it would happen to him in London and in Sydney. Stop him from going back to that role, David!"

David leaned his elbows on his desk, thinking a moment. As he fingered the coiled phone wire, he couldn't help but be impressed with her heartfelt arguments. "But it's not up to me," he finally said, stating the truth of the matter. "It's for Merle, Matthew, the theater manager, and their legal representatives to settle."

"But it's *your* show. You have influence!"

"I can't presume to interfere with Matthew's plans. He and I don't know each other well. Why would he listen to me? You've been with him all this time. You have more influence with him than I."

"No," she said, her voice subdued. "When it comes to this, he won't listen. The only way to stop him is for us to work behind the scenes and make the role unavailable to him. Find another actor."

"Merle says there aren't many to choose from."

"I'm begging you," she pleaded. "Won't you do this for *me,* if not for his sake?"

"For you?" David said, feeling a little appalled now. "You've forgotten me for years—not even a call or letter to tell me where you were—and now the only reason you phone me is because you want a favor."

"I know I'm selfish and self-centered," she admitted, her voice sounding more and more desperate. "You've always said that, and you're right. If not for me, then can't you do this for Matthew? Someone's got to save him from himself. I can't. I don't think his ex-wife can. Nor his doctors. He won't listen to anyone. Merle and the others just want him to come back because they know he'll make a lot of money for everyone. They don't care about *him.* I'm calling on you, because I thought you might care about him as a human being. I wish you were here to see him. He's so fragile right now, David. Matthew is such a unique and talented man. He has so much to give to the world. Don't let him destroy himself with this role. Take it away from him. Please, David."

David was quiet for a long moment, feeling as if a weight had fallen on his shoulders. He remembered the sight of Ned Holt's broken body in the orchestra pit. "I can hear how much you care for him. But I don't know what I can . . . . Look, I'll call Merle and tell him what you've said. But don't you see, when Merle speaks to Matthew himself, he'll believe Matthew?"

"Do what you can, David. I have to go now. I think Matthew's waking up."

"All right. I'll call Merle."

David hung up and walked into the living room. Harriet sat on his couch wearing a blue dress. "I'm sorry to keep you waiting," he told her.

"That's okay. Is it about the accident? I heard about it on the news. How is Ned Holt?"

"I called the hospital a little while ago. They say he's doing well, considering his injuries. We're working on a replacement. I'm afraid I have to make one more phone call. Do you mind waiting?"

"No, go ahead."

David returned to his office and quickly dialed Merle's number.

"David?" Merle said with jubilation in his voice. "I was going to call you. Matthew can't wait to come to Chicago! I've been on the phone all day negotiating a contract."

David took a long breath, not relishing the task of trying to burst Merle's bubble. "Yes, well—Darienne just called *me.*"

"She did?"

"She's with him in Switzerland, and she's very concerned. She says he hasn't recovered yet."

"Matthew told me he was feeling fine."

"Darienne says he's not. He hasn't even had time to rest his voice."

"Well, we can give him another week or two. It'll take a while to get the contract drawn up, rehearsals set, and so on."

"I have to tell you, Merle, she sounded extremely upset."

"Aw, women get emotional. My wife's like that, always wanting me to slow down and rest. It's the mother instinct. They like to take care of somebody. It's a nice quality, but men aren't little kids. If Matthew says he can do the job, I believe him."

"You don't know Darienne as well as I do," David said with a sense of irony. "She doesn't have much of a mother instinct. If she's this concerned, I'm afraid she may have good reason. We should consider that replacing one exhausted actor with another exhausted actor may not be wise."

"Matthew's a pro, David. He thrives on applause. When he sees the welcome back he gets in Chicago, it'll give him all the energy he needs. Darienne's in love with him, so she treats him like a hothouse plant. He's no withering lily. Has he ever let us down?"

"No," David had to agree. "But she's afraid he'll fall from the rope, too."

"Now, David, what are the statistical chances of an accident like that happening twice on the same stage? One in a million."

David didn't know how to argue with statistics. "Well, I promised her I'd convey her fears to you."

"Women," Merle said with amusement. "What would we do without 'em, eh?"

"Indeed," David replied in a resigned tone. They said goodbye and David hung up, feeling uneasy. He didn't know if Darienne's perceptions about Matthew, perhaps clouded by her love for him, were accurate or not. Well, he'd done as she asked. It was out of his hands.

He walked back into the living room. Harriet was sitting there, calm and patient as she looked up at him. It was nice to have a tranquil, down-to-earth woman, who wasn't connected with the frenzied world of entertainment, to talk to.

"I'm sorry," he said. "I pressed the button on my answering machine. I promise not to take or make any more calls tonight."

"Who's Darienne?" she asked. "I couldn't help but overhear. Veronica has mentioned her."

David smiled as he sat down beside her. "Darienne is a vampiress. I've known her for nearly four hundred years, since we were mortal adolescents in Paris. She loves luxury, jewels, travel, and clothes. When she feels like it, she visits me now and then."

"Veronica said she used to visit her, too, but she hadn't seen her in a long while."

David stroked his nose. "Yes, it always surprised me that the two of them formed such a friendship. She's the exact opposite of Veronica. I would have expected more jealousy, too, but they seemed to have worked that out."

Harriet's eyes looked a little concerned. "Jealousy?"

David tilted his head, wishing he hadn't let that slip. "Veronica knows about my long friendship with Darienne, and I think she understands. Veronica is the only one I love. Darienne is like a wayward sister, though I confess my relationship with her has not always been that of a brother. But Darienne is in love with someone herself now."

"Matthew McDowall?" Harriet asked.

"Do you listen at keyholes, too?" he said with pointed amusement.

Harriet looked contrite. "I'm sorry. Maybe it comes from having teenage kids. You have to keep track of them to be sure they're not falling in with the wrong friends. If I'm in earshot of a phone conversation, my ears just naturally try to pick up news."

"I don't think I should comment about her relationship with Matthew. I don't know all that much about it anyway."

"Is he really coming back to Chicago to replace Ned Holt?"

David laughed. "You missed your calling. You should have been a gossip columnist."

"I'd love to see him in *The Scarlet Shadow* again. He was so sensual . . . ," she said, her eyes taking on an appreciative light.

"Unlike your husband?"

The light in her eyes disappeared. "Ralph has no concept of what *sensual* means."

"I'll bet he does," David said. "He just doesn't understand it from a woman's point of view."

Harriet's face took on a look of serious deliberation, and she smoothed the skirt of her dress with her hand. "There's something I'd like to ask you, David." She swallowed and looked up at him with a certain lack of confidence, but yet with determination. "Veronica told me about what it was like to have a bond with you. I was wondering if . . . Would you do that for me? Initiate me?"

David's heart sank. He slumped one shoulder into the back of the couch, stunned to hear her ask this of him. "Why? Why would you want that?"

"What she described seemed so profound," Harriet said, her fingers trembling slightly as she folded her hands tightly in her lap. "She talked about how close she felt to you, how you and she could sense each other's feelings. Well, I've never had a relationship like that with anyone. Maybe my mother, but—that's different. Never with a man. I know how much you mean to Veronica and I have no intention of being her rival for your affection." She sat back a bit. "Though, lately, she's said some odd things."

"What has she said?" David asked, straightening.

Harriet hesitated. "Maybe I shouldn't have mentioned it, but—she misses you so much, she said if I had a relationship with you, she'd want me to tell her about it, so she could experience being with you vicariously. She said if she can't have you, then I might as well."

David felt like someone had punched him in the heart. He bowed his head and lifted his hand to his face. "Oh, God . . ."

"I know," Harriet said. "It upsets me, too. She told me just the other day she didn't know how she'd get through the remaining years you and she are to be apart." She grew quiet for a moment and her tone changed. "But that's between you and her. And maybe something will come about that will enable you two to be together sooner than that," she added with hopefulness in her voice.

Her tone made David lift his head. "What do you mean?"

"I don't know," she said with a smile and a shrug.

"You aren't thinking of that cure business, are you?" he asked, annoyed that she was still considering such nonsense when there were more important things to weigh. "Really, Harriet, you shouldn't put so much stock in psychics."

"Well, let's forget it then," she said easily. "As for Veronica, I have the feeling she wouldn't mind if you and I shared a bond. That is, a platonic bond. I'm not looking for anything more, both for Veronica's sake, and for mine, too. I don't want to be an unfaithful wife, even though I don't have the world's most perfect husband."

"But why have a bond with another man at all?" David asked, still trying to understand.

Harriet's brows contracted, as if searching for a way to explain herself. "I have women friends. I'm close to Veronica, for example. But I've never had a deep relationship with a man. My father was always working when I was a kid and he's dead now. I never had a brother. I hate to think I'm going to go through life never having experienced something on a deeper level with a man. Women, I understand. I need to understand the opposite sex better. You could help me with that. Look at it this way: If I can begin to fathom the male mind through you, it might help me understand Ralph better." Her tone changed. "Though I admit I can't see that you and he have much in common."

"It's an interesting theory," David said, stroking his eyebrow. Despite what his conscience was telling him, he found the notion of bonding with a woman without having a concurrent sexual relationship with her intriguing. Or was it just the offer of her blood that intrigued him?

"Besides," she continued, her voice and eyes brightening, "I don't think many women get the chance to get bitten by a vampire. When I saw those marks on Veronica's neck, I found myself feeling envious. There's something romantic about it, in a kinky sort of way. Though," she glanced downward, with a resigned expression, "maybe you wouldn't find the idea appealing. I may not be the type of woman you'd like to have a bond with."

David swallowed his growing desire to taste her blood and kept himself from eyeing her smooth, plump throat. Instead he gave her a reassuring pat on the hand. "Harriet, the more I'm with you, the more attractive I find you. But I'm amazed you're taking all this so calmly. You don't seem the least bit afraid of me or of what you're considering asking me to do."

"I've heard my grandmother's vampire stories since I was little. *They* were scary. But you aren't. You're too kind to be frightening."

David got up and took a turn about the room. Perhaps he'd learned to hide his sinister appetites too well. Finally he came up to her again and said with gravity in his tone, "You ought to be more frightened, Harriet. The vampire realm is a dark one, an unholy one, and you would be a part of it, once you're initiated. And the bond would last your whole life."

"But," Harriet said, leaning forward as she argued with increasing emphasis, "Veronica took that risk, and she's gone from a shy girl to a woman with profound passions and experiences. I don't want to die just having skimmed the surface of life. I have children, but they'll go off soon and have families of their own. Ralph will always be a good man, but . . . inept. I need something for *me*. I need it enough to have the nerve to ask you to do that for me."

Harriet got up from the couch and reached out to take hold of his arm. "I enjoy knowing you and admire you, and in many ways I'd like to be more like you. If I could attach my mind to yours—gosh, it would be a whole different world for me. Though it's asking a lot of you."

David studied her, her deep, sincere eyes and open features. He ought to just tell her *no* straight out. But he could see she needed him, and he'd grown fond enough of her to want to help her. It wouldn't cost him much to initiate her. On the contrary, the mere thought of her warm blood tantalized him.

His mouth began to water, and he looked away, ashamed, forcing himself not to dwell any further on that aspect. He had to think of Harriet and what the consequences would be.

Turning back to her, he took her hands firmly in his. "You'd constantly long to be with me, Harriet," he told her in a warning tone of voice. "You might experience the same unrelenting obsession for me that Veronica feels. Though, perhaps," he said, thinking as he spoke, "if we kept things platonic, our bond might develop along different lines." He stopped speaking to stare into her receptive eyes a moment and found his determination to dissuade her waning. "I confess, I find your proposition fascinating. I'm not sure what it would be like. It would be a step into the unknown."

Harriet's dark eyes brightened. "I'll take that step, if you will!"

"We must think about this further. I'll consider the matter," he said earnestly. "And so must you."

# 8

# You would be so magnificent

"NATALIE?" DARIENNE said when a sleepy woman's voice muttered hello. The long-distance wire to London was muffled with static. "It's Darienne."

"Darienne?" Natalie sounded surprised. "It's the middle of the night. What's wrong?"

"I'm sorry to wake you. I need your help. They want Matthew to do *Shadow* in Chicago. Did you read about the actor who was injured?"

"I heard it on the BBC. Matthew's not going—"

"He wants to pack tomorrow and fly to Chicago the next day."

"No! Can't you stop him?"

"He won't listen to me. But maybe the two of us could talk him out of it—"

"I'll be on the next plane!"

That night Darienne could hear voices as she approached Matthew's chalet, with its flower-planted window ledges. The front door was open. All at once Matthew, dressed in a Swiss sweater and jeans, hurried out with a purposeful stride, carrying two suitcases. Natalie followed him, standing by his small European rental car as he opened the trunk. Despite her neat skirt, turquoise sweater, and sleek silvery hair, she looked frazzled.

"God, Matthew, how can you do this to us again? I just had him convinced to let you meet him. Don't you see, if you go back to the States without seeing Larry, you'll be proving him right? He thinks you don't care. Apparently you don't!"

"Of course I care!" Matthew told her as he lifted a suitcase into the trunk. "But I didn't know you were making plans for a reunion. Everything's settled. I begin rehearsals in two days. All they've got in Chicago is the understudy."

"So what!" Natalie gestured sharply with her hands. "Can't you put relationships before your career for once in your life?"

Good for you, Natalie, Darienne thought as she quietly walked up the sidewalk toward them. They hadn't noticed her yet. Darienne congratulated herself on arriving at the perfect time to give Natalie support.

Natalie turned and noticed Darienne. Her expression showed her relief. "Thank God. I'm getting nowhere," Natalie said, apparently not caring that Matthew was there to hear. "See what you can do."

Having put the other bag in the trunk, Matthew walked around the car to the sidewalk and eyed them warily. "A conspiracy, is it?" he asked, his gaze sharpening as he looked from his mistress to his ex-wife. His eyes settled on Darienne. "You don't seem surprised Natalie is here."

"Oh, all right," Darienne said. "I called her and told her you were planning to leave. We have this evil plan afoot to keep you off the stage. Because we both care about you and don't want to watch you have a breakdown!"

"Somebody has to be sensible for you," Natalie told him, her tone more upbraiding than Darienne's. "You don't seem to have any common sense of your own. When you were young you could do stunts and play strenuous roles. But you're older now. You've proved you can play Sir Percy. Why do you have to do it all over again?"

Matthew looked as though he was trying to be patient. "I need to, that's all. You never did understand that. I *need* to be in a theater again. You saw that bag of fan mail. My fans care about me, too, and they want me back."

"Oh, for heaven's sake!" Natalie turned to walk back into the house in disgust.

"What bag of fan mail?" Darienne asked him.

Matthew strode through the door of the chalet and Darienne followed. In front of the couch, on the polished wood floor, was a very large cloth sack filled with letters. Piles of letters were spread out on the pine coffee table. Matthew picked up handfuls of them. "Look! My agent forwarded them and they arrived today. Letters from all over—Australia, the U.S., Britain, even Canada."

Darienne had seen him receive tons of fan mail at each theater in which he'd played *Shadow*. But somehow she'd thought all that would be left behind when he quit and came to Switzerland. "I must thank your agent. And your fans," she said very dryly. "They're all so conscientious."

"Be sarcastic, but the letters mean a lot to me. These people," he said, holding up the letters he'd grasped, "made me a success. If it weren't for them, I'd be nothing."

"They mean more to him than his own son," Natalie said, taking a seat on the couch. Her eyes looked hurt and hopeless.

Matthew tossed the letters down. "I knew you wouldn't understand."

"Oh, I understand more than you think," Natalie shot back. "Remember, I lived with you for five years. I know you belong to the world, Matthew. I'm not expecting you to be ordinary. I'm not expecting you to ignore your fans, either. But I would think you'd have enough sense not to ignore your health. And I'd hoped, I've even prayed, that you wouldn't ignore your own son!"

"She's right," Darienne said, taking a more conciliatory tone. "Your fans wouldn't *want* you to perform if they knew you hadn't recovered. And what have you gained if you trade a closer relationship with your only son for the distant adoration of your public?"

"Why does it have to be a trade?" Matthew argued, starting to pace the cozy room with its leaf-patterned wallpaper and braided rugs. "If Larry's willing to speak to me, why does it have to be right now? He can come to Chicago as my guest."

"He has a life in London, a job with the BBC," Natalie said.

"He can take a vacation."

"Matthew, he feels you deserted him. You need to go to *him*. He's willing to see you. You're here in Europe. It's logical for you to go to London now, when everything's been arranged."

He turned and pointed at his ex-wife. "Arranged without my knowledge."

"You knew I was going to see him," Natalie argued. "I told you I was going to try to talk him into meeting you."

"You didn't say it would be immediately. And I had no idea

this chance to go to Chicago would arise. They need me there. I can't let them down. David and Merle and the others—look what they've done for me, giving me the role of Sir Percy in the first place. I owe it to them."

"David would want you to consider your health first," Darienne told him, half-following him as he paced, her tone growing more impatient. "Why do you always think you have to save the show? It's been playing in Chicago for three years. It's got to close sometime."

"We're all making a lot of money on *Shadow*," Matthew said. "It pays to keep it going."

"Oh, now it's money," Darienne taunted. "As if you haven't made enough to last you a lifetime already, if you invest it wisely."

Matthew turned and stood squarely in front of her, his gray-green eyes so intense with bridled fury that Darienne found it difficult to look at him. "All right!" he said, his voice smooth and swift. "It's not the money. It's not because the show needs saving. It's because I *want* to do it. And that's all the reason I need!"

"You're obsessed with Sir Percy," Darienne retorted. "You say you admire his character because he cares about others, because you find something in him you don't see in your own life. But *you* could have a more fulfilling life if you'd try living *in* your life instead of through a stage character."

"Who made you a psychologist?" Matthew said, turning away abruptly.

"She doesn't need to be one," Natalie interjected from the couch. "What she said is plain to anyone who knows you. You're trading a life for the adulation of an audience. Where will they be when you're old and tired out and sick?"

"No one knows the future," Matthew said, pausing by the lace-curtained window. "But in the meantime, I'll live the life I need to live!"

"With your precarious health, you may not have much of it left," Darienne said with exasperation as she took a seat next to Natalie on the couch.

"*I* will be the judge of my state of health," Matthew said in a firm tone, staring them down from his position by the window.

"But she's right!" Natalie said. "You're too thin, and you

look worn around the eyes. You still take medications for all
your aches and pains. You should rest six months as your
doctors told you."

"I look and feel just fine, thank you," he said as he left the
window and walked toward them. "In fact, this opportunity
in Chicago has energized me. An audience is the best medicine
for any actor."

Natalie glanced at Darienne, her eyes glassy. "It's hopeless," Matthew's ex-wife said, her voice breaking despite the
finality in her tone. "I went through all this years ago. I'm not
going through it again."

Matthew's defiant posture changed, and he walked around
the coffee table to kneel beside Natalie. He placed his fingertips on her forearm. "It doesn't have to be like before. Have
Larry come to Chicago for my opening night. I'll pay all his
expenses. And you—come to Chicago, too. I want to get to
know you again."

Darienne averted her eyes, unable to look at his face as he
spoke so softly to his former wife. But she dared to look again
as she heard Natalie's response.

"No," Natalie said succinctly, shaking her head. "The last
thing I would ever do is follow you to Chicago. I don't want
to play second fiddle to a theater again. And more than that,
I wouldn't want Larry to go to Chicago and have to be pushed
aside while you play matinee idol. And most of all—most of
all—I'm not going to watch you kill yourself." Her voice grew
husky with unshed tears. "Because that's what will happen if
you go back to that show. It's all that's left to happen. You've
suffered injuries, you've pushed yourself far beyond your limits, you've collapsed from exhaustion. You won't let yourself
recover. All that's left is for you to fall off that rope yourself,
or have a heart attack, or catch pneumonia from standing at
a drafty stage door signing autographs late at night. I don't
want to be there to see it, Matthew." Tears spilled down her
cheeks. "I *won't* be there." She rose from the seat and, wiping
her eyes, turned to Darienne. "Sorry," she said. "I guess we've
failed."

Alarmed, Darienne grabbed her arm to detain her as Matthew rose to his feet. "You're not leaving. You're giving up
already?"

"Oh, yes," Natalie told her, nodding resolutely. "I have the good sense to give up. There's no way to pry him from a waiting audience. No way in the world. He was the same twenty years ago. It's best to cut your losses and split, believe me. Stay with him if you want, Darienne," she said, glancing at Matthew with eyes that were stunning in their pain and anger, "but you'll wind up with a broken heart!"

"Natalie—" Matthew said, following her as she took her arm out of Darienne's grasp and headed toward the door. "Don't go. Not like this!"

*"Déjà vu?"* Natalie taunted him. "You don't learn from experience, Matthew. But I do!"

Her hand was on the doorknob. Matthew took her by the shoulders and made her stop. "Don't leave me! We were just getting to know each other again."

"Just enough to remind me that placing any hope in you is a thankless proposition. Have a good life—whatever's left of it! I don't want to see you again."

She twisted free of his hold and walked out. "And don't phone me at my hotel," Darienne heard her tell him from outside the door. "I won't accept your calls."

"Natalie!!" Matthew stood on the threshold watching her walk away, his rib cage expanding and contracting with his harrowing breaths. After a few long minutes, when she'd apparently disappeared from his sight, he slowly closed the door. "I'll see her again somehow," he swore to himself, perhaps forgetting Darienne was nearby.

He leaned one shoulder against the door, curly head bowed, and stood there for a long moment, looking pale and distraught. Darienne felt like crying for him, even though his obvious feelings for his ex-wife made her insecure. She straightened, took a breath for strength, and walked up to him.

Slipping her arms around him, she said, "I'm still here, *cheri.* Darienne is still here."

He sniffed and pulled her closer. "She never did understand," he said, sounding too heartsick to be angry. "I need to work—to do what I can do, to sing, to perform, and then listen to the audience respond." He took a shaky breath, and then his voice sounded more firm, more sure. "There's nothing like it. Nothing in the world. It's better than ascending a mountain, better than winning ten million dollars, even better than sex. You understand at least a little, don't you?" He pushed her away a bit to look at her.

Tears blurred Darienne's vision as she gazed into his round, pleading eyes. "I . . . I try to, Matthew. But you must remember, you're only mortal . . . only human. You're not invincible."

His eyes flashed. "I am if I want to be."

"Matthew—"

"I get tired sometimes. I get sick. But I always rally again. I'm always back working sooner than anyone predicts, aren't I?"

"Yes, but—"

"It's all a question of willpower. And I understand willpower. I can make it work for me, just as I always have."

"Matthew, you're forty-six and you're worn out."

He raised one hand and pointed to his temple. "Not in here I'm not. I'm ageless, and as strong as I need to be. It's all a matter of the mind."

"You forget how exhausted you were only a few weeks ago, when you left Australia."

"Yes, I have forgotten. Because I don't dwell on the negative. You know that yourself, Darienne. You're a positive thinker. That's what I like about you. It's only lately you seem to have lost your optimism."

He took her by the upper arms and shook her soundly. She gasped at his strength and determination. In fact, despite her anxiety for him, it began to arouse her. His strength of character was partly what had made her admire him so when she first met him.

"There," he said, smiling as his gaze caught hers. "There's that shimmering light back in your eyes again. I love it when you look at me that way. I'd see that look when you had a front-row seat and I'd catch a glance at you while I sang. Or afterward in my dressing room. You always loved to watch me onstage. Well, I'm going back! Be happy for me. And for you."

He leaned in to kiss her, hard and with passion. Matthew had taken control again. And suddenly Darienne found she couldn't argue with him anymore.

* * *

A week later, Darienne was back in Chicago, the city where it all began. She had followed Matthew there from Switzerland, having again gone through the process of having herself shipped. She took up residence in her condominium on the ninety-first floor of the John Hancock, which was decorated with modern furniture in a white-on-white motif. In the daytime she slept in her white, enameled coffin lined with emerald-green velvet. At night she went to Matthew's hotel suite to be with him. Her first concern was for Matthew, and she hadn't even had a chance yet to contact David and let him know she was in town. But she meant to, soon. She hoped to find time to see Veronica, too.

Matthew had spent the day rehearsing at the theater. He appeared tired tonight in his denim shirt and jeans, but determined and somehow energized despite his returning gaunt look. Dressed in a lavender raw silk shirtdress with a long, full skirt, she sat on a stool by the wet bar in his spacious hotel suite. He was behind the bar, using a blender to mix some unpleasant-looking concoction.

"Brewer's yeast, banana, protein powder, vitamins, and mineral powders," he said, telling her the ingredients when she asked. "I had a nutritionist visit me at the theater. He recommended taking this as a supplement. He gave me eight different kinds of pills to take at different times of the day—bee pollen and ginseng and other herbs I never heard of."

"How long have you been taking these things?"

"Three days. I think it's working. At least, today I had more energy than I did yesterday. I got out of shape resting. I could hardly make it up the forty-foot ladder yesterday. Today, I handled it better."

"You look drawn and pale, Matthew."

"I don't want to hear talk like that," he said sharply. "I look fine."

"You need to face the truth!"

"The truth is," he insisted, turning off the blender, "I'm regaining strength and I'll be fine. I'm happy, Darienne. I sang great today. I can feel the energy coursing through me when I play Sir Percy. I feel his strength when I plant my feet on the floor, and his power moves up my body and out my breath as I sing, and out my fingers as I move. I've been meditating a couple of hours each morning when I get up. That gets me centered, so I can draw on that inner energy."

Darienne noticed the thick green candles at various places throughout his suite, all lit. One used to be enough for him. He used to think of his ritual of lighting a candle before each performance as barely more than a superstition. But ever since his collapse in London and his hospital stay there, he had come to place more and more psychological reliance on meditation techniques, the lighting of green candles to keep vigilance over his health, mood music with subliminal messages, a lucky penny in his pocket, and health fad diets. In Switzerland, he'd seemed to let go of these. But now Darienne was sad to see him returning to his old habits.

"What's the matter?" he said, studying her as he put down the glass he'd just finished drinking from. "Do I see disapproval in those bright eyes?" he teased.

"You didn't used to need things like this to keep you going," she said. "It shows how desperate you've become."

"It's not desperation. I'm just finding new ways to keep myself fit."

"Natalie was right." Tears clouded her eyes. "You're going to kill yourself doing this show."

His eyes widened with sudden hostility. "How dare you allow such a negative, poisonous thought into your mind!"

"Oh, Matthew," she said, gripping the edge of the polished wood bar. "If you could only step outside yourself and see yourself as Natalie and I do. You were always driven to perform, but it's gotten out of hand. You've lost your sense of balance."

Matthew shifted his weight in an edgy manner. "Look, I'm getting tired of hearing this, Darienne. If all you can do is weep and wail, then maybe we ought to call it quits. Your attitude even affects sex lately. You used to be so much fun, so carefree. That was why I loved sleeping with you—couldn't get enough. But lately, going to bed with you is a downer. You take everything so seriously, you practically mother me. It's a turnoff."

Darienne felt her face growing pale at his words. What was happening? Was she losing him? "I'm sorry," she whispered. "I didn't realize."

He reached over the bar to take her hand. "I don't like

hurting you," he said earnestly. "But our relationship used to be so wonderful. I used to get high just thinking about going back to my apartment with you after the show—your easy, fun-loving attitude and your delight in sex just for the sake of sex. I never knew a woman like you."

As he studied her face, his eyes took on a mystical, faraway sensuality. His voice grew soft and liquid. "Being with you was like drinking some powerful, exotic elixir. You never failed to take me to some stratosphere I never knew existed until I met you."

He let go then and lowered his eyes. His tone grew matter-of-fact. "But that magic's been lost lately. And I think it's you, not me, who's lost it."

"I've lost the man *I* once knew," she told him, turning tables on him to try to keep the control she felt she was losing. "You used to be so formidable that you kept me in circles. You used to understand yourself. You knew who you were. And you kept me from overpowering you. That's what I fell . . . what I found in you that attracted me so. But you've lost your way. You've lost your true self. And I've been trying desperately to help you find yourself again. And now you want to reject me because of that?"

Matthew didn't answer, but stood in front of her, the bar between them, his arms spread wide on the counter, his head down. She looked over his curly hair and the vulnerable aspect his face took on when his head was bowed like this. God, she loved him! How could she keep him? How could she find a new accommodation with him?

She stopped breathing for a moment and closed her eyes. There was a way. There was a way that would solve every-thing. Perhaps it was time to tell him the secret she'd kept from him for so long. She might as well risk it, for now there was nothing more she could lose.

"Matthew, would you sit down in the living room? There's something I need to tell you."

He lifted his head and looked at her, eyes round and ques-tioning. "What?"

"Just something I need to explain, something you don't know. It may be a little shocking. I'd like you to sit down and be comfortable," she said in a respectful voice. "Will you?"

He drew his broad shoulders up as he pulled his hands

toward each other along the edge of the bar. "Sure." He walked around the bar and into the living room of the hotel suite. Choosing a large, cornflower-blue upholstered arm chair, he sat down. Darienne sank to the floor in front of him, shifting her legs to one side and adjusting her long skirt. She draped her arms over his knee and took a long breath. How to begin?

"Matthew, I've often heard you tell reporters, when they ask about Sir Percy, that you don't believe in vampires. You usually make some joke about it."

He nodded, drawing his brows together and leaning his cheek on his fist, his elbow on the arm of the chair.

"Has it ever occurred to you that this might not be true?" she asked.

"What, that vampires may exist?"

She nodded.

"No."

"What if I told you that they do exist? That there are such human creatures who sleep in coffins during the day and can be out only at night?"

"I'd say you were off your rocker."

"Matthew, stop to think. Have you ever seen me during the daylight hours?"

He sat still for a long while, looking as if he was indulging her by thinking about her question. "I must have. I can't really remember."

"My darling, I know you never stopped to think about it, because you've always been so busy working, but you've only seen me at night. Do you really think I spend every day shopping? I know I adore clothes, but—"

"What are you saying?" he asked with amusement. "That *you* are a vampire?"

"I like to say *vampiress*. But, yes, *cheri,* that is what I'm saying."

Matthew gazed around the room in a comic way, mouth open, as if someone had just told him that the earth was flat. Then he looked at her sideways. "Darienne, what are you trying to pull? Is this some tactic?"

She straightened and looked up at him. "No, this is no game I'm playing. I am a vampiress. I was born in France almost four hundred years ago. I . . ." She sighed and lowered her eyes with a sense of embarrassment. "I don't eat. I drink blood obtained from medical sources. I spend each day in a coffin."

He suddenly started to get up, impatient now and angry. "I won't listen to any more of this—"

She stopped him from moving away by grabbing hold of his legs to keep him in place. Using her vampire strength, it was easy, since she was three times as strong as he. He looked down at her in shock when he found he couldn't move.

"Sit down, *cheri*. Please," she said, keeping her voice calm. "Sit down."

He sat down, paling as he stared at her with widening pupils.

She took his hand, palm up, stretched out his forefinger, and brought it to her lips. Opening her mouth, she made him touch her incisor, pressing the sharp tip of her tooth into his flesh.

"Ouch!" He pulled his hand away.

"I've always had to be careful when I kiss you, Matthew," she said with a wistful sadness. "My teeth could easily have drawn your blood. And that would have been dangerous, because I might not have been able to resist taking your blood. I've wanted to taste from you for years. But I've made myself be satisfied with coupling with you—which has been more than satisfying, *cheri*, especially for a mortal."

Matthew was testing his fingertip with his thumb. "You almost . . . drew blood *now*," he said, his voice a hollow whisper. He looked down at her. "I used to feel a sharpness sometimes when we kissed. I always wondered, but then I'd forget."

"In the passion of our lovemaking, have you ever noticed a glow in my eyes that seemed unreal?"

He nodded. "Sometimes I'd glimpse a radiance in your eyes. I thought I must have imagined it."

"It enters our eyes with any high emotion."

"I can't believe this! How can you be four hundred years old?"

"Like Sir Percy, I don't age. I was thirty-five when I died. I'll be thirty-five forever."

"But," he said, stirring in his chair, "if this is true, then how did you become one?"

She paused, wondering how much she should say. She didn't like to reveal David's secret, too. On the other hand, it would make everything so much more clear to Matthew. "David transformed me. We knew each other from the time we were teenagers in Paris in the late fifteen hundreds."

"Wait," Matthew said, raising his hand. "You're saying David de Morrissey is a vampire, too?"

"Why do you think he writes plays about vampires so convincingly?"

Matthew stared at her, sinking into himself slightly. "I've always felt as I sang the lyrics he wrote that he must have a profound understanding . . ."

"Now you know why."

"Go on."

"He studied with Shakespeare, you see." She told him David's story. "David is a much more noble vampire than I am," she said with a smile. "Anyway, after he'd been transformed, I met him again. When I discovered that he'd become immortal, I wanted that for myself, so I asked him to transform me. He did. And four centuries later, here I am."

Matthew rubbed his temple, then slid his hand over his eyes. "I . . . Why are you telling me all this? If this is true, why didn't you tell me before?"

"Because I was afraid you wouldn't accept me. I wanted to be your mistress, *cheri*. I didn't want to chance losing you. But now our situation has changed. You've changed, and maybe I have, too. But I have a solution to make everything right again. Matthew—" she said, taking both his hands in hers over his legs.

He stared down at her, as if half-afraid and half-fascinated at what she would say next.

"I can make you one of us," she told him. "You can be as David and I are. Immortal. Not only ageless, but more agile than even you can imagine, nimble as you are. And powerful, *cheri*. You would have all the strength you would need, more than you'd need, to play Sir Percy. You could play him forever and ever, and never tire, never become ill. You could be all you want so much to be. You could play a vampire as only an actor who is a vampire himself could."

Matthew stiffened in shock, as if wanting to bolt. "Are you suggesting—?"

"Yes." She slipped her hands up his forearms to keep him in place. "Stay calm, *cheri*. You're in no danger from me. I'm only asking you to consider the possibility."

He sank down again, but his eyes seemed riveted to hers. "I've been having sex all this time with a woman who is a vampire? And now you want me to become—" He turned his head and began to breathe in gasps, as if short of breath. "How do you expect me to believe this?" He tried to raise his hands. "Let me go!"

"No, my darling," she said, keeping him in place as gently as she could. "I need you to believe this, and I'm going to stay here with you until you're calm and you can think. Take a deep breath."

He did as she advised and leaned his head against the high back of the soft chair.

"You don't have to make this decision tonight," she told him. "I'd want you to think about it, to be sure. But imagine what it could mean for you. No more need for meditation and candles, no more health concoctions, no more worrying about climbing high ladders or swinging from a rope. Even if you fell off the rope and crashed into the pit, you would get up again, winded perhaps, but unharmed. You would have years to hone your skills as an actor and as a singer.

"Oh, Matthew," she said, pressing her cheek against his hand, "think how wonderful you would be onstage when you possessed a vampire's powers. No one would be like you, *cheri*. No one is like you now, but as a vampire, you would be beyond anything. No actor could compete with you. The talent you have, your charisma, backed with supernatural power—oh, you would be so magnificent, Matthew! I would sit in the audience and worship you every evening. And I would spend the rest of the night making love with you. And you would be my equal in strength and stamina. Sex in the superhuman realm is better than anything ordinary mortals can experience. That's why you thought sex with me was so special—because I could take you to levels mortal women can't."

She was encouraged to see Matthew looking at her now with a new light in his eyes. He seemed to be absorbing her words as if mesmerized with her promises.

"I thought the idea of power would appeal to you," she

said, running her hands up his arms as she raised herself to her knees. "I could do this for you, *cheri*. I would be thrilled to give you this power. It is a gift beyond price."

She hesitated. "But not without some cost. You would live as I do, only at night. You would have to rest in a coffin during the day, with some earth from the place where you were born. But these are simple things to arrange and I can help you. Travel is more difficult, but not impossible. You notice that I never was able to travel with you. I always had to arrange to have myself shipped in a coffin, unless I could be sure of getting from one place to another before dawn."

As he sat staring and contemplating, she paused to think. "Oh, yes. You wouldn't be able to play matinees, *cheri*. You'd have to write your contracts so that an alternate would play your roles in the day. You wouldn't be able to rehearse during the day, either. Have you signed the contract yet for the Chicago run?"

He blinked and looked at her as if being brought back to earth. "I . . . No. Still details to be worked out. I started rehearsals on a verbal commitment and a handshake."

"Then you can still have changes put in. I can transform you as soon as you like, perhaps the sooner the better, so that you can proceed as you will for the future."

He stared at her, confusion in his eyes. "This . . . transformation. What does it mean? What do you . . . ? You bite me on the neck? Like I do to Marguerite in the show?"

"Yes, only there's a bit more involved than David put in the script. We vampires call it the blood ceremony. I would drink from you," she said, reaching up tenderly to stroke the skin above the artery in his neck. "I would consume a great deal, *cheri*. Enough to cause your death."

When he jumped a bit, she tapped his cheek in a comforting manner. "Just before you died, I would make a cut in my breast and you would drink from me, my blood thus mingling with yours. This is what would transform you. You would die, briefly. And when you awoke, you would be like me. Immortal. Powerful. Sensual and strong on a superhuman level. Oh, think of it! From then on you would be invulnerable to disease and aging. I would teach you everything you need to know about our existence. You would be a wonderful vampire, Matthew. Just think, you could *be* Sir Percy. All those things you admire about him, you could become yourself. It's what you've wanted most, *n'est-ce pas?*"

She sank to the floor again, resting her hands on his knee, to give him a few moments to think. He sat still, eyes fixed at one of the candles burning on a table across the room. But soon he looked down at her again.

"I find myself wanting what you say I can be," he admitted in a strained voice. "But I don't like the idea of . . . of dying, of being dead and yet alive. This is how you exist, isn't it?"

"Yes. But we don't feel dead. I never felt more free or alive until after I'd died. The dying is nothing, *cheri.*"

He smiled to himself just slightly. " 'Dying is easy. Comedy is difficult.' A revered English actor said that on his deathbed."

She grinned. "You can be the one to prove his point."

Matthew's expression changed. "But aren't vampires connected with evil?"

"That idea came from some of the myths of folklore," she told him. "We aren't any more evil or good than any other human. We are just transformed."

"What about dying and going to heaven?"

Darienne glanced away. She never knew quite how to answer this question. "I don't know about heaven. Vampires don't die a normal death. We die and we stay here on earth. That's why, perhaps, we can't be seen in mirrors. We have gone against the laws of nature somehow, and we really shouldn't be here. In some strange way, the laws of physics demonstrate that, by not allowing our reflection to show."

He raised his finger at her. "I noticed I never saw you come into my dressing room. You'd always just appear next to me. It was because I was looking at the doorway in back of me through my makeup mirror."

She smiled because he seemed to be accepting her nature now. "Yes! I always stood next to the mirror when I talked to you, so you would be less likely to notice that I didn't reflect."

He nodded, growing quiet again. "And as Sir Percy sings in the show, 'The sun is my executioner,' I would perish if I saw the sun?"

"That is the knowledge that is passed from vampire to vampire. I don't know of any vampire who has actually perished in this way. Fire and, of course, a stake through the heart can destroy us."

"A stake through the heart," he repeated, sounding as if disbelief was haunting him again. "What about garlic and crosses?"

"We can look at a Christian cross. Garlic is merely an obnoxious smell. But then, all food is."

"I wouldn't eat?"

She shook her head. "Have you ever seen me eat?"

"No." He studied her. "But I've never seen you drink blood either."

"Of course, I never did that in your presence. We use blood bags. We don't go around attacking humans the way you see in some old movies. Most vampires nowadays are quite modern. There is the bloodlust," she told him with some seriousness. "You would need to get used to that. But you would learn to control it. You have so much command of yourself already, *cheri,* that these matters would not be difficult for you."

Matthew reached up with his fingertips and massaged his temples. "This is too much to comprehend all at once."

"I know, Matthew. Take your time. I'll be here whenever you need me. After dark, of course." She smiled. "I'm sure you'll see the wonders of this opportunity. The more I think about it, the more I wish I'd told you this before. You're taking it better than I used to fear you would." She ran her hand up his thigh. "Would you——?"

His expression froze and he stopped her hand with his. "Would you mind if we . . . if we skipped it tonight?"

Darienne sensed he was suddenly repulsed at the thought of sex with her, now that he knew what she was. Well, she could understand. He'd get over it. "All right, *cheri,"* she said, drawing her hand away. "We'll talk more tomorrow."

A mixture of discomfort and awesome speculation filled his eyes. "I understand why you didn't tell me this in the past. But I'm glad you have now. You . . . may be right. Maybe it's the solution I need. But I'll have to get used to the idea. And I'll have a lot of questions to answer before I . . . take any further step," he said with a convulsive swallow.

"I'll be here, Matthew. Just ask. I'll be happy to give you anything."

His expression changed and he smiled. He reached out to touch the tip of her nose with his fingertip. "I know," he whispered. "You always have. It makes me wonder now, why did you choose me?"

"In four centuries I've never known a man who could move me the way you do. You're the fantasy I didn't know I had until I saw you in *Shadow*. I wanted to possess that fantasy."

She grinned as she toyed with his hands. "Only *you* can't be possessed. But you've let me share, let me experience that part of you. You aren't like any other man. That's why," she said, taking his hand in hers almost reverently, "you must be preserved for the ages. What a shining fantasy you could be for all the women of the future who see you perform. I want you to be around for me, too, Matthew. To listen to you sing, to watch you command a stage—I've grown to depend on the thrill you give me. If you died a natural death—and you must someday unless I transform you—then where would I be? I'd be all alone with no Matthew to enrapture me. I might as well stay up and meet the sun!"

"Darienne," he whispered, a shimmer in his eyes. He stroked her cheek and ran his fingers through her hair. "You *are* a rare creature. You make me feel I'm more than I am. I do appreciate having you in my life."

She took his hand from the side of her face and kissed his palm in sheer adoration. "I appreciate *you, cheri*. More than you know." She would have told him she loved him. She longed to. But that was telling too much.

She'd given him enough to think about for one night.

# 9

# A firefly on a summer evening

USING HER vampire strength, Darienne climbed the rugged, sandstone blocks that formed the outer walls of David's mansion. Inserting her toes and fingers in the thick crevices between the rough-hewn blocks, she worked her way steadily upward. The building was easy to climb, which was one reason she enjoyed doing it. The other was that she liked to surprise David, so she literally dropped in on him by climbing through his third-floor living room's side window. She wore white pants and a low-cut, yellow-and-white sweater designed to please Matthew, whom she planned to visit later.

When she reached the window, she peered through the sheer drapery. She saw David relaxing on his couch, a manuscript in his hands. When she began to open the window, he looked up.

"Darienne!" He set aside the manuscript and rushed to help her climb in.

Once inside, she stood in front of him, held his hands in hers, and looked at him. "It's so good to see you, David!"

He smiled at her with some exasperation. "I heard Matthew's back in town, so I figured you'd show up one of these nights. How are you?"

"The same." She bowed her head. "Well, not exactly the same. I'm still in love with him." She put her arms around David and rested her head on his shoulder. "I guess I'll never be the same," she said against his thick cotton sweater.

"It shows you're human," David said, patting her back. "How is Matthew?"

She drew away a bit and shook her head. "Somehow he

154

finds the strength to get through his rehearsals. But it's taking its toll. He's losing weight again. His face looks drawn, almost gray sometimes. But he won't stop."

"You couldn't talk him out of it, I take it."

"Oh," she said with a wave of her hand, "there was no talking to him."

"You're afraid he'll have a collapse?"

"I'm sure that's what will happen unless . . ." She left off mid-sentence, realizing it might not be wise to confide to David that she'd offered to transform Matthew. Knowing David, he probably would not approve. "Unless he realizes his limits," she finished.

"I'm sorry I couldn't get anywhere with Merle. I called, but . . ."

"It doesn't matter," she said, stroking his cheek. "Matthew would have found a way to play the role no matter what." As she sighed, she found herself feeling reassured just looking into David's familiar blue eyes and seeing his handsome, aristocratic face again. She ran her fingers through his barely wavy rich brown hair. She was so used to tousled gray-and-brown locks, that feeling smooth dark hair seemed unusual to her now. She leaned against him again. "I'm so glad to see you, *cheri.*"

"I'm happy to see you, too, even if you have ignored me for three years."

"I'm sorry, David. Have you been lonely? You haven't seen Veronica in all this time?"

He closed his eyes and shook his head.

"If you'd just give up that pact and reunite with her—"

"I won't do that."

She gave him a sympathetic look. "I won't argue with you about that again. It's just that you could be with the one you love forever, if you wanted. I know now what that means."

"What about you and Matthew?" David asked, taking her elbow and walking with her toward the love seat. "Does he know? Have you initiated him?"

She lowered her eyes. "No, I haven't initiated him."

David seemed impressed. "You love him. How could you resist?"

Darienne thought this over a moment as she sat down. "I longed to taste his blood, of course. But . . . I didn't want him

to be under my power. I admire him for his strength to stand
up to me—not many men do."

"I know," David said ruefully. He picked up his manuscript
from the couch, set it on the table in front of them, and sat
down.

"If I'd initiated him, he wouldn't have been able to refuse
me anything. And, oddly enough, I didn't want that."

"I never expected you to be more sensible than me," David
said, looking at her in wonder. "I wanted the closeness with
Veronica that a bond brings."

Darienne studied him as she thought about her own point
of view. She realized she'd never thought through all this until
now when David asked her. "I think I was afraid of being that
close to Matthew. It's been difficult enough for me to get used
to being in love. If my mind and spirit were tied to his . . . I
can't imagine how I would have coped with that."

"But *you* are the vampire," David pointed out, as if surprised that he needed to state the obvious. "You would have
control."

"Yes," she agreed, taking his point with a feeling of irony.
"I could have willed him not to return to Chicago. I could
have made him love me. But if I could do those things, I would
be taking away what makes Matthew Matthew."

"But you wouldn't have to impose your will on him. Just
share his feelings and thoughts."

She shook her head and smiled sadly. "You know me,
David. If I had the power to control him, I'd use it. I'm not
noble like you."

David squeezed her wrist. "Then you were noble not to
initiate him."

"Was I?" She thought this over. "No. I was afraid of having
access to his mind and his feelings. I think I feared what I
might find there. Natalie, his ex-wife, says he's a genius. Anyone can see from watching him onstage how brilliant he is. If
I had access to his mind, I'm afraid I would be intimidated and
overwhelmed. I can deal with him as a man—he responds to
my sexual overtures as I expect. But as an artist, he has me in
awe. I couldn't deal with that on any closer level than I have
with him now." This was why she wanted to make him a
vampire through the blood ceremony rather than merely initiate him. As a vampire he would stay independent of her and

become her equal, but they would not share the mental and emotional bond that comes from initiation. She made a quick shrug of her shoulders in the French manner. "Besides, if I could know his mind and feel his feelings, I'd find out for certain that he doesn't love me. I'd rather not be that sure."

"He's not in love with you?" David said with surprise.

"No." She smiled. "He's very fond of me. But it's not love I see in his eyes. Only sensual adoration. I don't mind though. I understand sensuality. Love, I don't really understand. What would I do if he loved me? I'd probably run away."

David seemed to marvel at her words. "You encourage the love between Veronica and me, but you're afraid to have that for yourself?"

She tilted her chin as tears stung her eyes. "It's not that I don't want to be loved. It's that I'd feel like a piece of putty if I knew Matthew loved me. I'm used to being in charge of myself. What his love might release in me is too overpowering for me to cope with."

"You don't want to feel vulnerable."

"No." She pointed her forefinger and looked at him with warning eyes. "And don't try to change me. I'm happy this way."

David smiled sadly. "I can't change you. You must do that yourself."

They were interrupted by the distant sound of the brass door knocker on his front door.

"Harriet is here," he said. "I have to buzz her in."

"Harriet?" Darienne asked in puzzlement as David got up.

"She's Veronica's cousin," he explained as he pressed the button near the door frame. "I met her several weeks ago. She knows everything, by the way."

Darienne felt at sea for a moment, sorting out what David was telling her. "How did you meet her?"

"It's a long story," he said in a rush. "Let me go out and greet her." He went out onto the landing. In a few moments, he came back in with a nicely dressed, pleasant-looking woman. Darienne studied her, surprised. She didn't have Veronica's delicate beauty and ethereal sensuality, though Darienne did detect a suppressed sexuality in Harriet's ample, entirely feminine curves. Still, she seemed too ordinary to be the type David usually gravitated toward. Perhaps he kept contact with her so that he could have knowledge of Veronica.

Harriet stopped short when she entered the room. She turned to David with eyes that seemed to brighten. "Is this Darienne?"

"Yes. She dropped by to see me."

"Back from Europe?" Harriet asked as she walked up to Darienne.

Darienne was pleasantly surprised by Harriet's straightforward manner. "I arrived only a few days ago," Darienne told her, shaking her hand.

Harriet eyed her low-cut sweater and her hair, which Darienne had teased a bit and clippped back. "Gosh. You're certified gorgeous, all right!"

Darienne laughed, pleased with the compliment, and glanced at David.

"I've told her a little about you," David explained.

"I can imagine. You're Veronica's cousin?"

"Yes. Veronica has mentioned you to me, too. She said she misses seeing you."

Darienne felt crestfallen all at once, reminded that she had not only forsaken David, but Veronica, too. Veronica had probably needed someone to confide in the last few years, and Darienne hadn't been there to console her. "I've missed her," Darienne said with regret. "I'll try to see her soon. How did you meet David?"

They told her the story. Darienne listened with curiosity about the psychic and the supposed cure. But when Harriet explained she'd continued seeing David for advice about her husband, Darienne grew impatient. "An insensitive man is a drain on a woman," she told Harriet. "Divorce him."

"Darienne!" David admonished.

"I think of that as a last resort," Harriet explained.

"Oh," Darienne said, puzzled. "Do you still find him attractive?"

Harriet's expression was paradoxical. "I probably would if . . ."

"He was responsive to you. I know what you mean," Darienne said, quickly reading her thoughts. "My advice is stun him. Shock him. Do something to make him focus on you."

Harriet's eyes widened. "How?"

Darienne was beginning to like her. "Put on something

outlandishly sexy and flaunt yourself. You look like you have flesh appeal—use it! But be coy and feminine. It takes a little practice, but you can do it. Make him grovel. When men have to work and sweat to get what they want, they appreciate it more. And spell out what you expect. Some men have to be educated about sex. They think they know it all, but they're innocents, really. Take control. He'll follow like a lamb."

Harriet's mouth had dropped open in astonishment. And then they both glanced at David, realizing he was still present.

"Sorry, *cheri*," Darienne told him in the feminine, frivolous tone she saved for men. "I forgot you were here. But you already know my approach."

"Too well," David muttered. "I daresay you don't use it on Matthew."

"Matthew didn't need training," she said in a doting tone. "He was born sensitive. If all men were like him, Harriet wouldn't have a problem."

Harriet still seemed to be mulling over her advice. "I can see how that approach might work for you," Harriet said, gesturing toward Darienne in an admiring way. "You're so glamorous and worldly. But I'm just . . . me."

"A woman can be anything she wants. If you want to become a femme fatale, start thinking like one. Consider Scarlett O'Hara in *Gone With the Wind*. The author described her as not beautiful, but men seldom ever noticed."

Harriet nodded, as if she liked the notion, but couldn't believe she could acquire this skill. She turned to David, looking a little awed by Darienne's ideas.

"You may find some of what she said useful," he told Harriet in a dry tone. "She's more an expert on men than I, I suppose. But you also have to do what comes natural for you." He turned to Darienne. "Not every woman wants to be a seductress."

Darienne smiled, knowing better. But she did not openly disagree, so as not to undercut him in front of Harriet. Harriet had put her trust in him. And Darienne had to admit, Harriet could have done worse in choosing an advisor. David had a great deal of sensitivity, like Matthew, and she had always loved and appreciated him for that quality. But David was so altruistic and scholarly, she could only tolerate him for so long. Matthew, by contrast, possessed charisma and a quicksilver energy. Matthew challenged her constantly. David was like a comfortable old shoe.

Reminded that Matthew would be home from rehearsal soon, she shook hands with Harriet. "I have to go now, but I'm glad I met you. And if you want a woman's point of view regarding your husband, I'd be happy to talk to you again."

"Thank you," Harriet said, still looking a little stunned.

Darienne turned to David. "I'll see you again, soon."

"I hope so," he said as he walked to the door with her. "Give Matthew my regards. Tell him to let the understudy do matinees, so Matthew doesn't get overtaxed by the show."

"I've already suggested that," Darienne said. "I'll tell him you approve." She doubted David would approve of the rest of her suggestion to Matthew, but it didn't matter. David wouldn't know until it was too late.

Harriet watched as Darienne walked out with David to go down the spiral steps to the front door. What a stunning woman, Harriet thought—or rather, vampiress, as David had called her. So sexy and so French. She didn't think she could follow Darienne's advice, but she loved hearing it. Darienne would probably have Ralph straightened out in no time, if she had the chance. Except Ralph would never want to settle for me again, Harriet thought, growing depressed.

"What are you looking so sad about?" David asked when he came back upstairs.

"Darienne. She's so beautiful and she seems to know how to handle men. I wish I—"

"No, you don't." David settled his hands on her shoulders. "She may have had centuries to develop her skills, and it's true she can wrap most men around her finger. But she doesn't know herself well enough to get what she really needs. I think *you* do."

"*I* do?"

"You want to be loved and you're not afraid of being close to someone. In fact, you're seeking that from your husband."

"But I'm getting closer to you than to him," she said quietly, looking into his blue eyes, enjoying the feel of his hands on her shoulders. "Will you initiate me, David? Have you thought about it?"

"But I can't replace Ralph, Harriet. I can't be the loving husband you want."

"Maybe I'll never have what I want. But I could have a closer relationship with you. I want that experience," she told him emphatically. "I need something more than I have in my life. You could be like the brother I never had. Veronica can have all of you. I just want some permanent tie with you. You're the most wonderful man I ever met."

Tears filled her eyes. She stopped speaking and looked away. She hoped he wouldn't refuse, but was afraid he would.

"Like a brother," David repeated, as if pondering the notion.

"Yes." She looked up at him again. "I'd have your affection and support, but in a closer way than friends do. You said the bond doesn't have to be sexual."

David stroked his nose as if unsure. "I remembered since I saw you last that I once knew a vampire in England perhaps a hundred fifty years ago. He described a bond he had with a married woman who was connected with the royal family. He gave her support, he said, throughout an adulterous affair her husband was having, by initiating her and creating a bond with her. He said he admired her for the purity of her character and wanted to help her during a difficult time in her life. But she and the vampire never began a sexual relationship themselves. At least, he claimed they didn't. I knew this vampire to be an honorable fellow, so I had no reason not to believe him. I remember his story intrigued me at the time."

Harriet had to marvel again that David had lived so long and seen so much. "Could you do that for me?"

He stared at her for a while in his peculiar, still way. "You understand the bond is forever—until you die."

Or until *you* are cured, Harriet thought. She assumed that if he were no longer a vampire, their bond would disappear. "I understand," she told him.

"It will change you."

"That's what I'm hoping."

He smiled. "By that I mean, you'll want to be with me more than anyone else in your life. As I've told you, the bond can make a person obsessed with their vampire mentor."

Harriet thought of Veronica. "I'd love to know," she told him a bit breathlessly, "what it feels like to be obsessed."

"You shouldn't." His eyes grew troubled. "It's not a healthy state of mind."

"I don't care, David. I want to feel something strong for someone, even if it isn't natural. I need someone wonderful to support me. Everyone needs that."

"I can support you as I have been," he argued, "without initiating you."

"But it's not the same. I can only get away to see you once a week without arousing suspicion. From what Veronica described, if we had a bond, I could call on you anytime with my mind."

"Anytime after dark."

"That's good enough."

David seemed impressed with her sincerity and, by the rueful humor in his blue eyes, appeared to have run out of arguments. At last he said, "All right, Harriet. I'll initiate you."

Her heart leapt with joy. "You will? When?"

"Now, if you like."

"Oh, gosh," she said, suddenly feeling a little dizzy. "Okay." She swallowed. "What do we do?"

He eyed her closely. "Are you sure you want to go through with this?"

"Yes!"

"Then sit down with me on the love seat."

She did as he said, heart pounding. Did he mean it? Was he really going to—

"I hope your dress won't get stained," he said with concern. He seemed to be eyeing the collar of her pink cotton shirt-dress.

"S-stained?"

"This is real, Harriet, not a fantasy. I do draw blood."

"Y-yes." She unbuttoned the top two buttons of her dress and pulled the opened collar away from her throat with shaking fingers. "Will this be all right? What did Veronica do?"

David hesitated. "Veronica and I were already lovers. We were in the midst of . . . well, she had taken off her clothes."

"Oh," Harriet said, embarrassed. "I don't think I should . . ."

"No," David quickly agreed. "I think this will be fine." He reached to push her collar back even farther. "In fact, let me get you a small towel." He rose, went behind the wet bar, and came back with a clean, white linen towel. With gentle fingers, he arranged the towel over her shoulder, covering the pulled-back collar, so that her throat was exposed and the dress protected.

Harriet found her own pulse point at the side of her throat with her fingertips. "Should I dab it with some alcohol?"

He paused, looking totally puzzled. "Why?"

"To kill germs."

David shifted his eyes up to the chandelier and smiled slightly.

"Nurses always do that before they draw blood for lab tests," she explained, realizing he might not be familiar with current medical practices. "It prevents infection. Just like, if a kid comes home with a scraped knee, you put antiseptic on it."

"I see your point," David said, looking as if he was trying to be serious for her sake. "But I don't have any alcohol here, except for a bottle of port. In four hundred years, I've never known anyone I've initiated to become infected, so I don't think you need to worry."

Harriet felt a little foolish. A vampire ought to know his trade, she supposed. "Okay. Sorry."

"Don't apologize. It's a logical concern, especially for a woman who's been a mother. I'm glad you're taking such a levelheaded approach to this. I'm reassured that you aren't entering into this on a whim of passion, like most women I've dealt with—some of whom were sorry afterward because they didn't realize what they were getting into, they were acting so entirely on emotion."

"Because they were in love with you, like Veronica?"

"Yes."

"Well, I admit I'm half in love with you, or I wouldn't ask you to do this at all."

He smiled. "Half is about right, I think." His expression sobered. "I only hope it stays at that proportion afterward. You must fight becoming obsessed with me, once we have a bond."

"I will," she promised.

David nodded, as if satisfied with the seriousness of her reply. He pushed the towel and collar back from her throat

again, because the materials had crept forward a bit. Then he
began to lean toward her, tilting his head over her neck.

Harriet gasped as she felt the warmth of his breath on her
skin. I hope this isn't a sin, she thought fleetingly, envisioning
herself at church tomorrow in a dark confessional. Is this
something she'd need to ask forgiveness for? She didn't even
know.

"Relax," David said, settling his free hand gently on her
other shoulder.

Harriet realized how she'd tensed, but she calmed at the
sound of his soothing voice. When she felt his warm mouth at
her pulse point, she closed her eyes, but her eyelids fluttered
with a mixture of fear and eager anticipation, knowing what
was about to happen.

"Oh," she said softly as she felt a split second of swift, sharp
pain. But the pain gave way immediately to a warm, relaxing
delirium as she felt his mouth fasten onto her skin with sucking motions. The sensations reminded her of breast feeding.
She heard him swallow and she smiled, enjoying the idea that
she was giving him nourishment in return for the gift, the
bond, he was bestowing on her.

Soon she was aware, not only of her own calming heartbeat,
but also of another thrumming beat that seemed to give support to her own because it shared the same rhythm. The
nearness and oneness she felt with the beat began to make her
giddy. She wanted to giggle—like a young teenager sharing
secrets with her closest friend. Only the friend was male, not
female, and that created a different experience of intimacy
from what she'd ever known. Along with the euphoric feeling
of deep friendship, she felt a new, underlying well of maturity
and wisdom to draw from, a new source of life experience.
And most of all she felt a beautiful sense of reassurance, a
feeling that she was stronger because now she had a fatherlike
presence to lean on.

There was a sensual aspect, too—the flaming heat of his
mouth at her throat, the pulsing of combined heartbeats, the
solid warmth of his male nearness—but she forced herself not
to dwell on those feelings and consciously made herself focus
on the brother/father closeness, so new and comforting.

She was definitely lightheaded now, as though she were
floating in warm, balmy air, like a firefly on a summer evening.

As she felt him draw away from her neck, she objected. "No, not yet."

"It *is* pleasurable," he agreed, the liquid sensuality of his voice near her ear enriching the meaning of his words, "but I must stop before I take too much and you grow too weak." He took the towel and placed it with some pressure against her neck. Using his free hand, he picked up the lower edge of the towel and quickly blotted his mouth. He raised his head and looked into her eyes.

The startling cobalt blue of his eyes mesmerized Harriet, and she noticed he had high color in his cheeks. All at once she saw him as the most stunning, overwhelming male she'd ever seen. But despite the new intimacy with him she could now sense in the depths of her being, as though an invisible thread connected her heart to his, she reminded herself that she could not hope to experience him as her lover. That would betray Veronica, and David's love for Veronica. And it would betray Ralph, too. But already she wondered, how could she ever be satisfied living with Ralph, now that she had this intimate security, this link with David to rest in with such profound joy?

For joy is what she felt as she said, "David, I feel the bond already! Can I hug you?" She needed to feel close to him physically for a moment, because she'd begun to feel an ache the moment he took his mouth from her neck.

He enveloped her in his strong arms.

She relaxed against his shoulder, and the towel, which he'd let go of, slipped to her lap. She saw the bright bloodstains on it, knew they were her own, but didn't care.

*How do you feel?* She heard his voice, yet knew he hadn't spoken. Drawing back to look at him, she said, "How did you do that?"

"I can consciously transfer a thought to your mind now," he said. "And you can do the same. Try it."

"How?"

"Think what you want to tell me."

*I feel fine.* She looked at him but did not open her mouth.

"You feel fine," he repeated with a grin. "Good. Are you thirsty? I'd better get you some water. You need to drink liquids now, to replenish what's been lost."

As he began to get up from the couch, she instinctively took hold of his arm, not wanting him to move away from her. Gently, he unfastened her fingers gripping him. "The bond is new and you feel a strong need for my presence," he said. "But that will ease soon. I'm only going to get you a glass of water. I'll be back at your side in a moment."

Harriet nodded that she understood, but she felt the first unsettling pang of anxiety in the euphoria she'd so far been experiencing. She hadn't realized the bond would be this strong. It was more than a profound attachment to him, it was a need to be with him, near him, every second, to feel his heart next to hers, beating in unison with hers, as if they were twins that had never separated since birth.

So this was obsession. She could understand Veronica now. No wonder Veronica craved him so, having been his lover, too. Harriet immediately sensed the inherent danger—and the overpowering lure—of allowing herself even the thought of a sexual union with David.

In a moment, he was at her side on the couch, handing her a glass of water. As she drank—and she found she was indeed thirsty—David said, "I feel your anxiety. What are you thinking?"

"Don't you know?"

"I can't read your thoughts unless you consciously send them to me. I can only feel your feelings. And I know you've grown anxious."

She put down the empty glass. "I'm beginning to understand what you tried to tell me before. This bond is so profound," she said, tears of fear and deep love gathering in her eyes, "I don't know how I can go home tonight. I want to stay here with you."

He took her hand in both of his. "I know. But whenever you feel you need me after you leave here, you can call to me in your mind, and I will respond and reassure you, even if you're miles away. So we never have to be apart. Even during the day, Veronica used to tell me, she could feel my presence and it comforted her, though I was in a deep sleep."

Harriet nodded, remembering some of the things Veronica had said. "But Veronica lives alone. I'll have Ralph to contend with when I get home. And I don't even want to think about him. I want to be with you."

David squeezed her hand. "Remember, one reason you

wanted this bond was to better understand men, specifically your husband. Remember that objective."

"But I love you more than him. I think I did even before . . . this," she said, touching the place where David had drunk from her. "Now you're the only man I want to be with. How can I go home and be with Ralph?"

David's eyes grew pale, and she could feel his inner anguish and sense of guilt, a guilt she took on herself. "You loved Ralph, too, once," David said.

"Not like I do you."

"But that can change, perhaps." She could sense his doubt as he said the words.

Growing nervous and unsettled, Harriet looked at her watch. It was time to go. She began to cry, feeling helpless and bereft. "I don't want to leave you!"

"Shhh." David slipped his arms around her again and held her. "When you leave, you'll still have me near. As time goes on, this initial need for me will modify and I believe you'll find a comfortable balance. Your heart and your intentions are good. Now that my mind is connected with yours, I feel your innate goodness and sense of right and wrong. You can be strong away from me because you *are* strong. Be assured I care what happens to you. Now go home. Be patient with your husband. He cares for you, too, I imagine, though he may not show it."

"I don't know if I can wait until next week to see you."

"Then make an excuse and come to me, if you need to."

She looked at him with yearning. "Will you drink from me again?"

"Not for a long while. You must recover from the blood you've lost tonight." He lightly touched the side of her neck. "The bleeding has stopped. But the marks will be slow to heal. You'll have to find some way to conceal them. You must keep my secret, Harriet."

"I'd never betray you. I can put the collar of my dress up," she said as she buttoned the top button. She turned the collar up. "Does it show?" she asked.

"No," David said, though he still seemed concerned, as if a new thought had come to him. "What will you do when you go to bed? What if Ralph wants to make love? He might notice the marks."

Harriet stared at him, wondering why she hadn't thought of this herself. Though she still avoided sex with Ralph, she wasn't always successful. She let out a worried sigh. "I'd better start baking again."

# 10

## Let him touch you

SEVERAL NIGHTS later, about one A.M., Harriet stood
at her kitchen sink washing bowls and spoons she'd just used
for baking. It was about this time, during her late-night culi-
nary practices, when the kitchen was filled with a mouth-
watering scent, that she usually got very hungry.

But she had a new method to stick to her diet. She closed
her eyes, envisioned David, and called to him. *I'm dying to eat,*
she told him. *Help me.*

Immediately she felt his presence, as if he were near. Then
she began to feel just slightly nauseated as he transmitted to
her his vampire's aversion to food, which he'd told her he felt
at the very thought of eating. It was enough to kill Harriet's
appetite, and she sent back to him a mental *thank you.*

She had discovered he could do this for her the night after
she'd been initiated. Still longing to be with him, she'd called
to him late at night for comfort while she baked a coffee cake.
As she mentally communed with him, she again felt closer to
him than she had to any human being.

As David had promised, it *was* almost as good as being with
him at his home. They could exchange thoughts and feelings
better than if they'd known each other all their lives. In some
ways she felt as if she had a father again, this time a caring,
wise father who took time to make her feel nurtured and
appreciated, quite unlike her own father, who had spent little
time with her. And in another way, David was like a secret,
illicit lover, with whom she shared a male-female intimacy.
Though their bodies never touched, she still experienced him
as if he were within her, a psychic lover who gently penetrated
her and made her feel whole and happy.

169

Lonely as she felt the night after he'd initiated her, he'd come to her, his voice on the air molecules, caressing her ear, assuring her that he hadn't forgotten her. And when she'd felt the desire to indulge herself by tasting the warm coffee cake she'd just taken out of the oven, she'd fretted about her guilty urge. *I can help you with that,* David had told her, and transmitted to her his own distaste. In the days since, she'd lost four more pounds. David was better than any diet she'd ever tried.

After finishing at the kitchen sink, she crept soundlessly into her bedroom, where Ralph slept, took the new nightgown she'd sewn and its matching robe out of the closet, and brought them into the bathroom to change. She'd found a pattern for a sleeveless nightgown that had a high lace neckline. Harriet had bought a length of extra-wide lace and sewn it at the top as she made the garment, so that it covered the two small puncture wounds on her neck. The nightgown, which she'd made knee-length, was of soft cotton with a violet-and-leaf pattern. The longer, sleeved robe was made of the same material.

So far, she'd managed to avoid Ralph by sewing or baking well into the night. She hoped that could continue indefinitely, but if not, she could at least appease him by lifting the nightgown without unfastening the lace neck piece, thus hiding her secret. Ralph never insisted on complete nudity during sex. Whatever way was most direct was usually fine with him.

She walked out of the bathroom, dressed in her nightgown and robe, just in time to take the cookies she was baking out of the oven. Using two hot pads, she picked up the baking sheet and carried it to the counter. But as she set it down, one of the hot pads slipped, and the hot baking sheet dropped noisily onto the tiled counter. Oh, no, she thought, afraid she'd awakened Ralph.

She'd just begun putting the cookies onto wire cooling racks, when she heard Ralph's voice.

"Still up? Don't you ever come to bed at a decent hour anymore?" he said, coming up behind her, sounding sleepy and disgruntled.

"Sorry. I didn't mean to wake you up."

"I don't sleep well until you're in bed, too. I've told you that." He was scratching his chest through his blue pajamas.

She put the metal baking sheets in the sink.

"Done yet?" he asked.

"I have to wash these."

He fingered the sleeve of her robe as she worked. "This is new, isn't it?"

"I made it a few days ago."

"It's pretty."

"Thanks." She began to get nervous about his compliments.

"How about washing those in the morning and coming to bed now?" He ran his hand over her shoulder and massaged it.

She hesitated, trying to think of some way to put him off.

"C'mon Harriet. It's been over two weeks." He reached around and ran his hands over her full breasts through the nightgown material. She could feel his erection against her hip.

"Okay," she said, deciding not to argue. Perhaps it was better just to get it over with. Even her baking tactic wasn't working well anymore.

She followed him into the bedroom and turned out the lights. In the dark, she took off the robe, lay down, and pulled up her nightgown for him. Closing her eyes while he panted and thrusted, she waited till he was finished. It didn't take long.

But afterward in the dark, as she lay there while he fell off to sleep, tears streamed back from her eyes as she longed for David again. She called to him, breathing his name silently into the darkness, and as if on the wind through the open window, she heard his caring voice in her ear. *I'm here. I can feel your sadness. What happened?*

With her mind, she told him. And then she confessed how much she'd wished it had been him instead of Ralph.

The next evening, David listened intently as Harriet talked more about her husband. He wondered how he could advise her, she seemed so unhappy.

"I'm beginning to feel numb about sex now," she told him. "I want to avoid it or, if I have to do it, then get it over with. And yet I have the feeling that with another man"—she glanced at him as they sat on the couch—"it might be so different."

"But you don't want to have an affair, do you?"

"No," she said firmly. "But I wish I could."

"Did you always feel ambivalent about sex?"

"Not when I was a teenager. It was exciting. But even then, it was the idea of doing something adult and forbidden that was the exciting thing, not the physical contact so much. I never knew for sure how I was supposed to feel. I still don't."

"If you knew that, you could perhaps explain better to Ralph what you need. Have you ever—I don't mean to be indelicate—but have you ever had an orgasm?"

"On rare occasions. But even then it felt sort of out of synch with what Ralph was doing, and was less than earthshaking."

"Does Ralph notice your response?"

"I think he assumes that because he's enjoying it, I ought to be, too. To him sex is simple—and I'm making it complicated. That's his analysis of why I don't enjoy it."

David pondered this a moment. "I still think if you understood what you were missing, you'd be better able to direct him how to please you."

"How am I going to learn what I'm missing?"

He hesitated, debating with himself. Finally he said, "We could use our bond to try an exercise. I can imagine my relationship with Veronica and make you feel what I feel, the desire and sexual excitement. It won't bother you if I think of Veronica?"

"I'll feel like a mental voyeur," Harriet said, looking slightly shocked. "But then, *she* once suggested I sleep with you and report back to her, so she could experience *that* vicariously. I don't suppose she'd mind the reverse. She won't know, anyway, will she?"

"No." David drew his brows together as a new complication occurred to him. "Unless my mind unintentionally slips away from you and I connect with Veronica through my bond with her. I'm sure the temptation will be there. She's a very strong pull for me. This may be tricky."

"Just stop if things go wrong," Harriet said.

David was beginning to grow nervous. Maybe he shouldn't be doing this. He didn't want to break his pact with Veronica. Well, he'd be careful and give it a try, for Harriet's sake. "If I stop abruptly, you'll know it's because my mind has switched to Veronica. Then you must stop me from further

communion with her. Shake me or yell at me to break contact
with her."

"All right," Harriet said, sounding reluctant. "Are we
doing the right thing?"

"I don't know." David rubbed his cheek with his fingertips
in a worried manner. "Let's begin and see what happens. Take
hold of my hand," he said, reaching toward her. "That will
help keep me grounded to you while I think of her. Now close
your eyes and focus on me."

He watched Harriet follow his instructions. Holding her
hand, he tried to relax and recalled the long, lovely nights he
used to spend with Veronica on the window seat in the ballroom, their special place to make love. With some relief, he
found he was able to remember Veronica and yet keep his
mind focused on his mental connection with Harriet. As he
thought of Veronica, recalling her sweet, beautiful body,
marred only by his marks on her neck, her lustrous eyes
always yearning for him, her moist mouth ready for his kiss,
he began to grow aroused. His heart rate accelerated, his
temperature felt warmer, his breathing quickened. And within
him that long untapped electric excitement, that gnawing need
he'd pushed aside for years, soon grew to an ache. He felt the
stirrings in his groin, and then realized with some embarrassment that he was still channeling all these feelings to Harriet.

He opened his eyes and looked at her. Eyes still closed, she
was smiling slightly, her own breaths as quick and shallow as
his. Her eyebrows were contracted slightly, reflecting her own
inner ache for fulfillment. Suddenly she opened her eyes.

"You've stopped," she said, sounding abandoned. "Why?
It was so exciting. And so tender. I've never felt quite this
way." With fingers that trembled, she stroked the hand holding hers. "I wish you would touch me," she whispered.

In her dark eyes, deep and shining, he could see her un-
quenched sensuality, her ardent need. She looked rather beautiful now, he thought—eyes all filled with desire, her body's
rounded form full of pulsing femininity. Through their bond
they shared the same heightened heartbeat, and now he could
feel her body's aching desire, which he had ignited, psychically
transmitted back to him, shared like the beat of their hearts.

He lifted his hand, held by both of hers. As if at one with
his intention, her hands guided his to her breast. Her body felt

full and firm and warm. He could sense her hardening nipple through the thin material of her dress. He stroked the hidden peak with his thumb while he caressed the lower jutting contour of her breast with his hand.

She closed her eyes and gasped softly. With her free hand, she unbuttoned the top of her dress and pulled aside her collar, revealing his marks on her neck. "Drink from me again, David," she said in a needy voice. "And don't stop touching me." She brought his other hand to her other breast, which he fondled in the same way, enjoying her voluptuousness.

She tilted her head to one side and he leaned closer to her exposed neck. He kissed her skin and licked the puncture marks. He could feel her artery pulse, could almost smell her blood. Closing his eyes, he opened the wounds with his teeth and soon tasted the sweet richness of her blood. As she moaned with pleasure, he slid his hand into her unbuttoned dress, into her cleavage. His fingers played over her soft skin, delving beneath her clothing until he found her nipple. He teased and fondled it until she whispered an aching "Oh, David. Make love with me—"

And somehow the reality of her spoken need made him realize how far he'd gone. He pulled away from her throat, glad he'd come to his senses before he'd taken too much of her blood. He'd only drunk from her a week ago, and not enough time had passed for her to keep her strength. He took his hands away from her breasts.

"No." She tried to pull him close again.

"Harriet, I'm sorry. I never meant for this to happen," David said, suddenly weighted with guilt. He took out a handkerchief from his pocket, wiped his mouth, then refolded it to a clean side and pressed it against her throat.

Breathing hard, still looking a little lost in sensuality, she took hold of the handkerchief herself, and he drew his hand away. She looked down at her unbuttoned dress then. "Oh, my God," she said. "What happened?"

"That's what passion can do," he said in a rueful tone. He paused, collecting himself. "We must never do this again, Harriet."

"No," she said in agreement, and yet she looked so forlorn. "But it was so beautiful." She gazed up at him. "Could you send me these feelings while we're apart?" she asked as if with new hope.

David felt troubled. "It would leave us both frustrated, as we are now."

"Just once more?" she asked. "This is the first time in my life I've ever been so aroused and felt so sexy. I've never felt sexy. You made me feel that way, even though I'm not."

David rubbed his forehead. "Believe me, *you are.* Maybe Darienne was right when she told you to tease Ralph and make him work for sex. You've got the sensuality, in body and mind. You just need the confidence."

"You think so?"

"Yes!" he said with an ironic chuckle.

"But it was your desire for my blood, and my desire to give it, that turned us on, wasn't it?"

"Unfortunately that was part of it. But that wasn't all. It was your eyes and your lovely body that led me astray, even though I was aroused thinking of Veronica." He lowered his eyes, feeling ashamed. "God, I'm fickle."

"Maybe arousal is arousal. You know, any port in a storm?"

He looked up at her and his shoulders shook in silent laughter. As she smiled, he said, "It's been a long time since I've been with a woman. I should have known better than to test my willpower's low threshold with mental games."

"You were just trying to help me," she said, straightening her dress.

"Yes, my intentions were good anyway, if not my actions. Again, Harriet, I apologize. I feel I've broken your trust."

"Don't be sorry," she said softly, folding the bloodstained handkerchief. "I'll never regret it. You've given me the most beautiful memory I may ever have." She looked at her watch. "I'd better go. Can I keep this?"

"The handkerchief? Why?"

"A souvenir of the memory. Someday when you and Veronica are together and happy, I'll have this to remind me that I once had a few moments of bliss, too."

He looked at her with regret. "Have you given up on your husband altogether now?"

She hesitated, her eyes scanning the room, but focused inward. "Yes," she said at last. "Ralph could never give me even a speck of what I just experienced with you. I think I'll divorce him once Janet has graduated."

David felt deeply troubled. This was not at all what he'd hoped for. "But what would you do on your own?"

She shrugged. "Become a nun, maybe."

A few nights later, very late on a Saturday night, Harriet lay on her bed, wide awake and deliciously alone. Janet was at an all-night house party with a group of girls. Ralph had fallen sound asleep in his recliner after Harriet had been so considerate, he'd thought, to bring him a couple of beers while he watched the late-night movie. He'd slept all night in his recliner once before after a long Saturday, like today, when he'd mowed the lawn and worked in the backyard vegetable garden. She trusted the two beers would help him sleep extra soundly tonight.

And now she was blissfully alone, door closed, bathed in the pale light of the moon coming through the window, to commune with David. She'd longed to practice their private exercise to awaken her sensuality again, this time with the safety of distance between them. She closed her eyes and called to him, and soon she felt enveloped in his masculine, nurturing presence. *Just once more,* she asked. *Show me again what it's like to feel sensual.*

She detected some reluctance, but as if he couldn't refuse making her happy, he told her to open her mind to him and focus out all else.

And soon she felt warm and unsettled and her pulse began to accelerate. Her breathing grew labored. She felt her breasts grow sensitive to her nightgown as the rise and fall of her chest made her nipples rub lightly against the material. Her eyes grew heavy and dreamy while her mental ear heard David's low masculine voice and grew mesmerized with its sound.

*Caress yourself,* she heard him say. She slowly pulled up her nightgown until it was above her breasts. She ran her hands over her breasts, enjoying the sensation of her fingers over their round contours, over her increasingly sensitive nipples. With David's voice in her mind, she could almost feel as if it were him caressing her again with his beautiful, tender hands. She was starting to feel sexy and desirable again, the way David had made her feel before.

She writhed a bit on the cool sheets in a lazy, but restless, way, feeling a pleasurable swelling in her body's most intimate place.

*God, I feel your sensuality,* David told her, and she felt the ache within him, too.

*I wish you were here,* she told him with her mind. *I wish you could touch me and drink from me again. Oh, David. . . .*

The feminine place between her legs began to throb gently. Slowly she ran her fingers downward over her stomach, toward that exquisite point which begged to be touched.

Just as she was about to reach it, she felt another hand, a male hand, push her own hand away and then large fingertips slid into the slippery folds of tissue. The feeling was so intense and satisfying of her need, that she cried out softly and squirmed with pleasure. *David,* she thought and then wondered how he could actually be there with her. Her eyes flew open.

Ralph was kneeling beside the bed, watching her intently as he touched her. His eyes were wide and shining, almost like a child's.

"Can I play, too?" he asked, smiling yet with an uncertainty in his gaze.

Harriet sat up and pulled away from him. "What are you doing here?"

Disappointment took the light out of his eyes, but he seemed to want to keep his patience. "This is my bedroom, too. I'm *supposed* to be here at this time of night."

"I thought you were asleep in the living room."

"I guess you did. Do you always do . . . this, when I'm not nearby? Is that why you can avoid sex so easily?"

Harriet felt embarrassed. "I . . . no. I was just . . . experimenting. It's really none of your business."

Ralph nodded, the muscle at his jaw tightening for a moment. "Can I watch?" he asked in a more conciliatory tone. "What!?"

"Can I watch you? You looked so beautiful. Like a centerfold come to life."

Harriet had to laugh. "A chubby centerfold."

"No. I think you look just fine, all round and soft. Who wants to count ribs?" he said, running his hand over her rib cage.

She almost backed away again, but all at once she heard David's voice in her mind. *Let him touch you.* And suddenly she was aware that David was still with her, monitoring her feelings. All at once she was more confused than she'd ever been in her life. Here she was almost naked on a bed and dealing with two men, one beside her and one in her head. Her breathing grew unsteady, but from nervous confusion, not sensual arousal.

Ralph, however, could not know the difference. As his hand ran over her abdomen and up over one breast, he studied her reaction. "That really turns you on, huh?"

"Well . . . yes," she said, thinking, When David did it.

"I'll do that for you," Ralph offered.

"Why? You never wanted to bother with it much before."

"I didn't think it was necessary. I get turned on just looking at you. I figured, you ought to get turned on just looking at me. I didn't know . . . I mean, I never saw you like this before. You looked so sexy when I came in, writhing as you touched yourself. I didn't know you liked that so much."

"I tried to tell you."

"You did?"

"Yes! When I'd ask you to slow down. When I told you I wasn't satisfied. And you claimed it was all my problem. Well, I'm solving my problem myself!"

Ralph looked a little stricken, crestfallen. "All right. I can learn to do this. I'll be happy to, if I get this reaction."

Harriet felt a bit astonished. Was he serious? "It means you'll have to be patient and wait," she told him, remembering Darienne's advice to take the upper hand. "No consummation until *I'm* ready, until *I* say so."

"Okay." He sat there as if in suspension, eyes bright again, waiting for his next cue. He looked so cute, she almost laughed. And she began to feel something she'd never felt before, what Darienne seemed to know instinctively—power. The sexual power a woman can have over a man. This might be fun, she began to think.

*David,* she called, wanting some instant guidance. But David was no longer there. She couldn't reach him. Feeling a moment of panic, she wondered what was wrong. And then she remembered Veronica telling her that David blocked her from his mind whenever she tried to call to him. David must be blocking

Harriet now, probably wanting not to intrude while she dealt with her husband. Oh, God, it was all up to her now.

"What's wrong?" Ralph asked.

"Nothing," she told him. She put on a smile. "You . . . really want to 'help' me?"

"Yeah."

"Okay. Um, take off your clothes," she ordered.

In seconds, he was undressed. And already his arousal was blatant as he climbed onto the bed next to her. "He," she said, pointing to his most prized possession as if it were a third party, "he will have to wait a while!"

"He'll . . . try," Ralph replied, looking as if he wanted to be cooperative, but not quite sure he could be.

"Okay," she said, lying back, bringing her nightgown up above her breasts again, "g-go ahead. I'll tell you what I like."

He took hold of her breast and squeezed.

"Slow and gentle," she said, guiding his hand with hers in a motion that was similar to what David had done. "Yes," she whispered, growing calm and more relaxed as he took over the slow circular motion himself, giving her a surprisingly sweet, lulling feeling. Was this really Ralph? she thought, enjoying the slight roughness of his male skin, the large size of his hand. "This is beautiful," she told him softly.

"So are you," he said with an encouraged smile. "You're getting that dreamy look back." His eyes were shining with excitement. "What else do you want me to do?"

"Play with my nipples. Kiss them."

He did as she instructed. She'd never seen him so obedient in her life. Soon she was softly moaning with the deep electric sensation his mouth drawing on her nipple produced. His own breathing was growing heavy, and she began to feel nervous about making him wait. But somehow she knew Darienne would never let this make *her* nervous. Try to think like a femme fatale, Harriet instructed herself, remembering Darienne's advice. Make him work for it!

While he sucked at her breasts, she guided his hand slowly over her body, her stomach, her hips, her inner thighs. Soon he was moving very well on his own, and she forgot about guiding him, but merely lay back, squirming with excitement on the sheets as she enjoyed, enjoyed, enjoyed, for the first time in her life.

When that most exquisite point of her body ached to be touched, she guided his hand there. He slid his fingers into her, and she showed him the spot that craved touching the most. "Gently," she breathed. "Not rough. Ohhh, yes . . . Oh, Ralph, you're good at this," she said, closing her eyes in ecstasy as she felt hot, electric sensations quiver through her.

"Am I?" he said.

She opened her eyes and looked at him as he leaned over her. "Yes," she said with some surprise. "You've got a nice touch. I wish you'd used it years ago."

"Me, too," he said, and she saw a sheen of tears in his eyes. "You are so sexy! This is how I always hoped you'd be with me. I didn't know why you weren't. I thought all that talk about foreplay was women's lib stuff. I didn't want to believe it. Made me nervous, I guess. But it's not bad at all," he told her with a grin. "I'll be happy to do this for you anytime. For as long as I can hold out, anyway." He swallowed and glanced nervously at his very erect arousal.

"Not much longer," she told him. Indeed, his fingers were doing marvelous things that were almost bringing her to the brink. "I've never been this aroused before," she confessed. "This is like . . . ," she giggled, "well, almost like being a virgin again."

Ralph's eyes sparkled with humor and eager need. "I took that away from you once. I'll be happy to do it again. It's nice not being in the backseat of a car this time."

Harriet laughed, recalling the awkwardness of that night years ago at a drive-in theater when she'd given him what he'd wanted so much. "I'm sure glad I'm not seventeen anymore."

"Me, too. You're all woman now. And then some!"

"Ralph!" she said, chuckling at the way he was expressing himself.

"You don't believe me?"

"Well—"

"I never saw any woman in any movie or in any centerfold magazine that looked as sexy to me as you do right now. And you make me feel like I'm a great lover. I may have acted macho before, but underneath I knew you were unhappy and I didn't like to admit it to myself. But that's gone now. What a relief! And what a payoff! Soon, I hope?" He raised his eyebrows with comic helplessness.

She parted her legs and smiled at him. "Go ahead."

In the next moment he was on top of her and she closed her eyes with aching pleasure as she felt him ease into her. "Oh, gosh, you're so big," she whispered in his ear with delight. "I always did like that."

He smiled as he rose up on his elbows over her. "Now what do you want? Slow and gentle?" He began an easy back-and-forth movement.

"Oh, that's nice . . ." But it wasn't long before slow and gentle wasn't enough anymore. "Harder now," she said. "Nice, long thrusts. Oh, God . . . Oh, oh, oh . . ." His strong, rhythmic push and pull built such a tension, it almost made her crazy. She slipped her arms around him and held on tight. His powerful chest moved against hers as he panted, and she felt as if she were on a huge tidal wave of sensuality. And then all at once, her senses coalesced into a quiet moment, mysterious and eternal. She knew something was about to happen and there was no going back.

Suddenly, she cried out as sensation overtook her, and she writhed with each searing, delicious wave that rushed through her body. The jolts of ecstasy went on for several moments, and then her body quieted and she felt wondrously satiated, as she never had before. The feeling was so beautiful, it made her cry.

"What's wrong?" Ralph asked, fear in his voice, though he was still breathing hard from his own climax.

She sniffed as he held her in his arms. "I'm so happy," she said.

"Oh," he said, sounding relieved but puzzled. "This is happy?"

"Yeah," she said, wiping away her tears.

"Okay," he said, smiling. "Whatever you say. I'm happy, too."

She looked into his face. His eyes were—well, full of love. His blond hair was mussed and a bead of sweat rolled down the side of his forehead. He looked flushed and contented. Harriet thought he was handsomer than she'd ever remembered. And back in high school, she recalled, she'd thought he was the absolute *end* when it came to cute guys.

"This was nice, huh?" she said.

He laughed, apparently at her understatement. "I'd say so!"

She smiled coyly. "We'll have to do it again sometime."

"Anytime, honey."

They pulled up the covers to go to sleep. After they lay there close to each other for a few minutes in contented, peaceful silence, Harriet asked, "How come you woke up? I thought after two beers . . ."

"I don't know," Ralph said. "Suddenly I was wide awake. And I had this feeling that something was happening with you. So I got up and went to the bedroom to see if you were all right. And there you were—more than all right!"

"You had a feeling?" she said. "Like ESP?"

"Don't know."

"Have you had that happen before?"

"Years ago when you were pregnant with Janet. I was at work and somehow I knew you'd gone into labor. When your mother phoned, I knew before I picked up the receiver that that was what the call would be about."

"You never told me."

"Guess I forgot in all the excitement."

"Maybe you're psychic," she eagerly speculated.

"You know I don't believe in that stuff!"

"But it happened to you."

"Harriet, let's go to sleep before we're in another argument?"

She began to laugh, and she could feel his body shaking with laughter, too. "Good idea!" she said.

Before she fell asleep, she thought of David again. She'd felt abandoned when he'd blocked her call to him, but now she could see he'd wisely done it for her. Now her new experience with Ralph was all her own, all hers and Ralph's, and David had nothing to do with her response to her husband's love-making. And that was as it should be. Now she could truly appreciate Ralph's newfound prowess as a lover, as well as his obvious devotion to her despite their years of problems. David was still the most perfect man she'd ever met, all the more enhanced by his supernatural qualities. But Harriet wasn't a perfect woman and Ralph seemed more her speed. And David belonged to Veronica. Somehow, if Harriet could do anything about it, she would see to it that David and her cousin found a way to be happy together, as Harriet was now with Ralph.

# 11

# In a limbo of frustration

DAVID SAT in an easy chair by the window, feeling as if he were in a limbo of frustration. He felt heated, his pulse was fast, and a strategic part of his anatomy was swollen with need. He'd sensed Ralph had come in upon Harriet, so he had deliberately tuned her out of his mind, feeling her confusion in the situation. David didn't want to intrude on a husband and wife. Perhaps they could make some progress by themselves. So he'd left her with the advice to allow Ralph to touch her. Now David wondered what was happening. But he dared not channel his mind back to Harriet, for fear of intruding again. And he'd noticed that she only tried to contact him once after he broke their mental connection. Perhaps it was a sign that things were going well.

But David, unfortunately, remained alone in his home with his worked-up sexual needs. He'd conjured up memories of Veronica again in order to impart sensual feelings to Harriet. And now he wished he could go to Veronica's apartment, enter by her bedroom window while she slept, and make love with her. He could hypnotize her so that she wouldn't remember it, if he wanted to. But that wouldn't be right. Above all, he needed to treat Veronica with honesty and a pureness of heart.

But what was he to do with his increasingly frustrated sexual appetite? He used to appease his need with Darienne, but she'd been away so long. And now that she was back, all she could think of was Matthew.

Should he take a walk down Rush Street? There were plenty of attractive women there, and they were there hoping to meet men. It would be simple and convenient—a "one night stand" as they said nowadays. His need for blood was lessened because he'd drunk from Harriet so recently, so he wouldn't be so tempted to take their blood. He wouldn't even have to tell them who or what he was. Some heated, gratifying sex, and then good-bye.

But it seemed sordid and empty. He recalled Shakespeare's words, "The expense of spirit in a waste of shame is lust in action." David knew he would come home depressed afterward, however satiated he might be.

Why was he forced to live like this? If he were a mortal, he'd marry Veronica and have her beside him always. She would take away all his frustration and loneliness. But he wasn't mortal. And being a vampire, his choices were limited, both by his condition and by his sense of honor. Mesmerizing women solely for sex was not honorable. So what was there to do but live with his frustration?

David decided to take his mind off things by building a fire. It was not a particularly cool spring evening, but a fire would be nice, something to look at, something to do. He needed to work on his script, but if he did, he'd only have to contend with his vampire character's needs and frustration, which David had based, of course, on his own experience. It seemed there was no escape.

David placed logs on the fire, crushed a newspaper and stuck it in between, then struck a match and ignited the paper. He put the screen back into place in front of the fire and watched the flames take hold. There, that was done. What was there to do now? With displeasure he glanced at his script, lying on the coffee table. But then, all at once, he heard his window opening. Darienne, he thought, and rushed to the draped window.

In moments, she was climbing in, wearing a pale green dress with a short skirt and low neckline. "David," she said, smiling as he helped her in. "I thought I'd stop to see you again. Matthew was exhausted tonight from rehearsing, so I didn't stay with him long."

"I'm happy to see you," David told her with enthusiasm. "I was just telling myself I should work on my script. You've saved me!"

Darienne laughed, which made her shoulders shake and her

breasts bounce softly. The sight of her generous cleavage was enough to undo him in his present state. He took his eyes off her dress, yet couldn't help but wonder. She was devoted to Matthew now. Would she be willing—?

She always used to be. In fact, she used to come to him begging for sex. Darienne had always told David he was the only man in the world who could appease her vampire appetites, because he was a vampire, too.

"Sit down," David said, motioning her toward the love seat.

"Is something wrong?" she asked. "You seem a little nervous."

"No, uhm, no. How's Matthew? You said he was exhausted."

Darienne's beautiful face grew downcast. Her hair was fastened at the top of her head with a diamond clip, and she smoothed in a wisp of hair that had fallen loose from it. "He's got a lot on his mind—the show, and some serious choices he needs to make about his future. I think the mental strain is adding to his physical stress. But," her expression grew resolute, "I'm sure he'll make the right decision. And then everything will fall into place for him. Meanwhile, he . . . well, he wants me to visit him, but then he wants me to . . . to not stay long." She hesitated, tilting her head and averting her eyes. "There's been a change in our relationship. It's only temporary—while he's considering his future. But it's been difficult for me . . . and for him." She grew quiet, as if still thinking on the matter. David had never seen her so serious.

At the same time, David couldn't help but wonder, from what she'd just told him, if Matthew had been too tired or too distracted lately to engage with her sexually. Perhaps Darienne needed just what David needed right now. Or was he hoping that to justify his own lascivious ideas?

This was so strange, David found himself thinking. Usually it was Darienne coming up with all manner of excuses and reasons why David should have sex with her—usually she told him it was all to give *him* comfort, when really it was her own desires she wanted to quench. And now David found his own mind working in the same manipulative way. He'd always chastised her for her lack of moral values. But when push came to shove, his weren't much better, were they?

"I'm sorry things aren't going well," he said. "But in long relationships, problems inevitably develop. You've never been in one before, have you?"

"No. Except with you, of course. But that's different." Her expression grew amiable. "How's Harriet? I enjoyed meeting her the other night."

David hesitated over what to say. "At this very moment, I don't know. I had my mind tuned to hers and we were communing. But then I had to leave her. Even block her."

"Why?"

"Because her husband had come in on her unexpectedly."

"Oh. You felt he might suspect something, that was why you blocked her?"

David chuckled self-consciously. "It's all rather complicated." He explained how he'd conveyed sexual feelings to Harriet, so she'd understand what she was missing. Darienne listened with rapt attention, sex being her area of expertise. David finished by explaining what was going on just as Ralph apparently came in on Harriet, throwing her into confusion.

"I told her, *Let him touch you,* and then I cut communication with her. I hope I did the right thing."

Darienne sat in fascination, pondering for a moment. "I suppose you did. Though I wonder what's happened to poor Harriet. Her husband seemed so insensitive. Should you check?"

"Now?"

"Don't call to her, but just tune in on her, to see how she seems."

David glanced at his watch. "Well, it was over an hour ago. I suppose I could check." He concentrated and soon was in touch with Harriet's mind. And instantly he could tell how she was. "She's asleep," he said with some surprise. "Peacefully, I think. In fact, I feel a definite sense of wholeness with her."

"Whatever happened, she must be all right then," Darienne said. "I'll bet she followed my advice, got him to do right by her, and now she's blissfully exhausted."

David gave her a knowing look. "You would like to think it was *your* advice rather than my influence that made the difference."

"I'll gladly defer to your knowledge of literature, history, art, or civilization. But in matters of physical pleasure and sensual relationships, *cheri,* I do know more than you."

"Except when it comes to Matthew."

Her blond eyebrow quivered. "Yes, Matthew, perhaps, is my Achilles' heel. I fell in love with him. That's the problem."

"Love always presents a problem for our kind." He took Darienne's hand. "You said your relationship has changed and that Matthew hasn't wanted you to stay long lately. Does that mean you haven't been . . . intimate with him for a while?"

Darienne's mouth trembled and then tightened. "No, he hasn't wanted to couple with me for . . . for several days now. It's because he's deep in thought about something. I can't tell you what. Let's say it has to do with his career."

"Don't tell me then. I don't want you to divulge personal things," David said, nevertheless wondering what could be troubling Matthew. Perhaps it concerned Matthew's health again and his ability to do the show. Well, it was Matthew's business and David had no right to speculate. However, Darienne seemed to be hurting, and David decided he could legitimately make that his business. In the past, Darienne always made David's problems her concern—for reasons that suited her.

"I imagine you miss your intimacy with him."

"I do," Darienne said with a sigh, looking downcast. "He's like no other man."

David grew a bit downcast himself with that assessment. He pressed his fingers over hers. "Darienne, I know I'm not Matthew. But you used to enjoy sex with me. If you think I could help in that regard . . ." God, listen to me, he thought. Why not at least be honest about it?

When she looked up with slightly startled eyes, he said, "Look, the fact is, I could use a little recreation myself. All that conjuring of sensual feelings to demonstrate to Harriet has left me frustrated." His eyes dropped to her sumptuous cleavage. "And you look awfully delectable in that dress."

Darienne smiled and lifted her fingertips to one breast. "I wish Matthew had thought I looked delectable. He was so preoccupied, he didn't even seem tempted. I'm not sure he even noticed."

David insinuated his own hand beneath her fingers to caress

the softness beneath. "*I* could appreciate you tonight. I know you love Matthew. And you know I love Veronica. But, since neither of us can have the one we want at the moment—"

Darienne had closed her eyes as she pressed his hand between her breasts. "I think I'd like that, David," she whispered. She opened her eyes and looked at him with a brightening gaze. "It's been so long—years since we've coupled. I remember how good it was." She smiled and glanced at the thick Oriental rug. "On the Aubusson in front of the fire—as we used to!"

"All right," David said. He hesitated half a moment, but then leaned in to kiss her. Her mouth felt warm and eagerly clung to his. He slid his mouth across her cheek and down her chin and throat in a series of kisses while she reached up to take the clip out of her hair. As she raised her arms, her breasts lifted and plumped, and he pressed his mouth into her cushiony flesh. His mouth grew hot, and his hands began to tremble as they slid around her to unzip her dress. The ache in his loins became a throb.

"David," she said with a little laugh as he pushed down her dress and bra and licked her inviting, peaked nipple. The smooth, supple lushness of her soft flesh tantalized him, and he felt the vampire urge to bite. Cupping her large breast with his hand, he bit into the softness, his sharp teeth purposely drawing blood. Darienne squealed with exotic pleasure and urged him closer with her hands. The smell of blood alerted all his senses, and soon he was breathing hard with desire.

"Yes, David! Let me feel your teeth again. Again! It's been so long . . ." She took hold of his shirt and tore it open, sinking her teeth into his shoulder.

The pain mixed with intense pleasure made him cry out. "Damn it, I need you!"

"Hurry," she said, rising to pull off her clothes. David did the same. He pushed the coffee table out of the way. They fell together onto the plush Aubusson, the fire giving their skin a golden glow while red rivulets of blood from their bite marks trickled over their flesh.

Lying on her back, she wrapped her strong, long legs around him. Quickly she captured his hardness within her heated body. He immediately began urgent thrusts. Often in the past she had liked to be on top, but she seemed content to let him have the dominant position now. He kissed her again on the mouth, brutally, his sharp teeth drawing blood, which they both relished in flavor and feel. He bit into her shoulder then, all the while thrusting so hard he felt as if he could go through her.

She cried out with each lunge. "More! Harder! Harder!" and then, "How I've missed this! I'd forgotten . . ." she said in a swoon of ecstasy, her voice like heated honey. She began crying and laughing all at once, gasping for breath as she kept up with him thrust for thrust. David felt her dig her fingers into his hair, then run her nails down his back into his skin. She slid her hands down to his buttocks to make him push even harder.

David felt drunk with the pleasure of it, his long-repressed vampire lust for sex and the drawing of blood satiated in the rough, carnal coupling only a female vampire could give him. "Darienne," he breathed, sweating from exertion, running his mouth along her chin as she arched her head back. He knew by her frenzied gasps and the upward curving of her chest and neck that she was nearing climax. He rose up over her, resting on his elbows, and pushed against her with one, then another, savage thrust that would have injured any mortal woman. But they enraptured Darienne, who screamed with joy until her body shook with deep spasms of satiation. David felt himself explode with his own release while they rolled together on the rug.

They relaxed in temporary exhaustion, then drew apart. David smiled at her. "I needed that!"

Darienne's eyes were bright with their green, vampiric glow. "How could I have forgotten what it's like with you?" She ran her fingers through his hair, pushing it back from his perspiring face. "No one in the world satisfies me the way you can. Let me stay? Let's do this all night, the way we used to?"

He grinned, glancing down at her breasts, swollen from passion, streaked with blood from puncture marks already healing. Grabbing a handful of her long hair, he drew her beautiful, eager face close to his and looked into her smiling eyes. "You always did like orgies."

"Private ones, *cheri*. With you. You liked them, too, though you never wanted to admit it."

"I admit it now. Does that make you happy?"

"Yes," she said, leaning up to bite his lip. Immediately it reignited the spark of lust between them. "You always made me *so* happy this way."

She began to breathe deeply again in his arms, eyes aglow with erotic aggressiveness. She pressed her breasts against his chest and slid her smooth thigh over his hip. He could feel her body pulsing with impatient desire again.

Roughly, he pulled her to him, eager to enjoy her once more.

Hours later, as the night wore on toward dawn, Darienne violently writhed with David on the plush carpet as they headed toward yet another climax, each more frenzied than the one before. But while she held David in her arms, her body overwhelmed with dazzling sensations, a part of her mind drifted to Matthew. And wonderful as David was, she couldn't help but wish it were Matthew inside her and holding her, crying out with her, enjoying these moments of superhuman ecstasy.

But Matthew was still mortal and did not have the strength to savagely pleasure her the way David could. Now as she felt herself being drawn back up to that high, suspended plane of bliss by David's vampire thrusts and bites, she realized more and more how she needed this from Matthew. She must make Matthew an immortal, too, so she and he could enjoy coupling this way. If this was extraordinarily wonderful with David, how incredible, how deliriously rich and fulfilling an experience it would be with Matthew. Somehow she must convince him that letting her make him a vampire was the right, the only, choice for him.

He'd continued to seem so doubtful. When she answered one question, he came up with another. And while he remained doubtful, he also seemed to avoid sex with her, as if he feared it would cloud his thinking. She hadn't anticipated it would take him so long to make up his mind. If only he knew what he was missing by remaining a mortal. Somehow she must try to convey to him what sex as a vampire would be like for him, and for her.

The more she thought of Matthew, the more she imagined now in her mind that David was Matthew. And as his beautiful, manly body moved over hers, his engorged masculinity thrusting deep inside her, she clung to him, almost sobbing with the pleasure of it, thinking Matthew, Matthew, oh, I need this to be you with me. I need it to be you giving me this.

They rolled over until she was on top, astride him, making his hardness push into her more forcefully. She leaned over him, closing her eyes, crying out with joy as she felt him bite her breasts, pendulous between them. "Again, do that again. Oh! Press down on me," she said and then felt his hands grip her buttocks, as she had done to him, to make their thrusts more powerful. "Yes!" she cried out with frenzied pleasure. "Harder. Harder, Matthew." Her face contorted in anguish when she felt him stop for a moment. "Oh, God, don't stop! Please— Yes. Oh, yes! Oh, Matthew!" She lay down on top of him, holding him, kissing his neck, then biting, murmuring, "Matthew, Matthew, I need this from you."

She moaned and breathed his name as he rolled over with her so that he was on top. And then she clung to him, gripping him so tightly she felt she and he were one being, as her body climbed to that peak where she experienced that special moment of weightlessness and soaring bliss. And then her body burst into life, her muscles shuddering and contracting as a huge, deep vibration of pleasure convulsed her.

And while she clung to him, lost in Matthew's embrace, experiencing his manly sensuality, she whispered to him even as her body continued to orgasm, "Matthew, you must become a vampire," while she kissed the side of his face. "Let me make you a vampire so we can have this pleasure always—"

Her eyes fluttered open as she suddenly remembered, and indeed saw, it was David she was with. He'd drawn away a bit and was looking down at her with sharp blue eyes.

"Make Matthew a vampire?"

"I forgot. I'm sorry, David. I'm so used to Matthew, I began to imagine it was him instead of you. I'm sorry."

"All right. I understand. But what do you mean, make him a vampire? You haven't offered to—"

Darienne stared at him in confusion, pinned beneath him as she was. "What if I have? It's the only way he'll survive. He's exhausted, yet he's driven to play Sir Percy. I explained to him that if he were a vampire, he could play that role forever if he wanted."

David's face grew stern and he moved off of her. "But you're offering a desperate man the option of becoming a vampire as a way to solve his problems. That's taking unfair advantage. You want him to become a vampire for the sex he could give you. And so you could be with him forever."

"What's wrong with that?" she asked, sitting up.

"You're being selfish. You're not thinking of him first." He looked at her as if struck by a thought. "That's the choice about his future you were referring to earlier. And that's why he's been avoiding you. He knows you're trying to influence him!"

"I don't see why you have to be so righteous about it all," she said angrily, finding her hair clip to pin up her hair again.

"Choosing whether or not to become immortal is a huge decision with endless ramifications," he told her in a lecturing tone she didn't like. "I gave Veronica ten years to think it over, and even that's not enough. You look upon becoming a vampire as if it were a walk in the park on a Sunday. If you truly love Matthew, you should want him to choose what's right for *him.*"

Pompous sermonizer, Darienne thought. With tight silence she got up and went to the wet bar. She found a towel in a cupboard, turned on the faucet in the small sink, and began wiping the dried blood off her body.

David followed her, watching from the other side of the bar. "I know how much you love him," he said in a gentler tone. "I know you need him. Love and need can be painful things, especially for creatures like us. I love Veronica and I need her desperately, but I want above all to do what's right by her. If she decides, when our separation is over, that she wants to become a vampiress, then at least I can feel that it's a decision she's reached completely on her own after long years of consideration."

"Veronica loves you, and she'll choose you however long you make her wait," Darienne said, wiping her abdomen with the wet cloth. "But Matthew *doesn't* love me. Still, I want him!" She stopped and glared at David. "And I'll do whatever I can to convince him he should become one of us. I know him better than you, and I know he'll be happy once he's immortal. Matthew says he loves the feeling of power he has onstage playing Sir Percy. Well, I can give him that power for real and for eternity. I don't see any reason why I shouldn't urge him to take what I can give him. It's what he wants so much, he's destroying his mortal body to experience it for a few hours on a stage each night."

"But he doesn't know what being a *real* vampire is like!" David said, slamming his bloodied fist onto the wood bar. "And I don't think you would explain it to him in realistic terms."

"I've explained everything."

"Oh, I imagine you have. But you could make a tarantula sound like a funny, fluffy bug! You're clever about putting things in a way that makes people do what you want them to do."

*"You* asked me for sex tonight," she said, feeling defensive, wondering if he was now accusing her of seducing him.

David quirked his eyebrows. "I know I did! Don't change the subject. You musn't weave your glittering web around Matthew and lead him into a mode of existence he may regret for eternity. He'll never love you if he hates you for what you've made him."

Darienne felt hot tears sting her eyes and blur her vision. She threw the towel into the sink and walked to the love seat to put on her clothes. David followed.

"Listen to me, Darienne. This is the man, the one man, you've ever loved. You must do for him what's just."

"And what's that?" she said, venom in her tone as she zipped up her dress.

"Give him a decade alone to think about it, as I'm doing for Veronica."

"And during that time he'd kill himself trying to be a vampire onstage! I can give him what I know he wants *now*. And I intend to do that! Besides," she said, pointing at David, "what he does or what I do is none of your business."

As she turned toward the window to leave, David rushed across the room to detain her. "Darienne, you must be fair to him."

"I feel I am being fair. But I need to be fair to me, too. I want him, I need him, and I'll have him! I'm very grateful you asked me for sex tonight, David. It reminded me what I could have with Matthew. He keeps me in his life because he loves to go to bed with me. When I tell him in vivid detail how much more he'll love sex with me after I transform him, I think it just may be what he needs to be convinced. Thank you for showing me the way!" she said with spite. She turned toward the window and began to climb out.

"Darienne!"

"Good night, *cheri!*"

She dropped three floors to the ground, landing on her feet. It was nearing dawn and she needed to go home now. But tomorrow night she'd tell Matthew all she could about the glory of lovemaking between vampires.

When he arose from his coffin the next evening, David thought about Darienne's intentions toward Matthew. He felt he ought to warn the actor and contemplated trying to phone him at the theater, where he might still be rehearsing. But then David reconsidered, wondering if he should interfere to that extent. Darienne would never forgive him if he did. On the other hand, was David morally correct to look the other way while a mortal man was being seduced into a damned eternity by an amoral and clever vampiress?

David worried and fretted over the question all night, wondering if Darienne was with Matthew now, plying him like Scheherazade with sensually seductive tales of what sex could be like if only he'd let her transform him. Matthew appeared to have a deep sense of his own sensuality, judging by his stage performances. And he apparently was already hugely entranced with Darienne because of her evocative erotic nature. Could he resist the promise of passion with her beyond the mortal realm? When David returned to his coffin at dawn, he was plagued with guilt that he'd done nothing to warn the actor.

The next evening, just after he came up from his basement at dusk, the phone rang. David was surprised to find Matthew on the line.

"Merle gave me your number," Matthew explained in a hushed tone, as if he didn't want to be overheard. "I told him it was important."

"I'm so glad to hear from you."

"I'm calling from the theater. Rehearsal's just ending. Can I meet you somewhere? I need to talk to you. And I don't want Darienne to know."

"I think I understand. Would you like to come to my home?"

"No. We've got to meet at a place where she'd never think to look for me, where she'd never expect to find either of us. When she doesn't see me at my hotel, she may look for me, or decide to visit you."

David was surprised at the precaution Matthew was taking, but understood exactly what he was saying. "Where have you never been in Chicago?"

"Top of the Sears Tower?"

The idea of rushing up to the top of the world's tallest building in one of those modern elevators made David's head swim. "How about something at ground level? Oak Street Beach? No, that won't do," David said, thinking again. "Darienne and I used to go there for walks."

"What about that big fountain in Grant Park? I've seen it from Michigan Avenue."

"Buckingham Fountain."

"Right. I can get there in, say, half an hour."

"I'll catch a cab and be there." David hung up and rushed out of the house, relieved and anxious to have this chance to talk to Matthew.

David arrived at the fountain, surrounded by a pool, set in a garden, which looked very much like fountains he'd seen at Versailles, only larger. He began to walk around the fountain and soon found Matthew sitting on the low concrete wall that basined the pool. Matthew looked up and smiled as David sat down beside him. They shook hands.

The famed actor wore jeans and a simple blue shirt, looking not at all like a sought-after stage star, though it was said that women in Chicago were all a-twitter over the rumor that Matthew was back in town rehearsing. But despite the confidence and quiet, coiled energy David had always sensed in Matthew, David couldn't help but notice, even in the dim light, that the lines about the actor's eyes had deepened, he looked gaunt, and he seemed fatigued.

"Thanks for meeting me," Matthew said. "Darienne told me . . . about you."

David understood that to mean she had told Matthew he was a vampire. "I wondered if she had. When she visited me two nights ago she let it slip that she'd offered to make you one of our kind. I've been concerned about you ever since."

A hint of alarm flitted across Matthew's eyes. "Concerned?"

"It's a monstrous decision for anyone to make. I assume that's why you want to talk to me. To get my point of view on the matter?"

Matthew nodded. "Darienne makes it sound like the perfect solution for me. But I have some doubts that she has trouble answering."

"I wondered if Darienne had painted you a true picture of what you would become. What has she told you?"

"That I would be powerful, strong, ageless. I could be like Sir Percy, she says. He's a character I've grown to admire."

"And what is it about Sir Percy you admire?"

"His nobility. His self-sacrifice and his love for humanity. They're qualities I also sensed in you, though I never got to know you well."

David felt unworthy of Matthew's praise. "I don't know how you can say that."

"I've observed it in your manner whenever I've met you. And you wrote those qualities into the lyrics of the songs Sir Percy sings."

"But it's *your* sensitivity that brought those qualities to life in the character. You already have those traits, Matthew. You don't need to become a vampire to acquire them."

"I *don't* have those traits," Matthew argued with some impatience, as if he'd been told that before. "My personal life is a shambles. But when I'm playing Sir Percy, I become more than I am. The only way I feel truly happy anymore is when I'm playing him."

David shifted his position and scratched his temple. "How do you feel when you play him?"

"Powerful," Matthew replied in a hushed, yet resonant voice. "Sometimes it gets a little frightening. I even begin to *feel* superhuman. When I put Marguerite under my spell, I feel that authority and the lust to take from her and overpower her. I almost feel possessed and I love it, thrive on it!" He gave David a sharp glance. "What do you think that means? Am I connecting so much with the character that I lose touch with reality? Am I losing my own personality?"

David lowered his eyes, feeling acutely guilty. He tugged on his pants leg to loosen the material as he considered how to answer. "Matthew, do you remember long ago when you first began to rehearse for the role? I was there one evening, trying to convey to you what I felt Sir Percy should be like. You seemed to connect with him immediately and beautifully in almost all respects from the very first. You gave him more depth and color than even I could imagine. But," he glanced at Matthew to see his expression, "you had a bit of trouble relating to the vampire lust for blood, the feeling of superhuman power. I spoke to you about it. Do you remember?"

"Yes," the actor replied, seeming to marvel at the memory. "I didn't know then you were speaking from experience. I just thought you had a vivid imagination and a brilliant way of expressing yourself, of conveying feelings."

"It was more than words, Matthew. I looked in your eyes and . . . and hypnotized you." David looked down, rubbing his hands together slowly as he spoke. "Vampires have that power, you see. At least a male vampire can read men's minds and plant thoughts there. We can even make a person forget. But it only works with someone of the same sex. I don't have any control over women's minds, for example. Unless, of course, I've initiated the woman."

Matthew looked confused. "So what are you saying? You hypnotized me . . . for what? Why?"

"I transferred my own feeling of power and bloodlust to you, so you could feel it yourself and draw upon it as you performed. I did the same thing for Sam Taglia, when he was rehearsing *Street Shadows*. He never knew, either. But it enabled him to give a more stunning performance, because he truly felt how a vampire feels when he was in character. And it worked the same way for you. Though, other than that, your accomplishment in the role was entirely your own. I merely enhanced your darker side. And I suspect that's why, when you play Sir Percy, you feel so strongly that vampire power and bloodlust. I didn't realize then that it would enrapture you this way, so that you craved it. I'm sorry now. I can remove the feeling from your experience—make you forget it, if you wish."

Matthew stared at him, eyes round and stunned. "And you did that by looking into my eyes. L-like you are now?"

"Yes, but I'm not doing anything at this moment. I'll make you forget it, if you like," David said, repeating the offer, hoping Matthew would agree. "I hypnotized you without your knowledge or consent, and that was wrong of me. At the time, I felt it was a harmless way to get a better performance. I didn't realize it could affect your life the way it has. Let me make you forget—"

"No!" Matthew said, turning his head to break eye contact. "I . . . I'm not sure what I want yet."

"All right. I assure you I won't do anything mental to you without your consent. Please," David said with regret, seeing Matthew tensing, "don't be nervous around me. You're sensible to be afraid of my powers, but don't be. I'm trying to be as honest with you as I can. I've even admitted what I did to you in the past, so you'd understand and believe me. I want you to have a clear understanding of everything."

Matthew looked at him again, with eyes that were a bit hard. "I have no choice but to trust you. You and Darienne are the only two who can give me any information about this. But I believe you. I'd like to believe Darienne, too, but . . ." Matthew didn't finish the sentence, shaking his head instead.

"Darienne paints pictures in colors that suit her."

Matthew smiled in an ironic way. "I've noticed that. She's so anxious to transform me, it makes me uneasy. Not that the idea of becoming . . . one of you wouldn't make me uneasy anyway." Matthew glanced at pedestrians nearby, as if worried they would overhear.

"Would you like to walk?" David asked.

"That's a good idea."

They rose and began strolling around the large pond that surrounded the circular fountain. The water played in illuminating lights, looking like streamers of jewels in the dark night air. In the distance Chicago's tallest skyscrapers stood silently, like majestic guardians of the city.

"Does my explanation of why you have that feeling of vampire power onstage help you clarify anything in your mind?"

Matthew brushed his fingers roughly through his hair above his ear. "I don't know. I think so. Yes, I understand now that I wasn't going crazy when I felt that. But there are other things about the character, things that I felt after I quit playing him."

"What?"

"I remember telling Darienne in Switzerland that I thought of Sir Percy as a spirit hovering by me, like a friend waiting for me, that he was still with me even though I'd forsaken him. Did you hypnotize that into my mind, too?"

"No," David said, puzzled by what Matthew had described. "I don't quite understand what you mean."

"I felt like I'd left a part of myself on the stage in Australia. And yet that part, that alter-ego you might call him, was still near, like an invisible friendly ghost beckoning to me."

David rubbed the side of his forefinger over his lip as he thought through what Matthew was saying. "Then that must be your own personality."

Matthew turned his head. "Huh? What do you mean?"

"You said you felt as if you'd left a part of yourself onstage. You also said you think of your personal life as a failure. Yet the qualities you drew from to create Sir Percy—love, self-sacrifice, and sensitivity to others—must be buried within you. Perhaps you'd never tapped into them much in real life. But onstage, you found them. And when you left the role, you left those qualities you'd discovered in yourself behind, too, instead of taking them with you. You didn't leave Sir Percy behind so much as you left that newly discovered, untapped side of your own self—the part of your personality you buried, perhaps, to get ahead in a very competitive career. What you admire in Sir Percy is what you have within you. It's just as I told you when we began this conversation."

"Darienne has said that, too," Matthew murmured, sounding doubtful. "I didn't believe her."

"Darienne has a certain insight about people that's usually accurate," David admitted. "But you must be careful she doesn't use that insight to her own advantage."

They walked along a concrete path in a northerly direction away from the fountain, continuing through the huge city park toward the Art Institute. Matthew was silent for a long while, eyes on the walkway, hands in his pockets.

Finally David said, "What do you think about what we've discussed?"

Matthew rubbed his face and shrugged. "What the hell am I supposed to think? I'm more confused now than ever."

David hoped to help him straighten out his thoughts. "The main thing, if I understand correctly, is you need to decide whether or not to take Darienne up on her offer. Correct?"

"Right."

"How do you feel about the idea of becoming what I am?"

"Scared, but fascinated," Matthew said, smiling just slightly.

"That sounds normal. What fascinates you?"

"Having the power. Living forever."

"And what scares you?"

"The . . . having to live on blood. Never seeing daylight again. And," Matthew gave a hard chuckle, "living forever." He looked at David. "What's it like? Darienne thinks it's wonderful, but I'm not so sure you do, or you wouldn't have made Sir Percy such an anguished character."

"Darienne and I do have different perspectives," David told him. "I hate what I am. I loathe myself for choosing this. Did Darienne tell you how and why I became what I am?"

"Yes. I had to admire your reasons."

"Wanting to protect Shakespeare's works may have been an honorable reason, but what I've become is not honorable. I feel like a leech living off the blood of other humans. Even using blood from blood banks doesn't ease my conscience much. I might be taking blood that could save a life in a hospital. And the lust, the constant, never-ending craving to drink from a human! Blood tastes so much richer, like a strange, narcotic, crimson elixir, when it flows directly from a human vein. Once you become a vampire, the first thing you notice about every person you meet is their throat. Your eyes strain to find the subtle pulsing of their carotid artery, and when you find it, you have to force yourself not to become fixated on it. It's degrading to look upon others as a possible feast."

Matthew swallowed, looking as if he were slightly nauseated.

David decided to go on, seizing what seemed to be the opportunity to convince Matthew. "And spending your days in a coffin is not much fun either. You'll never see the sun again, because it would kill you the instant a ray touched your skin. So you must live in fear of dawn, and see the sun only through the moon's reflected light," he said, glancing at the half-moon above them. "You must keep your manner of living and your true nature secret from all but perhaps one or two mortals whom you trust. I've gone for decades with only Darienne as a confidant. There are always those who believe we exist, but look upon us as evil, and in their self-righteous notion of cleansing the world, they will seek to destroy us if our secret is suspected. So as a vampire, you must always be vigilant about keeping your secret and trust almost no one. To live like this certainly is not a way to make friends or have intimate relationships. Mine is the loneliest existence I can imagine."

Matthew nodded, looking very grave as he listened. "What about—you know, heaven and hell? Darienne couldn't answer my questions about that."

"I'm afraid I don't know much more about it than she, though I've thought a great deal more about it. Darienne prefers to be a happily oblivious agnostic."

"But what happens to the soul?"

"As a vampire? I believe we still carry our souls with us. We can't pass on to heaven, or hell if it exists, because we haven't died in the normal way. We're dead, but still here on earth. But—and this is what I believe to be the most crucial thing—if one *chooses* to become a vampire as I did, and as you are contemplating, I believe we commit the sin of pride—the sin Lucifer committed, of wanting to be like God. Consider that if you become a vampire, you have power over life and death. And you have immortality. Is this not becoming like God? And that is a sin I feel God would never forgive. Though I don't know for sure. But I'm afraid to find out. So I'm stuck here on earth forever, roaming this lonely planet, feeling acute guilt over what I've chosen to be, and even more guilt if I fall in love with a mortal woman—because when I do, I automatically involve her in my dark world, too."

David felt his throat closing with tears and paused to regain his composure. "But then," he said, "perhaps you aren't religious, and perhaps you're not worried about feeling lonely because you assume you'd have Darienne as a companion. You would have me as a friend, too." David smiled sadly. "For that reason I'd almost be tempted to talk you into it. I'd like you as a friend. But as a true friend, I absolutely cannot recommend this way of existing to you. And I hope to God that you'll choose not to become what I am."

Matthew appeared moved by David's heartfelt words, his eyes intense and moist. He seemed at a loss to say anything for a moment, looking at the trees they were passing by, dimly lit by the city lights and the moon. "I don't know what I think about religion," he said eventually. "I was brought up on it, coming from the Bible Belt. But I've fallen away from it, just never have time to think about it or study it anymore. But the idea of being alienated from God for eternity shakes me to the bones, I have to admit. And there's no going back?"

"No way I know."

"I'm grateful to you for telling me all this. You do paint a different portrait than Darienne does. The idea of becoming like Sir Percy doesn't seem quite so appealing anymore."

"You already have within you what you admired about his character," David repeated emphatically, wanting to convince him completely. "You can draw on that without becoming the lonely, godforsaken night creature that he is and I am. There's a romantic tragedy about alienated beings who are different. That's why movies and musicals about them are enduring and successful—*Beauty and the Beast, The Phantom of the Opera, The Scarlet Shadow.* It's one thing to spend a couple of hours identifying with and feeling the creature's sadness. It allows mortals to work out their own hidden neuroses, I suppose. But to live the life of one, if you can call it a life, is something altogether different. It's sordid and loathsome, dirty and often obscene. Develop yourself as you are. Becoming what I am won't solve anything for you."

Matthew nodded. "I think I'm convinced," he said in a quiet voice. But he paused then, as if a new thought had come to him, and glanced at David. "What about . . . Darienne has been telling me about sex between vampires. Is it true? Is it so out of this world?"

"The lust for sex becomes more acute, akin to our lust for blood. And because of our superior strength and stamina, we can reach greater heights than two mortals can, or even that heightened experience a mortal can reach when with a vampire. I expect you know what I mean."

Matthew nodded. "Darienne keeps saying that if I'm transformed, sex with her will be even better than it is now. I have to admit that intrigues me."

"I imagine it does," David said dryly. "Did she tell you about the biting?"

"Biting?"

"Along with the normal urges, we have the need to bite, to draw blood. The wounds heal fast. I imagine Darienne has told you that our bodies recover quickly from any damage. But can you envision a sexual encounter with two humans ramming each other with dreadful, bone-jarring power, biting each other to feel their fangs sink into flesh, to see and lick the blood, going on like this hour after hour because it takes so much to satiate their heightened needs? Once you are a vampire, yes, it's a powerful experience. But do you want to become a creature who has the unending lust to copulate in such a fashion? And if you wish to make love with a mortal, God, you have to be so careful not to hurt them. So it requires holding yourself back, which is not easy. Every now and then you have to find yourself another vampire just to get the lust for savage sex satiated for a while. Believe me, it's better never to have such a lust, because then you don't have to appease it."

Matthew was studying David intently. "Do you and Darienne . . . ?"

"Yes," David did not hesitate to tell him. He might as well know the whole truth. "Two nights ago, in fact. I imagine it may have prompted her to twist your arm even harder. You might be relieved to know that while we were at it, she began to imagine she was with you. She cares for you a great deal. But do you want to have sex with her as I've just described? It's what *she* wants, believe me."

Matthew's eyes seemed to fill with revulsion. "No, I can't imagine myself . . . doing that. I can't imagine her . . ."

"She craves it, Matthew. It's why she's always come back to me periodically over the centuries we've known each other. In most other ways I bore her. But she needs me for the sex. She doesn't have access to any other male vampire, and mortal men aren't enough for her. That's why she wants you to become a vampire. So you can take my place. She prefers you. You should be flattered."

Matthew looked nervous again. "What'll I do about her?"

David took a long breath and exhaled. "I don't know. You understand your relationship with her better than I. In some ways you may know her better than I. Be firm with her. If you decide to reject her offer, don't let her feminine wiles—and doesn't she have them!—dissuade you."

"You don't think she might . . . you know, transform me by force? She's demonstrated her superior strength. I imagine if she wanted to, I wouldn't have the muscle power to stop her."

David puckered his forehead as he considered this question. It came as a surprise. "I don't think Darienne would ever resort to force. It wouldn't be like her. She's a bit amoral, but she's not totally lacking a sense of ethics. I think you need to worry more about your attraction to her obvious charms fogging your logic. Because the moment you weaken, she'll take advantage and urge you into it in that cooing way of hers. And before you know it, you'll die and arise a vampire."

Even in the dim light of the evening, David could see Matthew's face grow pale. "I know exactly what you mean."

"Have I convinced you then to remain a mortal?" David asked with hope.

"You've certainly provided a far more realistic description than Darienne did. I'm probably ninety-five percent convinced. But there's still that five percent that fascinates." He looked at David with some admiration. "And if I wound up as a vampire like *you,* it's hard to see that that would be so bad, despite what you say. Your deep sense of humanity probably developed because you've lived so long and learned so much. Think what a great actor I could be if I had centuries to observe people and seek out new experiences. I could perfect my singing voice, too."

David's shoulders slumped. "Don't do it for that, Matthew. Please don't. It's not worth it . . ."

Matthew seemed to listen intently as David continued for yet another quarter of an hour trying to discourage him. But the quiet, charismatic actor said nothing more.

# 12

# An old shoe box, slightly smashed

"THIS IS it," Harriet said, showing Veronica the brown wrapped package she'd received that morning in the mail from Czechoslovakia. She'd called Veronica, who took the afternoon off from work to drive to Berwyn. Harriet had decided to wait until Veronica arrived, so they could open it together.

A few weeks ago they had written a letter to Aunt Maria, their aged relative who lived near the Bohemian Forest, asking for the recipe to cure a vampire. Anna had translated their letter for them, thinking it was all something of a joke, the silly curiosity of her granddaughters. But she liked the idea that they were taking an interest in corresponding with one of their distant relatives in the old country.

"Gosh, we just asked for the recipe," Veronica said, turning over the oblong package, held together with tape and string. "Did she send the ingredients, too?"

"Let's open it and see," Harriet said, taking it from her.

She got a pair of scissors out of a drawer beneath her sink counter, set the package on her kitchen table, and began carefully to cut the string and brown paper. Underneath she found what appeared to be an old shoe box, slightly smashed at the corners on its way from overseas.

She took off the lid and found a letter, handwritten in Bohemian on lined paper. Though neither Harriet nor Veronica had ever learned to read Bohemian, Harriet noted what appeared to be a listing of ingredients in the middle of the letter.

"Do you think this is it?" she asked Veronica.

"It must be," her cousin replied in an awed voice, looking at the letter over Harriet's shoulder. *"Babi* will have to translate this for us."

"I wonder what's in these?" Harriet picked up one of seven or eight packets, each wrapped with a half page of Czech newspaper folded over and over and neatly tied with string.

"Open one and see."

Harriet slipped off the string and carefully unfolded the newsprint, laying it flat on the table. In the center of the folds were what appeared to be dried, crushed leaves.

"Looks like oregano," Harriet said. She bent and sniffed it. "Doesn't smell like oregano, though."

"Must be some kind of herb. We'd better wrap it back up and take the whole box to *Babi."*

Forty minutes later they sat with their grandmother around the small table in her apartment. The packets were spread on the tablecloth, but unopened. Anna was adjusting her spectacles to read the letter. Veronica had a piece of paper and a pen in hand to write down their grandmother's translation.

"Aunt Maria says she dictated this letter to her daughter because she hasn't enough strength in her hand to write anything more than her signature," Anna told them. She looked up. "That must be why she's not sending Christmas cards anymore." She studied the letter again. "She says most of the ingredients are rare and she asked her daughter to go into the forest and get them all, because she knew we wouldn't be able to find them in the U.S.A. And then she lists them." Anna shook her head. "Some of these things sound familiar, but I don't remember them anymore. It's been so long since I've spoken Bohemian with anyone."

She began reading the list, but the names were all foreign to Harriet. Harriet glanced at Veronica, who gave her a blank look. The white paper she had in front of her was still unmarked.

"She says you pulverize each of the dried ingredients into a powder," Anna said, reading on.

Veronica began to take notes.

"Take a pinch of each and mix them all together with . . . oh-ho," Anna said, beginning to laugh, "with a pint of blood, preferably human. But cow's blood or sheep's blood will do." She glanced up with amusement at her granddaughters. "Aunt Maria really took your letter seriously! Well, she's very old and she probably didn't understand you were only curious."

"So what's supposed to be done with the mixture?" Harriet prompted her.

Anna found the place where she'd left off. "When the blood is thoroughly mixed with the powdered ingredients, the vampire is to drink it down one minute before the sun comes over the horizon at dawn." Anna stopped then and set the letter on the table.

"And then what?" Veronica asked, pen poised.

"That's all she says. There's a P.S. from her daughter saying she was glad you wrote and hopes you'll continue to correspond."

Harriet sighed, wishing as Veronica obviously did, that the letter had said something about what the vampire's reaction to the cure should be. "Well, let's open these packets. Maybe you'll recognize what's in them," she said to Anna.

Harriet and Veronica carefully took off the strings and unwrapped each paper. Inside they found various textures and colors of dried leaves. One looked as if it was the peeled bark of a tree. Another looked like dried mushrooms. "Do any of these look familiar?" Harriet asked her grandmother.

"This," she said pointing to one, "looks like an herb we used to put in soups. Some of these I think are herbs Aunt Maria used to use to make teas for different ailments. Aunt Maria used to be sort of a healer. If you came to her and said you had a congested chest, for example, she would put together some herbs she'd found in the forest and give them to you to make a tea from. They looked like these, but I never knew much about them. I just trusted her."

Anna adjusted her glasses as she scanned the various small piles of dried ingredients on pieces of newspaper. When she came to the one that looked like dried pieces of mushrooms, she gasped. "Oh, my! Now she shouldn't have sent you this!" She eyed the mushrooms more closely, as if to make sure. Then she shook her head in dismay and began wrapping up the newsprint that held the gray, twisted, dry pieces. "These are poisonous. I do know mushrooms, and these are very dangerous." She clicked her tongue as she got up from the table with the packet in her hand. "I'll throw them away, before someone eats them by mistake."

"No," Harriet said, taking the bundle out of her grandmother's hands. "Don't throw it away!"

"Harriet, the smallest speck of it could kill a person."

"We'll be very careful with it then. But we need all the ingredients. We can't throw anything away."

"What on earth do you need them for?" Anna said, obviously unsettled that Harriet wanted to keep the poisonous toadstools. "You aren't going to make up this recipe, are you?"

"Well . . ."

"Why? And where would you get the blood? I know you like vampire stories, but you're carrying things too far if you're going to keep something so deadly in your home. For all I know, some of these herbs may be poisonous, too." She spread her hands as she made an incredulous little chuckle. "You don't know any vampire to cure, so why keep this stuff?"

Harriet looked at Veronica, who returned the furtive glance. Veronica began folding up the packets. "We'll be very careful, *Babi,*" she said.

"But what will you do with it?" Anna persisted, though she sat down again.

"I'm thinking of writing an article about vampire lore for my magazine," Veronica said.

Harriet was impressed with Veronica's quick thinking. "I'm helping her do research," Harriet added, feeling only slightly guilty about lying.

"We may take the ingredients to an herbalist and have them identified," Veronica continued. "Magazine articles have to be factual, you know, even if it's about gypsy cures."

"Oh, well, if you must," Anna said, shaking her head worriedly. "But when you're done, burn all these things," she said, sweeping her hand over the packets Veronica and Harriet were putting back in the shoe box. "I'm sorry now I ever translated that letter you wrote Aunt Maria. What must her daughter—my cousin—think? The only correspondence they ever got from the younger generation of their relatives here in America is a letter asking for a cure for vampires. They must think Americans are nutty as fruitcakes!"

Now Harriet really did feel guilty. "I'll write them back a nice letter, and I won't even mention vampires, *Babi.*"

After leaving their grandmother's, Veronica and Harriet decided that Harriet should bring the box to David and tell him about the cure when she visited him tonight. Veronica left then, looking very concerned.

Harriet cooked supper—roast pork, sauerkraut, and dumplings, Ralph's favorite—and had it ready when her husband came home from work. She reminded him that she had her quilting class that night.

Ralph looked disappointed. "But Janet's studying with her friend again. When the kids are away, the parents can play," he said with a little grin. "Can't you skip the class? What do we need a quilt for anyway?"

Ever since they'd made love the night he'd found her alone in their bedroom, Ralph had had a one-track mind. And it wasn't that Harriet minded. In fact, it was as if they were kids again themselves. Harriet found that as long as she behaved like a sensation-seeking temptress, he was willing to do whatever she wanted. And sex with him was getting to be pretty darn good.

But tonight Harriet had David and the cure on her mind. "We need a special quilt for *fun,*" she said, reaching out to run her hand along his arm as she answered his question. "A love quilt. How about that?"

"I never heard of that. Is that a new thing?"

"Oh, it's the latest craze," Harriet said. "You sew in packets of potpourri that have special aromas to put you in the mood. Then when you lie down and make love on it, it heightens the experience." I'm getting as good at improvising as Veronica is, she thought with some chagrin.

"They teach that in your class?" he asked with astonishment.

"Oh, they teach *everything* nowadays."

"Sounds okay by me," Ralph said with a smile. "When's this class ever going to end? You've been going to it for months now."

"It takes a long time to make a quilt," Harriet told him, making a mental note to herself to go out and buy a romantic-looking quilt somewhere *and* some perfumed potpourri to sew into it.

* * *

David was waiting for Harriet to arrive when all at once he heard his living-room window opening. Darienne? he thought, hurrying to the window. In moments, Darienne was in the room, dressed in a stunning knit minidress, skintight and emerald green. Her diamond clip pinned up her loose curls, which fluffed out from the back of her head in a poufed pony tail. Diamond solitaires glistened from each earlobe. She seemed her old self again. Had Matthew given in to her quest to make him a vampire, despite all the things David had told the actor last night to dissuade him? Was that why she seemed so self-possessed?

"To what do I owe this visit?" David asked. "You left angry a few days ago."

"I'm on my way to see Matthew, but I came by to try to make peace with you. I don't like us being at odds. We've known each other too long to stay angry."

"All right, I agree." He rethought what he'd said. "That is, I don't agree with your plan to transform Matthew, but I agree we should try to overlook our differences and remain friends."

"I love him, and I still believe I only want what's best for him."

"I believe you believe that," David said in a dry tone.

Darienne made a face. "I suppose that's the best I'll get from you. Shall we kiss and make up?"

David grew leery and kept his distance.

"A handshake?" Darienne said, offering her hand instead. "My, you're suspicious of me! I told you I'm on my way to Matthew."

David took her hand. "That wouldn't stop you from indulging yourself with me, too, if you wanted to."

She withdrew her hand from his and pointed at him. "It was *you* who asked *me* for sex the other night—"

"Yes, yes, all right," David said. "I know I'll never hear the end of that!" He walked over to the love seat and sat down. "So, how is Matthew? Did you see him last night?"

"I see him every night."

"And?"

"He's . . . he seemed distracted last night. He came home very late from rehearsal. I was waiting for him at his hotel and had begun to worry. When he finally walked in he said there were problems at the theater and that he was too tired to talk. He asked if I would mind leaving and he promised that tonight he'd spend more time with me. He seemed very sincere. He also promised we'd talk more about his transformation."

"So that's why you're dressed to kill."

"You don't have to put it like that!" she said, pacing, her long slinky legs mesmerizing in their feminine rhythm as her high heels moved silently across the Aubusson. "I just want him to see what's his for the asking."

"And he still hasn't asked lately?"

"That's none of your business!"

So Matthew's continued to avoid her sexually, David surmised. Smart man. But Darienne had all her ammunition out tonight, from low-cut top to high-cut bottom. And she seemed to have confidence, too. "Do you think he'll agree to be transformed?" David asked, trying to sound as if it had ceased to matter to him one way or another.

"I think so. He said there were still some things he wanted to discuss with me, but he seemed set on making a decision. That alone makes me hopeful. He's been taking so long making up his mind, even avoiding the issue sometimes. He seemed to have a sense of purpose last night." She blinked and smiled to herself. "Yes, I think it's only a matter of hours." Her happy expression disappeared as she looked at David. "I suppose you'll give me another lecture now."

David spread his hands. "I've said all I can say."

"Good. I'm glad you can recognize when your opinion is irrelevant."

David shot her an impatient look just as the door knocker sounded downstairs. "That's Harriet." He rose to go to the door. "Try to be polite to me for her sake, will you? I'd hate for her to learn what a bitch you can be." He pressed the buzzer to allow Harriet to enter.

Darienne's blond head bowed as she took his reprimand. "Yes, of course. I'm sorry, David."

"It's all right," he said, taking a step toward her. "I know you're anxious about Matthew."

She looked up, her eyes bright with a sheen of tears. "Thank you for understanding, even if you don't agree with me." She moved up to him and kissed him on the cheek. "I really don't know what I'd do if I didn't have you to talk to."

David took her in his arms to comfort her for a moment. "Love is a difficult thing," he said softly.

She nodded as she drew away from him, dabbing at the corners of her eyes. "Thanks. I'm all right now," she said with a little smile.

David went back to the door. He walked out onto the landing to find Harriet climbing the spiral steps. "Harriet," he said, greeting her with a hug. An old box she was carrying got in their way. "What's that?"

"This is for you," she said, then stopped short when she saw Darienne. "Wow, what an outfit!"

Darienne grinned as Harriet moved around her to see her from all sides. "It's from Italy. You like?"

"If I had your body, I'd wear that all over town and let the men drool," Harriet said. Then she chuckled. "On second thought, I probably wouldn't have the nerve. But it's fun to know a woman who does! I'm happy to see you again."

"What's happening with your husband?" Darienne asked.

Harriet told her how much her married life had improved, owing in part to Darienne's advice, and she mentioned the "love quilt" she was supposedly making.

Darienne laughed, looking more genuinely gleeful than David had seen her in a long while. She gave Harriet a congratulatory hug. "I couldn't have handled him better myself! I'm proud of you."

"Thanks," Harriet said, seeming sincerely to appreciate the compliment. "I've had good help. From both of you," she said, glancing with smiling eyes at David.

David was elated to see Harriet looking so content and happy. Through their bond he could feel her inner peace, though he sensed some new anxiety. And he intuited that it had to do with him. "What's in this box? You said it was for me?"

"Yes," Harriet said, giving Darienne a worried glance. "Well, actually, there may be enough for both of you. This was sent to me by an elderly relative in Czechoslovakia. It contains the ingredients for an old gypsy cure."

"The cure you spoke of once?" Darienne asked. "To make vampires mortal again?"

David felt like laughing, even though Harriet looked so serious. "You're joking." But he could feel that she wasn't.

"It's supposed to be an ancient recipe." Harriet told them the story of her grandmother's Uncle Miklos and how they had written to Aunt Maria. "She sent a letter with instructions along with these ingredients from the forest," Harriet said, opening the box. "My grandmother translated it." She handed David a white sheet of paper.

David took in a quick breath as he recognized Veronica's handwriting. His fingers began to tremble, knowing the woman he loved had held the paper in her hands only hours ago. "Veronica wrote this," he whispered, his vision blurring slightly with tears as he looked up at Harriet.

Harriet nodded, and both she and Darienne stood in respectful silence while he composed himself.

"Sorry," he said, blinking hard. "I just suddenly felt so close to her."

"She misses you the same way," Harriet told him. "That's why I hope this cure will solve things for you and her."

"But how do you know it will work?" Darienne asked. "What *are* the ingredients, anyway?"

Harriet replied that she didn't know, that even her grandmother didn't recognize the names of the herbs. "But she did say one of the packets was dried mushrooms that are very poisonous. That is, to ordinary humans."

David was now concentrating on the words Veronica had written. "Pulverize each ingredient, take a pinch of each and mix with a pint of blood, human or animal," he said, abbreviating Veronica's notations. "Drink it one minute before dawn." He looked up. "And then what?"

Harriet lifted her shoulders. "That's what Veronica asked. But the letter didn't say anything more."

"You know," Darienne said, pushing back a wisp of hair by her ear, "I think I heard of this once, centuries ago, a few years after I became a vampire. I was traveling by carriage at night in the Carpathian Mountains. My driver and I came across a gypsy camp. They were colorful and they interested me, so I asked the driver to stop awhile. I sat with them around their camp fire and got them to tell me some stories. I asked what they knew about vampires—they never realized I was one. Eventually, an old woman said she knew a cure for vampires made from herbs and a certain mushroom. She said the vampire was made to drink the herbs mixed with blood just at the first rays of dawn. She swore she herself had cured two vampires with this formula. But she wouldn't tell me what herbs were used, because that was a closely held secret. I had no interest in becoming a mortal again anyway, so I didn't tax her for any further information."

David looked in the box, picking up the various packets of ingredients. This was all so preposterous, he thought. And yet, if only it were true. . . . The image of Veronica formed in his mind's eye, and he stood there a moment, holding the box, feeling transfixed. And then he realized he'd briefly tapped into his bond with her, and knew she was thinking of him at that very moment. He quickly disconnected. He must be clear-headed about this.

"What do you think?" he asked Darienne. "Do you believe in gypsy cures?"

Darienne shrugged her shoulders. "I don't know, David. My interests have always revolved around glamor and the idle rich. Other than that one time, when I happened upon their camp, I never took any interest in gypsies or fortune tellers or healers. I was happy with myself and my existence. I didn't need such people."

"I never put much trust in folk medicine. What if this formula doesn't work? The first rays at dawn would destroy me," David said, feeling more and more that, tempting though it was, this was much too risky to try. "In this modern age, with all we've learned from science, to trust in some ancient gypsy cure is . . . is really ridiculous. I appreciate your attempt to help, Harriet, but—"

"That's it!" Darienne exclaimed. "Science! Send the ingredients to Herman in Switzerland. Have him analyze them and see what he says."

David stared at Darienne with widening eyes. "Now that's good thinking on your part! An excellent idea."

"The Swiss vampire who's a scientist?" Harriet asked. "Veronica mentioned Darienne visited him." She turned to the vampiress. "Do you know his address?" Darienne nodded. "I could send him the material tomorrow by express delivery, if you want."

"Would you?" David asked.

"Sure," Harriet replied. "In fact, I'm glad you know someone like that who could check this out first. I was a little worried about it myself. Not that I don't trust my relative in Czechoslovakia. But she's very old and I've never met her."

"I'm sure this Aunt Maria is sincere, but the question is, does one put faith in ancient herbal remedies?" David said. "Especially for this. It's one thing for a mortal to drink mint tea to settle his stomach. It's another for a vampire to drink a concoction made from ingredients we don't even know and face the sun at dawn."

"I agree," Harriet said. She took the box from David's hands. "We'd better only send Herman a sample of each of these packets to do his analysis with. The instructions say you only need a pinch of each for the cure." She looked up at Darienne. "Unless you want to take it, too, if Herman approves. There's only a small amount of each, but I think there would be enough for both you and David, besides what we send to Herman."

Darienne smiled at Harriet as if Harriet were a sweet, thoughtful child. "Becoming a mortal again is David's dream, not mine. But thank you for considering it."

Harriet seemed a bit surprised, but said nothing more and set about spreading the packets on David's coffee table. "Do you have some envelopes," she asked him, "so we can divide these up to send to Switzerland?"

"Of course," David said, and turned to go into his office. As he went through his desk drawers, looking for a box of envelopes, he couldn't help but feel shaken by the events of the past several minutes—holding Veronica's notes, connecting with her through their bond for that tiny, unintentional moment, and now Darienne's statement that she had no wish to join David if reverting back to a mortal state were possible. He realized what an irrevocable gap it would create between himself and Darienne. And yet, he could have what he'd dreamed of for years, a normal life with Veronica. The pact could end, because if he became a mortal, too, there would no longer be any need for her to consider becoming a vampiress. He could be happy, truly happy! David could barely even comprehend what that meant, he'd been unhappy for so long.

But if he became a mortal again—or if he perished in the attempt to become one—he had another question to ponder.

Sooner or later he would have to deal with death, real death.
And that meant having to face God. What punishment
awaited him for his vile sin of choosing to become a vampire?

The thought of how God might deal with him made him feel
physically weak for a moment, and he grabbed the edge of his
desk for support. He closed his eyes as he recovered his
strength. To know a few years of happiness with Veronica, he
would willingly face His Maker's condemnation. It couldn't
be any worse than the hell he'd been living in since 1616, when
he made the awesome, repugnant decision to turn his back on
God's gift of life and become one of the earth's undead.

# 13

## Better odds than seventy percent

DARIENNE ENTERED Matthew's hotel room. He openly stared at her tight green minidress while he held the door for her.

"That is a remarkable garment!" he said with a smile, his eyes taking in everything.

"I'm glad you approve," she said, using her most frivolous French voice. She stood in front of him, after he'd closed the door, and ran her forefinger coyly up his chest. "I can leave it on or wriggle out of it, whichever you prefer. I have only a frail little lace panty underneath, delightfully easy for you to tear off me." Her voice grew more sensual and urgent. "Anyway you like it, Matthew. Anything you want, I'll do for you."

His eyes moved down to her cleavage as if he were tempted. But then, as though another thought had overtaken him, his expression changed and he stepped back from her. "You're stunning. Radiantly sexy tonight. But we need to talk about—"

"Your transformation?" she said with eagerness. "Of course, *cheri!* I'll do that for you first, and then our coupling will be even more wonderful."

"I haven't made up my mind," he said, his eyes growing stern. "I just want to *talk* about it some more."

Darienne tried to hide her disappointment. "All right. Shall we sit down?"

"No," he said, rubbing his fingertips together pensively. "I'd like to see where you live. How you live. If I'm to choose to live as you do, then I want to see what that's like. Especially since you've offered to let me share your place."

Darienne had indeed offered to let him stay with her if he were transformed. It was an offer she'd never made to anyone else, in all the centuries she'd existed. She'd always preferred to be independent, not even telling David where she lived. But she wanted to be near Matthew, as close as possible, sharing everything with him, always and forever.

"Of course, Matthew. I'd be happy to show you my condo," she said, very heartened by his interest. She grinned. "Remember when I first met you, I used to try to lure you to my place? But you always found some way to say no."

"Mmm," he said, not looking as amused with the memory as she would have thought he'd be.

"I was only trying to seduce you because you were so sensual and sexy, my darling." She curled a lock of his hair around her fingers. "You were happy when I finally succeeded—though it was at your place not mine. It's time you did see my place!"

Matthew nodded. "The John Hancock, right? I'll drive."

As they left together, Darienne wondered why he was taking such an unamused attitude. He didn't usually react like that to her teasing. But perhaps he was simply nervous because he was contemplating becoming an immortal. His reaction was probably perfectly natural. She decided she needn't worry. If she could manage to seduce him into sex three years ago—Matthew, the strongest-willed man she'd ever met—then she could find a way to talk him into this, too.

He drove his leased car to the Hancock and parked in Darienne's unused parking space. They took the elevator up to the ninety-first floor. When they walked into her condo and she turned on the lights, he blinked, for her decor was done in white on white with modern furnishings. The white wool carpet, white couches and chairs, silver-and-glass coffee table and lamps contrasted with the clear darkness of the night and the city lights outside her floor-to-ceiling windows. The only color in the living room came from the Impressionist paintings, by Renoir, Seurat, and Monet, on the white walls.

"I've never seen these," Matthew said as he looked at them in awe. "Are they real?"

"They're not reproductions or imitations," she assured him. "The art experts and museum curators don't know they exist. I bought them in France during the artists' lifetimes.

Except the one by Seurat," she said, pointing to a painting of Parisians in a park, done in the Divisionism style using dots of color. "It was given to me by the artist. I had a brief, but memorable, affair with Georges."

Matthew seemed impressed. "It's always so hard for me to believe you're as old as you are. David, too. You knew Seurat; he knew Shakespeare. It's incredible."

"When you are one of us, you will have the opportunity to meet all the famous people you want over the coming centuries," she told him with pride. "Especially since you will always be a famous actor, such important people will want to meet you. Oh, what an existence you will have, *cheri!*"

She saw his eyes grow luminous as he seemed to consider her words. He enjoyed the thought of remaining famous and moving in the circles of influential, creative people, she sensed.

"Why are you so sure I'd be a famous actor decade after decade?" he asked, looking doubtful. "I imagine even a vampire's career has ups and downs."

"But you possess immense talent and you would have a vampire's strength to carry that talent to its fullest potential. And the older you get, the more wisdom from experience you would acquire. You would have to pretend to retire every twenty or thirty years and then find some way to change your appearance, or go to another country, find a new name and begin again. But your talent and vampire resilience will always return you to the forefront. You would have one brilliant career after another." She chuckled. "In thirty years, when you reappear as a new actor, people will say, 'He's like a young Matthew McDowall!' And how we'll laugh together about it!"

Matthew smiled and rubbed the side of his nose. "I would get a kick out of that." His expression grew serious again and he began to look around her living room. "This is a beautiful condo." He gazed in the direction of her large windows, which overlooked a spectacular view of the city, almost as though they were in a stationary aircraft above Chicago. "The decor and the view are impressive. Sophisticated. It suits you and I like your taste. But where do you . . . spend the daylight hours?"

Darienne was happy he was getting down to basics, thinking it indicated he was truly serious about becoming a vampire. "I'll show you, *cheri,*" she said, putting her arm through his. She took him into another room, decorated in pastels, which she'd done in the manner of a boudoir with a sumptuous couch, long closets, and a vanity with several elaborate enameled jewel cases and crystal trays holding makeup compacts and brushes. But no mirror.

She took a key out of her handbag and unlocked an inner adjoining room. The room was intended to be a walk-in closet, but it contained only one thing—an immaculate white enameled coffin on a low, silvery pedestal. The coffin was closed, but Darienne lovingly lifted the lid so that Matthew could see its interior, which was of plush emerald-green velvet, the same color as the dress she wore tonight.

"I had this made in France and chose this material myself," she said, bending to run her hand over the soft, thick velvet. "Emeralds are my second favorite gem. Diamonds are my favorite, but they have no color, so I chose this. Beneath the material is a layer of French soil. I added that myself, of course." She turned to look at Matthew, standing beside her. "Would you like to try it out?"

Some color seemed to have drained from Matthew's face. He looked at her with startled eyes. "Try it?"

"Lie down in it, *cheri,* so you see how it feels. It's very comfortable."

"I . . ." He began to back away from the coffin. "N-no, I don't think so . . ."

Darienne laughed a bit. "Matthew, you aren't frightened of a coffin, are you? It's just enameled wood and velvet." She took hold of his arm again to urge him to come closer to the casket.

But Matthew quickly evaded her grasp and walked toward the door to go back into the boudoir room. "I can't do this, Darienne. This . . . It's not for me."

"Matthew," she said, alarmed at his reaction. She followed him into her boudoir. "You're behaving like a child who's heard a ghost story. Don't be silly."

"It's not silly," he snapped at her. "This whole idea suddenly makes my skin crawl. I feel nauseated. I don't want to spend my days in a coffin, velvet-lined or not. I'd rather actually *be* dead!" He sat down on her couch, hand at his stomach, looking as if he felt queasy and dizzy.

Darienne realized she'd have to find some patience and some way to talk him through his revulsion. She knelt on the floor at his feet. *"Cheri,"* she said, gently taking hold of his wrist, "I think I understand. Mortals grow up fearing death. And a coffin represents death. I'm used to the idea of being dead, so it doesn't bother me in the least anymore." She paused and stroked his hand with her thumb, looking at his bowed head, his tousled hair, as he took deep breaths, trying to recover. "This is just a little initial distaste that you'll get over quickly. Don't let your jittery stomach influence your mind. You must think about the overall lifestyle of a vampire. The coffin is only a small part of that. Think about the power you would have, immortality, increased stamina and sexual satisfaction."

"I don't give a damn anymore about all that—"

"Shhh!" she interrupted him. "You're just upset right now. You mustn't make any final decisions while you're feeling ill. Wait another day or two. Tomorrow night you'll feel better, and you'll be able to think more clearly. The benefits far outweigh any of the negative connotations mortals associate with coffins. You'll grow to love your private chamber, as I do. You can design yours any way you like. Varnished oak or walnut, if you like rich woods. Most men do, I think. And you could line it in whatever color or fabric pleases you. Maybe gray-green to match your eyes—"

Suddenly he got up and jerked his hand out of hers. "Stop it! I don't want to hear any more. I don't know how I let you intrigue me with this idea. My God, I was in there looking at your *coffin!"*

Darienne got up and rushed after him as he hurried into the living room. She'd never expected this reaction from him and didn't know what to do. All she knew was that she'd better not let him leave. If he did, she was afraid he'd never come back.

She grabbed hold of his elbow, made him turn, and encircled him in her arms. "Matthew, please, don't panic this way. Try to be calm."

"Let go!" he told her, trying to move out of her tightening embrace.

"No. You must listen to me."

"God!" he exclaimed, trying to wrench himself free of her superior strength. "Why didn't I listen to David?"

"David?" she repeated, holding him even more firmly.

Matthew's eyes flared with anger at her use of force. "I talked to David last night. He told me what being a vampire was *really* like. He almost convinced me, but I still had a damned trace of curiosity. I wanted to see how it would be, staying here with you as a fellow . . . ," his mouth flattened with distaste, *"vampire*. One look at that coffin, and that's all I needed to know David was right. The whole idea is repugnant and sick."

"You shouldn't have spoken to him!" Darienne chided, shocked that he'd done so without telling her. "David has a morbid, pessimistic view of everything, even love. You must believe what *I* tell you, Matthew. You'd be happy as a vampire. We'd be so happy together. Forever."

"No!" he said, taking advantage of an unintentional weakening of her grasp while she pleaded with him. He broke free of her hold and began running toward the door to escape to the hallway of the building.

But using her superhuman quickness and agility, Darienne was in front of him, barring his way, before he could even reach the door. "You aren't leaving here, Matthew!" Anger at David's influence on Matthew made her grow resolute. No more time to coddle him, she decided. "I know what's best for you. You're too confused now to think. I've helped you in the past when your mind had grown muddled from overwork. I've helped you plan your career, choose what cities to play *Shadow* in, bucked you up when you were too tired to see your fans, and told you when to rest. I saved your life by convincing you to quit the show because you were so exhausted. Now you're tired and confused again from more rehearsals. I see I must make *this* decision for you, too."

"What!" His eyes widened so that the whites showed prominently, and his lids seemed locked open with panic.

She took firm hold of him again, but softened her voice. "It's for your own good, my darling. You'll thank me for it afterward. And when we make love, you'll be eternally grateful for the astonishing experience." She was whispering seductively now, near his lips. Though he tried to back away, she warmly kissed his mouth. But his lips grew stiff with repugnance.

Turning his head to break free of the kiss, he said, "Let me go!"

"Shhh." She kissed the side of his chin, the corner of his jaw, and then down his neck. He brought his hands to her rib cage to try to shove her away, but she tightened her muscles and withstood him. Pushing back his shirt collar, her lips fastened onto his pulse point. She could feel the blood pumping from his racing heart, making the artery beneath his skin jump wildly, tantalizing her.

"Darienne, no!!" he cried out.

She barely heard him. Her breaths were coming faster as desire for his blood, for him, overtook her. "I've longed to drink from you for so long," she whispered hotly. "My darling Matthew. I want you so!"

She opened her mouth wide to bite, but just as her teeth grazed the tender skin of his neck, he shoved her with an incredible show of strength for a mortal. It was enough to throw her off balance.

But she kept hold of him as he turned to bolt for the door. She forced him to face her, his back against the door now. Ultimately he was helpless to outmaneuver her. She wanted to be as gentle as she could, but if he continued to resist, she'd do whatever she had to.

She looked him in the eye, those mystical gray-green eyes she'd grown to adore, often so full of humor or desire in the past. But now they only looked back at her with panic and resistance as he grew out of breath trying to break free. "Relax, Matthew," she instructed him. "This will be an exquisite sensual experience for us both. Don't fight me. Relax."

But as she pushed his chin to one side to reach his artery again, his eyes took on a new, inner determination. He looked the way she'd often seen him when he dominated a stage, his actor's eyes charged, mesmerizing in their intensity, as if he had focused in some internal way and channeled all his body's energy into his gaze. Though he wasn't much taller than she, he seemed suddenly to be looking down on her.

"Darienne, if you take this any further, I'll despise you!" His voice was low and smooth, frightening because of the control he seemed to have over his anger. "If you turn me into a vampire, the first thing I'll do is break you in two! And then

I'll stay up until the sun rises. I refuse to be what you want me to be!"

Darienne felt deeply shaken, but maintained her hold. "Don't say such things, Matthew. I know what's best for you."

"You aren't even giving me a chance to choose. No one, *no one,* makes a decision for *me.* I'll die first! And I mean a real death. I'll let the sun kill me."

"Don't say that!" she told him, her voice breaking as her mouth began to quiver. Suddenly, though she had him pinned against the door, she felt helpless. She let go, seeing it was meaningless now to use force in the face of his threats of suicide. He'd made the threats with such fierce intensity she believed him.

She sank down to the floor and wound her arms around his legs. "Don't talk about meeting the sun, Matthew. I couldn't bear it if you weren't somewhere on earth. I'm sorry I wanted to force you into the blood ceremony." She looked up at him. "It's only because I love you. I want to spend forever with you."

She swallowed and blinked tears out of her eyes. "But I'll wait," she said, as salty drops slid down her cheeks. "I know you'll realize someday that being a vampire is the only way for you to be all you want to be. But I won't force you. I'm sorry, Matthew. Please forgive me." She reached up and took hold of his hand. "Do you? Please say it, that you'll forgive me? Otherwise I'll cry all night. I can't stand to have you so angry with me." She pressed her wet cheek against the back of his hand. "I only love you, that's all. That's why I behaved so foolishly." She looked up at him, pleading for his forgiveness.

Matthew's eyes were still intense, but they seemed to have darkened with new insight. *"Love* me? You mean, you're *in* love with me?"

"Yes," she admitted, realizing this was the first she'd ever told him.

"Since when?"

"Since the night we first made love three years ago." She waited without breathing for his reaction. Perhaps, if he secretly returned her love, she'd have a new reason to use to convince him to become immortal.

His expression didn't change. "You never told me. Why?"

"I . . . I was afraid you'd leave. I know we promised each other no commitments, no big emotional involvement. And I meant that when I said it, before we made love that first time. But those hours I was in your arms—Oh, Matthew, how could I help but fall in love with you? I've loved you all this time and was always so afraid to tell you, because I knew you wanted to be free. But now I've told you. What else can I say? I worship you. I adore you. That's all I know."

Matthew closed his eyes, and she could see the muscles of his jaw clench. As she rose to her feet again in front of him, his eyes opened warily.

"I won't . . . do anything to you, Matthew. Not against your will," she said, ashamed now. "I promise. Please forgive me. You haven't said yet that you forgive me."

He stared at her steadily, and she wished she knew what was behind that powerful gaze. "I forgive you," he said, though there was no emotion in his tone. It was more a statement of fact. "I never knew you had such strong emotions for me. I was comfortable with our easy relationship. Seeing the true intensity of your feelings is . . . unsettling, to say the least. This is almost as much of a shock as finding out you weren't a normal woman." He paused and shook his head slightly. "I don't know what to say."

She sensed he was on his way toward saying he not only did not want to be a vampire, but also wanted her out of his life, now that he knew she loved him.

"Then don't say anything," she hurried to tell him. "You need time to think, don't you? Don't say any more until you've had a chance to rest and think through everything that's happened. And please don't . . . don't be afraid of me, because of what I tried to do a little while ago. I never would do anything that would cause you to want to destroy yourself. I want you here on earth, even if you remain a mortal. But I hope you'll think more about that, too. Don't make up your mind about anything yet. Please? Promise me?"

Matthew stared at her, much the way he had stared at her the moment David first introduced them to each other at the theater years ago. His eyes seemed to delve into the deepest recesses of her character with dispassionate assessment, and yet with a certain controlled admiration. He smiled just slightly. "You never give up, do you?"

"Not when it comes to you," she said, trying to smile, too.

"I'm going home now." Again it was a statement.

Darienne felt a surge of panic. Would she ever see him again? But when she saw his eyes flare with renewed, wary brightness as he apparently observed her emotion, she quickly tried to control herself. "All right. You . . . you do forgive me?"

"I told you I do," he said calmly.

"When will I see you again? Tomorrow night?"

His eyes shifted back and forth as he seemed to be thinking. "You wanted me to consider all this. I'll contact you when I'm ready to see you again."

"But—"

"Good night, Darienne."

He turned, opened the door, and walked out. Everything within her cried out to follow him and bring him back, but she stopped herself from doing so. That would be the most certain way to lose him forever, if she hadn't already.

She mustn't think that way, she told herself as she walked to the middle of her living room. Even if she had lost him for now, it was only a temporary situation. She'd think of some way to get him back. Was she not Darienne Victoire? Did not her last name mean *victory?* She was born and named to win! She hadn't lost a man yet and did not intend for Matthew to be the first.

Walking over to the huge windows, she looked out at the dazzling city lights spread before her. She'd have to be patient for a while and let Matthew recover from what he'd learned and what she'd attempted to do to him. How incredibly foolish and stupid she'd been! She should have known Matthew would never allow himself to be forced into anything. The thing she'd always most admired about him was his indomitable nature, his determination. She only could respect him even more now, and unfortunately, herself less.

If it weren't for David's interference, none of this would have happened! she thought with spite, remembering that Matthew had spoken to him. Had David called Matthew and deliberately sabotaged her plans? David was such a pompous moralist sometimes, she wouldn't put it past him.

That he would do such a thing to a friend, a friend he'd had for four hundred years! To undermine her happiness this way!

She was certain if Matthew had never heard David's miserable
view of a vampire's existence, she could have convinced him
to become one. It was all David's fault! He'd turned Matthew
against the idea, revolted poor Matthew to such an extent he'd
grown physically ill at the thought of it. And that in turn had
made Darienne so desperate, she'd tried to resort to force. Oh,
she'd have it out with David for this! she vowed, trembling
with anger. In fact, she ought to go right now and confront
him!

She almost turned to go out the door, but then thought
better of it. No, David would only say she was being illogical
and living by emotion. Oh, she could hear all his arguments.
She'd listened to them for centuries. He always told her she
had no common sense, no sense of morality, no sense at all!

She'd better wait until she calmed down, so she could confront him about this on the moralistic, rational level that he
understood best. She needed to make him realize that to betray a friend, as he'd betrayed her, was just as immoral as
anything he'd ever accused her of.

She closed her eyes and took a deep breath. Don't think any
more about this right now, she told herself. It was the advice
she'd often given Matthew, and she needed to follow it herself.
She peered down at the ribbonlike streets below, with the red
and white lines of car lights moving over them like trails of
slow-moving, glowing ants. Was Matthew's car one of those?
Was this the last she'd ever see of him?

She sighed and pressed her forehead against the thick pane
of glass. "Matthew . . . ," she whispered. "Don't leave
me . . ."

A week later, David was throwing some obsolete pages of
his screenplay into the fireplace when the telephone rang. He
went into his office and answered it. A male voice he'd never
heard before replied.

"Is this David de Morrissey?"

"Yes."

"I've heard of you through Darienne. I'm Herman, her
friend in Switzerland."

"Of course!" David replied. "She's often told me about
your scientific research."

"Darienne has told me so much about you, I feel as if I know you. I received a package from Harriet Dvorak—"

"The gypsy cure."

"Yes. She wrote that she'd sent it on your behalf and asked me to analyze the materials and call you. Well, I've been researching the contents all week, and I have some conclusions. Do you wish to hear them now?"

"Yes, very much," David said, sitting down and grabbing a piece of paper to write on.

"All of the contents, but one, are herbs which contain nutrients that purify and make the body strong. I'm speaking now of a mortal's body. The one remaining ingredient is a rare, poisonous mushroom. A small amount would kill a normal human within a few minutes of ingestion. This assortment of ingredients puzzled me at first, and I thought this is just some peasant folktale. In fact, I'd heard of a gypsy vampire cure over the centuries, but never was able to learn what all the ingredients were, so I was curious to analyze what Harriet sent."

"Yes," David said with a trace of impatience, for Herman seemed to have gotten a bit off track. "So you think it's all nonsense?"

"Not at all," Herman replied in his clipped, Germanic manner. "As I said, the poisonous ingredient puzzled me. But I did some tests using samples of my own tissues—hair and fingernail clippings, a bit of skin, and a sample of my own blood. I found that the poison had the effect of neutralizing what I call the vampiric agent that I've isolated in my years of analyzing human vampire cells. The vampiric agent, in turn, neutralizes the poison."

"Really," David said, fascinated.

"Yes, indeed, it's the very substance, this poison, that I've been searching for for decades. But to continue—this neutralizing effect will allow a few minutes during which the vampire's original life force can be restored. I could explain to you the chemical and biological reasons why I've drawn this hypothesis—for I haven't tested it on an actual vampire—but unless you have knowledge of chemistry and biology, I doubt you'd understand."

"No," David said with a chuckle, "science was never my strong point."

"All right then. To put it simply, my feeling is this neutralizing effect on the vampire's system would allow only a few minutes for the restoration of life to occur before the body began to degenerate. This is the reason the directions say the formula should be ingested only a minute before dawn. While this neutralizing effect is taking place, the vampire must allow his body to be exposed to sunlight, because the sun, with the help of the other herbal nutrients in the formula, allows the body's original life force to return and take over, and the vampire reverts to the mortal state. Now as I say, this is only my hypothesis based on my analysis, and is not proven. If you decide to try this formula, I'd be most grateful if you'd let me know your reaction to it."

"I certainly will—if I survive," David said with gallows humor. "How risky would you say trying this formula is?"

"Mmmm," Herman replied. "I haven't made any calculations along that line, but I imagine it would be somewhere around a seventy percent chance of success."

"Seventy percent," David repeated, not encouraged. "On that basis, would you recommend it?"

"I can't recommend anything to you, David. I don't know how badly you want to become a mortal again."

"Would *you* take it?"

There was a long silence from Herman's end of the line. "No, not at this point. I've gotten used to my vampire existence. I don't relish being one, but it has its advantages, especially nowadays with so many new discoveries in science being made. I like the idea of being around to see what happens in the next century. However, someday, I might want to return to the mortal state. I'd want better odds than seventy percent, I must admit."

"I see," David murmured, feeling the weight of decision settling over him. "What do you believe would happen if the formula didn't work?"

"If the vampire followed directions and exposed himself to the sun, and the poison did not have a strong enough neutralizing effect on his system, then the vampiric agent remaining in his body would cause the body to deteriorate under the sun's rays. I imagine in five minutes you would be returned to dust."

David said nothing for a long moment. "So, I have to weigh

whether trying to become mortal again is worth the risk of perishing altogether."

"Yes. And there's one more factor I ought to mention. Again, this is all speculation and hypothesis. But I have reason to believe that even if this formula were successful, the reversion might not be permanent."

"What do you mean?"

"It may be that the former vampire's liver might carry some residual trace of the vampiric agent. It might remain dormant or it might gradually spread through his mortal body, carried by the bloodstream, and return him to the vampire state."

David's shoulders slumped. "And what are the chances of that happening, if I survive the formula and the sun and become a mortal?"

"I believe that's a much lower risk—perhaps a five to ten percent chance that the cure wouldn't last. Chances are, if you successfully return to the mortal state, you would remain in that state. But I felt I should tell you, there is a risk that you wouldn't."

"Well . . . Thank you. I appreciate all the research you've done."

"It was my pleasure," Herman said. "Analyzing this folk cure has furthered my research immensely."

"Is there a chance you could perfect the formula, so that the risks would be lowered?" David asked, wondering if he should wait a few years before considering trying the cure.

"I certainly intend to investigate this to the utmost degree. But that could take decades, because it involves trial and error. And testing."

"Yes, I see," David said as he exhaled a long breath. "I would be the first to test it, wouldn't I?"

"The first that I know of. The stories I heard a century or two ago claimed that the gypsies had indeed cured vampires. But it's always difficult to know how much stock to put in folktales. I'm not urging you to test it, because such a huge decision must be entirely up to you, both as to whether or not you want to be a mortal again, and whether or not you wish to take the risk involved. My heart is with you, whatever you choose."

David had to smile silently at Herman, who sounded so logical, objective, and dispassionate that one wondered if he had any heartfelt emotions. "I appreciate that," David said. "Thank you for explaining my choices so thoroughly."

"Glad to be of service. Keep me posted."

David said good-bye and hung up. He sat at his desk for a long while, his face in the palms of his hands, his head swimming with the information Herman had given him. He reminded himself of Hamlet—"To be, or not to be: that is the question." And it *was* the question. Should he risk oblivion, or worse, the wrath of God, for the hope of a mortal's life with Veronica? Or should he continue to *be* as he was, one of the vile undead, whose only hope for eternal happiness was to transform the innocent, sweet, young woman he loved into a damned creature such as he was?

A seventy percent chance of success. What did that mean, exactly? That if there were ten vampires who each tried the formula, only seven would survive? Or was it that the formula itself might have a thirty percent chance of being defective or inadequate to the task? Oh, God, David thought. He was never good at numbers. He'd never been interested in gambling or understood how to play the odds. Especially not with his body and soul, if he still had one.

The real question was, how much should he risk to be with Veronica, as her mortal husband, not as her hideous vampire lover? What would Veronica want him to do? Should he ask her? But that would be breaking their pact . . . Was the pact worth keeping in view of this development, this possible cure? But in the end it was his decision, a decision which must be made rationally without the influence of the deeply felt emotion Veronica would bring if he spoke with her. He must keep his mind clear, and not burden her with a dreadful decision which must ultimately be his alone anyway.

While his head throbbed with these questions, he heard the distant sound of the brass front-door knocker. David paused, wondering who it could be. It wasn't Harriet's usual night to see him, but perhaps it might be her.

He rose and went through the living room, down the steps to his front door. When he opened it, he found Darienne standing in front of him, wearing a simple white blouse and a calf-length black skirt with high-heeled black boots.

*"Bonsoir,* David," she greeted him, but there was no smile in her eyes or on her lips.

"You're using the front door?" he said in an arch manner as he let her in.

"I don't consider you a friend anymore," she said coolly as he closed the door behind her, "so I felt I should follow the proprieties of people who are merely acquaintances."

David stared at her blankly. "What have I done to deserve this?"

"You spoke to Matthew behind my back," she said, eyes flashing with anger though her voice was level. "You turned his mind against the idea of becoming a vampire. Now he's turned away from *me*. In your pious quest to do the moral thing, which I'm sure is why you set out to warn him against me, you destroyed all my happiness. Therefore, I despise you." Her tone was cold, rigid. "I came here to tell you that."

"Can I explain my side of this?" David asked.

"If you wish."

"Come upstairs—"

"I don't want your hospitality. I'll hear what you have to say right here in your hallway, and then I'm leaving."

David felt disheartened by her impervious attitude. "First of all, I didn't seek Matthew out, or set out to dissuade him. He phoned and asked to meet me. It was *you* who told him I was a vampire. I could take you to task for telling my secret to a mortal without my permission."

Darienne lowered her eyes and said nothing.

"At any rate," David continued, "I agreed to meet him at Buckingham Fountain. He asked that we find a place where you wouldn't think to look for him."

Darienne glanced at David again, her eyes disillusioned and angry.

"He asked many questions," David went on, "and I answered them truthfully—the truth as I see it, anyway. He already had doubts. I didn't put them there. When we'd covered everything he wanted to know, I asked if I'd convinced him not to let you transform him. I admit, that is what I'd hoped to do. But he said, no, he wasn't entirely convinced, that the idea of power and living forever still intrigued him. Whatever happened between you and him after our meeting, I had nothing to do with. If he refused to let you transform him, then that was his choice."

"A choice based on revolting notions you'd planted in his

head! I showed him my coffin and he turned white and nearly became ill. You probably described our habits in some disgusting way that primed him to react as he did. And you influenced him behind my back—even found a secret place to meet. And all these centuries, I thought you were my friend!"

"It was Matthew who wanted secrecy. *He* suggested the fountain. Frankly, I had the impression he'd become a little afraid of you."

Darienne looked self-conscious then, leading David to wonder what had happened between them. "You didn't try to force him, did you? He asked if I thought you might, and I said *no*. Was I wrong?"

"What happened between Matthew and me is none of your business! All you need to know is that he refused to let me transform him, and I haven't seen or heard from him since. I'm afraid I've lost him for good. And it's all because of your interference! I used to be tolerant of your self-righteous, letter-of-the-law attitudes, even though I found them stifling and boring. But now I see how destructive they can be, how heartless and unfeeling *you* can be. And to *me,* after I've loved you and comforted you in your endless depressions all these years. You were perhaps the one person in the world I thought I could trust to never harm me. You always seemed too scholarly and altruistic to hurt anyone. But you have singlehandedly separated me from the one man I could ever love. And for that I'll never forgive you!"

Feeling limp, David took a seat on the second step of the spiral staircase, elbows on his knees, and rubbed his aching temples with the heels of his hands. "Darienne, I wish I could find the words to say to make you see this situation more objectively. But my head is still spinning from Herman's phone call."

"Herman called from Switzerland?"

He briefly told her the vampire scientist's assessment of the cure. "So I'm trying to consider whether I should risk self-destruction to have mortality. I can't even focus on your situation with Matthew. All I can say is, the things I told him weren't meant to separate you from him. I just tried to argue him out of choosing an existence I hate, to save him from someday having to face the sort of dilemma *I'm* in now. I didn't turn him against you; I tried to turn him against becoming a vampire."

"It amounts to the same thing," she snapped.

"No, it doesn't."

"Oh, I'm not going to argue with you! You always can dance circles around me with your high-flown logic and erudite explanations. But what it boils down to is that you've betrayed me. I have no further need of a friend such as you." She began walking to the front door.

David ran his hands roughly through his hair. "Well, if the formula fails and the sun destroys me, I can be relieved to know that you won't miss me."

Darienne turned and studied him. "You're going to try it?"

"I don't know. It will take me a while to decide. I was just . . . trying to be amusing."

"I don't find any of this amusing."

"You *used* to be the one with the sense of humor," David told her in an ironic tone. "You were the one always telling me that I was too serious. You were the one who knew how to have fun. All I knew how to do was brood, that's what you used to say. Maybe now you realize that being a vampire has a downside. If you were a mortal woman, this problem with Matthew would never have arisen. You might still be with him. It's your vampire-ness that got in the way, Darienne. Not me. You gave him a choice he didn't want. That's not my fault. Or his. Or yours, either, I suppose. None of us can help what we are or have become." David smiled to himself sardonically. "Unless, of course, one wants to take a folk remedy that has a seventy percent chance of working. There's enough for both of us. Perhaps now you'd like to become a mortal again, too. Then you might be able to get Matthew back."

Darienne set her teeth on edge and glared at him. Then she said, "Nothing would ever induce me to become mortal again. I have no wish to grow old, even with Matthew. If that's what you want, then go ahead. Even four-hundred-year-old friendships must end sometime." She turned and grasped the doorknob. "Good-bye, David."

The door slammed, and David remained on the steps, feeling a little numb. Everything was changing. And so fast! He felt his old way of life closing, like the door Darienne had just shut. And the choices that lay before him loomed perilous and unknown. He felt sad about losing Darienne's long companionship. But he had Harriet to confide in, and she at least was not given to flamboyant behavior, emotional outbursts, and unearthly lusts. Still, Darienne had brightened his existence, been a true friend who had indeed pulled him out of his depressions many times over the long centuries.

Well, Darienne was gone and the past was the past. Now he had the possibility of a peaceful, sweet future as a mortal with Veronica. Somehow he couldn't help but gravitate toward that radiant hope and want to grasp at it. There was only the sun to face, and possible destruction. And the possibility of meeting his Maker, which by rights should have happened four centuries ago. If he didn't survive the sun, just what would God have in store for him?

# 14

## It's not a normal case, don't you see?

DAVID WALKED along Rush Street late in the evening. It was a weeknight, and the Irish pubs were not quite so busy as they were on weekends, when the singles set invaded and took over the street. David decided to stop in one of the pubs and have a glass of port, the only thing other than blood that he imbibed. He knew he needed to continue his deep contemplation of his future and that he ought not to inject alcohol into his system. But the decision he faced weighed so heavily on him, he needed something to relieve his anxiety.

There were two empty stools at the bar, and he took one next to a young, dark-haired man in a plaid shirt. He wore thin-rimmed, tortoiseshell glasses and was drinking beer. David couldn't help but notice, from the young man's tense, hunched posture, that he seemed as wound up and morose as David was.

After David ordered the port, the husky bartender asked the young fellow if he wanted another beer.

"Yes," he replied as if distracted. "No. Well, yeah, why not?" He pushed his nearly empty glass mug forward. "If I'm going to stray from the straight and narrow, I might as well do a good job of it. Heck, I've never been really drunk. I should find out what it's like."

David and the bartender smiled at each other. "You haven't missed anything," David told the young man. "Just a blinding headache and nausea." He could still remember his own experiences as a young mortal.

"Well, who'd pay attention to a guy counseling against drunkenness if he's never been drunk himself?" the young man asked in a philosophic tone as he watched the bartender pour another beer. "It's like listening to a celibate priest advise a couple about their sex life. If I want to be a minister, maybe I ought to know more about the world before I try to set it straight."

"You want to be a church minister?" David asked.

The fellow shrugged. "I *thought* I wanted to be," he corrected himself. "I'm a PK."

"A what?"

"Preacher's kid. All my life, I've toed the line, lived in the world, but not of it. I assumed I wanted to be a minister like my dad. So, now I'm a seminary student. And sometimes, it's fine, and sometimes . . . I don't know what the hell I'm doing there. I get so mixed up about what I want and who I am, I sometimes wonder why I'm here. On earth. You know?" The young man's eyes seemed to go in and out of focus as he peered at David.

David guessed the beer had made him talkative. He seemed a type who would be a quiet, reflective, even shy fellow under ordinary circumstances. "Choosing to become a man of the cloth is a huge decision," David said, recalling his own youth, when he'd contemplated becoming a priest. "What's set you off on this mini-binge?"

The seminary student dabbed a finger at the bottom lid of his eye, as if he felt there were something in it. "Trying to persuade my sister not to run off with this guy she's nuts about who's into drugs. Dad doesn't know about him. I tried to counsel her, you know, use some of the techniques I've learned in seminary. Zero effect. She's on a plane at this moment flying to Vegas with him."

"She's your sister, so she doesn't see you as an authority figure. She probably thinks you don't know any more than she," David said, thinking of his relationship with Darienne, who was like a sister in some ways.

"I probably *don't* know any more than she does."

"I'm sure you would have been an effective counselor if it had been anyone else," David tried to reassure him. He realized then that he had an unusual opportunity to ask some questions of his own. He turned to the young man. "What's your name?"

"Kevin MacIntire."

"I'm David de Morrissey."

Kevin hesitated, his hazel eyes widening. "The playwright?"

"Yes. Have you seen my plays?"

"You bet! I loved them." He extended his hand and David shook it. "I like vampire stuff. You know those VCR tapes of the old 'Dark Shadows' soap opera? I've got the whole set."

"Impressive," David replied, though he'd barely heard of the soap opera. "If you don't mind, I'd like a theological opinion on something. You might consider it research for my next play."

"Oh." Kevin exhaled, and his shoulders sank as though he feared he was not up to the task. "I'll try."

"That's all I ask," David said. "Now, say a vampire had *chosen* to become what he was. Perhaps he thought he had good reasons, even noble reasons—say to protect some valuable manuscripts he was afraid would be lost to posterity. He wanted to live on through the centuries so a great artist's works wouldn't be lost. So, while still a mortal, he sought out a vampire and knowingly allowed himself to be transformed into a vampire himself."

"I like that," Kevin said with approval. "Sounds like a good premise for a plot."

"Does it really?" David wished it were only a plot device. He continued, "But after being transformed, he became acutely aware that he was horribly different from the rest of humanity, indeed that humans were now his source of sustenance—"

"The blood, right?" Kevin said, as if enjoying this.

"Exactly. The constant, degrading bloodlust," David said with distaste. "Not only did he suffer self-loathing over his lust, but he became terribly aware of being alienated from God. He felt a void, couldn't even pray, because he felt God had turned His back on him. By bypassing natural death, flaunting God's laws of nature, he was now outside the natural system of order that the Maker had created. In fact, he'd committed the sin of pride, of wanting to be like God—for, like God, a vampire has power over life and death, and he possesses immortality."

Kevin was smiling and nodding. "This is great stuff! You're going to put this in a play?"

"Perhaps. If I may continue . . ."

"Sure! Sorry I interrupted," Kevin said, picking up his glass again.

"Now, this vampire, who is guilty of the same sin for which Lucifer himself was cast out of heaven—"

"You know, you'd be great in a pulpit. You have a natural sense of drama when you speak."

"Thank you, but—"

"I interrupted again. Go on. I'll keep quiet."

"This guilt-ridden vampire has a chance to be cured," David went on. "That is, he's found a formula which might be able to make him revert into a mortal. Now, this is what this vampire wants more than anything. He's in love with a mortal woman, and . . . well, I needn't go into that part of it—"

"Romance, too! Let me tell you, this show's going to be a hit, just like your others."

"I . . . hope you're right," David said, wishing Kevin would curb his enthusiasm a bit. "As I say, he wants more than anything to be a mortal again. But—and this is what I'd like your opinion on—what happens if the formula doesn't work and the vampire perishes? Or, say it does work—what happens when the vampire-turned-mortal eventually dies a normal death? Since he's been outside of God's natural laws of order, would he go to meet his Maker? Or is he permanently outside God's domain? And if God *does* judge him, does the vampire, or ex-vampire, have any hope of being forgiven for his sin of pride?"

Kevin scratched his chin. "Well, the first part's easy. Nothing is outside of God's domain. As for the second part, I'd say if the vampire is repentent, God would forgive him."

David had been nothing but repentent for four centuries. Somehow he still felt it wouldn't make any difference. "But Lucifer was cast out of heaven *forever* for the same sin."

"Lucifer never asked forgiveness. He was too proud."

David felt a little astonished. In four hundred years he'd never thought of that. The idea had never entered his guilt-ridden mind. Still, David felt his situation was different. "But . . . but this vampire's been alienated from God for *centuries*. He's been *dead*, and yet not dead, walking the earth as if he were alive, feeding on human blood. He may still be in God's universe, but he hasn't fit into the *laws* of that universe. He's outside it. He's . . . *dead!*" David repeated, gesturing with his hand for emphasis. "It's not a normal case, don't you see? There's no precedent for it, at least, no parable or story that I know of that fits, that one could use as a guideline. How can I be certain that God would forgive me?"

Kevin seemed to stiffen. He turned slightly pale as he stared at David. His eyes focused on David's teeth. "Forgive *you?*"

"The vampire character in my play, I mean. I . . . I identify with my characters a great deal."

Kevin pushed his beer away, as if deciding he'd had too much. "You know," he said with hesitation, "I remember reading an article about you in the paper once. It said that you lived like a recluse and were never seen in the daytime. Do you do that to identify with your characters?"

"I write during the day." David felt guilty suddenly as he told his usual lie. Why not tell the truth for once? He could always make the young man forget this conversation afterward. Besides, he could tell that Kevin had already become suspicious.

David changed his tone of voice. "Would you like to go outside and walk a little?" he invited.

Kevin paled even more. "No."

"Do you believe in vampires?"

"Not . . . not until . . . Somehow I have the feeling *you* believe in them."

"I do." David leaned closer, reading his mind. "And, you're not too drunk to be imagining things. I *am* the type of creature we've been discussing."

Kevin began to back away to the point that he was almost ready to fall off the far side of his bar stool. David took gentle hold of his arms, caught Kevin's gaze through his glasses, and willed the young man to calm down.

"I have no wish to harm you. I've never had any wish to harm anyone. Do you believe me?"

Kevin nodded, wide-eyed and mute.

"All right," David said softly, "I won't keep you much longer. Just tell me what you think. Can someone who's been one of the undead for four centuries hope to ever fit back into God's plan for humanity?"

Perspiration had broken out on Kevin's forehead. He wiped it away with shaking fingers. "Well . . . ," he said, then swallowed. "How about this? Saint Paul said, 'I am convinced that neither death, nor life, nor angels, nor principalities, nor things present, nor things to come, nor powers, nor height, nor depth, nor any other created thing, shall be able to separate us from the love of God.' "

David sat transfixed. "Neither death nor life . . ."

"I think that statement covers your . . . situation." Kevin wet his lips. "Well, if I've answered your question, I think I'll be on my way—"

"Of course," David said, catching and holding Kevin's gaze before he could run off. He did a silent, quick hypnosis to make Kevin forget their conversation. "I hope things work out with your sister," David said then, in an easy tone of voice. "And don't worry, I think you've made the right career choice."

Kevin looked as if he felt bewildered suddenly, even a bit dizzy. He glanced at his glass of beer and shook his head. "Guess I had too much of that," he said with a laugh. "Sorry if I rambled on about the seminary. Is that what we were talking about?"

"Yes. I enjoyed our conversation. Will you be all right getting home?"

"Sure. Thanks . . . um . . . ?"

"David."

"David. 'Night."

"Good night." David watched him leave and then turned back to stare at his half-empty glass of port. *Neither death nor life.* Was there hope after all?

It was past five A.M. David knelt before his fireplace and held a lit match to a letter he'd just finished writing, addressed "To My Maker." The letter asked forgiveness for the terrible choice he'd made four hundred years ago. He still felt too unworthy to pray, but somehow writing the letter had felt comfortable to him. He watched the sheet of stationery curl into flame and then smoke, which moved up into his chimney and out to the sky above.

David glanced out his front window. Dawn was on its way, he thought with increasing anxiety. A few days had passed since his conversation with Kevin. Last night Harriet had come on her usual visit, and David had told her that after much contemplation he was ready to try the cure. She'd looked pleased and yet fearful.

"I'll get up early and come over to be with you, if you want," she offered.

David had agreed.

"Do you want Veronica to come, too?" Harriet asked then.

The idea at first elated David. But then he thought, What if I perish? He wouldn't want Veronica to witness him turning into a pile of dust under the sun's rays, if things went wrong. He requested that Harriet not even tell Veronica of his plans, fearing she'd worry herself sick.

"But she should know," Harriet objected.

"No," David insisted. "If all goes well, it will be a wonderful surprise. If not, then I'll be saving her as much pain as possible. He'd wondered if he should speak with Veronica before taking this last drastic step. But he feared if he saw her, or even communed with her from a distance, that he would be tempted to remain a vampire just to ensure that he would never be permanently parted from her. Indeed, she might even try to convince him not to drink the formula, out of fear of losing him forever.

He mustn't let their profound feelings for each other sway his sense of morality. The best thing for Veronica was to remain a mortal. And the best thing for David was to use this chance to try to become a mortal, too, or perish. Otherwise, they'd have to continue to abide by their pact. And when that was over, if Veronica chose to remain a mortal, then David would lose her. If she did choose to join him in the vampire existence, then David would transform her and suffer the guilt of that deed for century upon century. It had become clear to him, during these last few days of contemplation, that he would indeed rather perish than have to live with either outcome.

But if he had discussed all these things with Veronica, they both would have been led astray by their emotions and probably would have chosen a path that was best for neither of them.

He could sense Harriet was unhappy with his decision not to speak to Veronica, but she said nothing more.

Now David thought over all this again as he walked to the love seat to sit down and pass what might be the last minutes of his existence. He still felt he'd made the right decision in not even allowing Harriet to tell Veronica.

Earlier in the night he'd written a last will and testament to leave in Harriet's care. He left his mansion and all that was in it, including his rare books and manuscripts, to Veronica. He also left her his Swiss bank accounts.

To Darienne, though she hated him now, David left a jewel collection that had belonged to his mother. Darienne had always admired the collection, and he felt it should go to her out of respect for their long friendship.

To Harriet, he left a secret cache of gold hidden in the locked basement room in which his coffin was kept. David smiled at the thought that, no matter what happened at dawn, if he perished or became mortal, he would never have to rest in his coffin again.

Now there was nothing left to do that he could think of. He channeled his mind to Harriet's through their bond, and she told him she was driving to his home at that moment.

Relieved, able to relax a bit, David picked up yesterday's newspaper. He hadn't even looked at it yet, he'd been so distracted. After glancing over the front page, with its unending saga of world problems, he put that section aside and found the theater section. Merle had left an urgent message on his phone two days ago that Matthew was going to make a disastrous announcement to the press, and asked if David knew of some way to talk Matthew out of it. David had never replied.

As he perused the theater section, his eyes stopped at an article headlined, "McDowall bows out. *Shadow* to close." The article below read:

"Matthew McDowall announced today he would not, as previously reported, reappear in the title role of *The Scarlet Shadow*. Already in rehearsals and about to sign a one-year contract that had been under negotiation, the acclaimed actor did an unexpected about-face and said he would not do the show. He cited continuing health problems as his reason for not returning to the vampire role he'd made famous. 'During these past weeks of rehearsals, I've found I've not yet recovered from the exhaustion I experienced doing the show in England and then Australia,' the actor told reporters. 'I don't have the stamina to do the role justice. It's best to quit now and get the rest I need, rather than give less than my best to theater audiences. I'm sorry to disappoint my fans here, but I hope they'll understand.'

"The show's producer, Merle Larsen, said he regretted McDowall's decision, because it meant the David de Morrissey musical would close in Chicago, where it had opened three years ago to become one of the city's longest running shows and one of the most popular in theater history. Ned Holt, who had been playing the title role, is still recovering from a fall during a performance several weeks ago and is unable to return to the show. Alternating understudies are currently portraying the part of Sir Percy.

"When asked what he planned to do next, McDowall replied, 'Rest and reflect. A friend offered me a quiet place to stay in New York so I can thoroughly recuperate. By the time I've recovered maybe the film version will be under way, which I'm committed to do.'

*The Scarlet Shadow* closes in Chicago in two weeks."

That's the end of that, David thought, setting the paper down. Would the movie ever be made? David never had finished reworking the screenplay. He bristled to think that if he didn't survive the cure, some other writer would be hired to do the work. Then again, the powers that be in Hollywood might hire some other writer in any event. David probably need not regret it if he didn't live to see the movie version of *Shadow*.

He was relieved that Matthew had decided not to return to the stage show, however. He wished he could talk to the actor. It would be interesting to find out what had finally convinced him to turn down not only Darienne's offer to transform him into a vampire, but also the chance to play one on stage again, when he'd been so drawn to the role. Well, if David never saw Matthew again, at least he could perish feeling he'd helped dissuade the actor from making a terrible mistake, though he'd lost Darienne's friendship as a consequence.

Where was she now? David wondered. He hadn't seen her since she'd come over to reprimand him and tell him goodbye. She didn't even know what David had decided to do and probably didn't care.

But Harriet was on her way. David could feel her presence growing nearer. Somehow he could feel Veronica's presence, too, though he struggled to keep himself from making mental contact with her.

A sudden knock at the front door brought David to his feet. He knew Harriet had arrived and he rushed to press the buzzer. He walked out onto the landing as she climbed the spiral steps, carrying a blender.

"Hi," she said. "I brought this from my kitchen. I thought it would be the best way to pulverize the ingredients and mix them with . . . with the blood. You have some? I forgot to ask yesterday."

"Yes, in the refrigerator," David said, feeling relieved that she'd arrived in plenty of time before dawn. And yet he was growing short of breath from the knowledge of what he was about to do.

"I'll plug it in up here," she said, setting the blender on the bar and finding a wall socket below. "There. You have the ingredients?"

"Yes." David went into his office briefly and opened a desk drawer. He brought out the shoe box sent from Czechoslovakia.

Harriet seemed to gulp as she took it from him. She looked up at him earnestly. "Are you sure you want to do this?"

"I'm sure." But his heart was pounding.

She opened the box. "The directions said a pinch of each. So I'll just take a little out of each packet and put it in the blender. Maybe we should put the pint of blood in first."

David moved around to the inside of the bar and opened the refrigerator. He took out a plastic blood bag, which still had its label, stating the type and date of expiration. He handed it to Harriet.

Harriet took it carefully, as if with trepidation. Looking it over, studying the bag's tubed appendages, she asked, "How do you open it?"

"Oh," David said, taking it back. "That's easy." He bit into the top portion with his sharp incisors, making two holes which he enlarged by pulling the plastic against his teeth. "There," he said, handing it back to her.

She smiled as she carefully tipped the bag and poured the garnet-colored contents into the blender. "I wonder if your teeth will lose their sharpness when you're a mortal again."

"I suppose they may," David said. "They changed when I

was transformed, so they may go back to normal. I hope so. I've never enjoyed having teeth like an animal."

Harriet was taking a pinch of each ingredient out of each newspaper packet and tossing them on top of the blood in the blender. She ended with one of the dried mushroom chunks. "Did I get them all?" she asked worriedly.

"I think so. I watched you carefully."

"I'll put the cap on then," she said, twisting the blender cover into place. She turned the appliance on. As it made a whirring sound, David watched the blood swirl in the glass container. The rotating blades at the bottom minced the ingredients until he could no longer see their dark specks. Harriet turned the blender off. "I think we're finished," she said and looked up at him with wide eyes.

"What time is it?"

"Five-twenty. I read in the paper that dawn is supposed to be at five-twenty-six this morning."

"I have five minutes then."

Harriet nodded. "I lit a candle for you at church," she said, her voice slightly choked with emotion.

David blinked as tears started in his eyes. "Thank you. I appreciate all you've done for me, Harriet." He slipped his arms around her to hug her. And then he remembered. "I need to give you something—" he said, letting go to rush back to his office.

He came back with a sealed envelope and handed it to her. "I wrote down how I wish my possessions to be distributed if . . . if things don't go as planned. Most goes to Veronica, but there's something there for you—"

"I don't want anything," she said in a fretful tone, looking at the envelope as if it were evil. "I'm sure Veronica doesn't either. We want you to live."

"I know." David placed his hands on her shoulders. "But in case I don't survive, I want you both to be taken care of. One thing though. If I become dust, then you must somehow remove my coffin from my home. It's in a secret room in the basement. Veronica knows where. Then report me missing. The best thing perhaps is to say I'd talked of suicide. There may be some legal number of years to wait before I could officially be declared dead, because, of course, there won't be a body. Meanwhile, turn this will over to a lawyer."

Harriet shook her head as a tear rolled down her cheek. "David, maybe you shouldn't drink this."

David knew this was how Veronica would have reacted, too. But with Harriet, he could maintain his willpower. "I must. I've made the decision. I won't turn back now." He glanced at his watch. "Look, it's almost time."

He took the blender container by its handle and lifted it from the base. Taking off the cover, he looked down into the pint of crimson liquid mixed with herbs and poison. He carried the container across his living room to the bay windows at the front of the room. Shifting the draperies of the middle window, he looked up at the sky. "The stars are fading. Dawn is almost here. I can even smell it."

"It's . . . t-time," Harriet whispered, checking her watch.

David cradled the container in his hands, looking at the thick liquid again. "I'm grateful for one thing, no matter what happens—this is the last time I ever have to drink blood." He brought the rim of the glass to his lips and gulped down the contents quickly. Harriet took the container from him when he'd finished and set it on the small table between two armchairs in front of the bay windows.

"How do you feel?" she asked him, wringing her hands as she studied his face.

"Nothing yet," he replied. "Except my heart is pounding, but it was doing that before I drank . . ." He felt odd suddenly. He lifted his hand to his head.

"What's wrong?"

"I don't know. I feel heavy and lightheaded at the same time—as if the earth were pulling on me, and yet my head is floating." David looked out the window. City buildings blocked the horizon, but the sky had changed color just slightly and he knew. "It's dawn." He could hardly speak, his breaths were coming so shallow and fast. "I can feel the sun's rays, the way I could in my coffin. Only then I was protected." He felt absolutely, totally vulnerable, a speck of human flesh in the face of the sun's infinite fiery furnace. He began to grow warm.

"I can see the sunrise beginning," Harriet said, looking out the window, too. "There's a faint reddish cast to the sky now." She turned to him. "Are you okay?"

But David wasn't okay. "I'm burning up," he said, managing no more than a whisper. "Inside, I feel like I'm burning up."

Harriet gasped. "Your hands, David!"

He looked at his hands and saw what appeared to be a vapor or smoke rising from his uplifted fingertips. "My God!" he said with a shudder. He began to shake uncontrollably. Harriet ran to him and grasped his arm to try to steady him. "It's no use," David said, though he barely had a voice left. "I won't survive the sun." He sank to his knees as dizziness and a reeling, torturous feeling of internal flames overtook him. He tried to hold himself up with his hands on the floor. But he had no strength left in any of his limbs, and he fell on his side with a soft thud, onto the Oriental carpet. He could no longer see. Everything had turned bright, blinding red.

He felt Harriet taking his hand and heard her voice, as if in a faraway echo, and could not make out what she said.

"Tell Veronica," he whispered with his last ounce of strength, "I loved her . . ."

And then suddenly there was only blackness.

Harriet let go of his hand and got up. Frantically she threw open the side bay window and called to the car a few doors down the street. "Come up here!" she cried, waving her hands.

Immediately the car door opened and Veronica stepped out of the driver's seat. "What happened?" she yelled back.

"I don't know. Come up here. I'll buzz you in."

Harriet left the window after she saw Veronica running toward the house. The instant Harriet heard the brass door knocker, she pressed the buzzer button, then opened the door to find her cousin racing up the steps.

"What's hap—?" Veronica stopped short on the threshold and made a harrowing gasp as she looked into the room. "Oh, no!" Her face contorted as she grew hysterical. "No! Oh, God, no!" She brought her hands to her face and screamed.

Harriet grabbed hold of her. "Stop it! We don't know that he's gone, yet. I don't know what's happened." She took Veronica by the shoulders and walked with her to where David lay still as death on the floor, his eyes closed, his complexion gray.

Veronica fell to her knees beside him. "He's dead!" she cried with profound sorrow, tears flowing down her cheeks.

"But he's still here," Harriet said, trying to keep calm as she knelt on the other side of him. "He hasn't turned to dust. The sun didn't destroy his body." She picked up his wrist and felt it. "I can't find a pulse. But I never was any good at that."

Veronica clasped her hand to her mouth and stared frantic-eyed at David's inert form. She reached out and put her fingertips beneath his nose. "Is he breathing?"

"Got a makeup mirror? Wait," Harriet said, running to the couch, "I've got one." In a moment she was back, kneeling beside David again. She placed the mirror beneath his nose. "I saw this in a movie once. Oh . . . there's no vapor. He's not breathing."

"Mouth-to-mouth resuscitation?"

"It's worth a try," Harriet said. "Do you know how?"

"Not really," Veronica said, but nevertheless she pushed David from his side onto his back. Carefully, she opened his mouth. "Look," she said in awe to Harriet. "His teeth—"

Harriet leaned over to look. "They're not sharp anymore. And he reflects in the mirror," she said, holding it above him. "Maybe he'll be okay if we can just get him breathing. I'll push on his chest. Isn't that what they do? You do the mouth-to-mouth."

Harriet leaned over David, both hands flat on the white shirt over his rib cage. Veronica pulled his lower jaw forward a bit and then looked at Harriet.

"I'll push first," Harriet said. "Then you breathe into his lungs."

"Okay!"

Harriet pushed, then leaned back as Veronica bent over David, trying to breathe life into him. When Veronica's head came up, Harriet pushed down on his chest again.

"I think we're doing it right," Veronica said, her cheek near David's mouth. "I can feel the breath coming out when you push."

"Good. Let's keep it up," Harriet said, silently praying while she waited for Veronica to breathe into David's mouth again.

After about three pushes, Harriet thought David's com-plexion might not be quite so gray as it was, but she wasn't sure. It was hard to tell in the lamplight, though the sky was continuing to brighten.

"Wait," Veronica said after she'd completed another forceful exhale into his mouth. "I thought I felt him move." She looked at Harriet. "Did I imagine it?"

"I don't know," Harriet said, for she hadn't noticed any movement.

Veronica began tapping his cheek. "David? Do you hear me? It's Veronica. David?" She kept tapping. And all at once his eyes flew open. He stared up at Veronica, his eyes blue as stained glass windows in a cathedral.

"David, it's me!" Veronica said, her hands visibly trembling as she held his face. "It's Veronica. Can you talk?"

Harriet saw his chest rise and fall on its own. "He's breathing by himself now," she said to her cousin.

Veronica smiled down at him. "You're looking at me. Can you talk?"

Harriet watched them with eager fascination. David was indeed looking at Veronica, awe in his eyes now, as if he recognized her but couldn't believe what he saw.

His mouth moved and he spoke as if his tongue were dry. "Are we alive?" he asked Veronica.

"Yes!" Veronica replied, crying and laughing at the same time.

"Where?" he asked.

"We're here in your home. Harriet's here, too."

"Remember I gave you the cure to drink?" Harriet said, moving a bit to kneel by his shoulder.

He glanced at Harriet and then settled his eyes on Veronica again. "I remember drinking the blood. Then the sensation of burning. I thought I was turning to dust." He reached for Veronica's hand at his cheek. "I thought I'd never see you again."

"I was afraid, too," Veronica whispered, new tears falling from her eyes.

David squeezed her hand, then began to get up. The women helped support his back until he was sitting upright on the floor. Harriet thought his color looked good, but he seemed weak.

"Can we get you something?"

"I feel thirsty," he said, still speaking with some difficulty. "My mouth is so dry."

"What should we get you?" Veronica asked, her hand on his shoulder, looking at him with concern.

"Blood?" Harriet asked. "Or . . . water? If you're mortal now . . ."

"Do you really think I am?" David asked, glancing toward the window, where the sky had lightened to gray, with a pink brightness to the east. "My God, am I seeing a sunrise?"

"Yes!" Veronica told him with joy.

"Do you want to try drinking some water?" Harriet persisted.

"Like a normal human being? Well, I'll try it."

Harriet got up, found a glass in a cupboard beneath the wet bar, and filled it with water from the faucet. She brought it back to him.

David took it carefully in both hands and looked at it with trepidation. "I'm afraid it will make me ill. I haven't been able to drink water for centuries."

"Try a sip," Veronica said.

David lifted the glass to his mouth, sipped, and swallowed. Then, as if he were a man coming off a desert, he gulped the whole glass down, hands shaking.

Veronica took the glass from him and set it on the floor. "Are you okay?"

He sat still, a tentative expression on his face, as if monitoring his own system. "I think so. I started drinking and suddenly I felt so thirsty. I think I was dehydrated. Water feels so thin on the tongue compared to blood. But it tasted wonderful! Does that mean I'm really mortal now?"

Harriet picked up the makeup mirror she'd put aside. "Look at your teeth. In fact, look at your reflection!"

David took the mirror from her and held it in front of him. His head went back as if startled. "Is that what I look like? I'd forgotten. I look so young. Though I imagine I'll begin to age like everyone else now." He checked his teeth. "And my incisors are normal again." He grinned. "This is beyond wonder, to be like everyone else!"

As Veronica leaned her head on his shoulder, he gave the small mirror back to Harriet. Harriet untied the scarf at her neck and checked her throat in the mirror. Her skin was completely unmarred.

"Look," she said to them, "the marks are gone."

David and Veronica, arms around each other now, both peered at her throat.

"Thank God," David said.

"The bond is gone, too," Veronica said quietly in a thoughtful, almost disappointed voice. "I can feel that it's missing."

"I can, too," Harriet said, feeling regret, too. "I can't connect with you anymore. That psychic channel is all gone."

"You're right." David seemed astonished, even thrilled. "My special powers have disappeared!" He glanced from Harriet to Veronica. "Why are you both sad about that?"

"It's such a loss," Veronica said. "I always felt that special kinship with you through our bond, even when you blocked me from communing with you. As I sat in the car, I could feel that little part of me dying. I knew something had happened."

"I'll miss my bond with you, too," Harriet said, feeling rather ordinary again. "It was special."

"But you're both *free.* You're not under my power any longer."

"I loved being under your power, David." Veronica stroked his hair and gazed at him with adoring eyes. "I've never wanted to be free of you."

As she looked at them together, Harriet was beginning to feel in the way. The light in their eyes as they gazed at each other brought tears to her own eyes. She was so happy for her cousin and for David, that they were finally reunited.

"I think it's time I drove home," Harriet said.

"Why?" Veronica asked. "Ralph knows you stayed overnight with me."

"What?" David said to Veronica. "You mean, you knew that I—?"

Harriet felt self-conscious, but not guilty. "I told her, David. I thought she should know what you were going to do. After all, the psychic told Veronica about the cure, not me."

"Harriet explained why you didn't want her to tell me." Veronica smiled at him in a doting way. "It was just the sort of logic you've always used, and I could have predicted you'd say that. But neither of us agreed with you. I wanted to be here no matter what, so I asked Harriet if I could wait in her car while she went in. She was to signal me when . . . when whatever happened happened." Her chin began to tremble and David held her closer. "When I came in and saw you lying on the floor so still, I thought we'd lost you. But then Harriet pointed out that the sun hadn't turned you to dust. So we tried resuscitation."

"I thought somehow I'd made my way to heaven when I opened my eyes and saw your face hovering over me," David whispered, his voice full of emotion as he gazed into Veronica's eyes.

Harriet wished she could hear a man speak with such love to *her* just once in her life. Well, she could be happy for her cousin anyway, to have the experience of a profound love. And since they seemed to have forgotten she was still in the room, Harriet decided it was indeed time to go. She rose to her feet.

Veronica and David looked up. "Don't go yet," David said.

Harriet smiled, gratified to hear him say that to her with as much sincerity in his voice, if not adoration, as he'd shown her cousin. "I think you two should have some time alone. You've been apart so long. I'll see you again. Both of you. Together, I suppose—I hope! What will you do now? Live together? Get married?"

The couple looked at each other again. "Marriage sounds wonderful to me," David said to Veronica. "It's what I always wished for but felt I could never have, a quiet mortal's life with you as my wife. If I really am a mortal now, then that's what I want."

Veronica's warm brown eyes seemed to glow with joy through a sheen of tears. Too overcome to speak, she nodded her head, slid her arms around his neck, and pressed her cheek into his shoulder, looking just at that moment like a child who had found a lost parent. David pulled her closer, then smiled up at Harriet.

"Thank you," he said softly to Harriet. "None of this would have happened without you."

Harriet would have liked to thank him for the difference he'd made in her life. But now wasn't the time. "I'll call you. Maybe tomorrow." She grinned. "I can call during the day now, can't I?"

"Do!" David said.

Veronica looked up. "Are you really going?" she said to Harriet as she wiped tears from her face.

"Yes, I'm really going," she replied in an indulgent tone.

"Thanks, Harriet," Veronica said, her eyes dark and shining with happiness. The slightly hardened, sad look Harriet used to see so often in her cousin's eyes was all gone now.

Harriet was afraid of getting emotional now herself. She joked, "Well, I've cured a vampire and saved a romance. I think I'll take the day off and go on a shopping spree!"

"I'll walk you to the door," David said, beginning to get up.

Harriet paused, watching him rise to his feet. Veronica got up, too, and held onto his arm to steady him, but he didn't seem to need assistance. He moved toward the door, where Harriet stood.

"No, don't walk me down," Harriet said. "I just wanted to be sure you could stand. Veronica needs your attention more than me." She looked at her cousin as a new thought came to her mind. "You know, he may get hungry later. Mortal men always expect women to produce food for them. What'll you do?"

Veronica looked startled. "Is there a kitchen here?" she asked David.

"It's on the first floor, in disrepair. I never used it."

"We can go to my place," Veronica suggested.

"And start him out on frozen dinners?" Harriet said. She looked at David. "She's my cousin and I love her, but she can't cook worth a dime." She turned back to Veronica. "Better start him out with something simple. Bread and a little cheese maybe. Broiled chicken—you can get that at a deli. Some cooked vegetable. Or soup. Soup might be the best thing. Nothing creamed or real rich, though. See how his stomach reacts." Veronica nodded, seriously listening to Harriet's advice. "When he's ready for a good solid meal, well, you two can come over to my house then."

"I may finally get to eat one of those *kolacky* you were always bringing me."

"It's a deal!" Harriet said, turning to go out the door. "Bye, you two. Let me know if you need anything."

She hurried down the spiral staircase, waved up at them when she reached the front door, then went out to her car. Veronica would have to take a cab home, she realized. But Veronica, she knew, would not be in any hurry to leave David. Not today, or tomorrow, or ever. Veronica would have a whole new life now, Harriet thought with happiness as she started her car engine.

Inside the mansion, David and Veronica had not moved from the third-floor doorway, where they'd waved good-bye to Harriet. David couldn't stop looking at his beautiful, dark-haired Veronica, marveling that she was here with him. He could even hold her in his arms.

" 'How like a winter hath my absence been from thee,' " he said with feeling.

Veronica smiled, her eyes dewy with joyful emotion. "You're still quoting Shakespeare, just like you used to. I've missed that."

"I've missed you."

"Are you hungry?" she asked him.

"I don't think so."

"Thirsty?"

"I'll drink another glass of water in a little while. I just want to look at you now." He pulled her closer. "And kiss you."

The expression in her eyes changed and she melted against him. He brought his lips to hers and felt her feminine warmth as their mouths immediately fused in a gentle, tender kiss.

When they drew apart, he said, "I love you. That's the last thing I remember saying as I thought I was perishing."

Veronica's lustrous eyes widened. "I heard you—through our bond. And then, that opened channel between us vanished. And I knew you must either be mortal, or gone forever. I could hardly breathe, wondering what your fate had been." She burrowed her head into his shoulder. "I hope I never have to live through a moment like that again. If you had perished, I don't think I would have survived. These past years I've lived on the promise of seeing you again when the pact ended, knowing I could choose to be with you forever. But to know you didn't exist anymore—I wouldn't have had anything to live for."

David stroked her thick, dusky hair. "What about your career? Harriet said you've done well."

"I have, but it's nothing to live for. I did it because you wanted me to."

David felt curiously disheartened. "But the purpose of the pact was to let you develop yourself to your full potential on your own, without my influence, so you could choose wisely."

"I told you long ago that I'd choose you, no matter what. Thank goodness I didn't have to wait the full ten years. Being separated from you was so hard to bear, David."

"I thought years on your own would change you. But you seem the same," he said, not disappointed but curious. "You've barely changed at all. You only look the slightest bit older. Perhaps not quite the childlike creature you were when we met. But still, as you look at me now, I see those trusting, sweet eyes I fell in love with."

She smiled. "Because I *am* looking at you. At work, my boss says I've gotten to be tough as nails."

"Does he?" David asked with wonder.

"Sure. I call him Ed now, not Mr. Molloy, and I talk back to him when I feel like it. I get crabby and sarcastic sometimes at work. Because I'm really not happy there. But I write good copy and he's willing to put up with my out-of-sorts moods. I guess everyone else has had to put up with them, too."

She looked askance at David, as if feeling guilty. "I couldn't help it. I missed you so much. I didn't want to be impatient with people, but I was so unhappy."

"And Rob Greenfield?" David asked.

Veronica shook her head. "I never loved him. I went with him because it was what you told me to do, to see other men. When I was with him, I compared him to you in my mind constantly. And always found him lacking. He finally left. I felt bad that I'd led him on, but . . . even in that, I was trying to do what you wanted me to do. After Rob left, I never saw any other men. I didn't want anyone but you, and I didn't want to hurt anyone else."

David bowed his head. "I thought I was doing the right thing when I made you agree to the pact. Perhaps I was wrong. But it saved you becoming a vampiress, which is what you were ready to do when I made us part."

Veronica's eyes took on a languid, unblinking certainty as she gazed up at him. "I would have done or been anything for you, to be with you. I would, even now."

David had to marvel at her words. She wasn't under his power anymore. It wasn't the bond that made her say such things. "Why do you love me so much?"

"Because you were the only one who ever understood me.

You reassured me and comforted me. You were the first man I ever made love with. And that was such a powerful experience, it changed my life."

David chewed on his lip a moment, something he could do now, he realized, without injuring himself. "Sex with me was a powerful experience because I was supernatural then," he said, suddenly feeling a bit too ordinary. "But I'm a mortal now. I can't promise you such a heightened experience anymore. In fact, it waits to be seen whether I'm still functional at all." David was becoming aware of the fact that though he was holding the woman he loved in his arms and was overwhelmingly happy to be with her, he still felt no sexual stirrings.

Veronica looked at him wistfully for a moment, then kissed his cheek. "We'll wait a while until you're used to being a mortal. Until you've eaten a few meals and slept a normal sleep. Look," she said, turning toward the window. "It's morning now. Your first morning. And we're together. Everything will be all right now."

He smiled at her sweet reassurance as he looked at the beauty of the sunlight passing through the trees outside, flooding through the window where the draperies had been pushed aside. The light made patterns on the furniture and the Oriental carpet, bringing out their colors in the most vibrant hues he'd seen in hundreds of years. A gusty breeze came in through the window Harriet had opened earlier, billowing the sheer draperies and bringing in the refreshing smell of the lake.

David walked with Veronica to the middle window and he looked out on the street below, the new green leaves on the trees catching the sunlight, and the brownstones and the city skyscrapers behind them all taking on variations of color. In the night, they'd all looked like dark, opaque outlines, ominous sometimes, and mute. But in the sun, each building had character and detail and color. And finally, he looked again at Veronica, her soft skin radiant in the gentle morning light, her thick hair a richer brown than he'd ever realized, her trusting eyes a warm brown with golden specks he'd never noticed before, reflecting the light of outdoors.

"The world is a beautiful place after all," he murmured as

he ran his fingers over the reddish highlights playing in her hair. "And you are the most beautiful creation in it."

Veronica smiled, laid her head on his shoulder, and slid her arms around him. David settled his cheek on top of her head and felt that he finally knew the meaning of the word *happiness*. He thanked God he'd survived to see this day.

# 15

# Grass to cut and roses to grow

AROUND NOON that day, Harriet was spreading on the bed a new quilt she'd bought that morning. The quilt was made of country-print patterned swatches of material cut in the shape of hearts and arranged on a pale blue background that blended with the bedroom's wallpaper. She'd just spent an hour making tiny cuts in the quilt, stuffing in small amounts of perfumed potpourri, and sewing the slits back up again by hand so they wouldn't show. She poured what was left of the potpourri into an open dish on the bed stand, and now a lovely, romantic scent pervaded the room.

She was about to make herself a sandwich when she heard the front door open. Startled, she walked down the hall and saw Ralph come through the front door into the living room. What's he doing home now? she wondered.

"Something wrong?" she asked.

He set his briefcase on the couch and said, "No. I had a meeting with a client here in Berwyn, so I thought I'd stop home for lunch. Got anything to eat?"

"Sandwich meat and bread," she said.

"Great."

"Turkey or beef?" she asked with an inward sigh.

"Both."

"Wheat or rye?"

"Rye. You don't look too thrilled. Did I disturb your plans?" he asked, following her into the kitchen.

"No, I didn't have any plans. It's just a surprise. You rarely come home for lunch." It wasn't that she minded exactly. But she was used to having the day to herself these last few years since her kids were grown and at school. Having Ralph come home was like having a kid to feed again. She smiled as she remembered what she'd told Veronica that morning, that men always expected women to produce food for them.

"What's so funny?"

"Nothing," she said, getting out the sandwich fixings. "Just thinking of a conversation Veronica and I had."

"So, how is she? What was she so upset about that you needed to stay with her overnight?"

Harriet was glad she wouldn't have to cover her tracks with white lies anymore. "She was upset about her . . . boyfriend. But it's all worked out. She's going to get married."

"Married!" Ralph said with a grin as he took off his suit jacket and sat down at the kitchen table. "Well, it's about time. She's pushing thirty, isn't she? So who's the guy?"

Harriet considered what to say as she put together the sandwiches at the counter. "David de Morrissey. He's a writer, too. A playwright."

"You're kidding. *The Scarlet Shadow?*"

"Right."

"But isn't he a recluse? And he writes vampire stuff. Why would she want to hook up with a guy like that? I suppose he's got money from his stage shows."

"I've met him. He's very nice," she said, placing a plate with his lunch in front of him.

"But he's into vampires." Ralph shook his shoulders in a mock shiver before picking up his sandwich.

Harriet sat down at the table with her sandwich. "Women find vampires attractive."

"They do?" he said, chewing.

"Sure. They're strange and romantic and sad."

"I never knew you had a thing for vampires."

"Well, now you do."

They ate in silence then for a while. Harriet thought about David, how she already missed the closeness of the bond she'd had with him. She'd never again feel the profound sensations, the deep attachment, she'd known with him. Though it was over now, at least she had the memory of it.

"By the way," Ralph said, looking down at the kitchen linoleum, "this weekend I thought we ought to go out to some ceramic tile places and look for something to recover this floor."

"Ceramic tile? That's expensive."

"Well, this linoleum's beginning to wear out, just like the previous stuff we had, and we might as well put in something that'll last."

"But why make that investment in this house if we're going to move out of Berwyn?"

He looked at her. "I thought you didn't want to move."

"*I* don't. But you said you do."

He angled his chin a bit. "A few of the guys at the office were saying Berwyn's getting to be sort of a trendy place to live. There was even an article in *Chicago* magazine about it."

"Berwyn? Trendy?"

"It's a good location, close to the city, and it's got good solid old homes, like this one, that are affordable. So some of the young, upwardly mobile types from Chicago are moving in, fixing up these homes, and living here. They don't all quite fit in with the blue-collar families that have lived here all their lives, but we'll all get used to each other eventually. I always figured you and I were sort of halfway in between anyway. We're both from blue-collar families. I got a college degree and an office job, but underneath I'm still a beer and baseball type. And you like it here. So I figured, why not stay? Fix up this place. New floors, new kitchen cabinets, maybe a patio in the back. You might want to talk to a decorator and get some ideas to redo the living room really nice."

Harriet could barely believe all this. "Honest? What about the money? All of that will be awfully expensive."

"Well, we'll save a lot by not buying a new house. And I just got a raise. We don't have to do redo everything all at once. It may take a few years."

Harriet swallowed and looked at her sandwich pensively. "But it's always been save, save, save all these years."

"Because we're Bohemian, we've got that savings and loan mentality hammered into our noggins since birth. Nothing wrong with it. But at some point you begin to realize you can't take it with you. Life is to be enjoyed—like sex, as we've recently discovered," he said with a little grin.

Harriet sat still for a moment, trying to follow his train of thought. Feeling a little stunned, she picked up the second half of her sandwich.

They finished eating lunch, neither saying anything further. Ralph looked down and discovered a glob of white on his tie. "Sorry, I got a drip of mayonnaise on it," he said, looking at Harriet sheepishly as he dabbed at the spot with a paper napkin.

"I'll take it to the cleaners. Better put on another one."

Ralph got up and walked into the bedroom. "Smells nice in here," he said from the other room. "Is this bedcover new?"

"That's the quilt I b— made."

He stuck his head out the door. "In that class? The 'love' quilt?"

She smiled because he had so willingly believed what she told him. "Yeah."

"It's nice. Beautiful. Want to try it out?"

She was about to take a bite of her sandwich. "Huh?"

"I don't have to be back at work till two. We've got forty-five whole minutes."

Slowly she put the sandwich down. "But . . ."

"Janet's at school. You have something better to do now?"

"No," Harriet said, shrugging her shoulders and laughing.

"Well? I'll bite you on the neck like a vampire, if you want."

Harriet lowered her eyes as she got up from the table. "No," she said, a sense of sadness almost overtaking her. She'd known the real thing and couldn't abide the thought of a clumsy, joking imitation. "Plain old-fashioned sex will do," she told Ralph as she walked up to him, "since I don't know a real vampire." Anymore, she added to herself.

"You don't have to sound so disappointed."

Harriet smiled. "I'm not."

"Let's go then!" he said, unbuttoning his shirt. "I'm anxious to try out this quilt."

"Don't be in such a hurry," she said as he tossed his shirt onto the dresser. "You said we had forty-five minutes."

"Yeah, plenty of time," he said, unbuckling his belt.

"Well, if we're going to do this at all," she said, raising a cautionary finger at him, "then I want *all* forty-five minutes used up. No 'bam thank you ma'am' with the excuse that you have to get back to the office."

"Whatever turns *you* on is fine with me! It's a deal."

She laughed at their conversation. "This sounds like a negotiation."

"And you're getting to be some negotiator," he said, beginning to unbutton her dress. "Turns me on! So let's get this 'afternoon delight' under way. I'll even risk being late."

Harriet grinned as he tugged off her dress with gentle roughness. She might always miss her sublime experiences with David, her brief brush with the supernatural. But that was over, and now she was left with real life. As her husband playfully pushed her down onto the scented quilt, she decided maybe her real life wasn't so bad after all.

In the late morning, Veronica had gone out to buy some broiled chicken, bread, and a salad at a deli, as Harriet had suggested, and brought it back to David's house for them to share.

Eating had felt strange to David at first, chewing and swallowing actual morsels of food with different textures and flavors. They felt clumsy on his tongue and even a little uncomfortable sliding down his throat. But this discomfort only lasted a while, and soon he found he was enjoying the taste and the sensations. He ate modestly at midday, not sure how his body would react. But he suffered no ill effects; in fact, afterward he had an increased sense of well-being.

By mid-afternoon, David had a yearning to go out and see the city in the daylight, so he and Veronica left the house. They walked down Oak Street to North Michigan Avenue, which was sunny, busy with traffic, and noisy. His eyes were so unused to bright light that he began to squint a great deal, and Veronica loaned him her black-rimmed dark glasses.

The noise of the buses, trucks, and cars constantly passing them on the wide street seemed deafening compared to the relative quiet he'd grown used to at night. But the energy and life he felt and saw as he looked about him, the people hurrying to and fro, the soft gray skyscrapers with their gleaming windows, behind which people worked in offices, were a wonder to David. With Veronica beside him, he realized he was now a part of this vital, thriving city as he never had been before.

They shopped; they took a scenic boat ride on Lake Michigan, boarding the boat on the Chicago River near the Wrigley

Building for the hour-long ride. They walked as far south as the Art Institute, which David had always wished he could visit, but never had because of its inconvenient daytime hours. They went in to see the museum's famous collection of French Impressionist paintings by artists such as Renoir, Monet, and Manet, and the huge masterpiece "Sunday Afternoon on the Island of La Grande Jatte" by Georges Seurat.

"Darienne had an affair with Georges in 1884 or '85," David whispered to Veronica as they stood in front of the ten-foot-tall painting. "Didn't last long." He grew pensive thinking of the blond vampiress. "I wonder how she is. Where she is. Perhaps she's left Chicago."

When Veronica raised her dark brows in a questioning expression, he told her what had happened—Darienne's involvement with Matthew McDowall, the reason for their breakup, and her renouncement of David.

"She's all alone now," Veronica said, her face sad and concerned.

David stroked Veronica's long hair. "Yes, she is. But she'll recover her spirits." He hoped what he was saying was true. "She never remains alone for long. She always finds someone. Perhaps she'll go to Switzerland and visit Herman. Which reminds me," he added with a smile, "I need to call him tonight or tomorrow to tell him I tried the cure and I'm still here."

Veronica took his arm and leaned against him. "He'll be thrilled."

"No." David shook his head with amusement. "I doubt he's the type who's ever thrilled. Intrigued, mildly excited perhaps." He looked down at Veronica, clinging to him so lovingly. "God, it's wonderful to be out with you like this." He slipped his arm around her and they kissed.

They viewed more paintings, including "American Gothic" by Grant Wood, and "Nighthawks" by Edward Hopper, which David had previously seen only in reproductions.

It was late afternoon now, and David placed his hand at his stomach, where he was feeling an odd, gnawing, empty sensation. "Maybe I'm hungry," he said to Veronica, who was watching him closely.

"You probably are," she replied with a smile. "*I'm* hungry. Shall we find a restaurant?"

They walked up Michigan Avenue and found a small restaurant in one of the tall buildings. Both ordered fish and chips, which David ate with gusto. They ordered cheesecake for dessert.

"You'll gain weight at this rate," Veronica said, chuckling as he wolfed down the last bite.

" 'I see no objection to stoutness, in moderation,' " David quoted with amusement.

Veronica rolled her eyes. "Shakespeare?"

"Gilbert and Sullivan."

They left the restaurant and found they were near the theater where *The Scarlet Shadow* was playing. "Let's walk over. Maybe Merle, my producer, is there," David said. "I'm sure he's upset the show is closing."

When they reached the theater, they went in by the stage door. There had been a matinee, and some of the show's actors were there, passing time until the evening performance. David asked one of them about Merle and learned he had not come by that day.

Just as David told Veronica they might as well leave, he spotted Matthew, carrying a duffel bag, coming down the hall toward them. When the actor saw David, his pace slowed and his face went white.

"How can you be here . . . now?" Matthew asked with astonishment when David came up to him.

"Before dark? I'm cured of my malady," David said, not wanting to use the word *vampire* when there were other people around.

"Cured?"

"Is there a dressing room empty where we can talk?"

Matthew led them to one and closed the door. There David introduced him to Veronica and then went on to explain how he'd become mortal again.

"Incredible," Matthew said with wonder. "And how do you like it? Are you happy?"

"Deliriously." He slipped his arm around Veronica and, with a smile, added, "I'm even getting married."

"You knew?" Matthew asked her, eyes alight with curiosity.

"Yes. I thought I would become a vampiress so we could be together. Instead, David became mortal." She lifted her eyebrows in an expression David had always found charming. "I would have been happy either way, just so I could be with him."

Matthew smiled at her in the intense, genuine way David supposed women found so appealing. Instinctively, David pulled Veronica even closer. She was no longer under his power, no longer tied to him through their bond. He was only a mortal now and in equal competition with any other man who might pass her way and take notice of her ultrafeminine sweetness and beauty. But Veronica wrapped her arms around David's chest and seemed to be paying little attention to the famed actor.

"Hang on to *her!*" Matthew said, grinning at David.

David nodded, enjoying the comfortable feeling of being loved by a woman and envied by a man all at one time. He grew more serious then. "Have you seen Darienne?"

"Not since I . . . declined her offer."

"She told me what happened. She blames me for it, thinks I dissuaded you from choosing to be a vampire."

"No," Matthew said, shaking his head. He sat down on the empty makeup chair in the room. "I asked to see where she lived, thinking I might still go through with it. I'd weighed heavily all you told me. But the idea of permanently having that power I felt onstage, that power you said you'd instilled in my mind, of having that for real—well, I was very intrigued with that."

He shifted in the chair. "But when I saw her coffin . . ." He paused and seemed to breathe unsteadily for a moment. "I just couldn't handle it. All the things you'd told me became tangibly clear then. Power wasn't worth lying in a coffin all day and searching for blood sources at night. Darienne seemed to take it all in stride. In fact, she seemed proud to show me her casket, talked about the material that lined it and all . . ."

Matthew exhaled. "Suddenly being a vampire just seemed like the most revolting thing I could imagine. I could understand then why you said that you despised what you were. And after that even Sir Percy no longer seemed the shining, heroic figure I'd played for so long. I realized that the stage character was mostly fantasy, that a real vampire's existence is much darker and more horrible than I'd ever imagined. I was able to finally disengage from Sir Percy and give him up. I'd prefer never to play him again." He chuckled. "I'll have to, though, if they ever make the movie. I'm under contract. But that'll be different. Movies are shot out of sequence, in fits and starts. It won't be the intense experience it was playing him on a stage for two hours straight. I'm glad the contract for this play took so long to hammer out. I'd never signed it, so it was easy to drop out. Merle's not very happy with me, but—"

"Never mind Merle. You did what you needed to do to save your life. What will you do now?"

Matthew's eyes glimmered, seemed to grow warmer. "I'm catching the red-eye tonight for New York. I called my former wife and told her I'd decided to quit the show, which is what she'd wanted. She invited me to stay with her for a while to fully recover my health. I've always had a little flame burning inside for her. Maybe . . . I don't know. I don't want to hope for too much. If I can just get back a good relationship with her and get on speaking terms with my son, whom I haven't seen in twenty years, then maybe I can have some kind of life. I mean, a *real* life, a personal life. Not living from stage performance to stage performance with high doses of glamor and sex in between. For three years I've been sort of addicted—to Sir Percy and the high I felt playing him, and to Darienne and . . . well, all she provided. I need a quieter, more stable life. A home somewhere. Grass to cut and roses to grow. Sounds good, don't you think?"

"Sounds wonderful!" David readily agreed. "It's what I want, too."

"So you'll leave tonight without seeing Darienne?" Veronica asked, apparently concerned for the vampiress.

Matthew's face took on a guilty expression. "I know I ought to say good-bye to her. In her way, she took good care of me, especially when I was sick or depressed. But . . ." He glanced up at David. "To tell you the truth, I'm afraid of her now. When I told her I didn't want to be transformed, she almost attacked me. I talked her out of it, but I felt her sharp teeth grazing my neck. And my strength wasn't equal to hers. If I went to her to say good-bye, and she lost her cool again . . ."

"You might find yourself transformed whether you want it or not," David said. "No, it's best to avoid her. She's so infatuated with you, she's lost her sense of direction. She used to be quite calm and well adjusted. Love has changed her in a way I'd never have anticipated."

Matthew nodded thoughtfully. "She never told me she loved me until that last night. It came as a shock. I was fond of her, and I enjoyed her fun-loving nature. But we'd agreed our relationship was to be purely for pleasure. I think I've really been in love only once, and that was long ago when I met my wife. She eventually left me, with good reason. No one has ever really replaced her in my life, or in my heart. I may never be with her again permanently, but I can't see substituting her with anyone else. That's why I've drifted from one woman to another. I stayed with Darienne longer than anyone else because she was so free and easy. Or so I thought." Matthew looked at his watch. "Well, I need to go. I have to stop back at my hotel to pick up my luggage and then catch the shuttle to the airport."

"We'll walk out with you," David said, taking Veronica by the hand. As they walked out of the dressing room and down the hall, David added, "I'm glad I had this opportunity to talk to you. I'd wondered about your decision to leave the show."

The sun had set, and as they walked out the stage door, the moon was high above the tall buildings. "I'm glad it's all behind me now," Matthew said. "I'm looking forward to this next phase of my life."

As David listened, suddenly Veronica began tugging on his arm.

"David," she whispered, giving him a directional look up the street.

David turned, and so did Matthew, to see Darienne about twenty feet away, dressed all in white, walking up the sidewalk toward them.

# 16

## A sunshine in the shady place

DARIENNE WAS stunned to see who had come out the stage door, where she'd been headed. She'd read in the papers that Matthew was leaving the show. With waning hope, she'd waited for him to contact her. When he hadn't, she'd decided to try to find him at the theater.

And now, looking at her with grim faces, were not only Matthew, but David and—Veronica! Veronica began to smile at her hesitantly, and Darienne quickened her step.

"I haven't seen you in so long," Darienne said, genuinely pleased to see the dark-haired young woman. "I meant to visit you, but—"

"It's okay."

She glanced from Veronica to David. "But you're together. You've ended the pact?"

"No," David said. "The cure worked."

Darienne studied him with a sinking feeling. Much as she hated David right now, deep down she wanted him to be happy. But to see him so ordinary—she looked at his teeth, his eyes, his demeanor. All the subtleties of vampiric power that used to add silent force to him were gone. His vampire sexuality would be gone, too. Now he was just a commonplace, if aristocratic-looking, mortal.

Darienne had the feeling of being abandoned. But as she looked over the three of them, her eyes settling now on Matthew, she knew she didn't want to be one of them. She was more powerful now than any of them, poor weak mortals that they were. And yet, the sight of Matthew standing there with his intense eyes on her was enough to make her feel weak, too.

She raised her chin and straightened her posture before speaking to him.

"I read that you're leaving. Not only the show, but the city."

Matthew nodded. "I am."

"And you couldn't take time to even say good-bye to me?"

He didn't flinch, but stared at her steadily. "I would have. But I think you know why I haven't."

"I wouldn't harm you. Is that what you thought?" she asked, knowing in her heart that if he had come to her once more, she might not have had the willpower to stop herself from taking him by force.

"Then, you're right," he acquiesced, though she suspected he was humoring her. "I should have seen you again and said good-bye."

Darienne felt humiliated by his condescending manner, but she did her best to hide it. "You're going to New York, the paper said. The 'friend' you're staying with is Natalie, no doubt."

"Yes."

Darienne closed her eyes to keep tears from starting. Hearing him verify her suspicions hurt. "Well," she said, forcing a smile, "tell her hello for me. I always liked her, you know."

"I know," Matthew said, a hint in his voice of that reassuring tone that she'd always yearned for but somehow gotten little of during their relationship. "I'll tell her." He took Darienne off-guard by stepping forward then and extending his hand toward her. She took it with painful reluctance.

"Don't say good-bye," she whispered. "Please don't say that."

His gaze was empathetic now, and warm. "We had a remarkable relationship. I'll always be grateful for what you taught me about . . . enjoying life." His eyes took on a sensual sheen as he gazed deeply into hers, as if remembering the many hours of pleasure and passion they'd shared. "I'll never forget you," he said in a rare, whispery voice that made her bones feel weak. His eyes changed subtly and grew introspective. "But it's time for us both to move on."

"*You* may have to move on." Her voice broke despite her resolve. "I'm happy right here. Come back if you get bored. I think you will be bored without me and without the stage.

I'll always make myself available for you, *cheri.* Come back when ordinary life makes you feel constricted. I'll set you free again. Whether you stay mortal or not, I can give you more than any other woman. You know I can. So come back to Darienne when life grows dull. I'll make it exciting for you again."

He stared at her a moment as if mesmerized, but then lowered his gaze and let go of her hand. "I have to catch my plane." He slung the duffel bag he was carrying over his shoulder and turned to David. "Good-bye," he said, shaking hands. "I wish you and Veronica every happiness," he added, smiling at Veronica. He turned one last time toward Darienne, gave her a sharp, lingering look she couldn't interpret, and walked up the street.

Darienne watched until he turned the corner of the theater and disappeared from view. She lowered her gaze to the sidewalk then, for her eyes were filling with tears. She didn't want to look dejected in front of David, fearing he'd gloat. But she felt utterly dead inside, as if the glitter had been taken out of her existence. And the glitter was what she existed for. How could Matthew leave her? He craved excitement and challenge just as much as she did. And she could share the excitement and even create it with him better than anyone. Why would he leave her to go to some prosaic house in New York and live with Natalie, a lovely but, at best, ordinary woman? He'd regret it. He'd come back; she was certain. It was only a matter of time—

"Darienne?" Veronica stepped up and took her arm. "Are you okay?"

"Of course!" She quickly wiped away a tear as she looked up. "What's one man, more or less? There are so many. And I have all the time in the world." She glanced at David. "Unlike you, *cheri.*"

David came up and slipped his arm around Darienne's shoulders, while Veronica stayed at her other side.

"Unlike me, indeed," he said. "You'll recover from this. You're more resourceful than anyone I've known. And there *are* other exciting men in the world."

Darienne's shoulders slumped, giving in to David's comforting embrace. "But I only want Matthew," she admitted. "No other man will ever do. Just as Veronica," she said, squeezing the young woman's hand, "never wanted anyone but you. You have each other now, and I have no one."

"You have us," Veronica said. "We'll always be your friends."

Darienne smiled at her sweetness. "Thank you. I do appreciate that. I'm grateful to know you both. Yes, even you," she said, turning to David. "I know you meant well, painting Matthew such a negative picture of the vampire world. To be honest, which I'm not always, things hadn't been going well anymore between Matthew and me. Maybe my love for him was doomed anyway. I always sensed once he found out how much I cared, I'd lose him. He's what ordinary women would call a heartbreaker. And I wasn't any smarter than any of the others who've fallen for him. I'm hurt and alone now, too."

"Shall we take you home?" David suggested. "Though I still don't know where you live. You never would tell me."

For some reason, that made Darienne laugh. "The John Hancock, *cheri.*"

"Really? What floor?"

"The ninety-first."

David looked appalled. "Leave it to you to do what no other vampire would do," he muttered with humor. The three of them walked up Michigan Avenue in the brisk night air. The city was beautiful, and with her two friends beside her, Darienne began to feel better. She asked David what had happened when he took the cure and shuddered at what he described. Then she listened to him express his joy about being mortal again, but found she did not envy him in the least.

But she was glad he was happy and that Veronica, whom she'd always adored, was happy at last, too. She listened with rapt attention as they told her their plans for the future, to renovate his home, get rid of all the old furniture cluttering the first floor and the basement, and live in it as a respected playwright and his young wife.

When they reached the Hancock, David and Veronica—mostly Veronica actually—declined Darienne's invitation to come and see her apartment. She sensed Veronica had some intimate plan and did not press the matter.

"Another night," Veronica promised. "I've always wanted to see your closet. You have such beautiful clothes."

"I'd love to show them to you. David will be bored, but we'll ignore him."

Veronica laughed, and David seemed to take the comment with good humor.

"Will you be all right?" he asked in a serious tone.

"I'm fine. I'll just not think about Matthew, that's all."

"It would be best if you could let go of him emotionally," David said. "He told us earlier he wants to have a normal, quiet life now."

Darienne nodded. "I know. You're right. I have to forget him, somehow. Natalie will certainly take him back, now that he's quit the show. She'll probably reunite him with his son, and they'll be a family—"

Darienne stopped short as a thought sped through her mind. "Matthew's son . . . ," she said softly, to herself. The photo of Larry she'd seen in Switzerland came into her mind. He'd looked so much like Matthew. He probably had many of Matthew's qualities . . .

She glanced up at David and Veronica. "You know, I think I'll go to London for a while. I need to get away from here. I'll have to give you a raincheck on our spree through my clothes closet, Veronica."

"That's all right," Veronica said. "Maybe it *would* be good for you to get away."

But David didn't look so supportive of the idea. "Matthew's son is in London, isn't he?"

"He may be," Darienne replied in an airy tone.

"Darienne!"

She stopped her hedging and gave David a direct look. "You can't stop me, David. You couldn't stop me from doing anything before, and you certainly can't now, puny mortal that you are. Go home and be joyous with Veronica. I wish you both nothing but the best that mortal life has to offer. But as for me—I have my own splendid existence. And I'll fly to whatever city and look up whatever person I choose. Goodbye, my friends," she said, giving a mystified Veronica a kiss on the cheek. "I'll see you again someday." She kissed David, too. "Meanwhile, stay happy." She began to walk toward the entrance to her building, but turned once to say, "I intend to be happy, too! *Au revoir!*" She waved and then hurried toward the glass entrance doors.

When she reached her apartment on the ninety-first floor, she immediately got on the telephone, placing a call to an international airline. In minutes she'd made arrangements to have herself shipped to London, where, of course, she had a very chic flat in the poshest part of town.

"I'm afraid she'll go off to pursue Matthew's son, thinking he'll be a replacement for his father," David told Veronica as she drove them back to his home.

"She may be disappointed when she meets his son and will leave him alone," Veronica said, pulling up in front of David's mansion. She turned off the ignition. "No use worrying about it." She seemed to want to reassure him so he would take his mind off the matter.

They got out of the car. "You're right," he said in a resigned tone. "There's nothing I can do to stop her, in any case."

Veronica smiled and took his arm. She gazed at the upper windows as they walked up the sidewalk to his front door. "I'd often drive by here just to see your house and feel closer to you. You were always so firm in your resolve to keep our pact, that it made me angry sometimes, or afraid that you'd forget me."

"I'd never forget you. Never," he told her and leaned down to kiss her. "I've been so lonely without you."

He unlocked his front door. They walked into the entryway, their shoes sinking into the Oriental rug. "I like this oval hall," Veronica said, looking about. "I want to leave this just the way it is. Your living room, too. And your library on the second floor. But the old furniture you have stored in the first-floor rooms and the basement—"

"Will have to go," David said in a rueful manner.

"Not all of it. We should go through it and save the most valuable antiques. We'll need furniture for all the first-floor rooms anyway. I always wondered why you used the first floor for storage."

"I hated to throw my old furniture away, because it all meant something to me in other lifetimes. But I didn't want to haul it upstairs, either. And I wanted my living quarters to be as far from my coffin as possible, so I chose the third floor for my living room and office."

"What about your coffin? Will you throw it away?"

"No," David said, wishing he could answer differently. "I'd better keep it. Herman said there was a small chance the cure might not last."

"Not last?" Veronica said with some alarm. "You mean, you might change back into a vampire again?"

"There is a remote possibility of that, and I must be prepared."

"How would it happen, if it did? Would it be sudden, or gradual?"

"I have no idea," David replied. "And I'd rather not even think about it. By Herman's estimate, I have at least a ninety percent chance of remaining mortal, so let's think positively."

"It wouldn't matter to me, David. I'd love you either way."

David enfolded her in his arms and swayed back and forth, rocking her gently. "How did I ever deserve you?"

"I always wondered what you saw in *me*," Veronica said, holding onto him tightly.

"You were the most adorable, artless, feminine, sweet woman I ever encountered," he said, pulling her slender body closer to his. "In four centuries I'd never met your equal. For that reason I'm grateful I didn't stop existing as I should have in 1616. I've survived to hear Gershwin's music, see Gene Kelly dance, and to love you. It's more than I deserve."

Veronica looked up at him with luminous eyes. Her voice was hushed with expectant desire. "Will you love me now? Take me to the window seat in the ballroom. I want to be there with you now."

A feeling of inadequacy came over David. Though he was holding her close, enjoying her nearness, he still felt no sexual stirrings in his body. Had the transformation left some ill effect on his manliness?

"I was cured only this morning, Veronica," he said, feeling self-conscious and ill at ease with her now. "We've been out all day. I've only just gotten used to eating, to sunlight. I'm not sure I can—"

"Let's just go up to the ballroom. I want to see it again. It was a special place and it meant a lot to me. We first made love there. And you initiated me there. I just want to be there again with you."

Her eyes were so sincere and imploring, David couldn't

refuse. "All right," he told her. "But you may need to give me time before . . . before we regain all our former intimacy."

"I'll be patient," she assured him.

As they ascended the spiral staircase, David couldn't help but worry that he might not be able to be all that he formerly was to Veronica, that she might be disappointed. What if he found that he was no longer physically capable of making love with her? Would she leave him? Would he have been better off remaining a vampire?

When they reached the third-floor ballroom, Veronica's face grew radiant as she walked through the large wood double doors onto the polished parquet floor.

"Oh, it's just the same! It's so beautiful!" she exclaimed, her high voice echoing a bit in the vast empty room. David watched her gaze up at the three huge crystal chandeliers that hung from the ceiling, reflecting the moonlight that entered through the three sets of high, gold-draped bay windows, each with a velvet cushioned window seat beneath. She took him by the hand and pulled him eagerly toward the nearest window seat, where they always used to make love. "Let's sit down here, David," she implored him. "Just for a while."

He sat beside her and couldn't help but smile as he watched her look up at the glass above them, through which the moon and stars shone, and the glass to the back and on either side of the long, recessed seat.

"This *is* a special place, the loveliest place in the world to me," she told him, taking his arm and holding onto him with adoration.

"To me, too," David told her. He bent to kiss her upturned face, and she gently clung to his lips, though she let go of his arm. There was a sweet electricity in her kiss, and it warmed him and touched him emotionally. The intimate feeling was almost enough to replace the vampiric bond between them that had been lost. The love between them became a tangible thing he could feel like a warm aching knot in his abdomen, pure and poignant. She was life. She was his future. And yet, he began to grow anxious. He wanted to give her more, but his mortal's body didn't seem to want to cooperate.

"David," she whispered as she drew away and broke the kiss. "Look at me."

He opened his eyes to find she'd unbuttoned her blouse,

baring her small, exquisite breasts. As he looked on, mesmerized, taken by surprise, she slipped off the blouse, then stood
to remove her skirt. Her slim, fragile body was divinely feminine, delightful to watch as she gracefully turned and bent this
way and then that while she undressed. His heart began to
beat unsteadily and his breaths came faster.

She sat beside him again, her unclothed body smooth and
supple, her eyes shining with love and eagerness. Taking hold
of his hands, she pressed his palms over her breasts and closed
her eyes, smiling. "I wanted to feel your touch."

David's hands began to tremble as he fondled her soft
warmth. He felt her pink nipples hardening into pert nubs.
Slowly he slid his hands down her breasts, down her abdomen
to circle her small waist. She sat straight, looking at him with
happy, shining eyes, her thick brown hair falling over her
slender shoulders, her small, peaked nipples slanting upward.

Forgetting anxiety, David instinctively drew her to him,
held her tightly, and kissed her thoroughly, pleased that he no
longer had to be careful not to injure her. She kissed him back
with eagerness.

Veronica began to unbutton his shirt, and soon was tugging
his clothes away from his body, baring his chest. She ran her
hands provocatively over his nipples, then slowly down his rib
cage to his belt. After unbuckling that, she unfastened his
pants and slipped her hand inside.

"David!" she breathed with excitement as she caressed him.
It was only then that he realized his body was indeed cooper-
ating. Mortal arousal, he was discovering, was a more subtle
feeling than he'd grown used to as a vampire, for whom sexual
lust was so strong it became a burden to gratify. But what he
felt now was much more human and gentle.

"I've waited years to make love with you again," Veronica
whispered in breathless anticipation as he began to ease her
backward to lie with him on the window seat. "I've dreamed
of this, thought of nothing else sometimes."

She moaned and quivered with sweet urgency as he kissed
her breasts, then slipped his fingers between her thighs, feeling
her heated moistness. "Oh, David, I've wanted you for so
long," she said with a huge ache in her voice.

She looked so eager, her body ardently writhing against his,
her eyes glassy and delirious with need as she gazed at him,

that David felt he should warn her. "It may not be the experience for us that it used to be. I can't take you to that superhuman plane of sensuality I used to."

Her eyes grew sad and yet indulgent. "I know. But I still need you." She pressed her body even closer to him. "Make love with me, David."

He moved over her. As she parted her thighs for him, he slid into her, closing his eyes at the feel of her warm, tight body enveloping him. He opened his eyes to see her gratified smile as he began gentle thrusts within her.

"You're so lovely," he whispered, then kissed her as their bodies moved in instant, familiar unison, as if they'd never stopped making love together. And even more comfortable was the fact that David no longer had to withhold himself, curb his strength, in order not to hurt her. His mortal body was matched to hers now, and he felt a miraculous freedom in their lovemaking as he held her close and moved within her more and more urgently.

Veronica was breathing in gasps now. Her hand at the nape of his neck and the other at his lower back began to grip him more tightly. Meanwhile, David was finding that while he felt wonderfully free with her now, he no longer had the same control over his own body's reaction. He felt himself plunging toward climax, and there was little he could do to hold himself back, which he had always been able to do as a vampire.

But he felt Veronica's heated, lithe body grow even more agitated, her breathing increasingly labored and unsteady, and he knew it wouldn't be long for her, either.

Then, in the next moment, she cried out his name, "David!" in a triumphant sob. Her slim frame jolted beneath him as her chest and neck arched backward, her long hair falling off the edge of the cushion beneath her as her body was wracked with passion. He held her tightly as his own release came, a powerful spasm that at once brought comfort and energy, then profound relaxation.

They lay together for a long moment, holding onto each other. David drew upward and looked down at Veronica, gently stroking her hair back from her moist forehead. Tears stood in her eyes, and she looked both satisfied and sad.

David sensed why. "Was it so different from before? Are you disappointed?"

"No," she said, reaching up to touch his face. "Not disappointed. I'm so happy to make love with you again. But it *was* different. There used to be an extra magic, as if I were floating in a special sphere of lights just beyond reality, holding onto you. Now I'm holding onto you, but the room is the same, and I'm not floating. We're just here, you and I. But that's beautiful, too. And you're still a gentle, sensitive, wonderful lover. I'm happy. Really, very happy. That otherworld experience will be a magic memory of you that I'll always treasure."

"You'll still want me as an ordinary man?"

She laughed and blinked the tears out of her eyes. "You'll never be ordinary! You're handsome and brilliant, and more wise than anyone else I could ever meet. You may not be quite so overpowering anymore, but this way, *I* can be strong, too. I'm almost thirty. If we're going to stay mortal together, then I can't be your little girl, wrapped in your spell, forever."

David smiled, deeply heartened by her words. "I never wanted you to remain the child you were, adorable though you were. I'm glad to see you become more fully yourself, independent of me."

"Still, being mesmerized by your power *was* wonderful." Her eyes grew nostalgic. "Hearing your voice in my head, feeling your feelings, unable to think of anything but you, wanting you . . ." She slid her arms around his back and pulled him to her. "I *will* miss that, David. For a while, anyway . . ."

Eventually, they fell asleep together on the window seat. There was, as yet, no bed in the mansion, for David had always used his coffin as his resting place.

Hours later, when David awoke, the sun was already up, brightening the early morning sky. He looked through the glass above him to see white clouds skimming the blue sky on a brisk wind. Veronica soon awoke from her sleep in the hollow of his shoulder. She seemed slightly disoriented at first, but broke into a sleepy smile when she realized she was with David.

"You're lovely in the daylight," he said, running his fingers through her delightfully mussed hair, as she stretched her naked body beside him.

"You have a beard," she said, feeling the stubble on his chin. "Did you shave when you were a vampire?"

"Yes," he said. "Hair continues to grow even on people

who die a normal death. I shaved myself, which is tricky when you can't see yourself in a mirror. Finding a barber to come to my home in the evening to cut my hair was always a problem, too. Barbershops always have mirrors."

"There are so many things you can do, now that you're a mortal," she said, amusing herself by running her finger along his collarbone. "Eat pizza, for example."

"I can't wait," he said in a dour tone. "I've passed by pizza shops and it looks awful."

"It doesn't taste awful," she said, running her fingertip over his bicep now. "You know what else you can do?"

He gave her an indulgent smile. "What?"

"Make love with me in the daylight."

His smile became a tender one. "Now?"

"Now, under the fluffy clouds and blue sky." She took hold of his shoulders and began pulling him to her. "Let's do it for the first time in the sunshine, David," she said, her brown eyes dancing with lights as they reflected the golden rays streaming onto them through the windows.

As he looked down at Veronica, her bright sweet eyes and young face radiating love, he thought of words written four hundred years ago by Edmund Spenser, whom he'd known.

" 'Her angel's face,' " David murmured as he touched her soft cheek, " 'As the great eye of heaven shined bright, And made a sunshine in the shady place.' "

Tears glazed her eyes. "Will you always find such beautiful things to say to me, even when we're old?"

"Even then. For the first time, I look forward to the future with a sense of joy—because I know I'll be there with you."